Dear Readers,

Many  father said to me, "Bil_____ _____ you do in life. What's i_____ _____ am Johnstone you can ____

I've ne_____ ____ _ow, many years later, I like to think that I am still trying to be the best William Johnstone I can be. Whether it's Ben Raines in the Ashes series, or Frank Morgan, the last gunfighter, or Smoke Jensen, our intrepid mountain man, or John Barrone and his hard-working crew keeping America safe from terrorist lowlifes in the Code Name series, I want to make each new book better than the last and deliver powerful storytelling.

Equally important, I try to create the kinds of believable characters that we can all identify with—real people who face tough challenges. When one of my creations blasts an enemy into the middle of next week, you can be damn sure he had a good reason.

As a storyteller, my job is to entertain you, my readers, and to make sure that you get plenty of enjoyment from my books for your hard-earned money. This is not a job I take lightly. And I greatly appreciate your feedback—you are my gold, and your opinions do count. So please keep the letters and e-mails coming.

Respectfully yours,

WILLIAM W. JOHNSTONE

THE LAST MOUNTAIN MAN

RETURN OF THE MOUNTAIN MAN

PINNACLE BOOKS
Kensington Publishing Corp.
http://www.kensingtonbooks.com

PINNACLE BOOKS are published by

Kensington Publishing Corp.
850 Third Avenue
New York, NY 10022

Copyright © 2006 by Kensington Publishing Corp.
The Last Mountain Man copyright © 1984 by William W. Johnstone
Return of the Mountain Man copyright © 1986 by William W. Johnstone

All rights reserved. No part of this book may be reproduced in any
form or by any means without the prior written consent of the Publisher, excepting brief quotes used in reviews.

If you purchased this book without a cover, you should be aware
that this book is stolen property. It was reported as "unsold and
destroyed" to the Publisher and neither the Author nor the Publisher
has received any payment for this "stripped book."

This novel is a work of fiction. Names, characters, places, and inci-
dents are either the product of the author's imagination or are used
fictitiously. Any resemblance to actual persons, living or dead, or
events is entirely coincidental.

All Kensington Titles, Imprints, and Distributed Lines are available
at special quantity discounts for bulk purchases for sales promo-
tions, premiums, fund-raising, and educational or institutional use.
Special book excerpts or customized printings can also be created
to fit specific needs. For details, write or phone the office of the
Kensington special sales manager: Kensington Publishing Corp.,
850 Third Avenue, New York, NY 10022, attn: Special Sales Department, Phone: 1-800-221-2647.

Pinnacle and the P logo Reg. U.S. Pat. & TM Off.

First Pinnacle Books Printing: December 2006

10 9 8 7 6 5 4 3 2 1

Printed in the United States of America

THE LAST
MOUNTAIN MAN

We were victims of circumstances. We were drove to it.

Cole Younger, 1876

Author's note: The mountains and valleys and creeks and springs described in this novel are real. The rendezvous of aging mountain men at Bent's Fort reportedly did take place around 1865. The grave with the gold buried alongside the man supposedly exists, but it is not at Brown's Hole. To the best of my knowledge there is no town in Idaho called Bury. The story is pure Western fiction, and any resemblance to actual living persons is purely coincidental.

PROLOGUE

He was sixteen when his father returned from that bloody insurrection known to the North as the Civil War. The War Between the States to those who wore the gray.

Kirby Jensen was almost a man grown at sixteen, for he had worked the farm during his father's absence, taking over all the work when his mother fell ill and was confined to bed.

And it had been backbreaking work, attempting to scratch a living out of the rocky Ozark Mountain earth of southwestern Missouri. There never was enough food. The boy was thin, but rawhide tough, for the work had hardened his muscles and the pure act of survival had sharpened his mind. His hands were large and calloused from using an axe, handling trace chains on the mule team, and manhandling rocks from the rolling acres of land he, and he alone, had farmed since age twelve.

It was June, 1865; the war had been over and done for better than two months. If his father was coming home, he should be along anytime, now. *If* he was coming home.

Kirby wondered what his Pa would say when he learned his daughter had run off with a peddler? He wondered if he knew his oldest boy was dead? And he wondered what his reaction would be when Kirby told him of Ma's dying?

The plow hit a rock and jolted the boy back to his surroundings, popping his teeth together and wrenching his arms.

The boy swore. Made him feel more grown-up to cuss a little.

He unhooked the plow, running the lines through the eyes of the singletree, and left the plow sitting in the middle of the field. He was late getting the crops in, but no later then anyone else in the hollows and valleys of this part of Missouri. The rains had come, and stayed, making field work impossible. But he had to try to get something up.

It was a matter of survival.

Folding and shortening the traces, Kirby jumped on the back of one of the big Missouri Reds, the one called Ange, and kicked the mule into movement. It really didn't make any difference how much you kicked ol' Ange, for the mule would plod along at its own pace, oblivious to the thumping heels in its sides. But if you kicked too much, ol' Ange would dump a body on his butt, then stand over you and bray, kind of like mule laughter. Made you feel like a fool.

Then you had a devil of a time getting back on Ange.

Kirby plodded down the turn row on the east side of the field. Dust from the road caught his eyes. One rider pulling up to the house, leading a saddleless, riderless horse. A bay. The boy touched the smooth butt of the Navy .36 stuck behind his wide belt. A man just couldn't be too careful these days, what with some of those Kansas Jayhawkers still around, killing and looting and raping. But, he reminded himself, some of the Missouri Redlegs were just as bad as the Jayhawkers. Seems like war brought out the poison in some and the good in others.

Kirby's father hadn't held much with slavery, but he did feel a state had a right to set and uphold its own laws, so he had ridden off to fight with the Gray. His Pa's brother, up in Iowa, whom Kirby had not seen but one

time in his life, was a farmer, like most of the Jensen
men. But he had marched off to fight with the Blue. He
had gotten killed, so Kirby had heard, in Chancel-
lorsville, back in '63.

At sixteen, Kirby didn't believe a man had the right to
keep another in chains, as a slave, although there hadn't
been much of that in this part of Missouri: everybody
was too poor, just a day to day struggle keeping body and
soul together.

But he did believe, like his father, probably because of
his father, that the government in far-off Washington on
the river didn't have the right to tell a state what it could
and couldn't do in *all* matters.

Didn't seem right.

Had Kirby been old enough, and not had his Ma to
look after, he would have ridden for the Gray.

As Ange plodded closer to the house, Kirby could
make out a figure in the front yard. It was his father.

1

"Boy," Emmett Jensen said looking at his son, "I swear you've grown two feet."

Kirby had slid off Ange and walked to the man. "You've been gone four years, Pa." He wanted to throw his arms around his Pa, but didn't, 'cause his Pa didn't hold with a lot of touching between men. Kirby stuck out his hand and his Pa shook it.

"Strong, too" Emmett commented.

"Thank you, Pa."

"Crops is late, Kirby."

"Yes, sir. Rains come and stayed."

"I wasn't faultin' you, boy." Emmett let his eyes sweep the land. He coughed, a dry hacking. "I seen a cross on the hill overlookin' the creek. Would that be your Ma?"

"Yes, sir."

"When'd she pass?"

"Spring of last year. Doc Blanchard said it was her lungs and a bad heart." And grief, the boy thought, but kept that to himself.

"She go hard?"

"No, sir. Went on in her sleep. I found her the next morning when I brung her coffee and grits."

"Good coffee's scarce. What'd you do with the coffee?"

"Drank it," the boy replied honestly. "Then went to get the doc."

"Right nice service?"

"Folks come from all over to see her off."

Emmett cleared his throat and then coughed. "Well, I think I'll go up to the hill and sit with your ma for a time. You put up them horses and rub them down. We'll talk over supper."

Emmett's eyes flicked over the .36 stuck behind his son's belt. He said nothing about it.

"Pa?"

The father looked at his son.

"I'm glad you're back."

The father stepped forward, put his arms around his son, and held him.

Over greens and fried squirrel and panbread, the father and son ate and talked through the years that they had both lost and gained. There were a few moments of uncomfortable silence between them until they both adjusted to the time and place, and then they were once more father and son.

"We done our best," Emmett said. "Can't nobody say we didn't. And there ain't nobody got nothing to be ashamed of. I thought it wrong for the Yankees to burn folks' homes like they did. But it was war, and terrible things happen in war. But the bluebellies just kept on comin'. Shoot one and five'd take his place. They weren't near 'bout the riflemen we was, nor the riders, but they whipped us fair and square and now it's time to put all that behind us and get on with livin'." He sopped a piece of panbread through the juice of his greens. He chewed for a time. "You know your brother, Luke, is dead, don't you?"

"Yes, sir. I didn't know if you did, or not. I heard he was killed in the Wilderness, last year. Fightin' with Lee, wasn't he?"

Luke had always been Pa's favorite, so Kirby had felt.

Emmett nodded. "Yeah. Tryin' to get back to the Wilderness, so I heard." Something in his eyes clouded, as if he knew more about his son's death than he was telling. "I don't see no sign of your sister, Janey, and you ain't brought up her name. What are you holding back, Kirby?"

The moment the boy had been dreading. "She run off, Pa. Last year. Run off with a tinker, so he called himself. But he was a gambler, I'd say."

"Smooth-talker, I'd wager."

"Yes, sir."

"What'd his hands look like?"

"Soft."

"Gambler. How'd your Ma take it?"

"Hard."

"Probably helped kill her." He said it flatly, then shook his head. "Well, past is past, no point dwellin' on it." He rose from the table. "I've ridden a piece these last weeks—wanted to get home. Now I'm home, and I'm tired. Reckon you are, too, son. We'll get some sleep, talk in the morning. I got a plan." He covered his mouth and coughed.

Breakfast was meager: fried mush and coffee that was mostly chicory. A piece of leftover panbread.

"I don't think it good to stay here, boy," Emmett said, surprising the boy. "Too many memories. Land's got too many rocks to farm. I think it best for us to pack it up, sell what we can, and head west. We'll sell the mules, buy some pack horses. The mules is gettin' too old for where we're goin'. What is today, boy?"

"Wednesday, Pa." *West!* he thought. The frontier he'd read about in the dime novels. Buffalo and mountain men. Then he sobered as he thought: *Indians on the warpath.*

Emmett pushed his plate from him and put his elbows on the table. "We'll ride into town today, boy. Ask around some. Kirby, I brought that bay out yonder home for you."

Kirby mumbled his thanks, pleased but embarrassed. He had never had such a grand gift.

"How far you been from this holler, boy?"

"A good piece, Pa. I went to Springfield once. Took us a good bit of travelin' to get there, too."

Seventy miles.

Emmett stuffed his pipe and lit it, then pushed his rawhide-bottomed chair back and looked at his son. "Toward the end of the war, Kirby, some Texicans and some mountain men joined up with us. Them mountain men had been all the way to the Pacific Ocean; but they talked a lot about a place the Shoshone Indians call I-dee-ho. Or something like that. I'd like to see it, and all the country between here and there. I been all the way to the Atlantic Ocean, boy—you never seen so much water. You just got no idea how big this country is. But west is where the people's got to go. I figure we'll just head on out that way, too."

"Pa? How will we know when we get to where it is we're goin'?"

"We'll know," the man replied, a mysterious quality to his voice, as if he was holding back from his son.

Kirby met his father's eyes. "Whatever you say, Pa."

They pulled out the following Sunday morning, just as the sun was touching the eastern rim of the Ozark Mountains of Missouri. Kirby rode the bay, sitting on a worn-out McClellan saddle; not the most comfortable saddle ever invented. The saddle had been bought from a down-on-his-luck Confederate soldier trying to get back to Louisiana.

In Kirby's saddlebags, in addition to an extra pair of trousers, shirt, long handle underwear, and two pairs of socks, was a worn McGuffey's reader his Pa had purchased for a penny—much to Kirby's disgust. He thought he was all done with schooling.

The boy had no way of knowing that his education was just beginning.

The McGuffey's reader was heavy on his mind. As they rode, he turned to his father. "I can read and cipher." He knew his protests would fall on deaf ears. Once his father made up his mind, forget any objections . . . just do it.

"I 'spect you can," Emmett said, his eyes still on the little valley below them. His eyes lifted, touching the now tiny cross on the faraway knoll. He touched his boot heels to his mount and father and son headed west. "What's a verb?"

Kirby looked at him. "Huh? I mean, sir?"

"A verb, boy. Tell me what it is."

Kirby frantically searched his memory. "Well," he admitted. "Reckon I forgot. You brung it up, so you tell me."

"Don't sass me, boy." But there was a twinkle in the father's eyes. "I asked you first."

"Then I reckon we'll find out together, Pa."

"I reckon we will at that, boy." Emmett turned once, twisting in the saddle to look for the last time at the cross on the knoll. He straightened in the saddle, assuming the cavalryman's stiff-backed position. He asked his son, "You got any regrets, Kirby? Leavin' this place, I mean."

"Hard work, not always enough food, Jayhawkers, Yankees, cold winters, and some bad memories," the boy replied honestly, as was his fashion. "If that's regrets, I'm happy to leave them behind."

Emmett's reply was unusually soft. "You was just a boy when I pulled out with the Grays. I reckon I done you and your Ma a disservice——like half a million other men done their loved ones. I didn't leave you no time for youthful foolishness; no time to be a young boy. You had to be a man at twelve. I don't know if I can make up for that, but I aim to try. From now on, son, it'll be you and me." For a little while, he silently added. He coughed.

* * *

Together they rode, edging slightly northward as they went. They skirted Joplin, a town on the Ozark Plateau. It was a young town, only twenty-five years old in 1865. Joplin had a few years to go before it would become the metropolis of the three-state lead and zinc field. Kirby wanted to ride in and see the town; the only other big town he'd ever seen was Springfield. But his father refused, said there were dens of iniquity in there.

"What's a den of in . . . in . . . what'd you say, Pa?"

"You'll find out soon enough, I reckon."

"Why don't you tell me, Pa?"

"'Cause I ain't of a mind to, that's why." The father seemed embarrassed.

"Sure must be something pretty danged good."

Emmett smiled. "Some folks would say so, I'm sure. Never been to one myself. And don't cuss. It ain't seemly and you might slip and do so around a lady. Ladies don't like cussin'."

"You say hell's fire, Pa," he reminded.

"That's different."

"How come?"

"Boy, you sure ask a lot of questions. Worrisome."

"Well, how else am I to learn?"

"I can cuss now and then 'cause I'm older than you, that's why."

"How long will it be 'fore I can cuss, Pa?"

The father shook his head and hacked his dry cough. "Lord have mercy on a poor veteran and give me strength." But he was smiling as he said it.

They had left the cool valleys and hills of Missouri, with rushing creeks and shade trees. They rode into a hot Kansas summer. Only four years into the Union, much of Kansas was unsettled, with almost the entire western half the territory of the Kiowa and Pawnee; the Kiowa to the south, the Pawnee to the north.

The pair rode slowly, the pack horses trailing from lead ropes. The father and son had no deadline to meet, no place in particular to go . . . or so the boy thought.

They crossed through Osage country without encountering any hostile Indians. They saw a few—and probably a lot more saw them than they realized—but those the father and son spotted were always at a distance, or were not interested in the pair.

"They may be huntin'," Emmett said. "I hear tell Indians is notional folks. Hard for a white man to understand their way of life. I'm told the same band that might leave us alone today, might try to kill us tomorrow."

"Why, Pa?"

"Damned if I know, boy."

"You cussin' again."

"I'm older."

When they reached the Arkansas River, later on that afternoon, Emmett pulled them up and made camp early.

"We got ample powder and shot and paper cartridges, boy. I figure more'n we'll need to get through. According to them I talked with, from here on, it gets mean."

"How's that, Pa?"

"We're headin' west and north as we go. Like this." He drew a line in the dirt with a stick. "This'll take us, I hope, right between the Kiowa and the Pawnee. The white man's been pushin' the Indian hard the past few years, takin' land the Indians say belongs to them. The savages is gettin' right ugly about it, so I'm told."

"Who does the land belong to, Pa?"

Emmett shook his head. "Don't rightly know. Looks to me like it don't *really* belong to nobody. Way I look at it—and most other white folks—a man's gotta *do* something with the land to make it his. The Indians ain't been doing that. So I'm told. They just roam it, hunt it, fish, and the like."

"But how long have they been doing that, Pa?"

The man sighed. He looked at his son. "I 'spect forever, boy."

* * *

They rode westward, edging north. Several weeks had passed since they rode from the land of Kirby's birth, and already that place was fading from his mind. He had never been happy there, so he made no real attempt to halt the fading of the images.

Kirby did not know how much his Pa had gotten for the land and the equipment and the mules, but he knew he had gotten it in gold—and not much gold. His Pa carried the gold in a small leather pouch inside his shirt, secured around his neck with a piece of rawhide.

The elder Jensen was heavily armed: a Sharps .52 caliber rifle in a saddle boot, two Remington army revolvers in holsters around his waist, two more pistols in saddle holsters, left and right of the horn. And he carried a gambler's gun behind his belt buckle: a .44 caliber, two-shot derringer. His knife was a wicked-looking, razor-sharp Arkansas Toothpick in a leather sheath on his left side.

Kirby never asked why his father was so heavily armed. But he did ask, "How come them holsters around your waist ain't got no flaps on them, Pa? How come you cut them off that way?"

"So I can get the pistols out faster, son. The leather thong run through the front loops over the hammer to hold the pistol."

"Is gettin' a gun out fast important, Pa?" He knew it was from reading dime novels. But he just could not envision his father as a gunfighter.

"Sometimes, boy. But more important is hittin' what you're aimin' at."

"Think I'll do mine thataway."

"Your choice," the father replied.

Kirby knew, from hearing talk after Appomattox, the Gray was supposed to turn in their weapons. But he had a hunch that his father, hearing of the surrender, had just wheeled around and took the long way back to

Missouri, his weapons with him, and the devil with surrender terms.

His dad coughed and asked, "How'd you get that Navy Colt, son?"

"Bunch of Jayhawkers come ridin' through one night, headin' back to Kansas like the devil was chasin' them. Turned out that was just about right. 'Bout a half hour later, Bloody Bill Anderson and his boys came ridin' up. They stopped to rest and water their horses. There was this young feller with them. Couldn't have been no more than a year or so older than me. He seen me and Ma there alone, and all I had was this old rifle." He patted the worn stock of an old flint and percussion Plains' rifle in a saddle boot. "So he give me this Navy gun and an extra cylinder. Seemed like a right nice thing for him to do. He *was* nice, soft-spoken, too."

"It was a nice thing to do. You seen him since?"

"No, sir."

"You thank him proper?"

"Yes, sir. Gave him a bit of food in a sack."

"Neighborly. He tell you his name?"

"Yes, sir. James. Jesse James. His brother Frank was with the bunch, too. Some older than Jesse."

"Don't recall hearin' that name before."

"Jesse blinked his eyes a lot."

"Is that right? Well, you 'member the name, son; might run into him again some day. Good man like that's hard to find."

As the days rolled past, the way ever westward, father and son learned more of the wild country into which they rode, ever alert for trouble, and they learned more of each other. Becoming reacquainted.

They saw herds of buffalo that held them spellbound, the size and number and royal bearing of the magnificent animals awe-inspiring. Even though the animals themselves were stupid. And many times, as they rode, father and son came upon the bones of what appeared to be thousands of the animals, callously slaughtered for their hide, hump, and tongue, the rest left to rot and stink under the summer sun.

"Them is the Indians' main food supply," Emmett told his son. "And another reason why the savages is mad at the whites. I got to side with the savages 'bout this."

As they skirted the rotten bone yard, coyotes and a few wolves feasted on the tons of meat left behind. Kirby said, "This don't seem right to me."

"Ain't!" Emmett said, his jaw tight with anger. "Man shouldn't never take no more than he hisself can use. This is just pure ol' waste. Stupid."

"And the Indians had nothing to do with this?"

"Hell, no! Look at them shod pony tracks. Indians don't shoe their ponies and drive wagons that left them tracks over there. The white man did this."

They passed the slaughter, both silent for a time. Finally the boy said, "Maybe the Indians have a point about the white man comin' here."

His father spat a brown stream of tobacco juice from the ever present chew tucked in his cheek. "Reckon they do, boy. Not much is ever just black and white . . . always a middle ground that needs lookin' at."

"Like the War Between the States, Pa?"

"Yeah. Right and wrong on both sides there, too."

"Was you a hero, Pa?"

"We all was. Ever' man that fought on either side. It was a hell of a war. "

"Was you an officer?"

"Sergeant."

"Why was everybody a hero, Pa?"

"'Cause they'll never be—I pray God—another war like that one, boy. Don't know the final count of dead, but it was terrible, I can tell you that."

They plodded on for another mile before the father again spoke. "I seen men layin' side by side, some on stretchers, some on blankets, some just layin' on the cold ground—all of them wounded, lot of them dyin'. The line was five or six deep and it stretched for more'n three miles along the railroad track. You just can't imagine that, boy . . . not until you see it with your own eyes. Maybe one doctor for ever' five hundred men. No medicine, no food, no nothing. Men cryin' out for just the touch of a woman's hand before they died. Toward the end of the war there wasn't even no hope. We knew we was beat, but still we fought on like crazy men."

"Why, Pa?"

"Ask a hundred men, boy, and they'd give you a hundred different answers. They was some men that fought 'cause they really hated the nigras. Some fought 'cause they was losin' a way of life that was all they'd ever known. Some didn't fight at all till they seen the Yankees come through burnin' and lootin' and robbin' and rapin'. And some of them did that, too, boy, don't never let nobody ever tell you no different."

Kirby got a funny feeling in the area just below his belly at the thought of rapin'. He shifted in the saddle.

"I ain't sayin' the Gray didn't have its share of scallywags and white trash, 'cause we did. But nothing to compare with the Yankees."

"Maybe that had something to do with the fact that the Blues had more men, Pa."

Emmett looked at his boy, thinking: *boy's got some smarts about him.* "Maybe so, son."

They rode on, across the seemingly endless plains of tall grass and sudden breaks in the earth, cleverly disguised by nature. A pile of rocks, not arranged by nature, came into view. Kirby pointed them out.

They pulled up. "That's what I been lookin' for," Emmett said. "That's a sign tellin' travelers that this here is the Santa Fe Trail. North and west of here'll be Fort Larned. North of that'll be the Pawnee Rock."

"What's that, Pa?"

"A landmark, pilgrim," the voice came from behind the man and his son.

Before Kirby could blink, his pa had wheeled his roan and had a pistol in his hand, hammer back. It was the fastest draw Kirby had ever seen—not that he had seen that many. Just the time the town marshal back in Missouri had tried a fast draw and shot himself in the foot.

"Whoa!" the man said. "You some swift, pilgrim."

"I ain't no pilgrim," Emmett said, low menace in his tone.

Kirby looked at his father; looked at a very new side of the man.

"Reckon you ain't, at that."

Kirby had wheeled his bay and now sat his saddle, staring at the dirtiest man he had ever seen. The man was dressed entirely in buckskin, from the moccasins on his feet to his wide-brimmed leather hat. A white, tobacco-stained beard covered his face. His nose was red and his eyes twinkled with mischief. He looked like a skinny, dirty version of Santa Claus. He sat on a funny-spotted pony, two pack animals with him.

"Where'd you come from?" Emmett asked.

"Been watchin' you two pilgrims from that ravine yonder," he said with a jerk of his head. "Ya'll don't know much 'bout travelin' in Injun country, do you? Best to stay off the ridges. You two been standin' out like a third titty."

He shifted his gaze to Kirby. "What are you starin' at, boy?"

The boy leaned forward in his saddle. "Be durned if I rightly know," he said. And as usual, his reply was an honest one.

The old man laughed. "You got sand to your bottom, all right." He looked at Emmett. "He yourn?"

"My son."

"I'll trade for him," he said, the old eyes sparkling. "Injuns pay right smart for a strong boy like him."

"My son is not for trade, old-timer."

"Tell you what. I won't call you pilgrim, you don't call me old-timer. Deal?"

Emmett lowered his pistol, returning it to leather. "Deal."

"You pil . . . folk know where you are?"

"West of the state of Missouri, east of the Pacific Ocean."

"In other words, you lost as a lizard."

Emmett sighed, more a painful wheezing. "Back south of us is a tradin' post and a few cabins some folks begun callin' Wichita. You heard me say where Fort Larned was."

"Maybe you ain't lost. You two got names?"

"I'm Emmett, this is my son, Kirby."

"Pleasure. I'm called Preacher."

Kirby laughed out loud.

"Don't scoff, boy. It ain't nice to scoff at a man's name. Ifn I wasn't a gentle-type man, I might let the hairs on my neck get stiff."

Kirby grinned. "Preacher can't be your real name."

The old man returned the grin. "Well, no, you right. But I been called that for so long, I nearabouts forgot my Christian name. So, Preacher it'll be. That or nothin'."

"You the one left all them dead buffalo we seen a ways back?" Kirby asked.

"I might have shot one or two. Maybe so, maybe not."

"Seems like a waste to me."

"Did me too."

"That mean you ain't gonna kill no more?"

"Didn't say that, now, did I?"

Emmett waved Kirby still. "We'll be ridin' on, now, Preacher. Maybe we'll see you again."

Preacher's eyes had shifted to the northwest, then

narrowed, his lips tightening. "Yep," he said smiling. "I reckon you will."

Emmett wheeled his horse and pointed its nose west-northwest. Kirby reluctantly followed. He would have liked to stay and talk with the old man.

When they were out of earshot, Kirby said, "Pa, that old man was so dirty he *smelled.*"

"Mountain man. He's a ways from home base, I'm figuring. Tryin' to get back. Cantankerous old boys. Some of them mean as snakes. I think they get together once a year and bathe."

"But you said you soldiered with some mountain men."

"Did. But they got out in time. 'Fore the high lonesome got to them."

"I don't understand."

"They stay up in the high country for years. Don't do nothin' but trap and such. Maybe they won't see a white man once ever' two years—except maybe another mountain man. Sometimes when they do meet, they don't speak. All they've got is their hosses and guns and the whistlin' wind and the silence of the mountains. They're alone. It does something to them. They get notional . . . funny-actin'."

"You mean they go crazy?"

"In a way, I'm thinkin'. I don't know much about them—nobody does, I reckon. But I think maybe they didn't much like people to begin with. They crave the lonesomeness of space. The mountain men I was with, now, they were some different. They told me 'bout that old man's kind. They're brave men, son, don't never doubt that—probably the bravest men in the world. Got to be to live like they do. And what they've done well . . . ." He thought for a moment ". . . con*tri*bute to this country now that we fought the war and can put the nation back together."

"That's a real pretty speech, Pa."

Emmett reddened around the neck.

"What's con*tri*bute?"

"Means they done good."

Kirby looked behind them. "Pa?"

"Son."

"That old man is following us, and he's shucked his rifle out of his boot."

2

Preacher galloped up to the pair, his rifle in his hand. "Don't get nervous," he told them. "It ain't me you got to fear. We fixin' to get ambushed . . . shortly. This here country is famous for that."

"Ambushed by who?" Emmett asked, not trusting the old man.

"Kiowa, I think. But they could be Pawnee. My eyes ain't as sharp as they used to be. I seen one of 'em stick a head up out of a wash over yonder, while I was jawin' with you. He's young, or he wouldn't have done that. But that don't mean the others with him is young."

"How many?"

"Don't know. In this country, one's too many. Do know this: We better light a shuck out of here. If memory serves me correct, right over yonder, over that ridge, they's a little crick behind a stand of cottonwoods, old buffalo wallow in front of it." He looked up, stood up in his stirrups, and cocked his shaggy head. "Here they come, boys . . . rake them cayuses!"

Before Kirby could ask what a cayuse was, or what good a rake was in an Indian attack, the old man had slapped his bay on the rump and they were galloping off. With the mountain man taking the lead, the three of them rode for the crest of the ridge. The pack horses seemed to sense the urgency, for they followed with no pullback on the ropes. Cresting the ridge, the riders slid down the incline and galloped into the timber, down into the wallow. The whoops and cries of the Indians close behind them.

The Preacher might well have been past his so-called good years, but the mountain man had leaped off his spotted pony, rifle in hand, and was in position and firing before Emmett or Kirby had dismounted. Preacher, like Emmett, carried a Sharps .52, firing a paper cartridge, deadly up to seven hundred yards, or more.

Kirby looked up in time to see a brave fly off his pony, a crimson slash on his naked chest. The Indian hit the ground and did not move.

"Get me that Spencer out of the pack, boy." Kirby's father yelled.

"The what?" Kirby had no idea what a Spencer might be.

"The rifle. It's in the pack. A tin box wrapped up with it. Bring both of 'em, Cut the ropes, boy."

Slashing the ropes with his long-bladed knife, Kirby grabbed the long, canvas-wrapped rifle and the tin box. He ran to his father's side. He stood and watched as his father got a buck in the sights of his Sharps, led him on his fast-running pony, then fired. The buck slammed off his pony, bounced off the ground, then leaped to his feet, one arm hanging bloody and broken. The Indian dodged for cover. He didn't make it. Preacher shot him in the side and lifted him off his feet, dropping him dead.

Emmett laid the Sharps aside and hurriedly unwrapped the canvas, exposing an ugly weapon, with a potbellied, slab-sided receiver. Emmett glanced up at Preacher, who was grinning at him.

"What the hell are you grinnin' about, man?"

"Just wanted to see what you had all wrapped up, partner. Figured I had you beat with what's in my pack."

"We'll see," Emmett muttered. He pulled out a thin tube from the tin box and inserted it into the butt plate, chambering a round. In the tin box were a dozen or more tubes, each containing seven rounds, .52 caliber. Emmett leveled the rifle, sighted it, and fired all seven rounds in a thunderous barrage of black smoke. The Indians whooped and yelled. Emmett's firing had not dropped a single brave, but the Indians scattered for cover, disappearing, horses and all, behind a ridge.

"Scared 'em," Preacher opined. "They ain't used to repeaters; all they know is single shots. Let me get something outta my pack. I'll show you a thing or two."

Preacher went to one of his pack animals, untied one of the side packs and let it fall to the ground. He pulled out the most beautiful rifle Kirby had ever seen.

"Damn!" Emmett softly swore. "The blue-bellies had some of those toward the end of the war. But I never could get my hands on one."

Preacher smiled and pulled another Henry repeating rifle from his pack. Unpredictable as mountain men were, he tossed the second Henry to Emmett, along with a sack of cartridges.

"Now we be friends," Preacher said. He laughed, exposing tobacco-stained stubs of teeth.

"I'll pay you for this," Emmett said, running his hands over the sleek barrel.

"Ain't necessary," Preacher replied. "I won both of 'em in a contest outside Westport Landing. Kansas City to you. 'Sides, somebody's got to look out for the two of you. Ya'll liable to wander 'round out here and get hurt. 'Pears to me don't neither of you know tit from tat 'bout stayin' alive in Injun country."

"You may be right," Emmett admitted. He loaded the Henry. "So thank you kindly."

Preacher looked at Kirby. "Boy, you heeled—so you gonna get in this fight, or not?"

"Sir?"

"Heeled. Means you carryin' a gun, so that makes you a man. Ain't you got no rifle 'cept that muzzle loader?"

"No, sir."

"Take your daddy's Sharps, then. You seen him load it, you know how. Take that tin box of tubes, too. You watch out for our backs. Them Pawnees—and they is Pawnees—likely to come 'crost that crick. You in wild country, boy . . . you may as well get bloodied."

"Do it, Kirby," his father said. "And watch yourself. Don't hesitate a second to shoot. Those savages won't show you any mercy, so you do the same to them."

Kirby, a little pale around the mouth, took up the heavy Sharps and the box of tubes, reloaded the rifle, and made himself as comfortable as possible on the rear slope of the slight incline, overlooking the creek.

"Not there, boy." Preacher corrected Kirby's position. "Your back is open to the front line of fire. Get behind that tree 'twixt us and you. That way, you won't catch no lead or arrow in the back."

The boy did as he was told, feeling a bit foolish that he had not thought about his back. Hadn't he read enough dime novels to know that? he chastised himself. Nervous sweat dripped from his forehead as he waited.

He had to go to the bathroom something awful.

A half hour passed, the only action the always moving Kansas winds chasing tumbleweeds, the southward moving waters of the creek, and an occasional slap of a fish.

"What are they waiting for?" Emmett asked the question without taking his eyes from the ridge.

"For us to get careless," Preacher said. "Don't you fret none . . . they still out there. I been livin' in and 'round Injuns the better part of fifty years. I know 'em better— or at least as good—as any livin' white man. They'll try to wait us out. They got nothing but time, boys."

"No way we can talk to them?" Emmett asked, and immediately regretted saying it as Preacher laughed.

"Why, shore, Emmett," the mountain man said. "You just stand up, put your hands in the air, and tell 'em you want to palaver some. They'll probably let you walk right up to 'em. Odds are, they'll even let you speak your piece; they polite like that. A white man can ride right into nearabouts any Injun village. They'll feed you, sign-talk to you, and give you a place to sleep. Course . . . gettin' *out* is the problem.

"They ain't like us, Emmett. They don't come close to thinkin' like us. What is fun to them is torture to us. They call it testin' a man's bravery. Ifn a man dies good—that is, don't holler a lot—they make it last as long as possible. Then they'll sing songs about you, praise you for dyin' good. Lots of white folks condemn 'em for that, but it's just they way of life.

"They got all sorts of ways to test a man's bravery and strength. They might—dependin' on the tribe—strip you, stake you out over a big anthill, then pour honey over you. Then they'll squat back and watch, see how well you die."

Kirby felt sick at his stomach.

"Or they might bury you up to your neck in the ground, slit your eyelids so you can't close 'em, and let the sun blind you. Then, after your eyes is burnt blind, they'll dig you up and turn you loose naked out in the wild . . . trail you for days, seein' how well you die."

Kirby positioned himself better behind the tree and quietly went to the bathroom. If a bean is a bean, the boy thought, what's a pea? A relief.

Preacher just wouldn't shut up about it. "Out in the deserts, now, them Injuns get downright mean with they fun. They'll cut out your eyes, cut off your privates, then slit the tendons in your ankles so's you can't do nothin' but flop around on the sand. They get a big laugh out of that. Or they might hang you upside down over a little fire. The 'Paches like to see hair burn. They a little strange 'bout that.

"Or, if they like you, they might put you through what they call the run of the arrow. I lived through that . . . once. But I was some younger. Damned ifn I want to do it again at my age. Want me to tell you 'bout that little game?"

"No!" Emmett said quickly, "I get your point."

"Figured you would. Point is, don't let 'em ever take you alive. Kirby, now, they'd probably keep for work or trade. But that's chancy, he being nearabout a man growed." The mountain man tensed a bit, then said, "Look alive, boy, and stay that way. Here they come." He winked at Kirby.

"How do you know that, Preacher?" Kirby asked. "I don't see anything."

"Wind just shifted. Smelled 'em They close, been easin' up through the grass. Get ready."

Kirby wondered how the old man could smell anything over the fumes from his own body.

Emmett, a veteran of four years of continuous war, could not believe an enemy could slip up on him in open daylight. At the sound of Preacher jacking back the hammer of his Henry .44, Emmett shifted his eyes from his perimeter for just a second. When he again looked back at his field of fire, a big, painted-up buck was almost on top of him. Then the open meadow was filled with screaming, charging Indians.

Emmett brought the buck down with a .44 slug through the chest, flinging the Indian backward, the yelling abruptly cut off in his throat.

The air had changed from the peacefulness of summer quiet to a screaming, gunsmoke-filled hell. Preacher looked at Kirby, who was looking at him, his mouth hanging open in shock, fear, and confusion. "Don't look at me, boy!" he yelled. "Keep them eyes in front of you."

Kirby jerked his gaze to the small creek and the stand of timber that lay behind it. His eyes were beginning to smart from the acrid powder smoke, and his head was aching from the pounding of the Henry .44 and the screaming and yelling. The Spencer Kirby held at the ready was a heavy weapon, and his arms were beginning to ache from the strain.

His head suddenly came up, eyes alert. He had seen movement on the far side of the creek. Right there! Yes, someone, or something was over there.

I don't want to shoot anyone, the boy thought. *Why can't we be friends with these people?* And that thought was still throbbing in his brain when a young Indian suddenly sprang from the willows by the creek and lunged into the water, a rifle in his hand.

For what seemed like an eternity, Kirby watched the young brave, a boy about his own age, leap and thrash through the water. Kirby jacked back the hammer of the Spencer, sighted in the brave, and pulled the trigger. The .52 caliber pounded his shoulder, bruising it, for there wasn't much spare meat on Kirby. When the smoke blew away, the young Indian was face down in the water, his blood staining the stream.

Kirby stared at what he'd done, then fought back waves of sickness that threatened to spill from his stomach.

The boy heard a wild screaming and spun around. His father was locked in hand-to-hand combat with two knife-wielding braves. Too close for the rifle, Kirby clawed his Navy Colt from leather, vowing he would cut that stupid flap from his holster after this was over. He shot one brave through the head just as his father buried his Arkansas Toothpick to the hilt in the chest of the other.

And as abruptly as they came, the Indians were gone, dragging as many of their dead and wounded with them as they could. Two braves lay dead in front of Preacher; two braves lay dead in the shallow ravine with the three men; the boy Kirby had shot lay in the creek, arms outstretched, the waters a deep crimson. The body slowly floated downstream.

Preacher looked at the dead buck in the creek, then at the brave in the wallow with them . . . the one Kirby had shot. He lifted his eyes to the boy.

"Got your baptism this day, boy. Did right well, you did."

"Saved my life, son," Emmett said, dumping the bodies of the Indians out of the wallow. "Can't call you boy no more, I reckon. You be a man, now."

A thin finger of smoke lifted from the barrel of the Navy .36 Kirby held in his hand. Preacher smiled and spat tobacco juice.

He looked at Kirby's ash-blond hair. "Yep," he said. "Smoke'll suit you just fine. So Smoke it'll be."

"Sir?" Kirby finally found his voice.

"Smoke. That's what I'll call you now on. Smoke."

3

Preacher hopped out of the wallow and walked to a dead buck. He bent down and removed something from the dead Indian's belt. A Navy .36. He tossed the pistol to Kirby, along with a sack of shot and powder.

"Here, Smoke. Now you got two of 'em."

Kirby felt more than a little foolish with his new nickname. He did not feel at all like a man called Smoke should feel. Tough and brave and gallant and all that. But he smiled, secretly liking his new name.

Off another dead Indian, Preacher took a long-bladed knife, in a bead-adorned sheath. He tossed that to Kirby. "Man's gotta have a good knife, too."

Then he pulled his own knife and began scalping the dead bucks.

"Good God, man!" Emmett protested. "What in the hell are you doing?"

"Takin' hair," Preacher said. "I know a tradin' post that pays a dollar for ever' scalp lock a man can bring in. Fifty cents for a squaw's hair. But I don't hold with scalpin' wimmin. I won't do this to a Ute or a Crow—lived with 'em too long, I reckon—but I just purely can't abide a Pawnee."

Emmett grimaced at the bloody sight but kept his mouth shut. He had heard that Indians had not been the originators of scalping, but the white man. Now he believed the story.

Kirby looked on as Preacher took the Indian's hair. He was both horrified and fascinated.

Neither Emmett nor his son had ever seen a warlike Indian. There had been a few down-at-the-heels Quapaw Indians in Missouri when Emmett was growing up—and were still a few around—but they were not warlike. Father and son moved closer to take a look at their recent enemy.

Preacher had finished his grisly work. Surprisingly, to Kirby, at least, there was little blood from the close haircut.

"They don't look so mean to me . . . not now, anyways," Kirby said. "They just look . . . kinda poor."

"They ain't poor," Preacher contradicted. "Don't you believe that for a second. Most of the time they eat right well. Buffalo steak's nearabouts the best meat in the world, I reckon. And pemmican." He rolled his eyes and Kirby laughed at the old man's antics. "Well, you ever get a chance to eat some pemmican, you see what I mean. Tasty. Indian goes hungry, it's his own fault. They won't grow no gardens. They think that's beneath 'em. Warriors and hunters, not farmers. So to hell with 'em."

"Do you grow a garden, Preacher?" Kirby asked.

"I been known to from time to time. But I ain't no gawddamned sodbuster, if that's what you mean."

"See, Pa." Kirby looked at his father. "He can cuss. Why can't I?"

"Hush up, Kirby."

"What's that about cussin'?" Preacher asked.

"Never mind," Emmett said.

Kirby was growing accustomed to the dead braves. They did not bother him now. His stomach had ceased its growling. "What'd you call that food? Pem . . . what?"

"Buffalo meat, usually. Indians cut it into strips, dry it. That's called jerky. They take the jerky, crumble it, then beat hell out of it. Then they mix it with fleece—"

"With what?"

"Fat. Boilin' fat. Then you drop in a few berries, make it up in a brick, and wrap it. Best eatin' you ever put in your mouth. Don't spoil. Lasts for months. Shore do." He put his bloody scalps into a pouch on his wide belt and closed the flap.

"Won't those stink?" Kirby asked.

"They do get right ripe," the mountain man admitted.

"Do we bury these Indians?" Emmett inquired.

"Hell no!" Preacher looked horrified. "Plains' Injuns don't plant they dead like we do. 'Sides, they be back for 'em, don't you fret about that. Right now, I 'spect we better git from here. Put some country 'twixt us and them live Injuns. Let's go."

The trio rode at a steady gallop for several miles, then walked their horses, resting them as best they could. They repeated this several times, putting miles between them and the battle site by the creek. Late afternoon, they pulled up by a tiny stream and made a short camp.

"We'll make the fire small," Preacher said. "Use them dry buffalo chips we picked up. They don't hardly make no smoke. We'll have us coffee and beans, then douse the fire and make camp 'bout two-three miles from here. Place I 'member. We'll post guards this night, boys, and ever' night from here on in." He glanced at Kirby. "This is hostile country, Smoke."

Kirby sighed. He guessed it was going to be Smoke for the rest of his life. Or at least until Preacher left them. He looked at his Pa. Emmett was smiling.

Kirby said nothing until the fire was glowing faintly and the coffee boiling. The beans cooked, he sliced bacon into a blackened skillet then looked at Preacher.

"Why Smoke, Preacher?"

"All famous men got to have good-soundin' nicknames— impressive ones. Smoke sounds good to me. And believe me, Smoke, I have known some right famous men in my time."

"I'm not famous," Kirby said, a confused look on his face. Already a nice-looking boy, he would be a handsome man.

"You will be, I'm thinkin'," the mountain man said, stretching out on the ground. "You will be." And he would say no more about it.

They ate an early supper, then doused the fire, carefully checking for any live coals that might touch off a prairie fire, something as feared as any Indian attack, for a racing fire could outrun a galloping horse. They moved on, riding for an hour before pulling into a small stand of timber to make camp. Preacher spread his blankets, used his saddle for a pillow, and promptly closed his eyes.

Emmett said, "I'll stand the first watch . . . Smoke," and he grinned. "Then wake Preacher for the second, and you can take the last watch, from two till daylight. Best you go on to sleep now, you'll need it."

Just as Kirby was drifting off to sleep, Emmett said, "If you don't like that nickname, son, we can change it."

"It's all right, Pa," the boy murmured, warmed by the wool of the blanket. "Pa? I kinda like Preacher."

"So do I, son."

"That makes both of you good judges of character," the mountain man spoke from his blankets. "Now why don't you two quit all that jawin' and let an old man get some rest?"

"Night, Pa—Preacher."

"Night, Smoke," they both replied.

Preacher rolled the boy out of his blankets at two in the morning, into the summer coolness on the Plains. The night was hung with the brilliance of a million stars.

"Stay sharp, now, Smoke," Preacher cautioned. "Injun don't usually attack at night; bad medicine for them. Brave gets kilt at night, his spirit wanders forever, don't never get to the Hereafter in peace. But Injuns is notional, and not all tribes believe the same. Never can tell what they're gonna do. More'un likely, if they're out there, they'll hit us at first light—but you don't never know for shore." He rolled into his blankets and was soon snoring.

The boy poured a tin cup full of scalding, hot coffee, strong enough to support a horseshoe, then replaced the pot on the rock grate. Preacher had showed him how to build the fire, surrounded by rocks, larger rocks in the center to support a pan or pot, the fire hot, but no bigger than a hand. The air opening lay at the rear, facing the camp. The fire was fueled by buffalo chips, hot and smokeless, and the fire could not be seen from ten feet away.

While there was still light, Kirby (he could not bring himself to even think of himself as Smoke) had carefully cleaned and oiled the Navy Colt taken from the dead Indian. He had cut the flap off his holster and punched a hole in the front of the leather, threading a piece of rawhide through the hole, the loop to be placed over the hammer, securing the weapon. He did the same to a holster Preacher gave him, for his second weapon, then, using a wide belt—also given him by Preacher, from his seemingly never emptying packs—he buckled on his twin .36s. The right hand pistol he wore butt back, the left hand pistol, he carried butt forward, slightly higher than the other pistol. The big-bladed bowie knife was in its bead-adorned sheath, just behind the left hand Colt.

He had no way of knowing at this juncture of his young life, but with that action involving the pistols, and with what would follow in only a matter of hours, he was taking the first steps toward creating a legend that would endure as long as writers would write of the West. Men would fear and respect him; women would desire him but only one would ever find herself truly loved by him; children would play games, imitating the man called Smoke, and songs would be written and sung about him, both in the Indian villages and in the white man's saloons.

But on this pleasant night, Kirby was still some years away from being a living legend: He was just a slightly frightened young man, just a few months into his sixteenth year, sitting in the middle of a vast open plain, watching for savage Indians and hoping to God none were within a thousand miles of him. He almost dozed off, caught himself, and jerked back awake. He bent forward to pour another cup of coffee, rubbing his sleepy eyes as he did so.

That movement saved his life.

A quivering arrow drove into the tree where Kirby, just a second before, had been resting. Had he not leaned forward, the arrow would have driven through his chest.

Although Kirby had not yet practiced his gun moves, he had carefully gone over them in his mind. He drew first the right hand Colt, then the left hand gun, the heavy bark of one only a split second behind the first. Always a well-coordinated boy, his motions were almost liquid in their smoothness, the Colts in the hands of one of those few to whom guns seem almost an extension of the body. Two Pawnee braves went down in lifeless heaps. Kirby shifted position and the Navy Colts blasted the night in thunderous roars. Two more bucks were cut down by the .36 caliber balls.

Then the smoke-filled night was silent except for the fading sounds of Indian ponies racing away, away from the white man's camp. The Indians wanted no more of this camp: They had lost too many braves; too much death here.

"I ain't never seen nothin' like this!" Preacher exclaimed, walking around the dead and dying Pawnee. "I knowed Jim Bridger, Kit Carson, Broken Hand Fitzpatrick, Uncle Dick Wooten, and Rattlesnake Williams . . . and a hundred other salty ol' boys. But I ain't never seen nothin' to top this here. Smoke, you may be a youngster in years, but you'll damn shore do to ride the river with."

Kirby did not yet know it, but that was the highest compliment a mountain man could give another man.

"Thank you," he said to Preacher. He reloaded the empty cylinders.

Preacher scalped the Pawnee, then tossed the bloody scalp locks to Kirby. "They yourn, Smoke. Put 'em in that war bag I give you. They worth four dollars to you. Go on . . . four dollars ain't nothin' to sneeze at."

With his father watching him through eyes that had seen much, Kirby picked up the bloody hair and placed them in a beaded pouch Preacher had given him.

Emmett, who had ridden with the great Confederate Ranger, J.S. Mosby for a year, was the furthest from being a stranger to guns and gunplay. Although Kirby would not learn of it for years, his father had been with Mosby when they rode into the middle of a Union Army camp at Fairfax, Virginia, one night. They had asked their way to headquarters and there, Mosby awakened the Yankee general, Stoughton, by rudely and ungentlemanly slapping the man on his butt.

"Have you ever heard of J. S. Mosby," the Confederate guerrilla asked in a whisper.

Angry, the general replied, "Of course! Have you captured him?"

"No," Mosby said with a smile, "He's captured you."

The Confederate Rangers then kidnapped the Union general from under the noses of the general's own men.

"You're smooth and quick," Emmett complimented his son. "And I have seen some men who were smooth and quick."

"Thank you, Pa," Kirby said. He was just a little bit sick and embarrassed by what he'd done and all the attention he was receiving. The scalp locks in his war bag were not helping his stomach any.

"Be careful how you use your newfound talent, son," the father cautioned. "Use it for good, and not for evil. Temper your talent."

Then the man coughed and thought of his own mission westward. He wondered how and when he should tell his son.

"Yes, Pa. I will."

Preacher looked at the boy and wondered.

The trio rode for several days without encountering any more hostiles. They saw smoke, often, and knew they were being watched and discussed, but they rode through without further incident from the Pawnee. Three of them had killed more than twelve Pawnee, wounding several more in two quick fights. The Indian may have been a savage—to the white man's way of reasoning—but he was not a fool, and he was a first-class fighting man, many of the tribes the greatest guerrilla fighters the world would ever know. Part of that is knowing when to fight and when to back off. This was definitely one of the back-off times.

"This here is the Cimarron Cutoff," Preacher said. They had pulled up and sat their horses, the man and boy looking where he pointed. "The southern route to Santa Fe. Better for wagons and women, but the water is scarce. The northern route is best for water and graze, but it's tough. Lord, it's tough."

"Why?" Emmett asked.

"Mountains. Rocky Mountains. Make them mountains where I's born look like pimples."

"Where is that, Preacher?" Kirby asked.

"East Tennysee. Long time ago." His eyes clouded briefly with memories of a home he had not seen in more than half a century. At first the man had planned to return for a visit, but as the years rolled by, those plans dimmed, never becoming reality. Then he realized his Ma and Pa would be dead—long dead—and there was no point in going back.

The price many men paid for forging westward, opening up new trails for the thousands that would follow.

"I run off when I were twelve," Preacher said, looking at father and son. "That were, best I can recall, fifty-two year ago, 1813, I believe it was. I've spent the better part of fifty years in the mountains. And I reckon I've known ever' mountain man worth his salt in that time, and some that thought they was tough, but weren't."

"What happened to them that wasn't?" Kirby asked.

"I helped bury some of 'em," Preacher said quietly.

"You must know your way around this country, then," Emmett said.

"Do for a fact. I helped open up this here Santa Fe Trail, and I've ridden the Mormon Trail more'un once. Boys, I been up the mountain, over the hill, and 'crost the river. And I've seen the varmit." He looked hard at Kirby. "But Smoke, I swear I ain't never seen the likes of you when it comes to handlin' a short gun. It's like you was born with a Colt in your hands. Unnatural."

The old mountain man was silent for a time, his eyes on the deep ruts in the ground that signified the Santa Fe Trail. "I don't know where you two is goin'. Probably you don't neither. You may be just a-wanderin', that's all. Lookin'. That's dandy. Good for folk to see the country. So I'll tag along here and there, catch up ever' now and then see how you're a-makin' it. I usually don't much take to folk. Like to be alone. Must be a sign of my *ad*-vanced age, my kinda takin' a likin' to you two. 'Specially Smoke, there. I got a feelin' 'bout him. He's gonna make a name for hisself. I want to see that; be there when he do."

"We're heading, in a roundabout way," Emmett said, "to a place called I-dee-ho."

"Rugged and beautiful," Preacher said. "Been there lots of times. But were I you—'course I ain't—I'd see Colorado first. Tell you what: I got me a cache of fur not too far from here. Last year's trappin'. Ya'll mosey around, take it easy, and keep on headin' northwest. From here, more north than west. Ya'll will cut the northern trail of the Santa Fe in a few days. Stay with it till you come to the ruins of Bent's

Fort. I'll meet you there. See you." He wheeled his horses and rode off without looking back, pack horses in tow.

Emmett looked at his son. Preacher liked the boy. And if he would agree to see to him through the waning months of his boyhood . . . well, Emmett's mission could wait. The men he hunted would still be there. But for now, he wanted to spend some time with his son.

"How about it, Kirby—I mean, Smoke. Want to see Colorado?"

The boy-rapidly-turning-man grinned. "Sure, Pa."

Long before 1865, Bent's Fort lay in ruins. But from 1834 to 1850, the post ruled the fur trade in the southern Rockies. By 1865, the mountain men were almost no more. Time had caught up with them, and in most cases, passed them by. Civilization had raised its sometimes dubious head and pushed the mountain men into history. Those that remained were men, for the most part, advanced in years (for their time), heading for the sunset of their lives. But they were still a rough breed, tough and salty, not to be taken lightly or talked down to. For these men had spent their youth, their best years, and the midpoint of their lives, in the elements, where one careless move could have meant either sudden death or slow torture from hostiles. Mountain men were not easily impressed.

But the gathering of mountain men stood and watched as Kirby and his father rode slowly into the ruins of the old post, rifles across their saddles, pack animals trailing.

Kirby and his father did not know Preacher had spread the word about the boy called Smoke.

Kirby, as did many boys of that hard era, looked older than his years. His face was deeply tanned, and he was rawboned, just beginning to fill out for his adult life. His shoulders and arms were lean, but hard with muscle, and they would grow much harder and powerful in the months ahead.

"He don't look like much to me," an aging mountain man said to a friend.

"Neither did Kit," his friend replied. "Warn't but four inches over five feet. But he were a hell of a man."

The mountain man nodded. "That he were." His eyes were on Kirby. "Funny way to wear a brace of short guns."

"Faster than a snake, Preacher says."

The mountain man cocked an eye at his friend. "Preacher's been known to tell a lie ever' now and then."

"Not this time, I wager. That there kid's got a mean look to his eyes. Mayhaps he don't know it yet, but he do. Give him two-three years, I'd think long 'fore tanglin' with him."

That got him an astonished look. "Hell-fire, Calico. You fit a grizzly once!"

"Won, too," the old man said. "But I'm thinkin' that kid's part bear, part puma, part rattler. I'll go 'long with Preacher on this one."

"Does have a certain set to that squared-off jaw, don't he?"

"Yep. Big hands on him."

Kirby and Emmett sat their horses and stared. Neither had ever seen anything like this colorful assemblage. The men (only a few squaws were in attendance and they stayed to themselves), all of them sixty-plus in years, were dressed in wild, bright colors: in buckskin breeches and shirt, with beaded leggings, wide red or blue or yellow sashes about their waists. Some wore whipcord trousers, with silk shirts shining in a cacophony of colors. All were beaded and booted and bearded. Some held long muzzle-loading Kentucky rifles, or Plains' rifles, with colorfully dyed rawhide dangling from the barrel, the shot and powder bags decorated with beads.

This was to be the last great gathering of the magnificent breed of men called Mountain Man. Many of them, after this final rendezvous in the twilight of their years, would drift back into the great mountains they loved, never to be heard from or seen again, to die as they had lived—alone. Their graves the earth they explored, their monuments the mountains they loved, tombstones rearing above them forever. They were a breed of man that flourished but briefly, whose courage and light helped to open the way west.

When Emmett and Kirby spotted Preacher, they could not believe their eyes. They sat their horses and stared.

Preacher was clean, his beard trimmed. He wore new buckskins, new leggings, a red sash around his waist, and a light they had never seen sparkled from his eyes. "Howdy!" he called. "Ya'll light and sit, boys."

"I don't believe it," Emmett said. "His face is clean."

"Water to wash in over there," Preacher said, pointing. "Good strong soap, too. But you'd best dump what's in the barrel, though. It's got fleas in with the ticks."

When Emmett and son walked out into the final rendezvous of the mountain men, on this, their first day at the old post, they were greeted warmly, if with a bit of constraint.

"Gonna have us a feast," a one-eyed, grizzled old man told them. "Come on. Got buffalo hump, antelope, and puma. Preacher's gonna give up the message. Let's don't be late."

"Puma?" Kirby questioned.

"Mountain lion," the man told him. "Best, sweetest meat you ever did taste." He smacked his lips. "This is the first big rendezvous I've been to in more'un twenty year. Guess this will be the last one for many of us," he added, sadness in his voice.

"Why?" Kirby asked.

"Fur trade's damn near gone; pilgrims pourin' in over the trails me and all the others opened up. Hate to see it. Why, I seen five white people just last month. Five! Gettin' so's a body can't even be alone no more."

"When was your last rendezvous?" Emmett asked. Even he had never seen anything to compare with this gathering.

The mountain man stopped and scratched his head. "Let me ponder on that. Oh, back 'bout '40, I reckon."

"But this is 1865!" Kirby said.

"It is! Well, damn me. Time shore do get away from a body, don't it?"

"They'll be many more people behind us," Emmett said.

"Yep. I reckon there will be. Be a plumb ruination to the country, too." He shook his head and walked away to join a small group of aging mountain men gathered around several smoking pits just outside of what was left of the fort.

The fort, built in a sheltered bend of the Arkansas River, had been for years a welcome sight to trappers, traders, and the few travelers, representing a bit of safe haven for man and horse.

Sad, Kirby thought, his eyes taking in all the sights and sounds and good smells of cooking. It's sad. These men opened up this country, and now they're old, and nobody wants them around.

And that just did not seem right nor fair to the tall young man.

As if on silent cue, the men gathered in a circle. Preacher walked to the center of the circle, and the babble of voices fell silent

"Well, boys," he said in a somber voice. "I reckon this here rendezvous is 'bout gonna do it for most of us. Our time is past. We got to move over, make way for civilized folk: ranches and farms and plows and wire and pilgrims and the like.

"But boys, we can always 'member this: We saw it first and them few that come 'fore us. We seen it when it was glory. Untouched. We rode the mountains and the rivers, we made the trails for the pilgrims to foller, and we buried our friends—when we could find enuff of 'em to bury. Some of us was the first white man an eagle or bear or Injun ever seen. Now it's nearabouts time for some of us to see the elephant. But that's got to be all right. We done, I believe, what we was put on this here earth to do, and we can all be right proud we done it.

"Streams trapped out, purt-near. Fools comin' in a-killin' all the buffalo. In some parts they's stringin' wire all over God's creation. A-hemmin' us in."

He slowly turned, his eyes touching the gaze of all present.

"But where can we go?" Preacher asked.

No one could answer the question.

"We never married nobody 'ceptin' squaws. Got no white kin to go back to. Even if we did, they wouldn't have us. Can you see us livin' in a town? All cooped up like a wild animal? No, sir. Not me. Not for none of you, I'm thinkin'.

"For me, I'm gonna see to it that this here boy, Smoke," he cut his eyes to Kirby, "learns the true way of the wilderness. Might take me awhile, him being no more than a child. But . . . I reckon he's as old as we was when we come out here, green as a gourd and wet behind the ears.

"And when that's done, I'm gonna fork my horses and ride out to see this here much-talked about elephant.

"But, 'fore that happens, we all gonna eat, tell lies to one 'nother, and whoop and holler and dance. Then we just gonna ride out without lookin' back. 'Cause boys, it's all over for men like us, and for some of us, real soon-like, we got just one more trail to ride."

Kirby looked around him, seeing tears in some eyes of the mountain men. For they knew the words they were hearing were true.

Preacher took a deep breath. "Now, boys, bow your blasphemous old heads, 'cause I'm a-gonna talk to the Lord 'fore we feast.

"Oh, Lord," his voice was strong, carrying far beyond the

circle of men, "thanks for this grub we 'bout to partake of. We'll enjoy, I'm sure, 'cause them smells is startin' my mouth to salavatin'. But 'fore we start a-gummin' and a-gnawin' on this sweet meat, there's something I got to ask You. Do You ever think You maybe made a mistake in the way You set a man up to go down his final trail? Give it some thought, Lord. Here we are, old men past our prime, juices all dried up. Couldn't do nothin' with a woman 'cept think about it and some of us forgot what it was we could even think of. But we're a-smellin' all the good smells of cookin'. Point I'm makin', Lord, is this: If You ever want to do it again, do this: When a man gets our age, take his balls and give him back his teeth!

"Amen—let's eat."

4

Two days later, when Kirby awakened at dawn and kicked off his blankets, a curious silence surrounded him. A feeling of aloneness. Pulling on pants and boots over his long-handles, he looked around the ruins of the old post. Nothing. The mountain men were gone, having pulled out as silently as they had learned to live. He shook his father awake and told him what had happened.

On his feet, his father pointed. "Over there."

Preacher stood on the banks of the Arkansas, his face to the high mountains.

"What's he doin', Pa?"

"Sayin' goodbye, Kirby. In his own way." He glanced at his son. "That old man likes you, son. Listen to him, and he'll teach you things you'll need to stay alive in this country."

The son met the father's eyes. "I will, Pa."

The father patted the boy's shoulder and then coughed.

The three of them rode out the next morning. They headed for the tall, shining mountains.

"Where will your friends go, Preacher?" Kirby asked.

The day the mountain men had left, Preacher had spent to himself, speaking to no one. But on this day he was his usual garrulous self.

"They'll scatter, Smoke. Most of 'em will head back into the mountains, find 'em a lonely valley, and they'll never come out again. A few still got people back East, and they'll head there. But they won't stay; 'less they die there. It'll be too tame for 'em. And they own people won't want 'em around more'un four-five days. Then they'll want to get shut of 'em."

"That's sad. Why won't they want them?"

"Back East, Smoke, they got written laws a body's got to live by. Ain't none of us followed no law 'cept our own for more'un fifty years. Law of common sense. You don't put hands on 'nother man; don't steal from him; don't cheat him; don't call him a liar. Do, and you gonna get killed. Out here, Smoke, man purty well respects the rights of the other feller, and don't none of us need no gawddamned lawyer to tell us how to do that. It'll be that way out here for a while longer, till the fancy people get all het up and mess it all up. The worse is yet to come, Smoke. You wait and see. Thank Gawd I won't be around to see it. I'd have to puke."

"How do you mean: Mess it all up?"

"Lawyers readin' meanin's into words that ain't 'posed to be there. A-messin' up what should be left up to common sense. Hell's fire, Smoke. Rattlesnake crawls into your blankets with you, you don't ask him ifn he's gonna bite you. You kick him out and shoot him or stomp him. Same with man. Man does you a deliberate wrong—and don't never let no smooth-talkin' lawyer man tell you no different, Smoke, ever'body knows right from wrong— you go after that man; you settle up your way. To hell with lawyers—damn ever'one of 'em."

"I'll go along with you on that, Preacher," Emmett said. "That's one of the reasons I brought my son out here."

"Well . . . Smoke's got maybe twenty-five years 'fore this

country gets all worded up with them fancy-pants lawyers. After that, a man won't be able to be a man no more. And it's comin', boys, bet on it."

Preacher looked around him. "Well, ain't no use frettin' 'bout it now. 'Cause right now we got our hair to worry 'bout. We gonna be travelin' through hostile country, and the Sand Crick massacre is still fresh in the minds of the Injuns.

"Soldiers wiped out an entar Injun village: men, wimmin, papooses. Mostly Cheyenne and some Arapaho. Black Kettle was they chief. Happened last year and the Injuns still got hard feelins 'bout that. A Colonel Chivington was in charge, so I'm told."

"Will we pass by it?" Kirby asked.

"No. It's north and some east of here. But I seen it right after it happened. Damn near made me puke. There weren't no call for it. Black Kettle's brother, White Antelope, was killed that raid. And Black Kettle ain't no man to mess with. Left Hand, a chief of the Arapaho, showed his bravery and scorn of the white men by standin' in front of his tent with his arms folded crost his chest, refusin' to fight. Damn soldiers kilt him, too." Preacher spat on the ground.

"White men ain't no saints, Smoke. They can be just as mean and orne'y as they claim the Injuns to be."

"Where is Black Kettle now?" Emmett asked, his eyes on the huge mountains in front of them.

"On the warpath. So ifn either of you gets to feelin' your hair start to tingle, let me know, 'cause they's Injuns close by."

"I'll be sure to do that," Emmett said dryly.

For the next several days, they followed the Arkansas River, then cut northwest through the Arkansas valley. Kiowa country, Preacher told them. So stay alert. It was here that Kirby's frontier education really began.

"I ain't never seen the likes of this," the boy said, his eyes sweeping the panorama of nature.

"They's lots of things you ain't seen, Smoke," Preacher said. "But you will, I'm figuring. Ifn you don't get mauled by a bear, bit by a rattler, fall off your horse and break your neck, get caught up in a landslide or blizzard, eat bad meat or drink pisen water, shoot yourself in the foot and bleed to death, or get your hair lifted by Injuns."

Kirby swallowed hard. He pointed to plants on the desolate brown hills. "What's them things?"

"Them's prickly pear and ball cactus. In the spring, both have right purty flowers on 'em. Over there," he pointed, "is yucca. Them long tall white flowers on 'em is what the Spanish call Madonna Candles. Named after they momma, I guess, don't rightly know."

Emmett laughed at that and Preacher ignored him.

"You see, Smoke, most ever'thing the good Lord created can be used for something. The Injuns use the guts of them plants to make rope—good stout rope, too. I know; I been tied up with it a time or two. And ifn you feel in need of a bath—and a man ought to get wet with water two-three times a year—you can dig up some yucca root and use it for soap. Makes a good lather. Keep that in mind ifn you start to get real gamy. But don't overdo baths. I believe a body needs a chance to rest."

Emmett laughed and then coughed for a few seconds. His coughing had gotten worse the past week. But he offered no explanation for his cough and neither Preacher nor Kirby asked.

"Up here a ways," Preacher said, "we'll bear a little more west. Head for a tradin' post I know—called Pueblo."

Emmett looked at him. "I've heard that name."

"It's known a bit. 'Count of the Mormons, mostly. Back in ... oh ... '46 or '47, Mormons tried to make a settlement there. I come up on 'em time a two. They notional folk, don't believe like we do. Don't never talk religion with 'em—mess up your mind. I try to keep shy of 'em."

"What happened to the people who tried to settle there?" Kirby asked.

"Don't rightly know. I come back through there—me and Rattlesnake Williams—oh . . . I reckon it were '52 or '53, and we didn't see hide nor hair of 'em. I heared tell they went up north, back to Utah. Don't get me wrong; they good folk. Help you out ifn you need a hand. But you best know what you're doin' ifn you plan on tradin' with 'em. They good traders. And don't mess with they wimmin folk. They get real touchy 'bout they females."

The only thing Kirby knew about females was that they were different from men. Just exactly how they were different was still a mystery to him. He had asked his Pa a time or two, but Emmett got all red in the face and cleared his throat a lot. Said he'd tell Kirby when the time came. So far, the time had not yet come.

Kirby remembered the time, three years back, when a carnival came through his part of Missouri. One of the girls, just about his own age, had made a bunch of eyes at him. She'd cornered Kirby at the edge of the lot and told him for two dollars she'd make a man out of him. Then she reached down with her hand and grabbed Kirby. *Nobody* had ever grabbed him there. Scared him so bad he took off into the woods and was running so hard he ran right into a tree. Knocked himself unconscious for half an hour.

Kirby had never told anybody about that.

"Where's Utah?" Kirby asked.

"West of us. You'll see it one of these days, Smoke."

They pulled up to rest and Kirby's bay began tugging at the reins, trying to head off east. Kirby finally had to brutally jerk the reins to settle the animal.

"Smells water," Preacher told him. He pointed to a small water hole. "But that's bad water. Pisen. Horse sometimes ain't got no sense when it comes to water. Injuns call that water wau-nee-chee. Means no good."

Kirby rolled that word around his tongue, memorizing it. "How can you tell if water is no good?"

"Look for bones of small animals and birds close by. Can't always go by smell or taste." He swung his spotted pony. "You'll learn, Smoke. I'll teach you."

Emmett finally asked the question that had been on his mind for days. "Why, Preacher?"

"Gettin' old," the mountain man said simply and softly. "Like to leave something of what I know behind when I go see the elephant. Got no one else to leave it with."

"You were never married?"

Preacher laughed. "Hell's fire, yes! Five—no, six times. Injun ceremonies. I got twelve-fifteen younguns runnin' 'round out here. Half-breeds. But most of 'em don't know me for what I am, and I don't know them. That weren't the way I planned it; it just worked out that way. Wouldn't know most of 'em ifn I saw 'em. I'm just 'nother white man. They'd soon shoot me and take my hair as look at me. Probably rather shoot me than look at me, ifn the truth be told."

"Why?" Emmett asked.

"They breeds, that's why. Some tribes don't look with much favor on breeds. Then they's them that being a breed don't make no difference. Injuns ain't all alike, Smoke. They just as different in thinkin' as white men, and just as quarrelsome, too—with other tribes. Ifn the Injun would ever try to git along and unite agin us, the white man would have never got past Kansas. I think Injuns is the greatest fighters the world'll ever know. But they just can't get together agin us. Something I'm right thankful for," he added.

They took their time getting to Pueblo with Kirby learning more from the old mountain man each day. And he was eager to learn, retaining all the old man told him. The weeks on the trail had begun the transformation of the boy into the edge of manhood.

Sixteen, Emmett mused as they rode, and already killed half a dozen men. His son's quickness and ease with the Navy Colts had stuck in the man's mind. The father had handled guns all his life. Before taking up farming, he had been marshal of a small town in Missouri, on the Kansas border, and had killed two men during his tenure in office. God alone knew how many men he had killed in the war. But Kirby handled the Colts like they were an extension of his arms. And fast—God, the boy was fast.

Kirby practiced an hour each day drawing and dry-firing the Colts. In only a matter of weeks, his draw had become a blur—too fast for the eye to follow. And he was deadly accurate.

Well, Emmett mused, making up his mind, he was glad they had run into Preacher, and he was glad the mountain man had taken such an interest in Kirby. Smoke, he amended that. He was also glad the boy could take care of himself in a bad situation. For, although the father had not told the son, the move westward had not been pure impulse. Even had his wife not been dead, Emmett would have moved westward . . . he had given his word to Mosby.

If it took him forever, Emmett had sworn to Mosby, he would find and kill three men: Stratton, Potter, and Richards.

And he was sure Preacher had guessed there was a mission to fulfill in the back of the elder Jensen's mind.

Preacher was no fool—he was sharp. Emmett would have to confide in the old man—soon. For the three traitors and murderers, Potter, Stratton, and Richards, had said many times they were going to the place called Idaho when the war ended. And with the stolen Confederate gold, they would have ample funds to start a business. Ranches, more than likely, although one of them had expressed a desire to open a trading post.

Emmett knew, if he found the men at all, it might take

months, even years. But he also knew he didn't have years. But he had to find them. Had to kill them.

Or be killed, he reflected morosely.

While Kirby rode on ahead, his bay prancing, the boy taking to the new land like a colt to a field of clover, Preacher hung back to speak with Emmett, both of them keeping one eye on the boy.

"You got a burr under your saddle, Emmett," Preacher said. "Wanna talk about it?"

"I got things to do. And it might take me some time to do them."

"I figured as much."

"Thought you would have. I took no allegiance to the federal government after Lee surrendered. But I did swear to kill three men and get back as much of the Confederate gold they stole as possible. I'll do it, too."

"War's over," the old man observed. "Who you gonna give the gold to?"

"I might give it to Kirby. Maybe I'll just toss it in the river. Don't know. It's tainted." He looked at Preacher. "You'll take care of my boy?"

"You know that without askin'."

"Teach him what you know?"

"That's my plan. But they's more to this than you're sayin'. You had that cough long?"

"You're pretty sharp, Preacher."

"Don't know about that. Just keep my eyes and ears open, that's all."

"I caught a ball through the lung. Laid me flat on my back for weeks. Got infected. Then lung fever hit the other lung. Maybe—just maybe—if I stayed in a dry climate, I might make it, according to the doctors. But they didn't sound hopeful. I can't do that. I swore I'd find those men."

"Who are they?"

"Wiley Potter, Josh Richards, and a man named Stratton. They turned traitor and robbed some gold meant to keep the Confederacy going a while longer. That was bad enough, but they killed several men while stealing the gold. One of the men killed was my son, Luke."

Preacher grunted. "Smoke know about that?"

"No. He thinks his brother was killed fighting with Lee, in the wilderness. If I don't come back from this, you tell him the truth, all right?"

"Done."

"I'll be pulling out after I stock up with some supplies in Pueblo. I'll tell Kirby all I think he needs to know."

Kirby stood in front of the trading post at dawn, watching his father ride out, pack horse trailing. Emmett had taken only a few of the gold coins, leaving the rest with Kirby. The young man was conscious of the weight of the coins in the leather bag around his neck. His father stopped, spun his horse, and waved at his son. Kirby returned the wave, then his Pa was gone, dipping out of sight, over the rise of a small hill.

Preacher sat on the porch of the trading post, watching, saying nothing. Kirby turned, looking at the man who was to become his mentor.

"Will he be back?" The boy's voice was shaky.

"Ifn he can." Preacher spat on the dusty ground. "Some things, Smoke, a man's just gotta do 'fore his time on earth slips away. Your Pa has things to do. Smoke, ifn you wanna cry—and they ain't no shame in a man cryin'—best go 'round back and do it. Get it over with."

Kirby squared his shoulders. "I'm a man," he said, his voice firming. "I lived alone and worked the land and paid the taxes—all by myself. I haven't cried since Ma died."

Lot of weight on a boy's shoulders, Preacher thought. "Well, then, we'd best buy some salt and flour and beans and sich. Get you outfitted. Then we'll ride on outta here."

"Where will we meet up with Pa?"

"Brown's Hole—ifn he's lucky. Next year. Year after. He'll get word to us."

Kirby put a foot on the steps. "Let's get outfitted."

The man behind the counter at the trading post had given the boy ten dollars for the scalps in his war bag, winking at Preacher as he did so. Kirby had not seen the wink.

Kirby pointed to a shiny new Henry repeating rifle on the rack. "I want one of those," he told the man. "And a hundred rounds of .44s." He took a few coins from the leather bag. "For the Henry, I'll trade you this Spencer and pay the difference. Whatever is fair."

Man and boy haggled for fifteen minutes, the man finally throwing up his arms in an exaggerated gesture of surrender. The transaction was done.

Kirby bought an extra cylinder for his left hand .36, and a sack full of powder and shot.

They rode out.

Preacher told him he knew of a friendly band of Injuns up north of the post a ways. He'd see to it that Smoke got hisself a pair of moccasins and leggings and a buckskin jacket—fancy beaded.

"I ain't got that kind of money to waste, Preacher."

"Ain't gonna cost you nothin'. I know the lady who'll make 'em."

"She must like you pretty well."

Preacher smiled. "She's my daughter."

September, 1865

The pair rode easily but carefully through the towering mountains and lush timber. They had once again crossed the Arkansas and were now almost directly between Mt.

Elbert to the north, and Mt. Harvard to the south. They had nooned and nighted just outside a small trading post on the banks of the Arkansas—which would later become the town of Buena Vista—and picked up bacon and beans and coffee. They had left before dawn, both of them seeking the solitude of the high lonesome. It had not taken Kirby long to fall prey to the lure of the lonesome. The country was wild and beautiful, and except for Indians, sparsely populated.

"Where're we headin'?" Kirby asked.

"In a round 'bout way, to one of my cabins. On the North Fork. We'll have to winter there. It's gonna be a bad one, too."

Kirby looked around him. The day was pleasant, but cool. "How can you tell that this early?"

"Leaves on the aspen. Whenever they start turnin' gold this early in the fall, the winter's gonna be a bitch-kitty. Bet on it. But we'll have things to do, Smoke. Hunt, run traps, chop wood, and," he said grinning, "stay alive. That there is the mainest thing."

"Sometimes I get the feeling we're the first white men to see this country, Preacher."

"Know the feelin' well. But they's mountain men through here 'fore I was born. And not too many years ago an army man, named Gunnison, Captain Gunnison, as I recall, came through here. That was back in '52 or '53. He was chartin' the land."

"For what?"

"Railroad, I heared." He spat his contempt on the ground.

"When they gonna build it?"

"Not in my lifetime, I hope. I don't wanna see this here country all tore up. Pilgrims comin' in with their plows, a-draggin' they wimmin and squallin' kids with 'em." He shuddered. "Damn nuisance. Makes my skin crawl."

Kirby grinned. "That could be fleas, Preacher."

"Watch your mouth, boy—don't sass an old man."

Kirby laughed with his friend. "Some people might call the railroad progress, Preacher."

"Some people might paint wings on a pig and try to make it fly, too. No, sir. Land oughta be left the way God made it. Already folk in here pokin' holes in the ground, lookin' for gold and silver. They scarin' off the game, makin' the Injuns mad at ever'body. It's a damn shame and a dis-grace."

"Preacher?"

"Yep, Smoke."

"What happened back at the fort? Bent's Fort, I mean. Did the Indians destroy it?"

"Nope. Old Bent blew it up hisself. That was back in . . . oh . . .'52, I think."

They stopped, allowing their horses to drink and blow.

"Blew up his own fort? That's crazy. Why would he do that?"

Preacher chuckled. "Old Bill Bent was probably one of the finest men I ever knowed. I guess he just got discouraged when the fur trade kind of petered out. That'us back about '50. He tried to sell the fort to the government, but they fiddle-faddled around for two years tryin' to make up they minds. Far as I'm concerned, ain't been nobody in government had a mind since Crockett. Anyways, ol' Bill just blowed the damn thing up, loaded his goods on wagons, and moved down the Arkansas to Short Timber Crick. He set up two-three more places, but they weren't none of 'em nearabouts as grand as the first."

Kirby had gotten lost in the big hotel in Springfield; that was grand. He couldn't imagine anything to match that out here.

"Yes, sir, Smoke, Bent's Fort had nice livin' quarters, a bar, and a billiard room. That there bar served up a drink called Taos Lightning. And let me tell you, it were ever'thing it was cracked up to be. Struck your stomach like a fulminate cap to powder."

The old man and the young man rode on, climbing higher, the air cool as it pulled at their lungs. They rode for an hour without speaking, content to be surrounded by God's handiwork.

"Where is Mr. Bent now, Preacher?"

"Don't rightly know, Smoke. He were married two times—that I know of. Both times to Injun wimmin. First wife died . . . can't 'member her name. Then old Bill hitched up with her sister, Yellow Woman. Last I heard, he was livin' with one of his kids, on the Purgatoire River."

"Is he a legend?"

"Damn shore is. Just like you will be, Smoke. Someday."

The young man laughed. "I'll never be a legend, Preacher."

"Yeah, you will." Preacher's reply was solemn. "I can see it all around you, in ever'thing you do."

"Well, I guess only time will prove that, Preacher."

"As much time as the Good Lord gives you, Smoke."

5

That winter of 1865/66 was a brutal one, with days of snow that sometimes piled up to the shuttered windows of the cabin along the banks of the North Fork.

With time on his hands, Kirby read and reread, many times, the McGuffey's reader his father had bought for him. And he found, much to his surprise, that Preacher had a dozen or so thick volumes, including the selected works of a man called Shakespeare.

"I didn't know you read, Preacher," Kirby said, the howl of the winter winds muffled inside the small, snug cabin.

"Don't. Can't read airy word. But I wintered once with a feller who, as it turned out, had been a school teacher back East. Them books belonged to him."

"Belonged?"

"Thought hisself quite a ladies' man, that feller did. 'Bout twenty year ago—give or take some—he took a shinin' to a squaw over the mountain east of here. Only problem was that there squaw already had herself a buck, and that Injun didn't much cotton to that school teacher makin' eyes at his woman. He caught 'em together one afternoon. They was . . . ah . . ."

Kirby got his hopes up. At last!

". . . kissin' and things."

Damn! "What things?"

"Things. Don't interrupt. That buck killed the school teacher, cut off the woman's nose, and kicked 'er out. I got left with the books and the body. Buried the body. Didn't know what to do with the books, so I kept 'em. Used to be more'un them there. Rats et 'em over the years."

"Cut off her nose!"

"Injun way of divorce, you might call it. It varies from tribe to tribe."

"What happens to the man if he's unfaithful to the woman?"

"Some tribes, the woman can kick him and his goods right out of the wickiup, and he ain't got no say in the matter—none a-tall."

"Seems fair," the young man observed.

"Some bucks might not agree with you," Preacher said with a smile. "'Pecially this time of year."

The Chinook winds blew once in the late winter of '66, melting the snow and creating a false illusion of spring, confusing the vegetation and the animals. The warm winds also brought a stirring within the boy/man called Smoke.

"It ain't gonna last," Preacher told Kirby, now in his seventeeth year. "Likely be a blizzard tomorrow. Relax, Smoke, spring'll be here 'fore you know it." The mountain man smiled knowingly. "You act like you got the juices runnin' in you."

"What do you mean?"

Preacher cocked an eye at him. "Girls, boy. You know."

Kirby shook his head. "No, sir. I don't know nothin' about girls."

Preacher paled.

"I figured you'd tell me about females."

"Lord Gawd!"

"You mean I have to ask *Him*!"

"Don't blaspheme, young man," Preacher said sternly. "Come a time—and this ain't the time," he was quick to add, "you'll learn all there is for a man to know 'bout females." He grimaced. "And a bunch you don't want to know. Most aggravatin' creatures God ever put on this here earth. Can't live with 'em, can't do without 'em."

"That's what my father used to say. But he'd always grin at Ma when he said it."

"He better grin," Preacher replied.

Kirby read for a time while Preacher slept by the fire. When Preacher awoke, Kirby asked, "What do we do when spring does get here?" His thoughts were suddenly flung far, to his father, wondering where he was, if he was still alive.

"I start learnin' you good. And you start bein' a man."

"I wonder where my Pa is?"

"He's either on the way to doin' what he set out to do; he's already done 'er, or he's doin' it."

"Or he's dead," Kirby added.

"Mayhaps," Preacher's words were soft. "We all get to see the elephant someday."

"I don't know the whole story, Preacher. Pa said you'd tell me when it was time. I reckon it ain't time just yet."

"That's so, Smoke."

"All right. But I'll tell you this, Preacher: If those men he went after killed him, I'll track them down, one by one, and I'll kill them. And anyone who gets in my way." His words did not come from the lips of a boy; but a man grown in many ways.

Preacher had a sudden flash of precognition, the foreseeing coming hard, chilling the old mountain man.

"Yep," he said. "I reckon you will, Smoke."

The warm winds once again blew, and this time they were the real advance guard of spring. First to show their appreciation of the cycle of renewal were the peonies, bursting forth in a cacophony of color. The columbine, which would one day be the official flower of the yet-to-be-admitted state of Colorado, cast forth its contribution to spring, in colors of blue and lavender and purple and white. The valleys and foothills, the plains and mountains exploded in a holiday of technicolor.

And on that day, Preacher packed his gear and told his young friend to do the same. "Walls closin' in. Time to get movin'. Time for you to start learnin'."

With their Henry repeating rifles across their saddles, the pair rode out, heading northeast from the North Fork, into the timber and the mountains. Still, one hour each day, the boy called Smoke practiced with his deadly Colts, perfecting what some would later write was not only the first fast draw, but the fastest draw.

Those few who would get to know the man called Smoke would say he was even faster than the legendary Texas gunfighter, John Wesley Hardin; possessing more cold nerve than Wild Bill; meaner than Curly Bill; and as much a hand with the ladies as Sundance. But for now, Kirby was learning, and the mountain man taught him well.

Still spry as a cat and tougher than wang-leather, Preacher taught Kirby fistfighting and boxing and Indian wrestling. But more importantly, he taught him to win in a fight—and taught him that it didn't make a damn how you won. Just win. He taught him to kick, gouge, throw, and bite.

"Long as you right, Smoke, it don't make no difference how you win. Just be sure you in the right."

"Not knowin' the land and the animals can get a body dead," Preacher told him. "I'll start like you don't know nothin'. Which is not that far from the truth. Snakes."

"Huh?"

"Snakes. Tell me what you know 'bout 'em."

"I know to leave some of them alone."

"Wise, but not near enough."

"Well . . . I know a poisonous snake's got to coil before they strike."

"Wrong. A rattler can short-strike at you with just the power of his neck. You 'member that. And this, too: Rattler meat is good to eat. I've et a poke of it. Right tasty. But be damn shore the critter is dead 'fore you start to skin it. They get right hostile ifn you's to jerk the hide off 'fore they's dead."

Kirby smiled. "Wouldn't you?"

Preacher laughed. "'Spect so. Injuns was gonna skin me alive one time, up on the Platte. That's how I got my name, Preacher. I preached to them heathens for hours. Didn't think I knowed so many words. Even made me up a language that day and night. Called it the unknown tongue. But I made believers out of them savages. I reckon they thought I was crazy. Injuns won't harm a crazy man—most of 'em, that is. They think he's kind of a God. Finally that chief just put his hands over his ears and told his bucks to turn me a-loose. Said I's a hurtin' his ears something fierce. I got my pelts and rode out of there without lookin' back." He chuckled at the long-ago memory.

"And you've been called Preacher ever since."

"Yep."

Preacher had blindfolded the young man and spun him around like a top. Removing the sash, Preacher asked, "Which direction you facin', Smoke?"

Kirby shook his head, looking around him. "North."

"Wrong. You looked at that moss on yonder tree, didn't you?"

"Yes, sir."

"That kind of thinkin' can get you kilt. Moss, ifn there's light and water enough, can grow all the way 'round a tree. Man can wander 'round in circles and die believin' that moss only grows to the north."

"Then—"

Preacher answered the unspoken question. "Sun, stars, lay of the land, and a feel for them all. Come a time, Smoke, you'll just know. It won't take long."

The days passed into weeks, and Kirby's education grew, and so did he, gaining weight, filling out with hard muscle.

The young man pointed his finger at a bush full of berries. "I know about them—we got them in Missouri. Don't eat them, they're poison."

Preacher grinned. "But some birds do."

"Yes. But you said not to believe that old story that anything a bird eats a man can eat."

"That's right. See them flowers over yonder. Right purty and lots of birds eat 'em. But they can kill a man, or else make him so sick he'll wish he was dead. Oak tree yonder. I've knowed folk to boil the bark and make a bitter-tastin' tonic. Never cared for the stuff myself."

"Why?"

"'Cause it tastes like pisen water. And I just don't care to drink no pisen water."

As they traveled, they would occasionally encounter roaming bands of Indians, most of them friendly to Preacher. Once, after they had palavered with a band of Cheyenne, Kirby looked back in time to see one of the braves making a circling motion at his temple with a forefinger. He told Preacher.

"Sure. Sign for a crazy person. Let 'em keep believin' it. We'll keep our hair."

"Why do Indians think a crazy person is a God?"

"Well, they believe he's possessed by gods—nearabout the same thing to them. And the Injuns don't want no bad medicine with no God.

"They don't worship like we do, Smoke. Injun worships the sun, the stars, the trees, the moon, the rivers. Nearabouts ever'thing. Least the Injuns I know does.

They can't rightly tell you why they think a man crazy is thataway. I've heared twelve different versions from twelve different medicine men. Don't none of 'em make no sense to me."

During their wanderings, they met trappers and hunters, a few of whom rode from the west. Kirby would always ask about Emmett. But no one had seen him or heard about him. It was as if the man had dropped off the face of the earth.

"Idaho is wild, Smoke," Preacher told him. "Only a few places settled. We ain't heard nothin' by next spring, we'll strike out for the Hole."

1867

The pair spent the winter of 1866/67 in an old cabin on the banks of the Colorado River, with the northern slopes of Castle Peak far to the south, but visible on most days. Here, the pair ran traps, hunted, and on the bitter cold days and nights, stayed snug in the cabin built some forty years earlier by a long dead friend of Preacher's.

"What happened to the man who built this cabin?"

"He got tied up with a mountain lion one afternoon," Preacher said. "The puma won."

In the spring of '67, they sold their pelts at a post and rode out for the northwest.

"Show you where we used to rendezvous, Smoke. Back 'bout '30, I think it were. Worst damn place I ever been in my life. We called it Fort Misery. First time I ever et dog. Warn't too bad as I recall."

Kirby shuddered. "You've eaten dog since?"

"Shore. Many times. And so will you. That's why Injuns keep so many dogs 'round they camp. Come winter, food gets scarce, they cook up dog. It's right good."

Kirby hoped he would never eat dog. "This Brown's Hole—that where we're headin'?"

"Yep. On the Utah side of Brown's Hole, just west of Wild Canyon. Quiet there. I told your Pa 'bout it. Said ifn he could, he'd meet us there—somehow."

Kirby didn't like the sound of—somehow.

They had taken their time, riding through the Flat Tops Primitive area, past Sleepy Cat Peak, and into the Danforth Hills. They made camp at the confluence of the Little Snake and Yampa Rivers—and they stayed put for three weeks.

"What are we waiting for?" Kirby asked impatiently, the youth in him overriding his near manhood.

"Somebody'll be along directly." Preacher calmed him. "They always is. So you just hold your water, Smoke—we got time."

At the end of the third week, a mountain man rode in. He looked, at least to Kirby, to be as old as God.

"You just as ugly as I 'membered, Preacher," he said, in a form of greeting.

Kirby had learned that mountain men insulted each other whenever possible. It was their way of showing affection.

"You should talk, Grizzly," Preacher retorted. "I 'member what Elk Man told you thirty year ago: You could hire out your face to scare little children."

A pained look crossed the old man's face. "Hell, Preacher," he said in mock indignation, "I didn't ride seventy mile to get insulted."

"'Course you did. I'm one of the few that can stand to look at you. Light and sit, we got grub."

"You cook it?"

"Hell, yes, I cooked it!"

"That's even a worse insult," Grizzly said. But he dismounted, dropped the reins on the ground, and filled a plate with food.

After his second helping, piling his plate high with

venison, wild potatoes mixed with wild onions, and gravy, the old mountain man wiped his tin plate clean with a piece of Kirby's panbread, then poured a third cup of coffee. He belched contentedly and patted his stomach. "Bread was good, anyways. Boy must have made that."

Preacher glared at him. "I'd druther have to buy your traps than feed you for any length of time. You eat like a hog."

Preacher and Grizzly insulted one another for a full half hour, each one trying to outdo the other. Kirby had never heard such tall tales and wild insults. The men finally agreed it was a draw.

Grizzly said, "Do I talk in front of the boy?"

"He ain't no boy. He's a growed man."

Kirby poured himself a cup of coffee and waited.

"Man rode into the Hole 'bout two months ago. All shot up. Had a bad cough. He—"

"Is he still alive?" Kirby blurted.

Grizzly turned cold eyes on the young man. "Don't never 'rupt a man when he's a-palaverin'. Tain't polite. One thing 'bout Injuns, they know manners. They gonna 'low a man to speak his piece without 'ruptin'. 'Course they might skin you alive the minute you finished, but they ain't gonna 'rupt you while you's talkin'."

"Sorry." Kirby said.

"'Cepted. No, he's dead. Strange man. Dug his own grave. Come the time, I buried him. He's planted on that there little plain on the base of the high peak, east side of the canyon. You 'member it, Preacher?"

Preacher nodded.

Grizzly reached inside his war bag and pulled out a heavy sack. He tossed the sack to Kirby. "This be yourn, from your Pa. Right smart 'mount of gold." Again, he dipped into the buckskin and beaded bag, pulling out a rawhide-wrapped flat object. "This here is a piece of paper with words on it. Names, your Pa said, of the men who put lead in him. He said you'd know what to do, but for me to tell you don't do nothin' rash." Grizzly rose to his feet. "I done what I gave my word I'd do. Now I'll be goin' Thankee both for the grub."

Without another word, the old mountain man mounted his pony, gathered his pack horses, and rode off east. He did not look back.

"Ain't no point in movin' now," Preacher said. "Be dark in three hours. We'll pull out at first light."

At eighteen, Kirby had achieved his full growth: six feet, two inches tall, packing a hundred and eighty pounds of bone and muscle. His shoulders, arms, and hands were powerful, his legs long, his waist lean. His hair was long and ash-blond. His hands and face were deeply tanned. His eyes were an unreadable brown.

The bay his father had given him had not survived the first winter, slipping on ice and breaking a leg, forcing Kirby to shoot the animal. He now rode a tough mountain horse he had traded from an Indian, a huge Appaloosa, much larger than most of that breed. The Indian had ridden away chuckling, thinking he had gotten the better of the deal, for the Appaloosa would allow no one to ride it, refusing to be broken. But Kirby had slow-gentled the animal, bringing it along slowly and carefully, step by step. Now, no one but Kirby could put a saddle on the animal, much less ride him. He was a stallion, and he was mean, his eyes warning any knowledgeable person away. The Appaloosa had, in addition to its distinctive markings, the mottled hide, vertically striped hoofs, and pale eyes, a perfectly shaped seven between his eyes. And that became his name. Seven.

Gone was the McClellen saddle, replaced by a western rig, slightly heavier, but much more comfortable.

Smoke and Seven.

* * *

Emmett's horses had been picketed close to the base of Zenobia Peak. His gear was by his grave, covered with a ground sheet and secured with rocks. There were several more horses than Emmett had left with.

"You read them words on that paper your Pa left you?" Preacher asked.

"Not yet."

"I'll go set up camp at the Hole. I reckon you'll be along directly."

"Tomorrow. 'Bout noon."

"See you then." Preacher headed north. He would cross Vermillion Creek, then cut west into the Hole. Smoke would find him when he felt ready for human company. But for now, the young man needed to be alone with his Pa.

Kirby unsaddled Seven, allowing him to roll. He stripped the gear from the pack animals, setting them grazing. He picketed only the pack animals, for Seven would not stray far from him.

Taking a small hammer and a miner's spike from his gear, Kirby began the job of chiseling his father's name into a large, flat rock. He could not remember exactly when his Pa was born, but thought it was about 1815.

Headstone in place, secured by heavy rocks, Kirby built his small fire, put coffee on to boil in the blackened pot, then sat down to read the letter from his Pa.

Son,

    I found some of the men who killed your brother, Luke, and stolt the gold that belonged to the Gray. Theys more of them than I first thought. I killed two of the men work for them, but they got led in me and I had to hitail it out. Came here. Not goin to make it. Son, you dont owe nuttin to the Cause of the Gray. So don't get it in your mind you do. Make yoursalf a good life and look to my restin place if you need help.

Preacher kin tell you some of what happen, but not all. Remember: look to my grave if you need help.

I allso got word that your sis, Janey, leff that gambler and has took up with an outlaw down in Airyzona. Place called Tooson. I woodn fret much about her. She is mine, but I think she is trash. Dont know where she got that streek from.

I am gettin tared and seein is hard. Lite fadin. I love you Kirby-Smoke.

Pa.

Kirby reread the letter. *Look to my grave.* He could not understand that part. He pulled up his knees and his head on them, feeling he ought to cry, or something. But no tears came.

Now he was alone. He had no other kin, and he did not count his sister as kin. He had his guns, his horses, a bit of gold, and his friend, Preacher.

He was eighteen years old.

6

Having been born and reared on a farm, the earth was naturally a part of Kirby. So on the Utah side of the Hole, the tall young man planted several gardens: corn, beans, greens, potatoes. All carefully irrigated from a small stream. Preacher had scoffed at this, saying, "I'd be gawddamned ifn I'd bust any sod!" But Kirby noticed the old man ate up the vegetables on his plate, and usually helped himself to seconds, sometimes thirds.

Kirby had caught up with a band of wild horses, mustangs with some Appaloosa mixed in, and started raising horses. He now had a respectable herd.

Kirby no longer practiced with his Colts. He did not need to practice. He was a crack shot and blindingly fast.

Preacher, now pushing hard into his sixty-eighth year, was just as spry as when Kirby had first laid eyes on him—and just as cantankerous and ornery.

Kirby laid claim to all the land between Vermillion Creek to the east, and about two sections past the still ill-defined Utah state line to the west. All the land from Diamond Peak to the north, down to and including Brown's Hole. He rode once to a small town about a hundred and fifty miles from the Hole and filed on his claim. But the town died out a year later, becoming yet another ghost town on the western landscape, and

Kirby's claim was never recognized in the years ahead. It was illegal from the outset, since he was claiming far too much land, but Kirby figured—and figured correctly—that since the land was so desolate and in some instances, downright barren, no one else would want it.

Tucked away in the far reaches of the northwestern part of Colorado, Kirby and Preacher lived alone—and became something of a mystery, much as the hermit, Pat Lynch, would someday become. Pat, who later lived in the canyon with a pet mountain lion named Jenny Lind. Kirby and Preacher were not talkative men, sometimes going for days without speaking.

A wild and raging canyon cut down from the Hole: the Green River. It would later be named Lodore Canyon, by an army major, a geologist who was fond of quoting the poet Southey's "How the Waters Come Down At Lodore," as he shot the rapids.

Emmett Jensen's grave was now covered with a profusion of wild flowers, clinging stubbornly to the rocky soil. Kirby visited the grave weekly, sometimes standing for hours by the site. He spoke silently to his Pa, wishing he knew what to do. He always left with a mild feeling of discontent, as if he should be doing *something* about the men who killed his Pa.

At first, Preacher had told him, "You just too young yet to do much of anything 'bout them men who kilt your Pa. You got all the makin's, but you still need some seasonin'. Give it time, Smoke. Them folk be there when you ready to make your move."

But as the months marched into a year, then two, Preacher knew the boy was gone, and in its place, a man grown. He knew, too, from his half century and more on the trail, that the young man called Smoke was a potentially dangerous man: big and solid and steady and strong as a bear. A man whose draw with those old Navy Colts was so fast as to be a blur. And he never missed. Never.

The old mountain man knew little of the emotion called love. He had liked the squaws he had wintered with, sharing their buffalo robes—liked them all. He had enjoyed playing with his children. And somewhere in the back of his mind, he held a memory of his mother: a faded, time-worn retention of the woman, but without a clear face. He knew he must have loved her as a child. But the call of the open plains, the wilderness, the unknown, the high lonesome, the untraveled hills and mountains and trails, had been too much; overpowering love.

But with the man he called Smoke, the mountain man knew what he felt must be love, for in Smoke was everything the old man would want in a son: strength, daring, courage, eagerness to face the unknown, willingness to learn, to pit himself against the wilderness. Then, finally, the old man admitted the truth: He did not want Smoke to face the men on that list—for fear of losing him. He had been deliberately holding him back.

And that ain't right, he concluded. *The man is twenty year old,* Preacher thought. *Time to cut loose the tie-string and let him taste the world of people. He ain't gonna like it—just like me—but he got to see for hisself.*

The rattle of sabers and the pounding of hooves broke into Preacher's ruminations.

"Men comin'!" he called.

The young man known but to a few white men as Smoke stepped out of the cabin. His guns, as always, belted around his waist, the right hand Colt hanging lower than the butt-forward left gun. Had there been a woman with the detachment of cavalry, she would have called the young man handsome, and her heart might have beat just a bit faster, for he was striking-looking.

"Hello!" the officer in charge called. "I was not aware this area was inhabited by white men."

"You is now," Preacher said shortly.

"My name is Major John Wesley Powell, United States Army."

"I'm Preacher. This here is Smoke. An' now that we know each other, why don't you leave?"

The major laughed good-naturedly. "Why, sir, we've come to do a bit of exploring."

His good humor was not returned by either man. "What do you want to know 'bout this country?" Preacher asked. "Just name it, and I'll tell you—save you a mess of trouble. Then you can leave."

"May we dismount?"

"Dismount, sit, squat, stand, or kick your heels up in the air. It don't make no difference to me."

Major Powell laughed openly, heartily, then dismounted, telling his sergeant to have the men dismount and stand easy. "You old mountain men never cease to amaze me. And I mean that as a compliment," he added. His eyes turned to Kirby. "But you're far too young to have been a mountain man. Are you men related?"

"I'm his son," Preacher said with a straight face. "He fell in the Fountain of Youth a few years back, but he bumped his head doin' it and now he can't recall where it is. I'm waitin'."

Preacher glanced at the old scout with the army and then looked away.

"I got things to tell you, Preacher," the scout said.

"All right."

"Well," the major said with a smile. He cleared his throat. "Tell me, what do either of you men know about the river that flows through the canyon?"

"It's wet," Kirby said.

"And it ain't no place for a pilgrim," Preacher added.

"Then I take it that both of you have traversed the Green River?"

Preacher looked at Kirby for translation.

"Been down it," Kirby said.

"Hell yes, I been down it," Preacher said. "I been down it, up it, through it, crost it, and one time, back in '39, over it."

"The only man to ever shoot those rapids," a young lieutenant contradicted, "was General Ashley, back in '23 and '24."

"Yeah," Kirby said. "His name's still on the rock on the eastern side of the canyon wall. And don't never again call Preacher a liar."

The young officer stirred until the major called him softly down. "Stand easy, Robert." In a lower voice, heard only by a sergeant and the young officer, he said, "This is your first tour of duty out here, Bob—you know nothing of western men. Until you learn more abut the customs here, it would behoove you to curb your tongue. Calling a man a liar, or merely implying he is one, is a shooting matter west of the Mississippi. This is not Philadelphia, so just be quiet." He looked at Kirby. "He meant no offense, Mr. Smoke."

"Not mister—just Smoke."

"Unusual name," the major remarked.

"I give it to him," Preacher said. "After he kilt his first two men. I think he was fifteen, thereabouts."

The young lieutenant paled slightly.

The major said, "We saw a grave coming in. The name was Jensen."

"My father."

"I'm sorry, sir."

"Not nearly as sorry as the men who killed him will be."

Preacher looked at him. "You make your mind up?"

"About a half an hour ago."

"We goin' after 'em?"

"Yep."

"Figures."

Major stood quietly, not knowing what was going on. "I gather you men live here?"

"I own it," Kirby said.

"Own it? How much of it?"

Kirby told him.

"Why . . . that's hundreds of square miles!"

"We like lots of room."

"You have papers on this?"

"I filed on it, yeah. But I have no objections to you and your men staying here. Just don't trample my gardens or take my horses."

The major had stepped closer, standing by a large, flat rock. "I assure you, sir, we will leave the—"

No one saw the young man draw, cock, and pull the trigger of his right hand Colt. It was done as fast as a man could blink. The major looked down: A headless rattlesnake writhed at his boots.

"Sweet Molly!" a young cavalryman said. "I never even seen him draw."

Major Powell was a cool one; he had not moved. He kicked the squirming snake out of the way and said, "That was the most impressive shooting with a handgun I believe I've ever seen. I thank you, Smoke."

"Man can't be too careful out here," Preacher said, a bored look on his bearded face. "I take it upon myself to tell all pilgrims that."

The major smiled at this quiet slur. "I don't believe I've ever seen a man draw, cock, and fire a pistol that quickly. I'm sure I haven't. But I'm told the outlaw, Jesse James, is also quite proficient with a handgun."

"Who?" Kirby was startled.

"Jesse James. The Missouri bank robber and outlaw. Do you know him?"

"I've met him." Kirby drew his right hand Colt and tossed the weapon to the major.

The cavalryman inspected the pistol, noting the initials J. J. carved into the handles. Powell tossed the pistol back to Kirby. "I see," he said quietly, not quite certain where he now stood, for emotions concerning the James Gang ran both hot and cold, depending upon which side of the fence one stood. "And where are you from originally, Smoke?"

"That ain't a polite question to ask out here," Preacher informed him.

"I know," the major said. "I shouldn't have asked it. I withdraw it."

"It's all right," Kirby said. "I'm from the southwestern part of Missouri."

"Did you fight in the Civil War?"

"My Pa fought in the War Between the States," Kirby said with a smile.

"Ah . . . yes." The major returned the smile. He would say no more about James. He mounted, ordering his men to do the same. "We shan't disturb you, gentlemen. We'll bivouac on the other side of the canyon. Perhaps we'll see each other again."

"I doubt it," Kirby said.

"Oh?"

"Me and Preacher got things to do and places to go. Any horse you see around here with the SJ brand belongs to us. If you need a horse, take your pick of the mustangs and geldings, leave the mares alone. Just leave the money—what you think they're worth—in the cave at the Hole."

"Thank you," the major said. "You are a trusting man, Smoke."

"Not really. I just believe you don't want to cheat me."

Major Powell sensed in the young man a heavy, almost tangible aura of danger. The dark eyes gave no hint of what lay behind them.

"No," the army officer said. "I don't believe I want to do that."

The cavalrymen were gone in a cloud of dust, all but the old buckskin-clad scout who had guided them to this old post. He had not dismounted. He looked at Preacher.

"Thought you's dead," he finally said.

Preacher glared at him. "Yeah? That's what you get for tryin' to stir up that mess between your ears."

The scout grunted. "Walked right into that, I reckon." He shifted his gaze to Kirby. "Met a man who knowed your Pa in the war. One of Mosby's people. All stove up now—livin' over to the hot springs on the San Juan

Valley there. He heared 'bout your Pa gettin' lead in him west of here. His name is Gaultier. Don't ask me to spell it. He might know something that you wanna know. Told him I'd tell you ifn I saw you. I seen you. I told you. Good seein' you agin, Preacher."

"Right nice seein' you, Rio."

The scout wheeled his horse and was gone.

"Friend of yours?" Kirby asked.

"Not so's you'd know it. We fought over the same squaw back in '49. He lost. We ain't had much to do with each other since then. He's a sore loser."

"Can we trust him?"

"Oh, yeah. We don't cotton to one another, but you can trust him."

"Want to take a ride to the springs?"

"What do you think?"

Pagosa Springs, which translated means Indian healing waters, lies at the bottom of the state, not far from the New Mexico line, in what would someday become the San Juan National Forest. Several hundred miles, as the crow flies, from Brown's Hole, through some of the roughest and most beautiful country in the state. Late summer when the two men reached the hot springs. Preacher had groused and bitched the entire way.

"Gawddamned farmers! I never seen so many pilgrims in all my life."

They had seen half a dozen farms in a month.

For Preacher, it was his first encounter with barbed wire. He had cut his hand, ripped his shirt, and finally fell down before getting loose from the sharp tangle.

Kirby had sat his saddle and laughed at Preacher's antics, which only made matters worse and the profanity more intense.

Just east of the Uncompaghre Plateau, an irritated farmer's wife had threatened both of them with a double-barreled shotgun before Kirby could convince her they meant no harm to her, her pigs, or her kids.

"Woman!" Preacher had railed at her. "You put down that cannon. Why . . . I opened up this country. I—"

She waved the shotgun at him. "Get away from me, you dirty old man."

"Dirty old man! Why you lard-butt heifer, I—"

She stuck the Greener under his beard. "Git!" she commanded.

Preacher was fuming as they rode away. "Damned ole biddy," he cursed. "No respect for my kind. None a-tall."

Kirby grinned. "Civilization is upon us, Preacher."

Preacher violently and heatedly put together a long string of words which profanely contradicted his nickname.

They had stopped at mid-morning just west of the Needle Mountains to replenish their supplies. A wild, roaring mining camp that would soon be named Rico. It was an outlaw hangout in the early 1870s and would continue to be rough and rowdy until almost the turn of the century.

The population of the as yet unnamed settlement had rapidly diminished due to recent Indian raids, but there were still about a hundred men and half a dozen prostitutes in the camp when Kirby and Preacher dismounted in front of the trading post/saloon. As was his custom, Kirby slipped the thongs from the hammers of his Colts at dismounting.

They bought their supplies and turned to leave when the hum of conversation suddenly died. Two rough-dressed and unshaven men, both wearing guns, blocked the door.

"Who owns that horse out there?" one demanded, a snarl to his voice, trouble in his manner. "The one with an SJ brand?"

Kirby laid his purchases on the counter. "I do," he said quietly.

"Which way'd you ride in from?"

Preacher had slipped to the right, his left hand covering the hammer of his Henry, concealing the click as he thumbed it back.

Kirby faced the men, his right hand hanging loose by his side. His left hand was just inches from his left hand gun. "Who wants to know—and why?"

No one in the dusty building moved or spoke.

"Pike's my name," the bigger and uglier of the pair said. "And I say you came through my diggin's yesterday and stole my dust."

"And I say you're a liar," Kirby told him.

Pike grinned nastily, his right hand hovering near the butt of his pistol. "Why . . . you little pup. I think I'll shoot your ears off."

"Why don't you try? I'm sure tired of hearing you shoot your mouth off."

Pike looked puzzled for a few seconds; bewilderment crossed his features. No one had ever talked to him in this manner. Pike was big, strong, and a bully. "I think I'll just kill you for that."

Pike and his partner reached for their guns.

Four shots boomed in the low-ceilinged room. Four shots so closely spaced they seemed as one thunderous roar. Dust and bird's nest droppings fell from the ceiling. Pike and his friend were slammed out the open doorway. One fell off the rough porch, dying in the dirt street. Pike, with two holes in his chest, died with his back to a support pole, his eyes still open, unbelieving. Neither had managed to pull a pistol more than halfway out of leather.

All eyes in the black powder-filled and dusty, smoky room moved to the young man standing by the bar, a Colt in each hand. "Good God!" a man whispered in awe. "I never even seen the draw."

Preacher had moved the muzzle of his Henry to cover the men at the tables. The bartender put his hands slowly on the bar, indicating he wanted no trouble.

"We'll be leaving now," Kirby said, holstering his Colts

and picking up his purchases from the counter. He walked out the open door.

Kirby stepped over the sprawled, dead legs of Pike and walked past his dead friend.

"What are we 'posed to do with the bodies?" a man asked Preacher.

"Bury 'em."

"What's that kid's name?"

"Smoke."

They camped deep in the big timber that night, beside a rushing mountain stream, with the earth for a bed and the stars for a canopy. Over a supper of fresh-caught trout, Preacher asked, "How do you feel, Smoke?"

The young man glanced at his friend, a puzzled look in his eyes. "Why—I feel just fine, Preacher. How come you asked that?"

"You just kilt two men back yonder, Smoke. In front of twelve-fifteen salty ol'boys. And all they could do was a-gape at you with they mouths hangin' open. Now I ain't sayin' Pike and his friend didn't need killin', 'cause they did. They was bullies and troublemakers and trash. Pike's been in these mountains for years and he ain't worth spit. But the point I's makin' is this: Right now the story is being told in that there camp; tomorry night it'll be told 'round a dozen fires. This time next month, it'll be stretched to where you kilt five men, and that's where the salt gets spread on the cut."

"You mean I'll have a reputation?"

"Perzactly. And then ever' two-bit kid who thinks he's a gun-hand will be lookin' for you, to make a name for hisself."

"They'll never do it from the front."

"You that shore of yourself?"

"Yes, I am."

Preacher laid down his plate and poured a cup of coffee. "Yep, I reckon you is, at that."

7

THE MAN CALLED SMOKE

It was obvious to even the most uninitiated in medicine that Gaultier did not have much time left on this earth—in his present form.

"Cancer," he told them bluntly. "That's what the doctors say—and I believe them. Waters here help the pain, but I'm not going to make it." He looked at Smoke. "You have your father's eyes. And word is out that you are very good—perhaps the best—with a handgun."

"So I'm told," Smoke said.

"Well, you'd better be," the dying man said matter-of-factly. "Two of Pike's friends rode in yesterday afternoon. One claims to be his brother. Seems they tracked you southeast, then cut around, out of the wilderness, and came in from the south. Thompson and Haywood."

The young man remained calm. "I'm not worried about them. I'll deal with them when they confront me. What about the men who killed my father?"

Gaultier grinned. "You are a cool one, *jeune homme*. All right, I will tell you about your father—and your brother."

Smoke stepped out of Gaultier's tent along the creek an hour before sunset. He walked down the rutted street, the sun at his back—the way he planned it.

Thompson and Haywood were in the big tent at the end of the street, which served as saloon and cafe. Preacher had pointed them out earlier and asked if Smoke needed his help. Smoke said no. The refusal came as no surprise.

As he walked down the street, a man glanced up, spotted him, then hurried quickly inside.

Smoke felt no animosity toward the men in the tent saloon; no anger, no hatred. But they came here after him, so let the dance begin.

The word had swept through the makeshift town, and from behind cabin walls, trees, and boulders, the people watched as Smoke stopped about fifty feet from the tent.

"Haywood! Thompson! You want to see me? Then step out and see me."

The two men pushed back the tent flap and stepped out, both of them angling to get a better look at the man they had tracked. "You the kid called Smoke?" one said.

"I am." With instinct born into a natural fighter, Smoke knew this would be no contest. Both men carried their guns tucked behind wide leather belts; an awkward position from which to draw, for one must first pull the hand up, then over, grabbing the pistol, cocking it as it is pulled from behind the belt, then leveling it to fire. It is also a dandy way to shoot oneself in the belly or side.

"Pike was my brother," the heavier and uglier of the pair said. "And Shorty was my pal."

"You should choose your friends more carefully," Smoke told him.

"They was just a-funnin' with you," Thompson said.

"You weren't there. You don't know what happened."

"You callin' me a liar?"

"If that is the way you want to take it."

Thompson's face colored with anger, his hand moving closer to the .44 in his belt. "You take that back or make your play."

"There is no need for this," Smoke said.

The second man began cursing Smoke as he stood tensely, almost awkwardly, legs spread wide, body bent at the waist. "You're a damned thief. You stolt their gold and then kilt 'em."

Smoke, who had spent hundreds of hours practicing his deadly skills, thought that they were doing everything wrong. These men weren't gun-hands. He could smell the fear-sweat from the men.

"I don't want to have to kill you," Smoke said.

"The kid's yellow!" Haywood yelled. Then he grabbed for his gun.

Haywood touched the butt of his gun just as two shots boomed over the dusty street. The .36 caliber balls struck him in the chest, one nicking his heart. Haywood dropped to the dirt, dying. Before he closed his eyes, and death relieved him of the shocking pain, closing her arms around him, pulling him into that long sleep, two more shots thundered. He had a dark vision of Thompson spinning in the street. Then Haywood died.

Thompson was on one knee, his left hand holding his shattered right elbow. His leg was bloody. Smoke had knocked his gun from his hand, then shot him in the leg on the way down.

"Pike was your brother," Smoke told the man. "So I can understand why you came after me. But you were wrong. I'll let you live. But stay with mining. If I ever see you again, I'll kill you."

The young man turned, putting his back to the dead and bloody. He walked slowly up the street, his high-heeled Spanish riding boots pocking the air with dusty puddles.

"Cool, ain't he, Frenchy?" Preacher said.

"Yes," Gaultier said. "Too much so, perhaps. I wonder if killing the men who killed his father will then bring him happiness?"

"I don't know," Preacher replied. "I just wish to hell he'd find him a good woman and settle down."

"He will never settle down," the Frenchman said. "He might try, but he will always drift—like smoke."

"This here is your show, Smoke," Preacher said, as they rode away from the hot spring. "So you call the tune."

"La Plaza de los Leones. That's the closest name on the list."

"I been there. Reckon it's changed some, though."

"We'll soon see."

"Wanna answer me a question, Smoke?"

"Have I ever held back from you?"

"Reckon not. But you know I helt you back from doin' this for two years, don't you?"

"You didn't hold me back, you just didn't encourage me."

"All right. Have it your way. How come you made up your mind sudden like?"

"Because it was time, Preacher."

That hard flash of precognition again swept over the mountain man. "Son, have you taken a real clost look at the names on that paper? Now, I can't read airy one, but Frenchy read 'em to me. Them people is scattered over three states and territories. Chances of you finding them all is slim, at best."

"I'll find them."

Preacher nodded. "Well, I'll just tag along—keep you away from bad whiskey and bad wimmin. Both of 'em'll kill a body."

"Preacher? I've never known a woman—the way a man should know one."

"Well, your time'll come, Smoke. You'll fall in love one of these days—it happens to the best of us. Then you'll be walkin' into boulders and pickin' flowers and fallin' off your horse."

Smoke grinned. "Did you do that, Preacher?"

"Yep. For a squaw once. I guess I were in love—don't rightly know much 'bout it."

"What happened to her?"

"She died. And I just don't wanna say no more 'bout it."

La Plaza de los Leones, Square of the Lions, was only a few years away from being renamed Walsenburg. Built on the banks of the Cuchara River, the town, by 1869, was already a ranching and farming community with a city government. It was a hundred and fifty miles from the springs to La Plaza, but Smoke's reputation had preceded him.

The city marshal met them just outside of town, having been warned they were on their way.

"Just pull 'em up right there, boys," he told them. "I'm Marshal Crowell. If you boys are lookin' for trouble, then just keep on ridin'."

"There won't be any trouble in your town," Smoke assured. "I'm looking for a man named Casey."

"What do you want with him?"

"That's my business," Smoke said quietly.

"I'm the law." Crowell met the young man's eyes. "And I'm sayin' it's my business."

"Right," Preacher cut in. "You be the city marshal, shore 'nuff. But you ain't the sheriff. Matter of fact, you ain't nothin' outside of the town limits."

Crowell kept his temper. He knew the old man was right. Crowell was western born and reared, and he knew that here, unlike the East he had only read about, a man killed his own snakes, broke his own horses, and settled his affairs his way, without much interference from the law—to date.

"Start trouble in this town, young man," he warned Smoke, "and you'll answer to me."

"Casey," Smoke repeated. "Where is he?"

Crowell hesitated for a few seconds. "His ranch is southeast of here, on the flats. You'll cross a little creek 'fore you see the house. He's got eight hands. They all look like gunnies."

"You got an undertaker in this town?" Smoke asked.

"Sure. Why?"

"Tell him to dust off his boxes—he's about to get some business."

Crowell sat his horse and watched the pair until they were out of sight. He knew about Preacher, for Preacher was a living legend in Colorado when Crowell was still a boy. As much a legend as Carson, Purcell, Williams, or Charbonneau, son of Sacagawea. The young man with him—or was Preacher with the young man?—was rumored to be the fastest gun anywhere in the state.

A horse coming behind him broke the marshal's thoughts. "Tom?" A man's voice.

Crowell turned to look at the shopkeeper.

"You were deep in thought. Trouble?"

"Not for us, I hope."

"Who were those men?"

"One was the old curly wolf, Preacher. The other was the young gun-hand, Smoke."

"Here! Lord, Tom, who are they after?"

"He asked for Casey."

"Lord! Casey owes me sixty-five dollars."

Ten miles out of town, the pair met two hands riding easy, heading into town. Smoke and Preacher sat their saddles in the middle of the range and waited.

"You boys in on TC range," one of the riders informed them, his voice holding none of the famed western hospitality. "So get the hell off. The boss don't like strangers and neither do I."

Smoke smiled. "You boys been ridin' for the brand long?" he asked congenially.

"You deef?" the second rider asked. "We just told you to get!"

"You answer my question and then maybe we'll leave."

"Since '66, when we pushed the cattle up here from Texas—if it's any of your damned business. Now git!"

"Who owns the TC?"

"Ted Casey. Boy, are you crazy or just stupid?"

"My Pa knew a Ted Casey. Fought in the war with him, for the Gray."

"Oh? What be your name?"

"Some people call me Smoke." He smiled. "Jensen."

Recognition flared in the eyes of the riders. They grabbed for their guns but they were far too slow. Smoke's left hand .36 belched flame and black smoke as Preacher fired his Henry one-handed. Horses reared and screamed and bucked at the noise, and the TC riders were dropped from their saddles, dead and dying.

The one TC rider alive pulled himself up on one elbow. Blood poured through two chest wounds, the blood pink and frothy, one .36 ball passing through both lungs, taking the rider as he turned in the saddle.

"Heard you was comin'," he gasped. "You quick, no doubt 'bout that. Your brother was easy." He smiled a bloody smile. "Potter shot him low in the back; took him a long time to die." The rider closed his eyes and fell back to the ground.

"Let's go clean out the rest of this nest of snakes," Smoke said.

"There may be men at the ranch didn't have nothin' to do with your Pa and your brother dyin'."

"Yes. I have thought about that. I would say they have a small problem."

"Figured you'd say that, too."

"He that lies with the dogs, riseth with fleas," Smoke said with a smile.

"Huh?"

"It was in one of those books I read at the cabin on the Fork."

"Shoulda burned them gawddamned things. I knowed it all along."

Stopping in a stand of timber a couple of hundred yards from the ranch house, Preacher said, "There she is. Got any plans?"

"Start shooting."

"The house and out-buildin's?"

"Burn them to the ground."

"You a hard youngun, Smoke."

"I suppose I am." He smiled at Preacher. "But I had a good teacher, didn't I?"

"The best around," the mountain man replied.

The house and bunk house was built of logs, with sod roofs. Burn easy, Smoke thought. He yelled, "Casey! Get out here."

"Who are you?" a shout came from the house.

"Smoke Jensen."

A rifle bullet wanged through the trees. High.

"Lousy shot," Preacher muttered.

The rifle cracked again, the slug humming closer.

"They might git lucky and hit one of the horses," Preacher said.

"You tuck them in the ravine over there," Smoke said, dismounting. "I think I'll ease around to the back."

Preacher slid off his mustang. "I'll stay here and worry 'em some. You be careful now."

"Don't worry."

"'Course not," the old man replied sarcastically. "Why in the world would I do that?" He glanced up at the sky. "Seven, maybe eight hours till dark."

"We'll be through before then." Smoke slipped into an arroyo that half circled the house, ending at the rear of the ranch house.

Fifty yards behind the house, he found cover in a small clump of trees and settled down to pick his targets.

A man got careless inside the house and offered part of his forearm on a sill. Smoke shattered it with one round from his Henry. In front of the house, Preacher found a target and cut loose with his Henry. From the screams of pain drifting to Smoke, someone had been hard hit.

"You hands!" Smoke called. "You sure you want to die for Casey? A couple of your buddies already bought it a few miles back. One of them wearing a black shirt."

Silence for a few seconds. "Your Daddy ride with Mosby?" a voice yelled from the house.

"That's right."

"Your brother named Luke?"

"Yeah. He was shot in the back and the gold he was guarding stolen."

"Potter shot him—not me! You got no call to do this. Ride on out and forget it."

Smoke's reply to that was to put several rounds of .44s through the windows of the house.

Wild cursing came from the house.

"Jensen? The name is Barry. I come from Nevada. Dint have nothin' to do with no war. Never been no farther east than the Ladder in Kansas. Nuther feller here is the same as me. We herd cattle; don't git no fightin' wages. You let us ride out?"

"Get your horses and ride on out!" Smoke called.

Barry and his partner made it to the center of the backyard before they were shot in the back by someone in the ranch house. One of them died hard, screaming his life away in the dust of southeast Colorado.

"Nice folks in there," Preacher muttered.

Smoke followed the arroyo until the bunkhouse was between him and the main house. In a pile behind the bunkhouse, he found sticks and rags; in the bunkhouse, a jar of coal oil. He tied the rags around a stake, soaked it in coal oil, lighted it, then tossed it onto the roof of the ranch house. He waited, Henry at the ready, watching the house slowly catch on fire.

Shouts and hard coughing came from inside the ranch house as the logs caught and smoldered, the rooms filling with fumes. One man broke from the cabin and Preacher cut him down in the front yard. Another raced from the back door and Smoke doubled him over with a .44 slug in the gut.

Only one man appeared to still be shooting from the house. Two on the range, at least two hit in the house, and two in the yard. That didn't add up to eight, but maybe, Smoke thought, they had hit more in the house than they thought.

"All right, Casey," he shouted over the crackling of burning wood. "Burned to death, shot, or hung—it's up to you."

Casey waited until the roof was caving in before he stumbled into the yard, eyes blind from fumes. He fired wildly as he staggered about, hitting nothing except earth and air. When his pistol was empty, Smoke walked up to the man and knocked him down, tying his hands behind him with rawhide.

"What do you figure on doin' with him?" Preacher asked, shoving fresh loads into his Henry.

"I intend to take him just outside of town, by that creek, and hang him."

"I just can't figure where you got that mean streak, boy. Seein' as how you was raised—partly—by a gentle old man like me."

Despite the death he had brought and the destruction wrought, Smoke had to laugh at that. Preacher was known throughout the West as one of the most dangerous men ever to roam the high country and vast Plains. The mountain man had once spent two years of his life tracking down and killing—one by one—a group of men who had ambushed and killed a friend of his, taking the man's furs.

"'Course you never went on the hunt for anyone?" Smoke asked, dumping the unconscious Casey across a saddled horse, tying the man on.

The house was now engulfed in flames, black smoke spewing into the endless sky.

"Well . . . mayhaps once or twice. But that was years back. I've mellowed."

"Sure." The young man grinned. Preacher was still as mean as a cornered puma.

By the banks of a little creek, some distance outside the town limits, Smoke dumped the badly frightened Casey on the ground. A crowd had gathered, silent for the most part, watching the young man carefully build a noose.

"I could order you to stop this," Marshal Crowell said. "But I suppose you'd only tell me I have no jurisdiction outside of town."

"Either that or shoot you if you try to interfere," Smoke told him.

"The man has not been tried!"

"Yeah, he has. He admitted to me what he done," Smoke told the marshal.

"Lots of smoke to the southeast," Crowell observed. "'Bout gone now."

"House fire," Preacher said. "Poor feller lost ever'thing."

"Two men in the back of the house," Smoke said. "Shot in the back. Casey and his men did that. One died hard."

"That does not excuse what you're about to do," the marshal said. He looked around him. "Is anybody goin' to help me stop this lynchin'?"

No one stepped forward. Casey spat in the direction of the crowd. He cursed them.

"No matter what you call this," Crowell said, "I still intend to file a report callin' it murder."

"Halp!" Casey hollered.

"Vengeance is mine, sayeth the Lord!" said the local minister. "Lord, hear my prayer for this poor wretch of a man." He began intoning a prayer, his eyes lifted upward.

Casey soiled himself as the noose was slipped around his neck. He tried to twist off the saddle.

The minister prayed.

"That ain't much of a prayer," Preacher opined sourly. "I had you beat hands down when them Injuns was fixin' to skin me on Platte. Put some feelin' in it, man!"

The minister began to shout and sweat, warming up to his task. The crowd swelled; some had brought a portion of their supper with them. A hanging was always an interesting sight to behold. There just wasn't that much to do in small western towns. Some men began betting as to how long it would take Casey to die, if his neck was not broken when his butt left the saddle.

The minister had assembled a small choir, made up of stern-faced matronly ladies. Their voices lifted in ragged harmony to the skies.

"Shall We Gather At The River," they intoned.

"I personally think 'Swing Low' would be more like it," Preacher opined.

"He owes me sixty-five dollars," a merchant said.

"Hell with you!" Casey tried to kick the man.

"I want my money," the merchant said.

"You got anything to say before you go to hell?" Smoke asked him.

Casey screamed at him. "You won't get away with this. If Potter or Stratton don't git you, Richards will."

"What's he talkin' about?" Marshal Crowell said.

"Casey was with the Gray—same as my Pa and brother. Casey and some others like him waylaid a patrol bringing a load of gold into Georgia. They shot my brother in the back and left him to die."

Crowell met the young man's hard eyes. "That was war."

"It was murder."

"Hurry up!" a man shouted. "My supper's gittin' cold."

"I'll see you hang for this," the marshal promised Smoke.

"You go to hell!" Smoke told him. He slapped the horse on the rump and Casey swung in the cool, late afternoon air.

"I'm notifying the territorial governor of this," Crowell said.

Casey's boot heels drummed a final rhythm.

"Shout, man!" Preacher told the minister. "Sing, sisters!" he urged on the choir.

"What about my sixty-five dollars?" the merchant shouted.

8

The men road up the east side of the Wet Mountains, camping near the slopes of Greenhorn Mountain.

"Way I see it, Smoke," Preacher said, "you got some choices. That marshal is gonna see to it a flyer is put out on you for murder."

Smoke said nothing.

"Son, you got nothin' left to prove. I can't believe your Pa would want you kilt for something happened years back."

"I won't change my name, I won't hide out, and I won't run," Smoke said. "I aim to see this thing through and finished."

"Or get finished," Preacher said glumly.

"Yes."

"Well?"

"I head to Canon City."

"*We* head to Canon City," Preacher corrected.

"All right."

"Been there a time or two." Preacher had been *everywhere* in the West at least a time or two. "Son? You ain't gonna ride in there and hogtie them folk. That town's nigh on sixty year old. They got a hard man for a sheriff."

"But Ackerman's there."

"That's the one betrayed your brother? The one Luke thought was his friend?"

"That's him."

"Man like that needs killin'."

"That is exactly what I intend to do."

"Figured you'd say that."

A few miles outside of Florence, two riders stopped the pair early one morning. They were rough-looking men, with tied-down guns, the butts worn smooth from much handling. Their Missouri cavalry hats were pulled low, faces unshaven.

"Been waitin' here for you," one said. "Word of you hangin' Casey spread fast. They be warrants out on you 'fore long. You made that marshal look like a fool."

"What's your interest in this?" Smoke asked.

"I rode for the Gray. Know the story of what happened from a man that was there. What we wantin' to tell you is this: One of them hands that was on the range back at the TC beat it quicklike to Canon City. Seen him ride in, horse all lathered up and wind-broke. He ruined a good animal. Went straight to Ackerman's spread, few miles out of town, east. They waitin' for both of you."

"Much obliged to you," Smoke said. "Where you heading?"

"Back to Missouri. Got word that Dingus and Buck needin' some boys to ride with 'em. Thought we'd give it a whirl. You shore look familiar in the face to me. We met?"

"You was with Bloody Bill the night Jesse gave me this Colt. Tell him hello for me."

"Done. You boys ride easy and ready, now. See you." The outlaws wheeled their horses and were gone, heading east, to Missouri—and into disputed history.

"Now what?" Preacher asked his young partner.

"We'll just ride in for a look-see."

"Figured you'd say that."

* * *

"Welcome to Oreodelphia," Preacher said, as they approached Canon City from the south. They stopped, looking over the town.

"Oreo . . . what?"

"Oreodelphia. That's what one feller wanted to name this place—'bout ten year ago. Miners said they couldn't say the damned word, much less spell it. Never did catch on."

"Gold around here?"

"Right smart. Never got the fever myself. Found some nuggets once—threw 'em back in the crick and never told no one 'bout it."

"You may have found a fortune, Preacher."

"Mayhaps, son. But what is it I need that there gold for? Got ever'thing a body could want; couldn't tote no more. I got buckskins to cover me, a good horse, good guns, and a good friend. Had me a right purty watch once, but I had to give 'er up."

"Why?"

"One time a bunch of Cheyennes on the warpath come close to where I was hidin' out in a ravine. I plumb forgot that there watch chimed on the hour. Liked to have done me in. Thought I was dead for shore. Them Injuns was so took with that watch, they forgot 'bout me. I took off a-hightailin'." He laughed. "I bet them Injuns was mad when that watch run down and wouldn't chime no more."

They urged their horses forward. "One more thing I think you should know, Smoke."

"What's that?"

"I hear tell the state's gonna build a brand new prison just outside of town. They might be lookin' to fill it up."

The old mountain man and the handsome young gunfighter rode slowly down the main street of Canon

City. They drew some attention, for they were dressed in buckskins and carried their Henry repeating rifles across their saddles, instead of in a boot. And the sheriff and one of his deputies were among those watching the pair as they reined up in front of the saloon and stepped out of the saddle.

Boot heels clumped on the boardwalk as the sheriff walked toward them. Neither Smoke nor Preacher looked up, but both were aware of his approach, and of the fact that a deputy had stationed himself across the street, a rifle cradled in his arms.

"Howdy, boys," the sheriff greeted them.

He received a nod.

The sheriff looked at their horses. "Been travelin', I see."

"A piece," Preacher said.

The sheriff recognized him. "You're the Preacher."

"That's what I'm called."

"And you're the gun-hand called Smoke."

"That's what I'm called."

"You boys plannin' on stayin' long?"

Smoke turned his dark eyes on the sheriff and let them smolder for a few seconds. "Long enough."

The sheriff had seen more than his share of violence; he had seen more shootings, knifings, and hangings than he cared to remember. He had known, and known personally, men of violence: Clay Allison, Wild Bill, and others who were just as mean—or meaner—but never gained the reputation. But something in this young man's eyes made the sheriff back up a step, something he had never done before. And he silently cursed that one step.

"I heard what happened to Casey," the sheriff spoke in low tones. "Nothing like that is going to happen in this town. Don't start trouble here."

Smoke suddenly smiled boyishly and disarmingly. "You don't mind if we buy some supplies, have a few hot meals, and rest for a day or two, do you, sheriff? Take a hot bath?"

"Speak for yourself on that last part," Preacher said.

"Confine yourselves to doing that," the sheriff said, then brushed past the men.

"That lawman's salty, Smoke," Preacher observed correctly.

"But he backed up," the young man replied.

"Yep. They's something 'bout you that'll make a smart man get away from you. And that worries me, some."

"Why?"

"Might mean I ain't too smart."

They stabled their horses and told the stable boy to rub them down and give them grain. They went across the street to a small cafe and had steak, boiled potatoes, and apple pie for twenty five cents apiece.

"These prices," Preacher opined, "this feller'll be retired in a month."

As if by magic, the cafe had emptied of customers with the arrival of the buckskin-clad men. But when the regular diners—who, Smoke observed, ate for fifteen cents each—saw the pair meant no harm, the cafe once more filled with diners.

"Coffee's weak," Preacher bitched, as he sucked at his fourth cup.

"Any coffee that won't float a horseshoe," Smoke said grinning at him, "you'd claim was weak."

"True. What's your plan this time?"

"Check in at the hotel, then get some chairs and sit out front, watch the people pass by."

"Wait for them to come to us, eh?"

"That's right."

"And ifn they force our hand, the sheriff can't bring no charges agin us for defendin' ourselves."

"That is correct."

Preacher ordered another piece of apple pie and another cup of coffee. "To be so young, Smoke, you shore got a sneaky streak in you."

"It's the company I've been keeping for the past four years."

"Might have something to do with it, I reckon."

For two days Smoke and Preacher waited and relaxed in town, causing no trouble, keeping to themselves. Smoke bathed twice behind the barber shop, and Preacher told him ifn he didn't stop that he was gonna come down with some dreadful illness.

The mountain man and the gunfighter were civil to the men, polite to the ladies. Some of the ladies batted their eyes and swished their bustled fannies as they passed by Smoke.

"You boys sure takin' your time buyin' supplies," the sheriff noted on the second day.

"We like to think things through 'fore buyin'," Preacher told him. "Smoke here is a right cautious man with a greenback. Might even call him tight."

The sheriff didn't find that amusing. "You boys wouldn't be waiting for Ackerman to make a move, would you?"

"Ackerman?" Smoke looked at the sheriff. "What is an Ackerman?"

The sheriff's smile was grim. "What do you boys do for a livin'? I got a law on the books about vagrants."

"I'm retired," Preacher told him. "Enjoyin' the sunset of my years. Smoke here, he runs a string of horses on his ranch up to Brown's Hole."

"You're a long way from Brown's Hole."

"Right smart piece for shore."

"I ought to run you both out of this town."

"Why?" Smoke asked. "On what charge? We haven't caused you any trouble."

"Yet." The sheriff's back was stiff with anger as he strode away. The man knew a setup when he saw one, and this was a setup.

But his feelings were mixed. He owed Ackerman and

his bunch of rowdies nothing—they were all trouble-makers. Ackerman swung no wide political loop in this country. And there were persistent rumors that Ackerman had been a thief and a murderer during the war—and a deserter. And the sheriff could not abide a coward.

But, he sighed, if he was reading this young man called Smoke right, Ackerman's future looked very bleak.

A hard-ridden horse hammered the street into dust. A hand from the Bar-X slid to a halt. "Ackerman and his bunch are ridin' in, sheriff," the cowhand panted. "They're huntin' bear. Told me to tell you he's gonna kill this kid called Smoke—and anyone else that got in his way."

The sheriff's smile was grudgingly filled with admiration. The kid's patience had paid off. Ackerman had made his boast and his threat; anything the kid did now could only be called self-defense.

The sheriff thanked the cowboy and told him to hunt a hole. He crossed the street and told his deputy to clear the street in front of the hotel.

In five minutes, the main street resembled a ghost town, with a yellow dog the only living thing that had not cleared out. Behind curtains, closed doors, and shuttered windows, men and women watched and waited, ears atune, anticipating the roar of gunfire from the street.

At the edge of town, Ackerman, a bull of a man, with small, mean eyes and a cruel slit for a mouth, slowed his horse to a walk. Ackerman and his hands rode down the street, six abreast.

Preacher and Smoke were on their feet. Preacher stuffed his mouth full of chewing tobacco. Both men had slipped the thongs from the hammers of their Colts. Preacher wore two Colts, .44s. One in a holster, the other stuck behind his belt. Mountain man and young gunfighter stood six feet apart on the boardwalk.

The sheriff closed his office door and walked into the empty cell area. He sat down and began a game of checkers with his deputy.

Ackerman and his men wheeled their horses to face the men on the boardwalk. "I hear tell you boys is lookin' for me. If so, here I am."

"News to me," Smoke said. "What's your name?"

"You know who I am, kid. Ackerman."

"Oh, yeah!" Smoke said. "You're the man who helped kill my brother by shooting him in the back. Then you stole the gold he was guarding."

Inside the hotel, pressed against the wall, the desk clerk listened intently, his mouth open in anticipation of gunfire.

"You're a liar. I didn't shoot your brother; that was Potter and his bunch."

"You stood and watched it. Then you stole the gold."

"It was war, kid."

"But you were on the same side," Smoke said. "So that not only makes you a killer, it makes you a traitor and a coward."

"I'll kill you for sayin' that!"

"You'll burn in hell a long time before I'm dead," Smoke told him.

Ackerman grabbed for his pistol. The street exploded in gunfire and black powder fumes. Horses screamed and bucked in fear. One rider was thrown to the dust by his lunging mustang. Smoke took the men on the left, Preacher the men on the right side. The battle lasted no more than ten to twelve seconds. When the noise and the gunsmoke cleared, five men lay in the street, two of them dead. Two more would die from their wounds. One was shot in the side—he would live. Ackerman had been shot three times: once in the belly, once in the chest, and one ball had taken him in the side of the face as the muzzle of the .36 had lifted with each blast. Still Ackerman sat his saddle, dead. The big man finally leaned to one side and toppled from his horse, one boot hung in the stirrup. The horse shied, then began walking down the dusty street, dragging Ackerman, leaving a bloody trail.

"I heard it all!" the excited desk clerk ran out the door. "You were in the right, Mr. Smoke. Yes, sir. Right all the way. Why . . . !" He looked at Smoke. "You've been wounded, sir."

A slug had nicked the young man on the cheek, another had punched a hole in the fleshy part of his left arm, high up. They were both minor wounds. Preacher had been grazed on the leg and a ricocheting slug had sent splinters into his face.

Preacher spat into the street. "Damn near swallered my chaw."

"I never seen a draw that fast," a man spoke from his store front. "It was a blur."

The sheriff and a deputy came out of the jail, walking down the bloody, dusty street. Both men carried Greeners: double-barreled twelve gauge shotguns.

"Right down this street," the sheriff said pointing, "is the doctor's office. Get yourselves patched up and then get out of town. You have one hour."

"Sheriff, it was a fair fight," the desk clerk said. "I seen it."

The sheriff never took his eyes off Smoke. "One hour," he repeated.

"We'll be gone." Smoke wiped a smear of blood from his cheek.

Townspeople began hauling the bodies off. The local photographer set up his cumbersome equipment and began popping flash-powder, sealing the gruesomeness for posterity. He also took a picture of Smoke.

The editor of the paper walked up to stand by the sheriff. He watched the old man and the young gunhand walk down the street. He truly had seen it all. The old man had killed one man, wounded another. The young man had killed four men, as calmly as picking his teeth.

"What's that young man's name?"

"Smoke Jensen. But he's a devil."

9

There was a chill to the air when Smoke kicked off his blankets and rose to add twigs to the still smoldering coals. They were camped along the Arkansas, near Twin Lakes.

"Cold," Preacher complained, crawling out of his buffalo robe. "Can't be far from Leadville."

"How do you figure that?" Smoke asked, slicing bacon into a pan and dumping a handful of coffee into the pot.

"Coldest damn town in the whole country." Preacher put on his hat then tugged on his boots. "I've knowed it to snow on the Fourth of July. So damned cold ifn a man dies in the winter, best thing to do is jist prop him up in a corner for the season. Ifn you wanna bury him, you gotta use dynamite to blast a hole in the ground. Tain't worth the bother. And I ain't lyin', neither."

Smoke grinned and said nothing. He had long since ceased questioning the mountain man's statements; upon investigation, they all proved out.

"Them names on the list, Smoke. Any more of 'em in Colorado?"

"Only one more, but we'll let him be. He's in the army up at Camp Collins. An officer. Took the name of a dead man who was killed in the first days of the war. I can't fight the whole Yankee army."

"We goin' back to the Hole?"

"For the time being."

"Good. We'll winter there. Stop along the way and pack in some grub."

Major Powell and his detachment were gone when Preacher and Smoke reached the Hole in mid-September. Two horses were missing from the herd, and the money for them was in the cave. The soldiers had tended to the gardens, eating well from them. Emmett Jensen's grave had been looked after. But the flowers were dying. Winter was not far off.

The two men set about making the cabin snug against the winds that would soon howl cold through the canyon, roaring out of Wyoming, sighing off Diamond Peak. Preacher did a little trapping, for all the good it did him, and for awhile, the man called Smoke seemed to be at peace with himself.

Preacher was surprised and embarrassed that Christmas morning to find a present for him when he awakened. He opened the box and aahed at the chiming railroad watch with a heavy gold fob.

"That little watch and clock shop in Oreodelphia," Preacher recalled. "Seen you goin' in there." He was suddenly ill at ease. "But I dint get nothin' for you."

"You've been giving me presents for years, Preacher. You've taught me the wilderness and how to survive. Just being with you has been the greatest present of my life."

Preacher looked at him. "Oh, hush up. You plumb sickenin' when you try to be nice." He wound the watch. "Reckon what time it is." He turned his head so Smoke could not see the tears in his eyes.

Smoke glanced outside. "'Bout seven, I reckon."

"That's clost enough." He set the watch and smiled as it chimed. "Purty. Best present I ever had."

"Oh, hush up." Smoke smiled. "You plumb sickenin' when you try to be nice."

The winter wore on slowly in its cold, often white harshness. In the cabin, Preacher would sometimes sit and watch Smoke as he read and reread the few books in his possession, educating himself. He especially enjoyed the works of Shakespeare and Burns.

And sometimes he would look at the paper from his father and from Gaultier. And Preacher knew in his heart, whether the young man would admit it or not, he would never rest until he had crossed out all the names.

In the early spring of '70, as the flowers struggled valiantly to push their colors to the warmth of the sun, Smoke began gathering his gear. Wordlessly, Preacher did the same.

"Where we goin' in such an all-fired hurry?" he asked Smoke.

"I've heard you talk about the southwest part of this territory. You said it was pretty and lonely."

"'Tis."

"You know it well?"

"I know the Delores, and the country thereabouts."

"Many people?"

"Not to speak of."

"Be a good place to set up ranching, wouldn't it?"

"Ifn a man could keep his hair. That where we goin'?"

"What is there to keep us here?"

"Nothing a-tall."

Pushing the herd of half-broken mustangs and Appaloosa, the two men headed south into the wild country, populated mainly by Ute, but with a scattering of Navajo and Piute. They crossed the Colorado River just east of what would later become Grand Junction, then cut southeast, keeping west of the Uncompahgre Plateau. Out of Unaweep Canyon, only a few miles from the Delores River, they began to smell the first bitter whiffs as the wind changed.

Preacher brought them to a halt. While Smoke bunched the horses, Preacher stood up in his stirrups to sniff the air. "They's more to it than wood. Sniff the air, son, tell me what you smell."

Smoke tried to identify the mixture of strange odors. Finally he said, "Leather. And cloth. And . . . something else I can't figure out."

Preacher's reply was grim. "I can. Burnin' hair and flesh. You 'bout to come up on what an Injun leaves behind after an attack." He pointed. "We'll put the horses in that box canyon over yonder, then we'll go take a look-see."

Securing the open end of the canyon with brush and rope, the men rode slowly and carefully toward the smell of charred flesh, the odor becoming thicker as they rode. At the base of a small hill, they left their horses and crawled up to the crest, looking down at the horror below.

Tied by his ankles from a limb, head down over a small fire, a naked man trembled in the last moments of life. His head and face and shoulders were blackened cooked meat. The mutilated bodies of other men lay dead. One was tied to the wheel of the burned wagon. He had been tortured. All had died hard.

"You said you heared gunfire 'bout two hours ago," Preacher whispered. "You was right. Gawdamned 'Pache trick, that yonder is. They come up this far ever' now and then, raidin' the Utes."

"How did they get a wagon this far?" Smoke asked.

"Sheer stubbornness. But I hope they weren't no wimmin with 'em. If so, Gawd help 'em."

The men waited for more than an hour, moving only when necessary, talking in low tones.

Finally, Preacher stirred. "They gone. Let's go down and prowl some, give the people a Christian burial. Say a word or two." He spat on the ground. "Gawddamned heathens."

Smoke found a shovel, handle intact, on the ground beside the charred wagon. He dug a long, shallow grave, burying the remains of the men in one common grave, covering the mound with rocks to keep wolves and coyotes from digging up the bodies and eating them.

Preacher walked the area, cutting sign, trying to determine if anyone got away. Smoke rummaged through what was left of the wagon. He found what he didn't want to find.

"Preacher!"

The mountain man turned. Smoke held up a dress he'd found in a trunk, then another dress, smaller than the first.

Preacher shook his shaggy head as he walked. "Gawd have mercy on they souls," he said, fingering the gingham. "Man's a damned fool bringin' wimminfolk out here."

"Maybe one of them got away?" Smoke said hopefully.

"Tain't likely. But we got to look."

Almost on the verge of giving up after an hour's searching, Smoke made one more sweep of the area. Then he saw the faint shoeprints, mixed in with moccasin tracks. The prints were small; a child, or a woman.

"Good Lord!" Preacher said. "Mayhaps she got clear and run away." He circled the tracks until he got them separated. "Don't see none followin' her. Get the horses, son. We got to find her 'fore dark."

It did not take them long to track her. She was hiding behind some brush, at the mouth of a canyon. Movement of the brush gave her away.

"Girl," Preacher said, "you come on out, now. You 'mong friends."

Weeping was the only reply from behind the brush. Smoke could see one high-top button shoe. A dainty shoe.

"We're not going to hurt you," he said.

More weeping.

"They's a snake crawlin' in there with you," Preacher lied.

A young woman bolted from behind the brush as if propelled from a cannon barrel, straight into the arms of Smoke. With all her softness pressing against him, she lifted her head and looked at him through eyes of light blue, a heart-shaped face framed with hair the color of wheat. They stood for several long heartbeats, gazing at each other, neither of them speaking.

Preacher snorted. "This ain't no place for romance. Come on. Let's get the hell out of here."

Preacher griped and groused, but the young woman insisted upon returning to where the members of her family were buried. She stood for a few moments, looking down at the long, narrow grave.

"My aunt?" she questioned.

"Looks like the savages took her," Preacher said.

"What will they do to her?"

"Depends a lot on her. Was she a looker?"

"I beg your pardon?"

"Was she a handsome woman?"

"She was beautiful."

Preacher shrugged. "Then they'll probably keep her." He did not tell the young woman her aunt might have been—by now—raped repeatedly and then tortured to death. "They'll work her hard, beat her some, but she'll most probably be all right. Some buck with no squaw will bed her down. Then agin, they might trade her off for a horse or rifle."

"Or they might kill her?" she said.

"Yep."

"You don't believe I'll ever see her again, do you?"

"No, Missy, I don't. It just ain't likely. Down in Arizony Territory, back 'bout '51 or '52, I think it was, the Oatman family tried to cross the desert alone. The Yavapais kilt the parents and took the kids. A boy and two gals. The boy run off, one of the gals died. But Olive Oatman lived as a slave with the Injuns for years. They tattooed her chin 'fore she was finally traded off for goods. It's bes' to put your aunty out of your mind. I seen lots of white wimmin lived with Injuns for years; too ashamed to come back to they own kind even ifn they could."

The young woman was silent.

"What's your name?" Smoke asked.

"Nicole," she said, then put her face in her small hands and began to weep. "I don't know what to do. I don't have any family to go back to. I don't have anyone."

Smoke put his arms around her. "Yes, you do, Nicole. You have us."

"Just call me Uncle Preacher," the mountain man said. "Plumb disgustin'."

Smoke rummaged around the still smoldering wagon, looking for any of Nicole's clothing that might have escaped the flames. He found a few garments, including a lace-up corset, which she quickly snatched, red-faced, from him. He also found a saddle that had suffered only minor damage. Everything else was lost.

"Now, how you figure she's a-gonna sit that there saddle?" Preacher demanded. "What with all them skirts and petti-things underneath?"

"She's not. She found a pair of men's trousers that belonged to her uncle. She can ride astraddle."

"That ain't fittin' for no decent woman. Ain't nobody 'ceptin' a whore'd do that!"

"What the hell'd you wanna do? Build a travois and drag her?"

Preacher walked away, muttering to himself.

Nicole came to Smoke's side. "I can sit a saddle. I rode as a child in Illinois."

"Is that where you're from?"

"No. I'm from Boston. After my parents died, when I was just a little girl, I came to Illinois to live with my uncle and aunt. What's your name?"

"Smoke. That's Preacher." He jerked his thumb.

She smiled. She was beautiful. "Just Smoke?"

"That's what I'm called."

"At a trading post, we heard talk of a gunfighter called Smoke. Is that you?"

"I guess so."

"They said you'd killed fifty men." There was no fear in her eyes as she said it.

Smoke laughed. "Hardly. A half dozen white men, maybe. But they were fair fights."

"You don't look like a gunfighter."

"What does a gunfighter look like?"

She smiled, white even teeth flashing against the tan of her face.

"Carryin' on like children at a box social," Preacher muttered.

Nicole went behind a boulder to change out of her tattered and dusty dress. Preacher walked up to his young protégé.

"What are you aimin' to do with her?"

"Take her with us. We sure can't leave her out here."

"Well, hell! I know all that. I mean in the long run. Nearest town's more'un a hundred miles off."

"Well, I . . . don't know."

The mountain man's eyes sparkled. "Ah," he said. "Now I get it. Got your juices up and runnin', eh?"

Smoke stiffened. "I have not given that any thought."

Preacher laughed. "You can go to hell for tellin' lies, boy." He walked off, chuckling, talking to himself. "Yes, siree," he called, "young Smoke's got hisself a gal. Right purty little thing, too. Whoa, boy!" He did a little jig and slapped his buckskin-clad knee. "Them blankets gonna be hotter than a buffalo hunter's rifle after a shoot." He cackled as he danced off, spry as a youngster.

Smoke's face reddened. What the young man knew about females could be placed in a shot glass and still have room for a good drink of whiskey.

"What is Preacher so happy about?" Nicole asked, walking up behind him.

Smoke turned and swallowed hard. Luckily, he did not have a chew of tobacco in his mouth. The men's trousers fitted the woman snugly—very snugly. The plaid man's shirt she now wore was unbuttoned two buttons past the throat, and that was about all the young man could stand.

Smoke lifted his eyes to stare at her face. She was beautiful, her features almost delicate, but with a stubborn set to her chin.

She had freshened up at the little creek and her face wore a scrubbed look.

"Uh . . ." he said.

"Never mind," Nicole said. "I'm sure I know what he was laughing about."

"Ah . . . I've saddled a little mare for you. She's broke, but hasn't been ridden lately. She may kick up her heels a bit."

"Mares do that every now and then," Nicole said coyly, smiling at him.

"Uh . . . yeah! Right."

"Smoke?" She touched his thick forearm, tight with muscle. "I'm not trying to be callous or unfeeling about . . . what happened today. I'm just . . . trying to put it—the bad things—behind me. Out of my mind. Do you understand?"

"Yes." He touched her hand. Soft. "Come on. We'd better get moving."

When Nicole swung into the saddle, the trousers stretched tight across her derriere. Smoke stared—and stared. Then his boot missed the stirrup when he tried to mount and he fell flat on his back in the dust.

"I knowed it!" Preacher said. "Knowed it when I seen 'em a-lookin' at one 'nother. Gawd help us all. He'll be pickin' flowers next. Ifn he can git up off the ground, that is."

The trio pushed the horses and followed the Delores down to its junction with Disappointment Creek. There, they cut slightly west for a few miles, then bore south, toward a huge valley. They would be among the first whites to settle in the valley. Long after Smoke had become a legend, the town of Cortez would spring up, to the south of the SJ Ranch. Midway in the valley, by a stream that rolled gently past a gradually rising knoll, Smoke pulled up.

"Here?" Preacher looked around, approval of the site evident in his eyes. He had taught the young man well.

"Right here," Smoke said. "We'll build the cabin on that small knoll." He pointed. "Afford us the best view in the valley and give us some protection as well. See that spring over there?" he asked Nicole. "It feeds into the creek. Comes out under the knoll. We can dig a well and tap into it, or its source."

"It's so beautiful," she said, looking around her.

"Yep," Preacher teased. "Be a right nice place for a man to start raisin' a family. Shore would."

Smoke blushed and Nicole laughed. She had grown accustomed to the mountain man's teasing, and liked him very much. But it was to the tall young man she more often cast her blue eyes. The thought of him being the much-talked about and feared and hated gunfighter was amusing to her. Smoke was so gentle and shy.

Nicole had a lot to learn about the West and its men. And she was to learn very quickly and harshly—in the time left her.

10

First a house was built, of adobe and logs and rocks, with rough planking and sod for a roof. Smoke would not settle for a dirt floor; instead he carefully smoothed and shaped the logs, which had to be dragged from the forest, which lay to the northeast. The work was hard and backbreaking, but no one complained, except Preacher, who bitched all the time, about almost everything. Neither Smoke nor Nicole paid any attention to him, knowing it was his way and he was not going to change.

Nicole never spoke of leaving, and Smoke never brought it up. Preacher just grinned at them both.

Twice during the summer of '70, the trio came under attack from the Utes, and twice they were beaten back, with the Utes taking heavy losses from the rifles in the fortlike home on the small hill. Nicole, to the surprise of the men, proved not at all reluctant to learn weapons, and became a better than average shot with a rifle. On the final attempt by the Utes to drive the whites from the land, Nicole showed what backbone she had by knocking a brave off his circling pony, wounding him slightly, then calmly finishing him off with another round. Turning from the peephole, she saw two braves attempting to chop their way in through the back door. She killed them both.

The Utes in the huge valley never again attacked the home, choosing instead to live under a wary peace with the two men and the woman they came to call Little Lightning.

But it was with awe in her eyes that Nicole watched Smoke handle his guns: with calmness and cold deliberation. Death at the end of his arms. Even in haste, he never seemed to hurry, choosing his targets, almost never missing, even at the most incredible range.

Arriving too late to plant a garden, Smoke and Preacher hunted for food, drying and curing the meat for the harsh winter that was ahead of them. When the rough house was up, the well dug, close to the house, and food to last them, Preacher saddled his horse one morning and rigged a pack horse.

"Headin' east," he told them. "Over to the Springs, maybe. Mayhaps beyond. They's things we be needin'. Pump for the kitchen; pipe—other things. I'll be back—maybe—'fore the first snow. Ifn I ain't, I ain't comin' back till spring. I may decide to winter in the mountains with some old cronies still up there. Don't know yet. See you younguns later."

He rode off, not looking back, for if he had done that, Smoke and Nicole would have been able to see the twinkle of mischief in the eyes, the eyes full of cunning and knowledge—of a man and woman and a long winter ahead.

Preacher had decided the young folks needed some time to themselves, and he was going to give it to them. He also wanted to test the wind; see if the legend of Smoke had grown any since the shootings of the past summer. He suspected the stories had mushroomed—and he was right.

Nicole touched Smoke's arm. "When will he be back?"

"When he feels like it." Smoke was experiencing a rush of emotions; a sense of loss in the pit of his stomach. This would be the first time in five years he and

Preacher would be separated for any length of time. And Smoke knew, although he could never put it into words, he loved the cantankerous old mountain man—loved him as much as he had his own father.

"Why did he leave like that?" Nicole asked. "Without even a fare-thee-well?"

"Lots of reasons." The young man's eyes were on the fast disappearing dot in the valley. "He knows he doesn't have many winters left, and he wants to be alone some—that's the way he's lived all his life. And he wants us to have some time together."

He looked down at the petite woman. She met his gaze.

The wind whistled through the valley, humming around them, touching them, caressing them with a soft, invisible hand, making them more conscious of their being together.

A flush touched her face. "I'll . . . I'd better see to the breakfast dishes."

"I've got to check on the herd," Smoke said, keeping his eyes averted. "Keep a gun close by. I'll be back by midday."

"I'll be waiting for you," she replied, her voice husky.

He again met her gaze, for the first time seeing a fire among the gentle blue.

It scared the hell out of him.

Smoke spent the morning checking on his herd, looking over the new colts, crisscrossing the valley floor, his eyes alert for any Indian sign. He knew he was stalling, putting off the trip back to the house—and to Nicole. He was not expecting any trouble from the Utes, for when they saw he was not going to be run off the land, and was not—at this time—the forerunner of more whites, they had made gestures of peace toward him, and he had accepted that offer.

Twice he had shared meat he had killed with the Utes. And once he had come upon a young Ute boy who had been badly injured in a fall near Ute Peak. Smoke had spent two lonely nights with the boy, watching over him, tending to his injuries. He had then constructed a travois and carried the boy to his camp.

The years with Preacher had stood Smoke well, for he had slept in countless Indian camps and had learned their ways—as much as any white man could—and Smoke knew sign language, which seemed to be universal among the many tribes.

The next morning he had ridden out of the Indian camp, as safely as he had ridden in. There had been no more trouble from the Utes. But the Ute were not the only tribe in this part of the country; there were Piute, and to the south, Navajo and some Apache. And the Apache were friends to no white man—and damn few other Indians.

In this section of the young nation, if one grew careless, one could get suddenly dead.

He turned Seven's nose north. Toward the cabin. Toward Nicole.

He stabled the Appaloosa, rubbed him down, and forked hay for him. Then Smoke washed at the stream behind the hill.

Nicole was silent as she ladled beans and venison on their plates, then sat down across the rough-hewn table from Smoke. There was unexpected tension between them. They had been alone before, several times, when Preacher was off wandering; but this was different. They were *really* alone.

"How's the stock?" Nicole asked, her eyes fixed on the plate.

"Fine. Two colts growing like weeds. No sign of Apaches. Saw some deer. Didn't think to shoot. We got food enough for a time."

After that, conversation did not lag—it died.

Smoke was aware of his heart thudding heavily in his chest. Nicole was nervous, twice dropping her fork. The meal seemed to be taking a lot longer than usual. Smoke suddenly noticed she had changed her dress since his leaving that morning. She had put on her best dress.

Usually she wore men's britches she had tailored to fit her. The dress seemed to bring out her womanhood.

Smoke reached for the honey pot to sweeten his coffee and knocked over the clay jug.

"I'll get it," they spoke in unison, as honey dripped from the table to the floor.

They both rose and bent down, banging their heads together. Smoke put his hand on the edge of the table for support and it toppled over, dumping him to the floor, everything on the table spilling and pouring on his head and all over her.

"Oh—hell!" Nicole said.

That startled Smoke. It was the first time he'd ever heard a lady swear.

They looked at each other: Smoke, with beans and venison on his head; Nicole, with honey and gravy dripping off her chin. They began laughing and pointing at each other.

He offered his hand and she took it, both of them rising to their feet, slipping in the mess on the floor. He took off his shirt and headed for the door.

"Where are you going?" she asked.

"To the creek, to take a bath. I'll holler when it's all clear."

She smiled, and Smoke was not at all sure he liked the look in her eyes.

Standing in the water, with lather from the waist up, Smoke could not believe his eyes when Nicole appeared on the bank, towels in her hand. He closed his eyes and turned his back, speechless, when she began taking off her stained dress. Then she was by his side.

"Give me the soap," she said. "I'll scrub your back."

"Nicole . . ." he managed to croak.

"Turn around, Smoke—look at me."

He turned, and she laughed when she saw his eyes were tightly closed.

"You'll have to open them sometime," she whispered. He did.

And there was no more need for words.

* * *

Full dark when he slipped from her side to step out into the coolness of Colorado night. He left Nicole sprawled in sleep in his bed. Smoke rolled a cigarette and lit it, the match explosive in the night. He inhaled deeply.

He felt drained, but yet, ten feet tall. He felt weak, but yet powerful. They had made love, and told each other of their love, for what seemed like hours, on the cool grass of the creek bank. They had bathed and soaped each other, then walked naked back to the house where they made love again. Then they had slept.

In all his young but eventful life, the man called Smoke had never before experienced anything to compare with the sensual events of that afternoon and early evening with Nicole, in the quiet valley.

He stepped back into the house, pulling on his boots and buckling his guns around his lean waist. Shirtless, he stepped back out into the purple night.

He checked the grounds around the house, then the corral and the lean-to that served as a barn. Quiet. It really was an unnecessary move, since Seven would sound an alarm if a stranger approached, but it made Smoke feel better to double check. He went back into the house and stoked up the fire, putting on coffee to boil, the pot hanging on a swivel iron, attached to the fireplace wall. He sensed, rather than heard, Nicole enter the room.

She was barefoot, wearing one of his shirts, and he thought she had never appeared more beautiful.

"Would you like me to fix supper?"

He rose and shook his head. She came into his arms.

"I love you," he said.

Her reply was a loving whisper; a commitment spoken from the heart.

* * *

Preacher did not return that winter of 1870/71, and although Smoke did not admit his feelings aloud, Nicole knew he was worried about the old mountain man, fearing he might be hurt, or dead.

And it was Nicole who finally eased his mind, calming the unrest in him.

"How old is Preacher?" she asked one evening. A steady rain fell in the valley, occasionally mixed with sleet and snow. The winter had been a hard one, requiring brutal work from both of them just to stay alive.

"He's pushin' seventy. Least that's what he'll admit to bein'. Getting old."

"And he's lived a very long, exciting, and fruitful life. He wouldn't want to die in a bed, would he? He'd want to pass this life the way he's lived—in the wilderness. And wouldn't he be sad if he knew you were sad?"

He smiled, his mood lifting from him. He looked at her, something he never tired of doing. "Yes, Nicole, you're right. As usual."

She came to him, sitting very unladylike in his lap, in the wood and rawhide chair, the frame covered with a bearskin. "We've got to get married, Smoke."

"We are. We said we wanted to wait until Preacher came back."

"Well . . . I'm pretty sure we're going to have a baby."

He sat stunned in the chair. "Nicole, we're better than a hundred miles from the nearest doctor."

"I went to nursing school, honey. There is nothing to worry about. All I want is for us to be married. I want the baby to have a legal name."

"Preacher told me there was a little settlement of Mormons just west of here—over in Utah Territory. It'll be a week there and a week back. Can you stand the ride?"

She smiled and kissed him. "Just watch me."

* * *

The air was still cool when they rode out of the valley, heading for Utah. But spring was in the air, evident in the leafing trees, the plants, and the flowers that grew wild, coloring the valley. Nicole sat her little mare; Smoke rode Seven.

Nicole looked back at the cabin she had called home for months. "How dangerous is this trip?"

"We might go there and back without seeing an Indian. We might be ambushed ten miles from the cabin. No way to answer that question. I don't know much about Utah Territory, so we'll be seeing it for the first time—together."

They camped on the third night just north of the Hovenweep, near Keely Canyon. They had seen a few Indians on the third day—the first since leaving the valley—Weminuche Ute. But they did not bother the man and woman, but only watched through obsidian eyes, faces impassive. They were armed with ancient rifles and bows and arrows, and perhaps they did not want to risk a fight against the many-shoot rifles of the man and woman; perhaps they did not feel hostile that day; perhaps they were hunting and did not want to take the time for an attack. With an Indian, one never knew.

On the fifth day, Smoke figured they were in Utah Territory—probably had been all day—and the settlement of Mormons should be in sight. But all they found were rotting, tumble-down cabins, and no signs of life.

"Preacher said they were here in '55," Smoke said. "Wonder where they went?"

Nicole's laughter rang out over the deserted collection of falling-down cabins. "Honey, that's sixteen years ago." Her eyes swept the land, spotting an old, weed-filled graveyard. "Let's look over there."

The last faded date on a rotting headmarker was fourteen years old.

In the largest building of the more than a dozen cabins, they found a rusting tin box and pried open the lid. They found rotting papers that crumbled at the touch.

Smoke took Nicole out into the sunlight. "I know what I'll do," he said.

He took a small hammer and a nail from the side pack of his packhorse, carried in case an animal threw a shoe. He built a fire and spent an hour heating and hammering the nail into a crude ring. When it cooled, he slipped it on her third finger, left hand.

"It'll have to do," he said. "Close as I can make us to being really married."

She kissed him and said, "Let's go home."

11

Preacher was sitting on the rough bench in front of the cabin when they rode into the yard. He was spitting tobacco juice and whittling on a piece of wood.

"Howdy," he greeted them, as if he had been gone only a day instead of months. "Where you two younguns been?"

"We might ask you the same question," Smoke replied.

"Ramblin'. Seein' God's country in all its glory."

"We got married," Nicole said proudly, showing him her nail ring.

"Right nice," he acknowledged, looking first at the ring, then into her eyes. "You with child, girl?"

She blushed. "Yes, sir."

"Figured ya'll get into mischief while I's gone. Tain't no big deal; I helped birth dozens of papooses in my time. Woman does all the work; man just gets in the way. Who spoke the words?"

"Nobody," Smoke said. "Couldn't find a minister. Went all the way into Utah Territory looking."

"Well . . . I always believed it was what was in your hearts that counted. Knowed you was in love when I seen you fall off your horse."

"I didn't fall off my horse!"

"Did, too."

"Did not!"

"I'll go fix supper," Nicole said.

When she had closed the door to the cabin, Preacher said, "Good thing you didn't ride east, boy—warrants out for you all over the place."

They walked to the lean-to and stabled the horses, rubbing them down with burlap. Preacher gave Smoke the news.

"Got warrants for you with your pitcher on 'em at the Springs and at Walsenburg. Don't ride no further east than the Los Pinos—you hear?"

Smoke looked at him, then opened his mouth to protest.

"You married now, son. You got 'sponsibilities to that there woman who's a-carryin' your child. And you got men huntin' you. That there Potter and Richards . . . 'mong others. Price on your head, too. Big money. They some 'fraid of you, boy—or something like it."

"It's a mystery to me. What'd you hear about Potter and Stratton and Richards?"

"They all up in Ideeho Territory. Up in the wild country. All live in or around a town called Bury."

"B-e-r-r-y?"

"No. Like you plant somebody in the ground. Way I got the story, Smoke, your Pa rode in that there town like a wild man, reins 'tween his teeth, both hands full of Colts. Kilt three or four, wounded two-three more, and took a right smart 'mount of gold them men took from the Rebs. Way I heared it, no one knowed him up there in Bury, so he hung around for a week or two 'fore he made his move, listenin' till he learned where the gold was."

"Wonder what he did with the gold?"

Old eyes studied the young man. "You interested in it?"

"Not in the least."

"I hoped you'd say that."

"If they leave me alone, I'll leave them alone."

"It ain't gonna work thataway, boy."

"What do you mean?"

"You got bounty hunters sniffin' your back trail. They's at least three thousand dollars on your head, dead or alive. All of it put up by them three men up in the territory. That's big money, boy—big money. That's why I come back so soon. Got to have somebody watchin' your back."

"Don't those bounty hunters know the truth about me? About what happened to Pa and Luke?"

"They don't care, son. They after the money and to hell with how they earn it. Most bounty hunters is scum. I'd shoot a bounty hunter on sight—take his hair."

"We're going to raise horses here, Preacher. Run some cattle directly. You and me and Nicole. We're going to raise a family, and our children will need a grandfather—that's you, you old goat."

"Thank you. Nicest thing you've said to me in months."

"I haven't seen you in months!"

"That's right. You keep them guns of yourn loose. When the girl gonna birth?"

"November, she thinks."

"Just like a woman. Don't never know nothin' for sure."

The summer passed uneventfully, with Smoke tending to his huge gardens and looking after his growing herd of horses. Preacher hunted for game, curing some of the meat, making pemmican out of the rest.

In the first week of July, much to Preacher's disgust, Nicole sent him off to the nearest town for some canning jars.

"What the hell is a cannin' jug?"

"Jars," she corrected. "They have screw-down, airtight lids. They keep food fresh and good tasting for months."

"Well, I'll be damned."

"Probably," Smoke said, saddling Preacher's pony.

"And don't forget the lids," Nicole reminded him. "And the vinegar. And you come right back, now, Preacher. No dillydallying around, you hear?"

"Yes, ma'am," he said sourly. "And don't fergit the lids!" he mimicked under his breath. " Shore hope none of my compadres see me doin' this. Never live it down."

He continued to mutter as he rode off. "I fought a grizzly bear and won one time," he said. "Now I'm runnin' errands to git jug lids. Ain't nobody got no respect for an old man."

If anyone else had called him an old man, Preacher would have dented his skull with the butt of his Henry.

The nearest town of any size—other than the Springs, and Preacher could not go there; too many people knew him and might try to track him back to Smoke—was Del Norte, located just a few miles south of the Rio Grande, on the eastern slopes of the San Juan Forest.

He knew of a town being built at the site of old Antoine Robidoux's trading post, up close to the Gunnison, but he doubted they would have any canning jars and lids, so he pointed his pony's nose east-northeast, to avoid settlements as much as possible. He rode through the western part of the San Juan's, across the Los Pinos, through the Weminuche, then followed the Rio Grande into Del Norte—a long bit of traveling through the wilderness. But Preacher knew all the shortcuts and places to avoid.

As Preacher rode into town, coming in from the opposite direction, deliberately, his eyes swept the street from side to side, settling on a group of men in front of a local saloon. Most were local men, but Preacher spotted two as gun-hands.

He knew one of them: Felter. An ex-army sergeant who had been publicly flogged and dishonorably discharged for desertion in the face of the enemy; the enemy being the Cheyenne up in the north part of the state. But Preacher knew the man was no coward—he just showed uncommon good sense in getting away from a bad situation. After his humiliation and discharge from the army, Felter had turned bounty hunter, selling his gun skills—which were considerable—to the highest bidder. He was an ugly brute of a man, who had killed, so it was said, more than twenty men. He was quick on the draw, but not as quick as Smoke, Preacher knew. Nobody he had ever seen or heard of was that quick. He cut his eyes once more to Felter. The man had been accused of rape—twice.

The other man standing beside Felter looked like Canning, the outlaw. But Preacher was not sure of that. If it was Canning, and he was riding with Felter, they were up to no good—and that was fact.

In a general store, Preacher sized up the shopkeeper as one of those pinch-mouthed Eastern types. Looked like he might be henpecked, too.

Preacher bought a little bit of ribbon for Nicole to wear in her hair, and some pretty gingham for a new dress—she was swellin' up like a pumpkin.

"Got any cannin' jars?"

The shopkeeper nodded. "Just got a shipment of those new type with the screw top. Best around."

"Can you pack 'em for travel over some rough country—headin' east?" Preacher lied.

"I can."

Preacher ordered several cases and paid for them. "Put 'em out back. I'll pick 'em up later on. My old woman is 'bout to wart me plumb to death. Up to her bustle in green beans and sich. Know what I mean? Never should have got hitched up."

"Sir." The shopkeeper leaned forward. "I know *exactly* what you mean. By all that is holy, I do."

"Walter!" A shrill voice cut the hot air of the store. "You hurry up now and bring me my tea. Stop loafing about, gossiping like a fisherwoman. Hurry up!"

Preacher cringed at the thought of being married to someone who sounded like an angry puma with a thorn in its paw. *God!* he thought, *her voice would chip ice.*

"Walter!" the voice squalled from the rear of the store, causing the short hairs on the back of Preacher's neck to quiver.

Black hatred flashed across the shopkeeper's face.

"Git you a strap," Preacher suggested. "Wear 'er out a time or two."

The man sighed. "I have given that some thought, sir. Believe me, I have."

"Good luck," Preacher told him. He walked out into the street, his Henry cradled in his arms.

A young man in a checkered shirt, a bright red bandanna tied about his neck, dark trousers tucked into polished boots, and wearing two pearl-handled pistols, grinned at the mountain man.

"Hey, grandpa! Ain't you too old to be walkin' around without someone to look after you? You likely to forget your way back to the old folks' home."

The barflies on the porch laughed. All but Felter. He knew the breed of men called mountain man, and knew it was wise to leave them alone, for they had lived violently and usually reacted in kind.

Preacher glanced at the young would-be tough. Without slowing his stride, he savagely drove the butt of his Henry into the loudmouth's stomach. The young smart aleck doubled over, vomiting in the street. Preacher paused long enough to pluck the pistols from leather and drop them in a horse trough.

"You run along home, now, sonny," Preacher told him, over the sounds of retching and the jeering laughter of the loafers on the porch. "Tell your Ma to change your diapers and tuck you into bed. You 'pear to me to need some rest."

Preacher stepped into the dark bar, allowed his eyes to

adjust to the sudden gloom, and walked to the counter, ordering whiskey with a beer chaser.

The batwings swung open, boots on the sawdust-covered floor. The marshal. "Trouble out there, old-timer?"

"Nothin' I couldn't handle, young-timer."

The marshal chuckled. "Calls himself Kid Austin. He's been overdue for a comedown for some time. Thinks he's quite a hand with those fancy guns."

Preacher glanced at the lawman. "He'll never make it. They's a lot of salty ol' boys ridin' the hoot-owl trail that'll feed them guns to him. An inch at a time."

The marshal ordered a beer, then waited until the barkeep was out of earshot. He put his elbows on the bar and said softly, "You're the Preacher; man who rides with the young gun, Smoke. Don't talk, just listen. The bounty's been upped on your friend's head. That's the word I get. Someone up in the Idaho Territory is out to get Smoke."

"Potter, Stratton, and Richards."

"That's right. Potter is big . . . politically. Richards is in mining and cattle. Stratton *owns* the town of Bury. Those two gunfighters on the porch, Felter and Canning, work for those three men. They got a bunch of hardcases camped just north of town. When you leave, and I hope it's soon, ride out easy and cover your trail."

"Thanks."

"No need for that. I just know what happened in the war, that's all. Can't abide a traitor."

Preacher glanced at him.

"Since that first shooting, back at the mining camp, the story's spread. I reckon all the way to the Idaho Territory. But there's more. Your friend has a sister named Jane—right?"

"He don't speak none of her."

"Well, she's up in the territory now."

"Let me guess: She's in Bury."

"Yeah. She's Richards's woman. He keeps her."

"I'll tell him."

When Preacher rode out of Del Norte, he did so boldly, not wanting to implicate the shopkeeper, maybe leaving him open to rough treatment from Felter or Canning. Poor fellow had enough woes to contend with from that braying wife. Preacher picked up his jars, secured them well, then rode out to the east.

He didn't think he was fooling anybody, for Felter knew him; knew he was friends with the young gunfighter. He would be followed.

Preacher rode easy, constantly checking his back trail. He rode across the San Luis Valley, slowly edging north. No one alive knew Colorado like the Preacher, and he was going to give his followers a rough ride.

By noon of the second day, Preacher had spotted his trackers. He grinned nastily, then headed his horses toward the Great Sand Dunes. If any of those behind him had any pilgrim in them, this is where Preacher would cut the sheep from the goats.

He skirted the southernmost part of San Luis Creek, filled up his canteens and watered his horses, and grinning, headed for the dunes. On the east side of the lake, Preacher pulled into a stand of timber, carefully smoothed out his trail with brush and sand droppings, then slipped back and waited.

He watched two men, neither of them Felter or Canning, lose his trail and begin to circle. Leaving his horses ground reined, he worked his way to the edge of the timber until he was close enough to hear them talking.

"Damned ol' coot!" one of them said. "Where'd he go?"

"Relax," his partner said. "The boss's got twenty men workin' all around. We got him boxed. He can't get out."

Old coot! Preacher thought. *Your Ma's garters I can't get out!*

"Relax, hell! I want that five thousand dollars."

The ante was going up.

"How much is on the ol' fart's head?"

Old fart! Preacher silently raged.

"Nothin'," the meaner-looking of the pair said with a grin. "It's the gunfighter Richards and them want. That old man ain't worth a buffalo turd."

Buffalo turd! Preacher almost turned purple.

"We'll take the old man alive, make him tell where the kid's at, then kill him."

You just dug your own grave, Preacher thought.

The two men sat their horses. They rolled cigarettes. "How come all this interest in this Smoke? I ain't never got the straight of it."

"Personal, way I heard it. The kid's sister is Richards's private woman up in Bury. I ain't never been there so I can't say if she's a looker. Probably is. Then they's the gold.

"Seems the kid's brother was a Reb in the war, on a patrol bringin' gold in for the South. Richards and them others killed the Rebs and took the gold—'bout a hundred or so thousand dollars of it. 'Bout three-four years back, the kid's Daddy comes a-bustin' into Bury—'fore it was a town proper—and killed some of Richards's men. Took back some of the gold. 'Bout forty thousand of it, so I heard—but some of it was dust that had been recently washed. Richards thinks the kid has it . . . wants it back and the kid dead."

Preacher grinned. He had thought all along Emmett buried the gold with him. Smart man.

Preacher jacked back the hammer of his Henry and blew both men out of the saddle. "Call me an old fart and a buffalo turd, will you!"

Preacher rode hard to the north, following the creek, going from first one side to the other, many times riding down the middle of the creek to hide his horses' tracks. Just south of the small settlement called Crestone, Preacher headed west, across the valley, undercutting another settlement between the San Luis and the Saguache Creeks. He was out of supplies when he reached Saguache. Picketing his pack animals just outside of town, he rode in, just in time for a hanging.

In the early 1870s, almost every third building in the town was a saloon, and it was a rough and rowdy place. Preacher rode to a general store, got his supplies, and asked who was getting hanged, and for what?

"Some tinhorn gambler named Anderson. Killed a man last night during a card game. Fellow caught him cold-deckin' and braced him. Gambler had one of them little belly guns. Had the trial this mornin'. Judge and jury and all. Lasted forty minutes. Jury deliberated for five minutes. You wanna come watch him swing?"

"Thanks. I best be travelin'. Headin' east," he lied.

"Best be glad you ain't headin' west, lots of hardcases thataway. Lookin' for that outlaw gunfighter and murderer Smoke Jensen. Got six thousand dollars on his head and the ante's goin' up."

"I'm too old for that kind of nonsense," Preacher said. "Leave the hard ridin' and the gunsmoke to the young bucks."

"I know what you mean." The shopkeeper laughed, patting his ample belly. "'Sides, with me it'd be unfair to the horse!"

Outside of town, Preacher swung wide and headed west, into the Cochetopa Hills, then south into the wilderness, then angled southwest, straight through some of the wildest and most beautiful country in the world. Days later, in the Needle Mountains, he was ambushed.

He felt he was being watched as he rode, but figured it was Indians—and Indians didn't worry him, since most of them thought him to be crazy, and he could usually ride through them, singing and cackling.

The slug that almost tore him from the saddle hit him in

the left shoulder, driving out his back. Preacher slammed his heels to his pony's side and, keeping low in the saddle, headed for a hole he knew in the mountains. Through his pain, he could hear men yelling off to his right.

"Get him alive! Don't kill him."

But "getting Preacher" took more doing than the men chasing him had. Another rifle barked, the slug hitting him in the leg, deflecting off his leg bone and angling upward, ripping a hole when it exited out his hip, taking a piece of bone with it. Savagely reining his pony, Preacher leveled his Henry. He emptied two saddles and shot the horse out from under a third rider, grinning with grim satisfaction as the horse fell on the man, crushing him. The man's screamings ripped through the mountains. Preacher slipped away, hunting a hole where he could tend to his wounds; he was losing a lot of blood.

Preacher rode hard, barely able to see, barely able to hang on to his saddle horn. The pack animals trotted along, keeping pace, frightened. Finally, in desperation, he tied himself in the saddle.

All through the afternoon he rode, half conscious, until he reached a small lake just west of the Animas. There he slid to the ground, dragging his bad leg. In a fog of pain, Preacher loosened the saddle cinch, allowing air to flow between saddle and hide. What he did not need now was a galled-up horse. He was fearful of removing the saddle; didn't know if he would have the strength to swing it back on the pony. He put on his pickets, and collapsed to the earth.

All through the cold night he dreamed of his Indian wives and his kids, as his wounds festered and infected, fevering him. Their images were blurred, and he could not make out their faces.

He dreamed of the mountains and the valleys as they were when he first saw them, close to sixty years back. Lush and green and wild and beautiful. And he dreamed of his compadres, those men who, with Preacher, blazed the trails and danced and sang and whooped and hollered at the rendezvous . . . back when he—and they—were full of piss and vinegar and fire.

But most of them were now dead.

He dreamed of the battles he'd had, both with white and red men. And he wondered if his life, as the way of life of the red man, was ending.

When the chill of dawn touched him with her misty hand, Preacher knew he was close to death.

12

His babbling and shouting woke him, jerking him into a world filled with pain. "Got to get to Smoke!" he was saying as he opened his eyes. "Got to get to my boy!"

And he knew his feelings toward the tall young man were just as parental as if he were his own flesh and blood.

And he knew he loved the young man with the dark brooding eyes and the cat-quick guns.

Dragging himself to the lake, he washed his wounds and bound them, the sight of them sickening him. He had been hit much harder than this, but that was years back, when he was younger and stronger. He knew he should prepare poultices for his wounds, but didn't know if he had the strength, and, more importantly, the time.

He dragged himself to his pony and tightened the cinch and swung into the saddle. "I'm seventy year old," he muttered. "Lived past my time. Turned into a babblin' ol' fool—maybe I am touched in the head. But I got to warn my boy they's comin'. And I got to cover my tracks better than an Injun."

Having said that, he touched his heels to the pony's side and moved out, gritting his stubs of teeth against the waves of pain that ripped through him.

* * *

Modern day doctors would have said what the old man did was impossible for a man half his age. But modern day doctors do not know and will never know the likes of the mountain men who cut the trails of the way west.

A chill was in the morning air when Preacher rode up to the cabin on the knoll in the valley. He was a gaunt shell of the man who had ridden out in the middle of the summer. Through sheer iron will, stubbornness, and hard-headed cantankerousness, he had brought the pack animals with him.

"Howdy, purty thing." He grinned at Nicole. "I brung your durned ol' cannin' jugs." Then he fell from his pony and into the arms of Smoke.

They tended to his wounds, as best they could, for his leg had become infected and it was swollen and grotesque. Nicole turned a tear-stained face to her husband.

"I think he's dying, Smoke."

"Bend down here, son," Preacher said. "I got something to tell you—and don't argue with me. I ain't time for no debate."

Smoke squatted beside the bed.

"I covered my back trail," Preacher whispered. "So you be safe for a time." Slowly and with much pausing for breath, he told Smoke and Nicole what he knew, and about the gold in the bottom of his father's grave at the Hole.

"When your woman births the baby, wait till spring and then get the hell out of this country. Find you a safe place to live out your lives. Right now, you get my fancy buckskins out of that there trunk over in the corner and then leave me be for a while."

On the porch, Nicole asked, "What is he going to do?"

Smoke sighed heavily, a numbness gripping his heart. "Get all dressed up in his fancy buckskins and sash and such, prepare himself to die, mountain-man style."

Smoke and Nicole sat on the porch of the cabin and waited, listening as Preacher hummed a French song as he dressed.

"I don't know why he's doing this," Nicole said, tears running down her face.

"He's doing it because he's a mountain man." Smoke's eyes were on the mountains in the distance. "I've got to do something." He rose and walked to the lean-to.

He selected a gentle horse, a mare, too old for breeding. He saddled her and took her back to the cabin. Preacher was waiting with Nicole on the porch.

Preacher's eyes touched the horse, returned to Smoke. "I see you didn't forget ever'thing I learned you."

"No, sir," Smoke said, fighting back tears. "Preacher? What is your Christian name?"

The old man smiled. "Arthur was my first name—why?"

"Because if we have a son, I want to name him after you."

"That'd be right nice. Now help me on that nag yonder and stand back."

Preacher was dressed in clean, beaded buckskins. His dying suit. He wore new leggings and moccasins and a wide red sash around his waist. A cap of skunk hide and hair on his head.

"You look grand," Smoke said.

"You tell lies, too," Preacher retorted. "Help me on the mare."

In the saddle, Preacher looked at Smoke. "You know I'm gonna shoot this horse, don't you, son?"

Smoke nodded. Nicole put her face in her hands and wept. "I don't understand," she said.

"So I can have something to ride when my human body is gone, girl. So don't you fret and carry on. One old life is endin', but you carryin' new life. That's the way of the world." He looked at Smoke. "You be mindful of what I learned you, boy, you hear?"

"Yes, sir."

He rode off without looking back, riding toward the high, far mountains. There, he would select his place to die. He would go out of this world as he had lived in it—alone.

"You know what?" Smoke said to Nicole, as they stood and watched him disappear. "I never even knew his last name."

Autumn touched the valley under the shadows of the great mountains, painting the landscape with a multicolored brush: the grass a deep tan, the trees golden, the sky blue, and the flowers white and purple and red. On a huge rock by the banks of the creek, Smoke chipped Preacher's name, when he died, and his approximate age. The course of the creek has long since shifted, the bed now part of grazing land, but the huge rock remains. And far in the mountains, high above the West Delores, time and wind have scattered the bones of man and horse. But some locals say that in early fall, on a clear night, if one listens with ears and heart, you can hear the sounds of a slow-moving old mare, carrying a grizzled old mountain man. The old man is singing a French song as he completes his circle, before dismounting to rest for another year, his eyes on a valley far off in the distance.

Of course, that's just a myth. A local legend. Folklore. Certainly isn't *real.* But in the 1930s when the CCC boys were working in the valley, they tried to move the huge boulder with four names chipped deep into it. Something frightened them so badly none of them would ever again go near the boulder. Work was halted at the site.

The local rancher would only say, "I told you so."

And some say Preacher did not die of his wounds, but lay near death in an Indian village for months, while one of his daughters took care of him. Some say the old man returned to help the man called Smoke in his vendetta. Many people *insist* that is the way it happened. That Preacher and Smoke . . .

Well, that's another story.

As the winds changed from cool to cold, and the first flakes of snow touched the valley, Nicole gave birth to a boy.

While Smoke paced the cabin floor, feeling totally inadequate—which, in this situation, he was—a tiny squall of outrage filled the bedroom, as breath was sucked into new lungs. Nicole's hair was stuck to her head from sweaty, painful exertion, and her face was pale.

"Take the knife," she told her husband. "And cut the cord where I show you."

His hand trembled and he hesitated for a second. Her sharp command brought him back.

"Do it, Smoke!"

The umbilical lifeline severed, the baby washed, the tiny wound on his belly bandaged, Nicole wrapped the boy in clean white cloths and the baby nursed at her breast.

"You look like you're going to be sick," Nicole told him. "Go outside."

He did and thought, *what I know about birthing babies would fill volumes. And what I know about the inner strength of women would, too.*

When he again entered the house, Nicole was nursing the child at her breast, and Smoke thought he had never seen a more beautiful sight. He stood in speechless awe.

Fed, warm, and secure, the child then slept beside its mother.

"You sleep, too," Smoke told her. "I'll stand watch."

"If baby Arthur starts to cry," she said wearily, "just take him."

"What am I supposed to *do* with it?"

She smiled at him. "It will come natural to you. Just keep your hand under his head for support."

"Oh, Lord," Smoke said.

Nicole drifted off into sleep and after an hour, the child awakened. With much trepidation, the young man took his son in his big, work-hardened hands and held him gently.

"Now what do I do?" he said.

The baby looked up at him.

"Arthur," Smoke said. "You behave, now."

And the baby, like his namesake, promptly started squalling and grousing.

Winter locked in the valley and Smoke knew, as long as the hard winter held, the three of them would be safe from the stalled pursuit of the bounty hunters. But in the spring, their coming would be inevitable and relentless. Smoke would have to move his family to a safer place.

But where?

His smile was grim. Sure, why not. Right under their noses would be the last place they would look. Idaho. He would have to hang up his .36s—maybe get a new Remington or Colt—carry just one gun. Use Seven for breeding, never for riding. Maybe, he thought, they could pull it off.

Preacher drifted into his mind. God, how he missed that ornery old man, so full of common sense and mountain wisdom. He would have been a great companion for the baby.

Smoke shook his head. But Preacher was gone. And the living have to go on living. Preacher told him that.

He struggled to remember what Preacher had told him about Idaho Territory. He recalled Preacher telling him there was a lake on the eastern pan (Gray's Lake). So wild and beautiful and lonely it had to be seen to be believed. No white men lived there, Preacher said. So that's where Smoke would take his family to live, hopefully, in peace.

But he wondered if he could ever live in peace. And that ever present speculation haunted him, especially when he looked at his wife and son.

If anything ever happened to them . . .

Baby Arthur cooed and gurgled and grew healthy and strong and much loved during the winter of 1871/72. He would be big-boned and strong, with blond hair and blue eyes that flashed when he grew angry.

The three of them waited out the winter, making plans to leave the valley in late spring, when the baby was six months old, and they felt he could stand the trip. They both agreed it would be taking a chance, but one they had to take.

In a settlement that would soon wear the name of Telluride, in the primitive area of the Uncompahgre Forest, bounty hunters also waited for spring. They were a surly, quarrelsome bunch as the cold days and bitter nights drifted toward spring. With them, a young man who called himself Kid Austin. Kid was quick with a pistol— perhaps the quickest of them all—but the only man he had ever killed was a drunken old Mexican sheepherder. Even with the knowledge that the Kid was untested, the bounty hunters left him alone. For he was uncommonly fast and quick-tempered. And because the man they hunted was a friend of the old mountain man who had humiliated the Kid in front of that saloon, Kid Austin thus hated the man called Smoke. He dreamed of killing this Smoke, of facing him down in a street, beating him to the draw, and watching him die hard in the dirt, crying and begging for mercy, while men stood on the boardwalks and feared him, and women stood and wanted him. Those were his dreams—all his dreams. Kid Austin was not a very imaginative young man. And he would not live to dream many more of his wild dreams of glory and power.

Felter was a patient man, who shared none of the Kid's dreams. Felter didn't know how many white men he had killed. He thought it to be around twenty-five, and nobody gave a damn how many Indians. He slowly spun the cylinder of his Colt. "They got to be in that valley, southwest of the San Juan's. Everything points in that direction."

"That old Ute we talked to," Canning said. "He said something 'bout a blond-haired woman called Little Lightning. That could be Smoke's woman." He grinned. "You boys can have the gunfighter; I'll take me a taste of his wife. I'd like to hump me a yeller-haired white woman. Man gits tired of them greasy squaws."

"You rape all the squaws you take a mind to," a bounty hunter named Grissom told him. "Don't nobody give a damn 'bout them. But you bother a white woman, you gonna get yourself hung."

Canning's grin spread across his unshaven face. "Not ifn I don't leave her alive to talk about it, I won't."

"That there is a thought to think about," Grissom agreed. "But that Ute said she was all swole up with kid, gettin' ready to turn fresh."

"So?"

"What about the kid?"

Canning shrugged that off. "I 'member the time up in north Colorado when we hit an Injun camp—surprised them. That were fun. After we had our fun with some young squaws, I found me a papoose just a-hollerin' and grabbed him up by the heels. Swung him agin a tree. Head popped like a pistol shot."

"That were a Injun kid. This here be a white baby."

"No never-mind. Richards said to kill 'em all. Don't want to leave no youngun around to grow up and git mean."

The bounty hunters all agreed that made sense. And they would pleasure themselves with the woman—then kill her.

"I want Smoke," Kid Austin said. The older bounty hunters smiled. "I want him face on so's I can beat him at his own game. You all just watch me."

"Yeah, Kid," a man called Poker said. "You a real grizzly, you are."

"I just need one chance."

It's probably the only one you'll get, too, Felter thought. *'Cause if the Preacher took him under his wing and taught him right, this Smoke will be a ring-tailed tooter.*

The first week in April, a violent pre-season thunderstorm, spawned by a week of abnormally warm weather, struck the valley, scattering the herd of breeding horses.

"I've got to get some of them back," Smoke said. "We've got to have them for breeding stock. But I hate to leave you and Little Preacher alone." His face was worry lined, for he knew with the warm weather, the bounty hunters would be riding hard to get him.

She laughed away his fears. "We have to get that cow back for milk, and there is no telling where that fool cow ran off to. And don't forget, I'm a pretty good shot."

"I might be gone for several days."

"Honey," she said touching his face, "it was the hand of Providence that brought us that cow—Lord knows how it got out here. But you've got to get it back for the baby." She pressed a packet of food on him. "I'll be packing while you're finding the herd—and the cow." She laughed. "You always look so serious when you're milking."

"Never *did* like to milk," he said.

He left reluctantly, knowing he had no choice. As he rode away on Seven, he stopped once, turning in the saddle, looking back at his wife, holding their son in her arms. The sun sparkled off her hair, casting a halo of light around the woman and baby. Smoke lifted a hand in goodbye.

Nicole waved at him, then turned and walked back into the cabin.

To the northeast, still many hard miles away, just leaving the last fringes of heavy forest and tall mountains

behind them, rode the bounty hunters. Since the middle
of March they had fanned out in the mountains, asking
questions of any white man and several friendly Indians.
The Indians told them nothing, but several white drifters
told them of a cabin in the valley, on a knoll, with a little
creek running behind it. Where the Delores leaves the
San Juans, head southwest, you can't miss it.

Canning's thoughts were of the yellow-haired woman.
Felter thought about the money.

Kid Austin thought of being the man who killed the
gunfighter/outlaw Smoke. What a name he'd have after
that—and all the women he wanted.

Smoke worked long hours, gathering his precious
herd of mustangs and Appaloosa, tucking them in a
blind canyon, holding them there while he searched for
the others. He found the cow and the old brindle steer
that had wandered up with her, probably, Smoke concluded, the only survivors of an Indian attack on a
wagon train.

During the late afternoon of the second day out,
Smoke thought he heard the faint sounds of gunfire carrying on the wind, blowing from the north, but he could
not be certain. He listened intently for several moments.
He could hear nothing except the winds, sighing lonely
off the far mountains. He returned to his work.

"Fine-lookin' woman," Canning said, looking at Nicole.
She was sprawled in semi-awareness on the floor. His eyes
lingered on her legs where her dress had slid up when she
was knocked to the floor. The bodice of the dress was
ripped open, exposing her breasts. Canning licked his
lips.

The bounty hunters had destroyed the interior of the
cabin, looking for gold that was not there.

One bounty hunter sat in a chair, cursing as he bandaged a bloody arm. "She can shoot," he said. "Damn near tore my arm off. Somebody see ifn you can find a bottle of laudanum."

Felter's eyes found the body of Stoner lying in front of the cabin. "Yeah, she sure can shoot. Just ask Stoner."

"If he answers you," Kid Austin said, "the back door's mine."

They all laughed at this.

"Drag his body out of sight," Felter said. "Don't want to spook this Smoke when he rides up. And hide your horses. We'll take him when he comes in."

Kid Austin opened his mouth to protest.

"Shut up," Felter cut him off. "Maybe you'll get a crack at him, maybe not. I'd like to take him alive, torture him, find out where the gold is."

He knelt down beside Nicole, his hands busy on her body.

Arthur began crying.

"Shut that kid up!" Felter snarled. "'Fore I shoot the little snot."

Canning picked up a blanket and walked to the cradle. He folded the wool and held it over the baby's face for several minutes. The child kicked feebly, then was still as life was smothered from it.

Nicole was stripped naked and shoved into the bedroom. Her hands were tied to the bedposts. Arthur was silent, and Nicole knew, with the awareness mothers seem to possess, her son was dead.

She began weeping.

She opened her eyes, and through the mist of tears, watched Canning drop his trousers to the floor.

The perverted afternoon and evening would wear slowly for Nicole.

And Smoke was a day's ride from the cabin on the knoll in the valley.

13

On the morning of the third day out, Smoke pushed his horses closer to the cabin, a feeling of dread building within him. Some primitive sense of warning caused him to pull up short. He left the cow, the steer, and the horses in a meadow several miles from the cabin.

He made a wide circle of the cabin, staying in the timber back of the creek, and slipped up to the cabin.

Nicole was dead. The acts of the men had grown perverted and in their haste, her throat had been crushed.

Felter sat by the lean-to and watched the valley in front of him. He wondered where Smoke had hidden the gold.

Inside, Canning drew his skinning knife and scalped Nicole, tying her bloody hair to his belt. He then skinned a part of her, thinking he would tan the hide and make himself a nice tobacco pouch.

Kid Austin got sick at his stomach watching Canning's callousness, and went out the back door to puke on the ground. That moment of sickness saved his life—for the time being.

Grissom walked out the front door of the cabin. Smoke's tracks had indicated he had ridden off south, so he would probably return from that direction. But

Grissom felt something was wrong. He sensed something; his years on the hoot-owl back trails surfacing.

"Felter?" he called.

"Yeah?" He stepped from the lean-to.

"Something's wrong."

"I feel it. But what?"

"I don't know." Grissom spun as he sensed movement behind him. His right hand dipped for his pistol. Felter had stepped back into the lean-to. Grissom's palm touched the smooth wooden butt of his pistol as his eyes touched the tall young man standing by the corner of the cabin, a Colt .36 in each hand. Lead from the .36s hit him in the center of the chest with numbing force. Just before his heart exploded, the outlaw said, "Smoke!" Then he fell to the ground.

Smoke jerked the gun belt and pistols from the dead man. Remington Army .44s.

A bounty hunter ran from the cabin, firing at the corner of the cabin. But Smoke was gone.

"Behind the house!" Felter yelled, running from the lean-to, his fists full of Colts. He slid to a halt and raced back to the water trough, diving behind its protection.

A bounty hunter who had been dumping his bowels in the outhouse struggled to pull up his pants, at the same time pushing open the door with his shoulder. Smoke shot him twice in the belly and left him to scream on the outhouse floor.

Kid Austin, caught in the open behind the cabin, ran for the banks of the creek, panic driving his legs. He leaped for the protection of the sandy embankment, twisting in the air, just as Smoke took aim and fired. The ball hit Austin's right buttock and traveled through the left cheek of his butt, tearing out a sizable hunk of flesh. Kid Austin, the dreaming gunhand, screamed and fainted from the pain in his ass.

Smoke ran for the protection of the woodpile and crouched there, recharging his Colts and checking the

.44s. He listened to the sounds of men in panic, firing in all directions, hitting nothing.

Moments ticked past, the sound of silence finally overpowering gunfire. Smoke flicked away sweat from his face. He waited.

Something came sailing out the back door to bounce on the grass. Smoke felt hot bile build in his stomach. Someone had thrown his son outside. The boy had been dead for some time. Smoke fought back sickness.

"You wanna see what's left of your woman?" a taunting voice called from near the back door. "I got her hair on my belt and a piece of her hide to tan. We all took a turn or two with her. I think she liked it."

Smoke felt rage charge through him, but he remained still, crouched behind the thick pile of wood until his rage cooled to controlled venom-filled fury. He unslung the big Sharps buffalo rifle that Preacher had carried for years. The rifle could drop a two thousand pound buffalo at six hundred yards. It could also punch a hole through a small log.

The voice from the cabin continued to mock and taunt Smoke. But Preacher's training kept him cautious. To his rear lay a meadow, void of cover. To his left was a shed, but he knew that was empty for it was still barred from the outside. The man he'd plugged in the butt was to his right, but several fallen logs would protect him from that direction. The man in the outhouse was either dead or passed out; his screaming had ceased.

Through a chink in the logs, Smoke shoved the muzzle of the Sharps and lined up where he thought he had seen a man move, just to the left of the rear window, to where Smoke had framed it out with rough pine planking. He gently squeezed the trigger, taking up slack. The weapon boomed, the planking shattered, and a man began screaming in pain.

Canning ran out the front of the cabin, to the lean-to,

sliding down hard beside Felter behind the water trough. "This ain't workin' out," he panted. "Grissom, Austin, Poker, and now Evans are either dead or dying. The slug from that buffalo gun blowed his arm off. Let's get the hell outta here!"

Felter had been thinking the same thing. "What about Clark and Sam?"

"They growed men. They can join us or they can go to hell."

"Let's ride. They's always another day. We'll hide up in them mountains, see which way he rides out, then bushwhack him. Let's go." They raced for their horses, hidden in a bend of the creek, behind the bank. They kept the cabin between themselves and Smoke as much as possible, then bellied down in the meadow the rest of the way.

In the creek, the water red from the wounds in his butt, Kid Austin crawled upstream, crying in pain and humiliation. His Colts were forgotten—useless anyway; the powder was wet—all he wanted was to get away.

The bounty hunters left in the house, Clark and Sam, looked at each other. "I'm gettin' out!" Sam said. "That ain't no pilgrim out there."

"The hell with that," Clark said. "I humped his woman, I'll kill him and take the eight thousand."

"Your option." Sam slipped out the front and caught up with the others.

Kid Austin reached his horse first. Yelping as he hit the saddle, he galloped off toward the timber in the foothills.

"You wife you don't look so good now," Clark called out to Smoke. "Not since she got a haircut and one titty skinned."

Deep silence had replaced gunfire. The air stank of black powder, blood, and relaxed bladders and bowels, death-induced. Smoke had seen the men ride off into the foothills. He wondered how many were left in the cabin.

Smoke remained still, his eyes burning with rage. Smoke's eyes touched the stiffening form of his son. If Clark could have read the man's thoughts, he would have stuck the muzzle of his .44 into his mouth and pulled the trigger, insuring himself a quick death, instead of what waited for him later on.

"Yes, sir," Clark taunted him. He went into profane detail of the rape of Nicole and the perverted acts that followed that.

Smoke eased slowly backward, keeping the woodpile in front of him. He slipped down the side of the knoll and ran around to the side of the small hill, then up it to the side of the cabin. He grinned: The bounty hunter was still talking to the woodpile, to the muzzle of the Sharps stuck through the logs.

Smoke eased around to the front of the cabin and looked in. He saw Nicole, saw the torture marks on her, saw the hideousness of the scalping and the skinning knife. He lifted his eyes to the back door, where Clark was crouching just to the right of the closed door.

Smoke raised his .36 and shot the pistol out of Clark's hand. The outlaw howled and grabbed his numbed and bloodied hand.

Smoke stepped over Grissom's body, then glanced at the body of the armless bounty hunter who had bled to death.

Clark looked up at the tall young man with the burning eyes. Cold slimy fear put a bony hand on his shoulder. For the first time in his evil life, Clark knew what death looked like. "You gonna make it quick, ain't you?"

"Not likely," Smoke said, then kicked him on the side of the head, dropping Clark unconscious to the floor.

When Clark came to his senses, he began screaming. He was naked, staked out a mile from the cabin, on the plain. Rawhide held his wrists and ankles to thick stakes driven into the ground. A huge ant mound was just inches from him. And Smoke had poured honey all over him.

"I'm a white man," Clark screamed. "You can't do this

to me." Slobber sprayed from his mouth. "What are you, half Apache?"

Smoke looked at him, contempt in his eyes. "You will not die well, I believe." He mounted Seven and rode back to the cabin.

"Goddamn you!" Clark squalled. He spat out a glob of honey. "Shoot me, for God's sake! It'll take me days to die like this. You're a devil—you're a devil!"

The ants found him and Clark's screaming was awful in the afternoon.

Smoke blocked the screaming from his mind as he rode back to the cabin, across the plain, so lovely with its profusion of wild flowers. Nicole had loved the wild flowers, he recalled, often picking a bunch of them to brighten a shelf or the table.

By the cabin on the knoll, Smoke found a shovel and began his slow digging of graves, one smaller than the other. Seven would warn him if anyone approached from any direction.

He paused often to wipe the tears from his eyes.

14

Smoke covered the mounds of earth with armloads of wild flowers from the meadow. He asked God to take mother and son into His place of peace and love and beauty.

But Vengeance is Mine, Sayeth the Lord, popped into his brain.

"No, Sir," Smoke said. "Not this time."

Clark's screaming had hoarsened into an animal bellow.

Smoke fashioned two crosses of wood and hammered the stakes into the ground at the head of each grave. He walked down to the creek bank, to the boulder where he had chipped Preacher's name. He added two more names.

Smoke gathered up all the weapons of the dead bounty hunters and put them in the cabin. He had made up his mind to change to the Army .44s. He would pick out the best two later; there would be ample shot and powder. He dragged the bodies of the dead bounty hunters far out into the plain, leaving them for the wolves, the coyotes, and the buzzards, the latter already circling.

It was late afternoon, the dark shadows of blue and purple were deepening. On a ridge to the northeast, Felter watched, as best he could, through field glasses, until it became too dark to see.

"He buried his wife and kid," Felter told the others. "Drug the other bodies out in the plain, buzzards gatherin' now. And he staked out Clark on an anthill."

"The bastard!" Canning cussed.

But Felter chuckled. "He ain't no more bastard than us. He's just tougher than rawhide and meaner than a grizzly, that's all. Madder than hell, too."

Kid Austin moaned in pain.

Felter gazed down into the dark valley. He could not help but feel grudging admiration for the man called Smoke. That would not prevent him from killing Smoke when the time and place presented itself, but it was good to know, at last, what type of man he would be going up against. Felter was one of the best at the quick-draw, but, he reasoned, why tempt fate in that manner when shooting a man in the back was so much safer?

But with this man called Smoke, he pondered, he would have to be very careful how he set up the ambush. For Smoke had been trained by the old mountain man, Preacher, and now Felter knew Smoke was as dangerous as a cornered grizzly. It would not be easy, but it could be done.

The bounty hunters made a cold camp that night. "Look sharp," Felter told the first night guard. "We up against a curly wolf. If any of you doubt that, just listen when the wind changes, and you can hear Clark squallin'."

No one spoke. They had all heard the howling of Clark. He was dying as hard as if he had been taken by Apache.

The Kid had never seen a man staked out before, but the others had come upon several.

The head would swell to twice its normal size from the ant stings; the eyes would be blind; the genitals would be grotesquely swollen; the lips would be swollen, turned inside out, and the tongue would finally swell up, blacken, and the man would choke to death, usually going insane long before that happened. It usually took two to three days.

Kid Austin shuddered in the night. He lay on his stomach on his blankets. "Smoke's crazy!" he said.

Felter chuckled. "No . . . he's just got a touch of mountain man in him, that's all."

On a mesa opposite the timber where Felter and the others slept, Smoke made his cold camp. Seven was on guard. Sleep finally took the young man in soft arms . . . almost as soft as the arms of Nicole.

And he dreamed of her, and of their son.

Long before first light touched the mountains and the valley, creating that morning's panorama of color, Smoke was up and moving. He rode across the valley. Stopping out of range of rifles, by a stand of cottonwoods, he calmly and arrogantly built a cook fire. He put on coffee to boil and sliced bacon into a pan. He speared out the bacon and dropped slices of potatoes into the grease, frying them crisp. With hot coffee and hot food, and a hunk of Nicole's fresh baked bread, Smoke settled down for a leisurely breakfast. He knew the outlaws were watching him; had seen the sun glint off glass yesterday afternoon.

"That bastard!" Canning cussed him.

But Felter again had to chuckle. "Relax. He's just tryin' to make us do something stupid. Stay put."

"I'd like to go down there and call him out," Kid said. His bravado had returned from his sucking on the laudanum bottle all night.

Felter almost told him to go ahead, get the rest of his butt shot off.

"You just stay put," he told Austin. "Rest your butt. We got time. They's just one of him, four of us."

"They was twice that yesterday," Sam reminded him.

Felter said nothing in rebuttal.

The valley upon which the outlaws gazed, and upon

160   *William W. Johnstone*

which Smoke was eating his quiet breakfast, as Seven
munched on young spring grass, was wild in its grandeur.
It was several miles wide, many miles long, with rugged
peaks on the north end, far in the distance, snow-
covered most of the time, with thick forests. And, Smoke
smiled grimly, many dead end canyons. One of which was
only a few miles from this spot. And he felt sure the
bounty hunters did not know it was a box, for it looked
very deceiving.

Clark had told Smoke, in the hopes he would only get
a bullet in the head, not ants on the brain, that it was
Canning who scalped his wife, Canning who first raped
her, Canning who skinned her breast to make a tobacco
pouch with the tanned hide.

Smoke cleaned up his skillet and plate and then set
about checking out the two Remington .44s he had
chosen from the pile of guns. Preacher had been after
him for several years to switch, and Smoke had fired and
handled Preacher's Remington .44 many times, liking
the feel of the weapon, the balance. And he was just as
fast with the slightly heavier weapon.

He spent an hour or more rigging holsters for his new
guns, then spent a few minutes drawing and firing them.
To his surprise, he found the weapon, with its sleeker
form and more laid-back hammer, increased his speed.

His smile was not pleasant. For he had plans for Canning.

Mounting up, he rode slowly to the northeast, always
keeping out of rifle range, and very wary of any ambush.
When Smoke disappeared into the timber, Felter made
his move.

"Let's ride," he said. "Let's get the hell out of here."

But after several hours, Felter realized *they* were being
pushed toward the northwest. Every time they tried to
veer off, a shot from the big Sharps would keep them
going.

On the second day, Canning brought his horse up

sharply, hurting the animal's mouth with the bit. "I 'bout
had it," he said.

They were tired and hungry, for Smoke had harassed
them with the Sharps every hour.

Felter looked around him, at the high walls of the
canyon, sloping upward, green and brown with timber.
He smiled ruefully. *They* were now the hunted.

A dozen times in the past two days they had tried to
bushwhack Smoke. But he was as elusive as his name.

"Somebody better do something," Felter said. "'Cause
we're in a box canyon."

"I'll take him!" Canning snarled. "Rest of you ride on
up 'bout a mile or two. Get set in case I miss." He grinned.
"But I ain't gonna do that, boys."

Felter nodded. "See you in a couple of hours."

Smoke had dismounted just inside the box canyon,
ground reining Seven. Smoke removed his boots and
slipped on moccasins. Then he went on the prowl, as
silent as death. He held a skinning knife in his left hand.

"No shots," Austin said. "And it's been three hours."

Sam sat quietly. Everything about this job had turned
sour.

"Horse comin'," Felter said.

"There he is!" Austin said. "And it's Canning. By God,
he said he'd get him, and he did."

But Felter wasn't sure about that. He'd smelled wood
smoke about an hour back. That didn't fit any pattern. And
Canning wasn't sitting his horse right. Then the screaming
drifted to them. Canning was hollering in agony.

"What's he hollerin' for?" Kid asked. "I hurt a lot
more'un anything he could have wrong with him."

"Don't bet on that," Felter told him. He scrambled
down the gravel-and-brush-covered slope to halt Canning's frightened horse.

Felter recoiled in horror at the sight of Canning's blood-soaked crotch.

"My privates!" Canning squalled. "Smoke waylaid me and gelded me! He cauterized me with a runnin' iron." Canning passed out, tumbling from the saddle.

Felter and Sam dragged the man into the brush and looked at the awful wound. Smoke had heated a running iron and seared the wound, stopping most of the bleeding. Felter thought Canning would live, but his raping days were over.

And Felter knew, with a sudden realization, that he wanted no more of the man called Smoke. Not without about twenty men backing him up, that is.

Using a spare shirt from his saddlebags, Felter made a crude bandage for Canning. But it was going to be hell on the man sitting a saddle. He looked around him. That fool Kid Austin was walking down the floor of the canyon, his hands poised over his twin Colts. An empty laudanum bottle lay on the ground.

"Get back here, you fool!" Felter shouted.

Austin ignored him. "Come on, Smoke!" he yelled. "I'm goin' to kill you."

"Hell with you, Kid," Sam muttered.

They tied Canning in the saddle and rode off, up the slope of the canyon wall, high up, near the crest. There they found a hole that just might get them free. Raking their horses' sides, the animals fought for footing, digging and sliding in the loose rock. The horses realized they had to make it—or die. With one final lunge, the horses cleared the crest and stood on firm ground, trembling from fear and exhaustion.

As they rested the animals, they looked for the Kid. Austin was lost from sight.

They rode off to the north, toward a mining camp where Richards had said he would leave word, or send more men should this crew fail.

Well, Felter reflected bitterly, *we damn sure failed.*

Austin, his horse forgotten, his mind numbed by over-doses of laudanum, stumbled down the rocky floor of the canyon, screaming and cursing Smoke. He pulled up short when he spotted his quarry.

Smoke sat calmly on a huge rock, munching on a cold biscuit.

"Get up!" the Kid shouted. "Get on your feet and face me like a man oughta."

Smoke finished his meager meal, then rose to his feet. He was smiling.

Kid Austin walked on, narrowing the distance, finally stopping about thirty feet from Smoke. "I'll be known as the man who killed Smoke," he said. "Me! Kid Austin."

Smoke laughed at him.

The Kid flushed. "I done it to your wife, too, Jensen. She liked it so much she asked me to do it to 'er some more. So I obliged 'er. I took your woman, now I'm gonna take you." He dipped his right hand downward.

Smoke drew his right hand .44 with blinding speed, drawing, cocking, firing, before Austin could realize what was taking place in front of his eyes. The would-be gun-fighter felt two lead fists of pain strike him in the belly, one below his belt buckle, the other just above the ornate silver buckle. The hammerlike blows dropped him to his knees. Hurt began creeping into his groin and stomach. He tried to pull his guns from leather, but his hands would not respond to the commands from his brain.

"I'm Kid Austin," he managed to say. "You can't do this to me."

"Looks like I did, though," Smoke said. He turned away from the dying man and walked back to Seven, swinging into the saddle. He rode off without looking back.

"Momma!" the Kid called, as the pain in his belly grew more intense. "It hurts, Momma. Help me."

But only the animals and the canyon heard his cries

for help. They alone witnessed his begging. The clop of Seven's hooves grew fainter.

His intestines mangled, one kidney shattered, and his spleen ruptured, the Kid died on his knees in the rocky canyon, in a vague praying position. He remained that way for a long time, until his horse picked up its master's scent and found him, nudging him with its nose, toppling the Kid over on his side. The horse bolted from the blood smell, running down the canyon. One Colt fell from a holster, clattering on the rocks, to shine in the thin sunlight filtering through the timber of the narrow canyon.

Then the canyon was quiet, with only the sighing of the wind.

Smoke rode back to the cabin in the valley and packed his belongings, covering the pack frame with a ground sheet. He rubbed Seven down and fed him grain and hay, stabling him in the lean-to.

He cleaned his guns and made camp outside the cabin. He could not bear to sleep inside that house of death and torture and rape. His sleep was restless during those starry nights of the first week back in the valley; his sleep troubled by nightmares of Nicole calling out his name, of the baby's dying.

The second week was no better, his sleep interrupted by the same nightmares. So when he kicked out of his blankets on this final morning in the valley, his body covered with sweat, Smoke knew he would never rest well until the men who were responsible for this tragedy were dead—Potter, Stratton, Richards.

Smoke bathed in the creek, doing so quickly, for the creek and the mossy bank also held memories. He saddled Seven and cinched the pack on a pack horse, then went to the graves by the cabin, hat in hand, to visit with his wife and son.

"I don't know that I will ever return," he spoke quietly. "I wish it could have been different, Nicole. I wish we could have lived out our lives in peace, together, raising our family. I wish a lot of things, Nicole. Goodbye."

With tears in his eyes, he mounted Seven and rode away, pointing the nose of the big spotted horse north.

But in a settlement on the banks of the Uncompahgre, Felter and Sam and Canning were telling a much different version of what happened in the cabin in the valley.

15

"I'm tellin' you boys," Felter said to the miners, "I ain't never seen nothin' like it. Them murderin' Utes raped the woman, killed her and the baby, then scalped 'em. It was terrible."

"Yeah," Sam picked up the lie. "Then that outlaw, Smoke Jensen, he all of a sudden comes up on us—shootin'. He kilt Grissom and Poker and Evans right off. Just shot 'em dead for no reason. He went crazy, I guess. Stampeded our horses and Felter and me took cover in a waller. He took our horses."

"Time we worked our way out," Felter said, "this Smoke had killed the rest of our crew and staked out Clark on an anthill, stripped him nekked and poured honey all over him." He hung his head in sorrow. "Wasn't nothin' we could do for him. You boys know how hard a man dies like that."

The miners listened quietly.

"I found Canning," Felter said. "You all know what was done to him. Most awfullest thing I ever seen one white man do to another. Kid Austin was shot in the back; never even had a chance to pull his guns."

Some of the miners believed Felter; most did not. They knew about Smoke, the stories told, and knew about Felter and his scummy crew. Some of them had known Preacher, and knew the mountain man would not take a murderer to raise as his son. The general consensus was that Felter and Sam and Canning were lying.

Felter had not told them of the men riding hard toward the camp; men sent by Richards and Stratton and Potter. That message was waiting for Felter when he arrived at the miners' camp.

Several miners left the smoke-filled tent, to gather in the dusky coolness.

"Pass the word," one said. "This boy Smoke is bein' set up. We all know the story as to why."

"Yeah. The fight'll be lopsided, but I sure don't wanna miss it. I hear tell this Smoke is poison with a short gun."

"I heard it myself. See you."

Although the trail of Felter was three weeks old, it was not that difficult to follow: a bloody bandage from Canning's wounds; a carelessly doused campfire; an empty bottle of laudanum and several pints of whiskey. And Indians told him of sighting the men.

It all pointed toward the silver camp near the Uncompahgre. And it also meant Felter was probably expecting more men to join him—probably more men than had attacked his cabin. How many brave men does it take to rape and kill one woman and a baby?

That thought lay bitter on his mind as he rode, following the trail with dogged determination.

Just south of what would soon be named Telluride, in the gray granite mountains, two miners stopped the young man on the spotted horse—stopped him warily.

"I was told you'd be ridin' a big spotted horse with a mean look in its eyes," a miner said. "I ain't tryin' to be nosy, young feller, but if you're the man called Smoke, I got news."

"I'm Smoke." He took out tobacco and paper and rolled a cigarette, handing the makings to the miners.

"Thanks," one said, after they had all rolled, licked, and lit. "'Bout fourteen salty ol' boys waitin' for you at the silver camp. Most of us figure Felter lied 'bout what happened at your cabin. What did happen?"

Smoke told them, leaving nothing out.

"That's 'bout the way we had it figured. Son, you can't go up agin all them folks—no matter how you feel. That'd be foolish. They's too many."

"If they're gunhands for Potter or Richards or Stratton, I intend to kill them."

"'Pears to me, son, they 'bout wiped out your whole family."

"They made just one mistake," Smoke said.

"What's that?"

"They left me alive."

The miners had nothing to say to that.

"Thanks for the information." Smoke moved out.

The miners watched him leave. One said, "I wouldn't miss this for nothin'. This here is gonna be a fight that'll be yakked about for a hundred years to come. You can tell your grandkids 'bout this. Providin', that is, you can find a woman to live with your ugly face."

"Thank you. But you ain't no rose. Come on."

How the tall young man had managed to Injun up on him, the miner didn't know. He was woods-wise and yet he hadn't heard a twig snap or a leaf rustle. Just that sudden cold sensation of a rifle muzzle pressing against his neck.

"My name is Smoke."

The miner almost ruined a perfectly good pair of long johns.

"If you got friends in that camp," Smoke told him, "you go down and very quietly tell them to ease out. 'Cause in one hour, I'm opening this dance."

"My name is Big Jake Johnson, Mr. Smoke—and I'm on your side."

Smoke removed the muzzle from the man's neck.

"Thank you," the miner said.

"Do it without alarming Felter and his crew."

"Consider it done. But Smoke, they's fourteen hard-cases in that camp. And they're waitin' for you."

"They won't have long to wait."

The mining camp, one long street, with tents and rough shacks on both sides of the dusty street, looked deserted as Smoke gazed down from his position on the side of a sloping canyon wall.

The miners had left the camp, retreating to a spot on the northwest side of the canyon. They would have a grandstand view of the fight.

Felter knew what was happening seconds after the miners began leaving, and began positioning his men around the shacky camp.

The owners of the two saloons had wrestled kegs of beer and bottles of whiskey up the side of the hill, and were now doing a thriving business. A party atmosphere prevailed. This was better than a hanging—lasted longer, and would have a lot more action. But when the first shot was fired, the miners and the barkeeps would head for pre-picked out boulders and trees. Watching a good gunfight was one thing; getting shot was quite another.

"Felter!" Smoke called, his voice rolling down the hillside. "You and Canning want to settle this between us? I'll meet you both—stand-up, two to one. How about it?"

In a shack, an outlaw known only as Lefty looked at Felter. "You ain't never gonna take this one alive, Felter. No way."

Felter nodded. "I know it." He was crouched behind a huge packing crate. No one in his right mind would trust the thin walls to protect him. A Henry .44 could punch through four inches of pine.

"Give us the gold your Daddy stole!" Felter yelled. "Then you just ride on out of here."

"My Pa didn't steal any gold. He just took what your bosses stole from the South—after they murdered my brother. And I don't have it," Smoke said truthfully.

Smoke shifted positions, slipping about twenty-five yards to his right. He had seen a man dart from the camp, working his way up the side of the hill.

Smoke watched the man pause and get set for a shot. He raised the Henry and put a slug in the man's belly, slamming him backward. The man screamed, dropped his rifle, and tumbled down the embankment, rolling and clawing on his way down. He landed in a sprawl in the street, struggling to get to his feet. Smoke shot him in the chest and he fell forward. He did not move.

The miners across the way cheered and hollered.

"Thirteen to go," Smoke muttered. He again shifted positions, grabbing up the dead man's Henry, shucking the cartridges from it, putting them in his pocket.

Smoke watched as men fanned out in the town, moving too quickly for him to get a shot. Just to keep them jumpy, Smoke put a round in back of one man's boots. The man yelped and dived for the protection of a shack.

"You boys ridin' with Felter!" Smoke yelled. "You sure you want to stay with this dance? The music's gonna get mighty fierce in a minute."

"You go to hell!" the voice came from a shack. A dozen other voices shouted curses at Smoke.

Two men sprang from behind a building, rifles in their hands. They raced into a shack. Smoke put ten .44 rounds into the shack, working his Henry from left to right, waist high.

One man screamed and stumbled out into the street, dropping his rifle. He died in the dirt, boot heels drumming out his death song. The second man staggered out, his chest and belly crimson. He sat down in the street, remained that way for a moment, then toppled over on his face.

Smoke shifted positions once more, reloaded, and called out, "Any more of you boys want to dance to my music?"

Canning looked at Felter, both of them crouched behind the packing crate. "Hell with the gold. I'll settle for the eight thousand. Let's rush him."

Felter was thoughtful for a moment. This whole plan was screwed up; nothing had worked right from the beginning. Smoke was pure devil—right out of hell. The cabin they had searched had been clean, but poor in worldly goods. Smoke didn't have the gold. For all Felter knew, his Pa might have spent it on whiskey and whores.

Felter knew only that he could not fail twice. He could never set foot in the Idaho Territory if he botched this job, and the way it looked, it was going to be another screw-up.

"All right," he said to Canning. "Can you ride?"

"I'll do anything just so's I can take him alive; so's I can use my knife on him. Listen to him scream."

Felter doubted Smoke would give any man the pleasure of screaming. But he kept that thought to himself. He also kept other thoughts to himself. He was sorry he ever got mixed up in this, and for the first time he could recall, he knew fear. For the first time in his evil life, Felter was really afraid of another man.

"All right," Felter said. "This time, by God, let's take him."

He passed his orders down the street, from shack to shack. Three men to the right, three men to the left, three to stay in town, and two to circle around Smoke, coming in from the rear.

But Smoke had other ideas, and he was putting them into play. His guns roared, a man screamed.

"Damnit, Felter!" Lefty yelled, running across the dusty street. "The hombre's in *town!*"

Smoke's .44s thundered. Lefty spun in the street, a cry pushing out of his throat as twin spots of red appeared on his shirt front. He stumbled to the dirt.

"I'll kill him!" a short hairy man snarled, running down the side of the street, darting in and out of doorways. He was shooting at everything he thought he saw.

"Over here," Smoke called.

The outlaw spun and Smoke pulled both triggers of a shotgun he removed from under the counter of a tent saloon. The blast lifted the man off his feet, almost cutting him in half.

Smoke reloaded the sawed-off as he ducked down an alley, behind a shack, and up that alley. He came face to face with an ugly bounty hunter. The bounty hunter fired, the lead creasing Smoke's left arm, drawing blood. Smoke pulled the triggers of the sawed-off and blew the man's head from his shoulders.

He stepped into an open door just as a man ran toward him, his fists full of .45s. Splinters from the door frame jabbed painfully into Smoke's cheek as he dropped the shotgun and grabbed his .44s. He shot the man in the chest and belly, the bounty hunter falling into a water trough. He tried to lift a .45 and Smoke shot him between the eyes at a distance no more than five feet. The trough became colored with red and gray.

The street erupted in black powder, whining lead, and wild cursing. Horses broke from their hitch-rails and charged wild-eyed up and down the street, clouding the air with dust, rearing and screaming in fear.

Smoke felt a hot sear of pain in his right leg. The leg buckled. He flung himself out of the doorway and to the protection of the trough as Canning hobbled painfully into the street, his hands full of guns belching smoke and flame, his eyes wild with hate.

One of Canning's slugs hit Smoke in the left side, passing through the fleshy part and exiting out the back as he knelt on his knees, firing. The shock spun him around and knocked him down. Smoke raised up on one elbow and leveled a .44, taking careful aim. He shot Canning in the right eye, taking off part of his face. Canning's legs jerked out from under him and he fell on his back, his left eye open and staring in disbelief.

Smoke jerked pistols from the headless outlaw's belt

and hand just as Sam and another man ran into the smoky, dusty street, trying to find a target through the din and the haze. Smoke fired at them just as they found him and began shooting. A slug ricocheted off a rock in the street, part of the lead hitting Smoke in the chest, bringing blood and a grunt of pain.

Smoke dragged himself into an alleyway and quickly reloaded all four .44s. He was bleeding from wounds in his side, his leg, his face, and his chest, but he was also mad as hell. He looked around for a target, shoving the fully loaded spare .44s behind his belt.

Sam was on his knees in the middle of the street, one arm broken by a .44 slug. The outlaw screamed curses at Smoke and lifted a pistol, the hammer back. Smoke shot him in the chest. Sam jerked but refused to die. He pulled the trigger of his pistol, the lead plowing up the street and enveloping the man in dust. Smoke shot him again, in the belly. Sam doubled over, dropping his pistol. He died in the center of the street, in a bowing position, his head resting on the dirt, his hat blowing away as a gust of wind whipped between the tents and shacks.

Lead began whining down the alley, and Smoke limped and ran behind a building, pausing to reload and to catch his breath. It has been said that it's hard to stop a man who knows he's in the right and just keeps on coming. Smoke knew he was right—and he kept on coming.

Another of Felter's men ran across the street and down the dirt walkway and into the open alleyway just as Smoke stepped away from the building.

Smoke shot him twice in the belly and kept on coming.

The miners were shouting and cheering and betting on who would be the last man on his feet when the fight was over. Bets against Smoke were getting hard to place.

Sam's partner stepped out and called to Smoke, firing as he yelled. One slug spun Smoke around as it struck the handle of a .44 stuck behind his belt. Pain doubled him over for a second. He lifted his Remingtons and dropped the man to the dirt.

The sounds of a horse galloping hard away came to Smoke as Felter's last man still on his feet ran out of a shack behind Smoke. Smoke coolly lifted a .44 and shot him six times, duckwalking the man across the street, the slugs sending dust popping from the man's shirtfront with each impact.

It was almost over.

Smoke reloaded his Remingtons, dropped the spare .44s to the dirt, and took a deep breath, feeling a twinge of pain from at least one broken rib, maybe two.

Felter had sat behind kegs of beer in the tent saloon and watched it all. He had had a dozen or more opportunities to shoot Smoke from ambush—but he could not bring himself to do it. Jensen was just too much of a man for that. He poured himself a glass of whiskey and shook his head.

What he had seen was the stuff legends are made of; it was rare—but it was not unknown to the West for one man to take on impossible odds and win.

He stood up. "I believe I can take you now, Smoke," he muttered. "You got to be runnin' out of steam."

"Felter!" Smoke called. "Step out here and face me." Blood dripped from his wounds to plop in the dust. His face was bloody and blood and sweat stained his clothing.

Smoke carefully wiped his hands free of sweat just as Felter stepped out of the tent saloon. Both men's guns were in leather. Felter held a shot glass full of whiskey in his left hand. Smoke's right thumb was hooked behind his gunbelt, just over the buckle. Twenty-five feet separated them when Felter stopped. The miners were silent, almost breathless on the hillside, watching this last showdown—for one of the men.

"I seen it, but it's tough for me to believe. You played hell with my men."

Smoke said nothing.

"You and me, now, huh, kid?"

"That's it, and then I take out your bosses."

Felter laughed at him and sipped his whiskey. "I just don't think you can beat me, kid."

"One way to find out."

"I think you're scared, Smoke."

"I'm not afraid of you or of any other man on the face of this earth."

His words chilled the outlaw. He mentally shook away that damnable edge of fear that touched him.

Felter drained the shot glass. Whiskey and blood would be the last thing he would taste on this earth. "Your wife sure looked pretty nekked."

Smoke's grin was ugly. "I'm glad you think so, Felter—'cause you'll never see another woman."

Felter flushed. Damn the man's eyes! he thought. I can't make him mad. "You ready, Smoke?"

"Anytime."

Felter braced himself. "Now!"

The air blurred in front of Felter, then filled with the thunderous roar of gunfire and black smoke. The bounty hunter was on his feet, but something was very wrong. There was something pressing against his back. He felt with his hands. A hitch-rail.

Empty hands! Empty?

My hands can't be empty, he thought. "What . . . ?" he managed to say. Then the shock of his wounds hit him hard.

Why . . . I didn't even clear leather, he thought. The damn kid pulled a cross-draw and beat me! Me!

Felter steadied his eyes to see if he could be wrong. Smoke's left hand holster was empty. He watched the kid shove the .44 back into leather.

"No way!" Felter said. He reached for his Colt and lifted it. His movements seemed so slow. He jacked back the hammer and something blurred in front of him.

Then the sound reached his ears and the fury of the slug

in his stomach brought a scream from his lips. Felter again lifted his Colt and a booming blow struck him on the breastbone, somersaulting him over the hitch-rail, to land on his backside under the striped pole of a tent barber shop.

But Felter was a tough, barrel-chested man, and would not die easily. Unable to rise, he struggled to pull his left hand Colt. He managed to get the pistol up, hammer back, and pointed. Then Smoke's .44 roared one more time, the slug hitting Felter in the jaw, taking off most of the outlaw's face. The slug whined off bone and hit the striped barber pole, spinning it.

The street was quiet. The battle was over.

The barber pole squeaked and turned, then was silent.

Smoke sank to his knees in the dirt.

"You hard hit, son," a miner told him. Unnecessary information, for Smoke knew he was hurt. "You can't just ride out bleedin' like that."

Smoke swung into the saddle, gathering the reins in his left hand, the pack horse rope in his right. "I'll be all right."

He had cleaned his wounds in town; now he wanted the high country, where he would make poultices of herbs and wild flowers, as Preacher had taught him.

The mountain man's words returned to him. "Nature's way is the best, son. You let old Mother Nature take care of you. They's a whole medicine chest right out there in that field. All a man's gotta do is learn 'em."

"When you boys plant them," Smoke told the crowd, "put on their headboards that Smoke Jensen was right and they were wrong."

He rode off to the west.

"Boys," a miner said. "We just seen us a livin' legend. You remember his name, 'cause we all gonna be hearin' a lot more about that young feller."

EPILOGUE

For a month Smoke tended to his wounds and rested at his camp on the banks of the San Miguel, on the west side of the Uncompahgre Forest. He rested and treated his wounds with poultices.

He ate well of venison, fished in the river, and made stews of wild potatoes and onions and rabbit and squirrel. He slept twelve to fifteen hours a day, feeling his strength slowly returning to him. And he dreamed his dreams of Nicole, her soft arms soothing him, melting away the hurt and fever, calming his sleep, loving him back to health.

At the beginning of the fifth week, he knew he was ready to ride, ready to move, and he carefully checked his guns, cleaning them, rubbing oil into the pockets of his holsters, until the deadly .44s fitted in and out smoothly.

Then he packed his gear and rode out.

In the southwestern corner of Wyoming, a wanted poster tacked to a tree brought him up short.

WANTED
DEAD OR ALIVE
THE OUTLAW AND MURDERER
SMOKE JENSEN
10,000.00 REWARD
Contact the Sheriff at Bury, Idaho Territory

Smoke removed the wanted flyer and carefully folded it, tucking it in his pocket. He looked up to watch an eagle soar high above him, gliding majestically north-westward.

"Take a message with you, eagle," Smoke said. "Tell Potter and Richards and Stratton and all their gun-hands I'm coming to kill them. For my Pa, for Preacher, for my son, and for making me an outlaw. And they'll die just as hard as Nicole did. You tell them, eagle. I'm coming after them."

The eagle dipped its wings and flew on.

RETURN OF THE
MOUNTAIN MAN

To my friend who answers my endless questions
concerning weapons of the old west:
Hollis Erwin.

Back of the bar, in a solo game, sat Dangerous Dan McGrew, And watching his luck was light-o'-love, the lady that's known as Lou.

—Robert W. Service

1

The man called Smoke looked at the new wanted poster
tacked to a tree. This one had his likeness on it. He smiled
as he looked at the shoulder-length hair and the clean-
shaven face on the poster. The artist had done a dandy job.

But it in no way resembled the man who now called
himself Buck West.

Kirby Jensen had been sixteen years old when the old
mountain man called Preacher hung the nickname
Smoke on him. Preacher had predicted that Smoke
would turn out to be a very famous man. And he had. As
one of the most feared gunfighters in all the west.

It was not a reputation Smoke had wanted or sought.

Smoke now wore his hair short-cropped. A neat, well-
trimmed beard covered his face. He no longer wore one
pistol in cross-draw fashion, butt-forward. He now wore his
twin .44s butt back and the holsters tied down low. He was
just as fast as before. And that was akin to lightning.

He had turned his Appaloosa, Seven, loose in a valley
several hundred miles to the east. A valley so lovely it was
nearly impossible to describe.

Nicole would have loved it.

Seven had gone dancing and prancing off, once more
running wild and free.

Nicole.

He shook his head and pushed the face of his dead wife from his mind. He turned his unreadable, cold, emotionless brown eyes to the west. The midnight-black stallion he now rode stood steady under his weight. The man now called Buck stood six feet, two inches, barefooted. He weighed one eighty: all hard-packed muscle and bone. His waist was lean and his short hair ash-blond.

The stallion shook his head. Buck patted him on the neck. The stallion quieted immediately. The animal's eyes were a curious yellow/green, a vicious combination that vaguely resembled a wolf's eyes. The stallion had killed its previous owner when the man had tried to beat him with a board. Smoke had bought the horse from the man's widow, gentled him, and learned to respect the animal's feelings and moods.

The stallion's name was Drifter.

Smoke had carefully hidden his buckskins, caching them with his saddle and other meager possessions in the valley where the Appaloosa, Seven, now grazed and ran free with his brood of mares.

Smoke had very carefully pushed all thoughts of the past behind him. He had spent months mentally conditioning himself not to think of himself as the gunfighter Smoke. His name was now Buck. Last names were not terribly important in the newly opened western frontier, and it had been with a smile that Buck chose West as his last name.

Buck West. Smoke was gone—for a time.

Buck laughed. But it was more a dark bark, totally void of humor.

Drifter swung his head around, looking at the man through cold killer eyes. Buck's packhorses continued to graze.

High above, an eagle soared, pushing and gliding toward the west. Buck could have sworn that it was the same eagle he had seen months back, after the terrible shoot-out at the silver camp not far from the Uncompahgre. At least fourteen men had died under his guns that smoky, bloody day. And he had taken more than his share of lead, as well. It had taken him months to fully recover.

Many months back, in the southwestern corner of Wyoming, he had seen the first wanted poster.

WANTED
DEAD OR ALIVE
THE OUTLAW AND MURDERER
SMOKE JENSEN
10,000.00 REWARD
CONTACT THE SHERIFF
AT BURY, IDAHO TERRITORY

He had removed the wanted poster and tucked it in his shirt pocket. He knew he would see many, many more of the dodgers as he made his way west. He had looked up to watch an eagle soar high above him, gliding majestically northwestward.

He had said, with the big skies and grandeur of the open country as witnesses, "Take a message with you, eagle. Tell Potter and Richards and Stratton and all their gunhands that I'm coming to kill them. For my Pa, for Preacher, for my son, and for making me an outlaw. And they'll die just as hard as Nicole did. You tell them, eagle. Tell them I'm coming after them."

The eagle had circled, dipped its wings, and flown on.

Buck shook away the memories, clearing his head of things dead and buried and gone. He let the smoldering coals of revenge burn on, deep within his soul. He would fan the coals into white-hot flames when branding time arrived. And he would do the branding—with hot lead.

The man who had earned the reputation as one of the most feared gunfighters in the newly opened west spoke gently to Drifter and the big cat-footed stallion moved out through the timber.

Buck was just west of the Rockies, skirting south of the Gros Ventre Range. He would—unless he hit some sort of snag—make Moose Flat in two days. Once at the Flat, he would camp for a few days and rest Drifter. Then he would ride for Bury, Idaho Territory.

Bury was a good name, Buck thought. For that is exactly what I intend to do to Stratton and Richards and Potter: bury them!

It was cool during the day and flat-out cold at night; early spring when Buck crossed the still ill-defined line into Idaho Territory. He had seen several bands of Indians, but they had left him alone. He knew they'd seen him, for this was their country, and they knew it as intimately as the roots of a tree knows the earth that nurtures it. But Indians, as Preacher had once put it, were notional critters.

Buck moved out, slowly. He would take his time, get accustomed to the country, and eyeball everything in sight. For if he made it out of Bury alive, he was going to need more than one back door and one hell of a good hiding place.

Buck wore gray pin-striped trousers tucked into soft calfskin boots. Black shirt. His hat was black, low-crowned, and wide-brimmed. His leather vest was black. His belt was silver-studded with a heavy buckle. A jacket and slicker were tied behind the saddle, over the saddle-bags. A Henry repeating rifle rested in a boot, butt forward instead of the usual fashion of the butt facing back. He did not ride in the usual slump-shouldered manner of the old mountain men, but instead sat his saddle ramrod straight, cavalry fashion. Because of this, many who saw the handsome, cold-eyed young man believed him to be ex-cavalry. He let them think it, knowing that helped to further disguise his past.

He carried a two-shot derringer in his left boot, in his right boot a long-bladed, double-edged dagger—that knife in addition to the Bowie he wore on his gunbelt, behind his left-hand gun.

Buck was an expert with all the weapons he carried. The legend growing around the man stated there was no faster gunhand in all the west. He was faster than the Texas gun Hardin; even more steel-nerved than Wild bill; meaner than Curly Bill; when he was in the right, crueler than any Apache; as relentless in a hunt as any man who ever lived.

The old mountain man, Preacher, who helped raise him from a lad, had taught him fistfighting and boxing and Indian wrestling. But even more importantly, Preacher had taught him how to win, teaching him that it don't make a good gawddamn how you win—just win.

The old mountain man had said, and the boy had remembered, "Long as you right, Smoke, it don't make no difference how you win. Just be sure you in the right."

And Lord God, how fast the young man was with those deadly .44s.

Buck gave Drifter his head, letting the horse pick his own way at his own pace, staying close to the timber, away from open places, always edging slightly south and west. He wanted to enter the mostly uncharted center of the Territory from the south. Just north of the Craters of the Moon, Buck would turn Drifter's nose north until he hit the Big Lost River. He would follow that through some of the most beautiful and wild country in the Territory. He would then track the Big Lost for a time, then head more north than west until reaching the new town of Challis. There, he would resupply and head north, following the Salmon River for about thirty-five miles. Bury was located about midway between the Salmon and the town of Tendoy.

But if Buck had his way, the town of Bury would soon cease to exist.

It would be several more years before the toll road would be started between Challis, reaching to Bonanza, with a spur to Salmon. Only then would the big-scale silver mining at Bay Horse get underway.

But that was future. This was now. And Buck was not heading for Bury to pan for gold, search for silver, or start a ranch. And he really didn't care all that much if he died doing what he'd set out to do—just so long as he got it done. The men now living and prospering in and around Bury had directly killed his brother. They had ordered out the men who had killed his father; raped, tortured and murdered Buck's wife, Nicole; killed his baby son; and killed his best friend and mentor, the old mountain man, Preacher.

And then they had done their cruel best to kill the man who now called himself Buck West.

Stratton, Potter, and Richards had thrown their best gunhands at the young man. He had killed them all.

Thus far, Stratton, Potter, and Richards had failed to stop Buck.

Buck had no intention of failing.

2

Buck was being followed. He had yet to catch a glimpse of his pursuers, but he knew someone was tracking him; knew it by that itchy feeling between his shoulder blades. Twice in as many days he had stopped and spent several hours checking his backtrail. But to no avail. Whoever or whatever it was coming along behind him was laying way back, several miles at least. And they were very good at tracking. They would have to be, for Buck not to have spotted them, and Preacher had taught the young man well.

Puzzled, Buck rode on, pushing himself and his horses, skirting the fast growing towns in the eastern part of the state, staying to the north of them. Because of the man, or men, tracking him, Buck changed his plans and direction. He rode seemingly aimlessly, first heading straight north, then cutting south into the Bridger Wilderness. He crossed into Idaho Territory and made camp on the north end of Grays Lake. He was running very low on supplies, but living off the land was second nature to Buck, and doing without was merely a part of staying alive in a yet wild and untamed land.

The person or persons following him stayed back, seemingly content to have the young man in sight, electing not to make an appearance—yet.

Midafternoon of his second day at Grays Lake, Buck watched Drifter's ears prick up, the eyes growing cautious as the stallion lifted his head.

Buck knew company was coming.

A voice helloed the camp.

"If you're friendly, come on in," Buck called. "If you want trouble, I'll give you all you can handle."

Buck knew the grizzled old man slowly riding toward his small fire, but could not immediately put a name to him. The man—anywhere between sixty-five and a hundred and five—dismounted and helped himself to coffee and pan bread and venison. He ate slowly, his eyes appraising Buck without expression. Finally, he belched politely and wiped his hands on greasy buckskins. He poured another cup of coffee and settled back on the ground.

"Don't talk none yet," the old man said. "Jist listen. You be the pup Preacher taken under his wing some years back. Knowed it was you. Ante's been upped some on your head, boy. Nearabouts thirty thousand dollars on you, now. You must have a hundred men after you. Hard men, boy. Most of 'em. You good, boy, but you ain't that good. Sooner 'er later, you'll slip up, git tared, have to rest, then they'll git you." He paused to gnaw on another piece of pan bread.

"The point of all this is . . . ?" Buck said.

"Tole you to hush up and listen. Jawin' makes me hungry. 'Mong other things. Makes my mouth hurt too. You got anything to ease the pain?"

"Pint in that pack right over there." Buck jerked his head.

The old mountain man took two huge swallows of the rye, coughed, and returned to the fire. "Gawddamn farmers and such run us old boys toward the west. Trappin's fair, but they ain't no market to speak of. Ten of us got us a camp just south of Castle Peak, in the Sawtooth. Gittin' plumb borin'. We figured on headin' north in about a week." He lifted his old eyes. "Up toward Bury. We gonna take our time. Ain't no point in gettin' in no lather." He got to his feet and walked toward his horses. "Might see you up there, boy. Thanks for the grub."

"What are you called?" Buck asked.

"Tenneysee," the old man said without looking back. He mounted up and slowly rode back in the direction he'd come.

"You're not any better lookin' than the last time I saw you!" Buck called to the old man's back, grinning as he spoke.

"Ain't supposed to be," Tenneysee called. "Now git et and git gone. You got trouble on your backtrail."

"Yeah, I know!" Buck shouted.

"Worser'n Preacher!" Tenneysee called. "Cain't tell neither of you nuttin'!"

Then he was gone into the timber.

Fifteen minutes later, Buck had saddled Drifter, cinched down the packs on his pack animal, and was gone, riding northwest.

He wondered how many men were trailing him. And how good they were.

He figured he would soon find out.

Staying below the crest of a hill, Buck ground-reined Drifter and scanned his backtrail. It was then he caught the first glimpse of those following him. Four riders, riding easy and seemingly confident. He removed a brass spyglass from his saddlebags and pulled it fully extended, sighting the riders in. He did not recognize any of them, but could see they were all heavily armed. Hardcases, every one of them.

Buck looked back over his shoulder, toward the west. He smiled at the sight. Blackfeet. And the way they were traveling, the gunhands and the warlike Blackfeet would soon come face to face.

The Blackfeet had not always hated the white man. Long before the Lewis and Clark expedition, the Blackfeet had been in contact with the French-Canadian trappers of the Hudson's Bay Company. For the most part, they had gotten along. But in 1806, when the Lewis and Clark expedition split up, Clark turning southward to explore the Yellowstone River, Lewis taking the Blackfoot Branch as the best route to the Missouri, Lewis had encountered a band of Blackfeet. No one knows who started the fight, or why, and the journals of Lewis don't say, but the battle had a long-lasting effect. Since the Blackfeet were the most powerful and warlike tribe in the Northwest, their hatred following the battle closed both rivers to American travel.

Buck was puzzled why so many Blackfeet were in this part of the Territory, somewhat off their beaten path. He concluded, after looking them over through his spyglass, that they were a war party, and had been quite successful, judging from the scalps on their rifles and coup sticks and wound into their horses' manes.

Buck smiled as the Blackfeet spotted the white men first. Within seconds, the Blackfeet had vanished, the war party splitting up, lying in silent wait to spring the deadly ambush.

Buck didn't wait around for the fun. He quickly mounted up and took off in the other direction. Blackfeet had a reputation for being downright testy at times.

And from the north, a pair of old eyes watched as Buck rode out. The eyes followed the young man until he was out of sight.

Buck heard the shots from the short battle as he continued to put more distance between himself and the Blackfeet. The old man waited almost an hour before leaving his hiding place. Leading a pack animal, he slowly rode after Buck. He was in no hurry, for he knew where Buck was going and what he was going to do. He just wanted to be there to help the young man out.

1874 in most of Idaho Territory was no place for the faint-hearted, the lazy, the coward, or the shirker. 1874

Idaho Territory was pure frontier, as wild and woolly as the individual wanted to make it. It would be three more long, bloody, and heartbreaking years for the Nez Percé Indians before Chief Joseph would lead his demoralized tribe on the thirteen-hundred mile retreat to Canada. There, the chief would utter, "I am tired; my heart is sick and sad. From where the sun now stands I will fight no more forever."

But in 1874, the Indians were still fighting all over Idaho Territory, including the Bannocks and Shoshones. It was a time for wary watchfulness.

It had been fourteen years since an expedition led by Captain Elias D. Pierce of California had discovered gold on Orofino Creek, a tributary of the Clearwater River. It wasn't much gold, but it was gold. Thousands had heard the cry and the tug of easy riches, and thousands had come. They had poured into the state, expecting to find nuggets lying everywhere. Many had never been heard from again. As Buck rode through the southern part of the state, heading for the black and barren lava fields called the Craters of the Moon, even here he was able to see the mute heartbreak of the gold-seekers: the mining equipment lying abandoned and rusting, the dredges in dry creek beds. Now, in early summer, a time when the creeks and rivers were starting to recede, Buck spotted along the banks a miner's boot, a pan. He wondered what stories they could tell.

He rode on, always checking his backtrail. He had a vague uneasy feeling that he was still being followed. But he could never spot his follower. And that was cause for alarm, for Buck, even though still a young man, was an expert in surviving in the wilderness.

He skirted south of the still-unnamed village of Idaho Falls, a place one man claimed "openly wore the worst side out."

Buck rode slowly but steadily, coming up on the south side of the Big Lost, north of the Craters of the Moon.

He stopped at a trading post at what would someday become a resort town called Arco. Inside the dark, dirty place, filled with skins and the smell of rotgut whiskey, Buck bought bacon and beans and coffee from a scar-faced clerk. The clerk smelled as bad as his store.

Buck's eyes flicked over several wanted posters tacked to the wall. There he was.

"Last one of them I seen had ten thousand dollars reward on it," he said, to no one in particular. He noticed several men at a corner table ceased their card playing.

"Ante's been upped," the clerk/bartender said with a grunt.

"Man could do a lot with thirty thousand dollars," Buck said. He walked to the bar and ordered whiskey. He didn't really care for the stuff but he wanted information, and bartenders seldom talked to a non-drinking loafer. "The good stuff," he told the bartender. The man replaced one bottle and reached under the counter for another bottle.

He grinned, exposing blackened stubs of teeth. "This one ain't got no snake heads in it."

Buck lifted the glass. Smelled like bear piss. Keeping his expression noncommittal, he sipped the whiskey. Tasted even worse.

"Have any trouble coming from the east?" the bartender asked.

"How'd you know I come from the east?"

"That's the way you rode in."

"Seen some Blackfeet two-three days ago. But they didn't see me. I didn't hang around long."

"Smart."

"You see four men, riding together?" the voice came from behind Buck, from the card table.

"Yeah. And so did the Blackfeet."

"Crap! You reckon the Injuns got 'em?"

"I reckon so. I didn't hang around to see."

"You mean you jist rode off without lendin' a hand?"

"One more wouldn't have made any difference," Buck said quietly, knowing what was coming.

"Then I reckon that makes you a coward, don't it?" the cardplayer said, standing up.

Buck slowly placed the shot glass of bear piss back on the rough bar. He eyeballed the man. Two guns worn low and tied down. The leather hammer thongs off. "Either that or careful."

"You know what I think, Slick? I think it makes you yellow."

"Well, I'll tell you what I think," Buck said. "I think you don't know your bunghole from your mouth."

The man flushed in the dim light of the trading post. His dirty hands hovered over his guns. "I think I'll jist kill you for that."

"Bet or fold," Buck said.

The man's hands dipped down. Buck's right-hand .44 roared. The gunhand was dead before he hit the floor, the slug taking him in the center of the chest, exploding his heart.

"I never even seen the draw," the bartender said, his voice hushed and awe-filled.

"Any of you other boys want to ante up in this game?" Buck asked.

None did.

The dead man broke wind as escaping gas left his cooling body.

"He were my partner," a man still seated at the table said. "But he were in the wrong this time. I lay claim to his pockets."

"Suits me," Buck said. No one had even seen him holster his .44. "He have a name?"

"Big Jack. From up Montana way. Never spoke no last name. Who you be?"

"Buck West. I been trackin' that damned Smoke Jensen for the better part of six months."

Big Jack's partner visibly relaxed. "Us, too. I would

ask if you wanted some company, but you look like you ride alone."

"That's right."

"Name's Jerry. This here's Carl and Paul. Don't reckon you'd give us a hand diggin' the hole for Jack?"

"I don't reckon so."

"Cain't much blame you."

"Bury him out back," the bartender said. "Deep. If he smells any worser dead than alive I'll have to move my place of business."

3

The men watched as Buck rode away, ramrod straight in the saddle. Jerry said, "That young feller is faster than greased lightning."

"Faster than Jesse, I betcha!"

"Ain't no faster than Wild Bill, though," Paul said.

Jerry spat on the ground. "Wild Bill ain't crap!"

"You don't say!" Carl turned on his friend. "I suppose you gonna tell us Wild Bill didn't clean up Abilene?"

"He sure as hell didn't. I know. I were there. Me and Phil Coe. I seen Wild Bill shoot him with a pair of derringers after Phil done put his gun away. Then he turned around and shot the marshal, Mike Williams. Wild Bill better not ever try to brace that there Buck West. Buck's a bad one, boys. Cold-eyed as a snake."

It would be almost exactly two and one half years later, on the afternoon of August 2, 1876, in Deadwood, South Dakota, when a cross-eyed, busted-nose wino named Jack McCall would blow out Hickok's brains as he studied his poker hand of Aces and Eights. Wild Bill would be thirty-nine years old.

"I think Potter ought to know about this here Buck West," Jerry said. "Think I'll take me a ride later on. Let Buck get good and gone."

"We'll tag along."

Late that afternoon a stranger rode up to the trading post and walked inside. He cradled a Henry repeating rifle in the crook of his left arm. "I seen the fresh grave out back," he said to the barkeep. "Friend of yourn?"

"Hell, no! Don't git me to lyin'."

"Man ought to have a marker on his grave, don't you think?"

"I'll git around to it one of these days. Maybe. Big Jack was all they called him."

"Better than nothin'. I don't reckon he died of natural causes?"

"Not likely. You gonna talk all day or buy a drink of whiskey?"

The buckskin-dressed old man tossed some change on the wide rough board that passed for a counter. "That buy a jug?"

"And then some. No, sir. That Big Jack fancied hisself a gunhand, I guess." He placed a dirty cup and a clay jug of rotgut on the counter. "But he done run up on a ringtailed-tooter this day. Feller by the name of Buck West. You heard of him?"

"Seems I have, somewheres. Bounty hunter, I think. But he's a bad man to mess with."

"Tell me! Why, he drew so fast a feller couldn't even see the blur! Big Jack's hand could just touch the butt of his .36 when the lead hit him in the center of the chest. Dead 'fore he hit the ground."

The old man smiled. "That fast, hey?"

"Lord have mercy, yes!" He eyeballed the old man. "Ain't I seen you afore? You a mountain man, ain't you? Ain't so many of you old boys left."

"Not me, podner. I'm retared from the east. Come out here to pass my golden years amid the peace and tranquility of the High Lonesome."

The bartender, no spring chicken himself, narrowed his eyes and said, "And you jist as full of shit now as you was forty year ago, you old goat!"

The old man laughed. "Wal, you jist keep that information inside that head of yourn and off your tongue. You do that and I won't tell nobody I know where Rowdy Jake Kelly was retared to. You still got money on your head, Rowdy."

"Man, I heard you got kilt! Shot all to hell and gone over to Needle Mountains."

"Part of it's true. I got all dressed up in my finest buckskins, rode an old nag up into the hills, and laid me down to die. Lordy, but I was hurtin' some. Longer I laid there the madder I got. I finally got up, said to hell with this, and rode off. Found me one of my Injun kids—or grandkids, I ain't real sure which—and she took care of me. You keep hush about this, now, you hear?"

"I never saw you afore this day," Rowdy Jake Kelly said.

The old man nodded, picked up his jug of whiskey, and rode off.

Buck had left the trading post and followed the Big Lost River north. He pushed his horses, rested them, then pushed them hard again, putting as many miles as possible between himself and the trading post. He had a hunch the men back at the trading post would be hell-bent for Bury. They were bounty hunters; he knew from the look. He smiled grimly at what they might think if they knew they had been within touching distance of the man called Smoke.

Buck found himself a hidden vantage point where he could watch the trail, and settled in for the evening. He built a hand-sized fire and fixed bacon and beans and coffee. Using tinder-dry wood, the fire was virtually smokeless. He kept his coffee warm over the coals.

Just at dusk, he heard the sounds of riders. Three riders. He watched as they passed his hiding place at a slow canter, heading north, toward the trading post at Mackay. He watched and listened until the sounds of steel-shod hooves faded into the settling dusk. Using his saddle for a pillow, Buck went to sleep.

Just as the first rays of dawn streaked the horizon, Buck was fording the Big Lost, heading for the eastern banks and the Lost River Range. He did not want to travel those flats that stretched for miles before reaching Challis, preferring to remain in the timber.

He wanted to take his time getting to Bury for two reasons: One, he wanted the story of the shoot-out at the trading post to reach the right ears—namely, Potter, Stratton, and Richards. Men like that could always use another gun, and Buck intended to be that other gun. Two, he still had that nagging sensation of being followed. And it annoyed him. He knew, *felt,* someone was back there. He just didn't know who.

The eighty-mile ride from the trading post to Challis passed slowly, and Buck took his time, enjoying the sights of new country. Buck was a man who loved the wilderness, loved its great beauty, loved the feeling of being alone, although he knew perfectly well he certainly was not alone. There were the eagles and hawks who soared and glided above him. The playful camp-robber birds, the squirrels and bears and puma, the breathless beauty of wild flowers in early summer. No, he was not alone in the wilderness. Alone was just a state of mind. Buck had only to look around him for company, compliments of nature.

Sensing more than hearing movement, Buck cut toward the west and into the deep timber of the Lost River Range. He quieted his horses and waited in the timber. Then he spotted them. It was a war party, and a big one. From this distance—he couldn't risk using his spyglass, for it was afternoon and he was facing west, and didn't want to risk sunlight bouncing off the lens—he could only guess the tribe. Nez Percé, Bannock—maybe Sheepeater. Preacher had told him about the little known but highly feared Sheepeaters.

Buck counted the braves. Thirty of them, all painted

up and looking for trouble. He cursed under his breath as they reined up and dismounted, after sending lookouts in all directions.

Were they going to make camp? Buck didn't know. But he knew it was awfully early for that.

To the south, Borah Peak, almost thirteen thousand feet high, loomed up stark in the high lonesome. The highest peak in the state, Borah dominated matters for miles.

Buck sat it out for several hours, watching and waiting out the long minutes. The horses seemed to sense the urgency of the moment and were very quiet. Occasionally, Buck would slip back to them to pat and water them, whispering gently to the animals, keeping them still and calm.

Returning from his last trip to the animals, Buck looked out over the valley he was high above. He grunted, not in surprise, but rather an "I should have known" grunt.

The Indians were gone, having left as swiftly and silently as they had come. Buck lay still for another ten minutes, mulling the situation over in his mind.

The war party had built no fires, either cook or signal. They had met with no other Indians. Why had they stopped? Buck had no idea. But he knew one thing: he damn sure wasn't going to head out after them. Whichever direction the war party had taken, he planned to head in the other direction. And he did. Before two minutes had passed, Buck had tightened cinches and was heading out. He found where the war party had ridden south, so he swung Drifter's head and pointed his nose north, toward the muddy, brawling town of Challis, located just to the northwest of the Salmon River. Buck would hang around Challis for a few days, listening to the miners talk and attempting to get the feel of what the townspeople thought of Bury, some thirty-five miles north and slightly east.

Challis was one short business street, more saloons than anything else, with tents and shacks and a few permanent-looking homes to the north. Most of the shacks appeared to have been tossed in their location by some giant crap-shooter.

Buck stabled his horses—he wasn't worried about anyone stealing Drifter, for the stallion would kill anyone who entered his stall—and taking his Henry repeating rifle, a change of clothing, and his saddlebags, Buck walked toward the town's hotel.

After checking in, Buck went to a barber shop and took a hot bath, a young Chinese man keeping the water hot with additional buckets of water. After Buck had soaped off the weeks of dirt and fleas, he dressed in dark trousers, white shirt, and vest. He left his boots to be shined and settled in the barber chair.

"Short," he told the barber. "And trim my beard."

"Passin' through?" the barber asked.

"Could be. Mostly just drifting."

The barber had noted Buck's tied-down guns. Being an observant man, and one raised on the frontier, he knew a fast gun when he saw one. And this man sitting in his chair was a gunhand, and no tinhorn. The butts of his .44s were worn smooth from handling, with no marks in the wood to signify kills. Only a tinhorn did that, and tinhorns didn't last long in the west.

But there was something else about this young man. Confidence. That was it. And a cold air about him. Not unfriendly, just cold.

"If it's silver you're huntin'"—he knew it wasn't—"big strike north and east of here. Close to the Lemhi River."

"Not for me," Buck told him. "Too much work involved in that."

"Uh-huh. You be handy with them .44s?"

"Some folks say that."

"You head north from here, follow the Salmon until the river cuts through the Lemhi range, then head east. You'll come up on the town of Bury."

"Hell of a name for a town."

"It's right proper, considerin' the size of their boot hill. You'll see."

"Why would I want to go to someplace called Bury?"

"Maybe you don't. Then again, you might find work up there."

"Might do that. How's the law in this town?" Buck set the stage with that question.

"Tough when they have to be. Long as it's a fair fight, they won't bother you."

"I never shot no one in the back," Buck replied, putting it just a bit testily.

"You don't have that look about you, that's for sure." The barber's voice was very bland.

"Where's the best place to eat?"

"Marie's. Just up the street. Beef and beans and apple pie. Good portions, too. Reasonable."

They weren't just good portions; they were huge. The food simple but well-prepared. The apple pie was delicious. Buck pushed the empty plate away and settled back, leaning back in his chair, his back to a wall. He lingered over a third cup of coffee and watched the activity in the street through the window.

He was waiting for the marshal or sheriff to make his appearance. It didn't take long.

The town marshal entered the cafe, a deputy behind him. The deputy held a sawed-off double-barrel twelve-gauge express gun in his hands. And it appeared he had used it before.

The marshal was not a man to back up or mince words. He sat down at Buck's table, facing him, and ordered a cup of coffee. He stared at Buck.

Buck returned the stare.

"Passin' through?" the marshal asked.

"Might stay two or three days. I'm in no big hurry to get anywhere."

"You got a name?"

Buck smiled. "I'm not wanted."

"That don't answer my question."

"Buck West." Buck then placed the man. Dooley. He'd been a lawman over in Colorado for years. A straight, no-nonsense lawman. But a fair one.

Dooley pointed up the street. "Them houses with paint on them beginning at the end of the street is off-boundaries for drifters. Decent folks live there. The dosshouses is on the other end of the street." He pointed. "Thataway." He jerked his thumb. "The road out of town is thataway. Feel free to take it as soon as possible."

"I don't intend to cause you or your men any trouble, Marshal," Buck said softly.

"But you will," the marshal replied just as softly. "You just got that air about you."

"You're a very suspicious man, Marshal."

"Goes with the job, son." The marshal drained his coffee cup, stood up, and started to leave. He looked once more at Buck. "You sure look familiar, mister."

"I just have a friendly face," Buck said solemnly.

"Yeah," the marshal said drily. "I'm sure that's it."

4

As he stood facing the two men in the saloon, it occurred to Buck that perhaps the marshal just might have been right. Buck had entered the saloon, ordered a beer, and had nursed it for about fifteen minutes before the cowboy with a loud and arrogant mouth had begun needling him.

"You gonna drink that beer or stand there and look at it with your face hangin' out?"

Buck ignored him.

"Boy, you better talk to me!" the cowhand said.

"I intend to drink this beer," Buck said, "in my own good time. Not that it's any of your business."

The cowboy took a step backward, a puzzled look on his face. Buck knew the type. He was big and broad and solid with muscle. And he was used to getting his way. He had been a bully all his life. He belittled anything he was too stupid to comprehend—which was nearly everything.

"That's Harry Carson, stranger," the barkeep whispered.

"Is that supposed to mean something to me?" Buck said, not bothering to keep his voice to a whisper.

"And his buddy is Wade Phillips," the barkeep plunged ahead.

"I wonder if either one of them can spell unimpressed," Buck said. He felt the old familiar rage fill him. He had never been able to tolerate bullies; not even as a boy back in Missouri.

The deputy who had been with Marshal Dooley earlier that day leaned against the bar, silently watching the show unfold before him. Carson and Phillips were both loud-mouthed troublemakers. But he felt he had pegged this tall young man right. If he was correct in his assumption, Carson and Phillips would never pick another fight after this night.

The deputy slipped out of the line of possible gunfire and sipped his beer.

"What'd you say, buddy?" Carson stuck his chin out belligerently.

Buck fought back his anger. "Go on, Carson. Back off, drink your drink, and leave me be."

"You got a smart mouth, buddy." Phillips stuck his ugly, broad-nosed and boozy face into it.

Upon entering the place, Buck had slipped the hammer thongs off his .44s. He slowly turned to face the twin loudmouths.

"I'm saying now I'm not looking for trouble. But if I'm pushed into it, so be it."

"Talks fancy, don't he?" Phillips's laugh was ugly. But so was he, so it rounded out.

"Yeah," Carson said. "And got them fancy guns on, too. But I betcha he ain't got the sand in him to duke it out."

Buck's smile was faint. He had pegged the men accurately. Both men probably realized that neither one of them could beat Buck in a gunfight, so they would push him into a fight with fists and boots. And if he didn't fight them at their own game, he would be branded a coward.

The bully's way.

Buck took off his gunbelt and laid it on the bar. Spotting the deputy, he slid the hardware down the bar to him. "Look after those, will you, please?"

"Be glad to, West. Watch 'em. They're both dirty at the game."

Buck drained his beer mug and said, "Not nearly as dirty as I am."

Then Buck smashed the mug into Carson's face. The heavy mug broke the man's nose on impact. Buck then jabbed the jagged broken edges into the man's cheek and lips, sending the bully screaming and bleeding to the sawdust-covered floor.

Buck hit Phillips a combination left and right, glazing the man's eyes with the short, brutal punches. Buck did not like to fight with his bare fists, knowing it was a fool's game. But sometimes that was the only immediate option. Until other objects could be brought into play.

Phillips jumped to his boots, in a crouch. Buck stepped close and brought one knee up, at the same time bringing both hands down. As his hands grabbed the man's neck, his knee came in contact with the man's face. The crunch of breaking bones was loud in the saloon.

The fight was over. Carson lay squalling and bleeding on the floor beside the unconscious Phillips. Buck turned around. Marshal Dooley was standing by his deputy.

"Any law against a fair fight, Marshal?" Buck asked. "It was two against one."

"And they were outnumbered at those odds," Dooley said. "No, West, there is no law against it. Yet," he added. "But someday there will be."

Buck retrieved his guns and buckled them around his waist. "Not as long as there are people so stupid as to place and praise physical brawn over the capacity of reason."

Dooley blinked. "Who are you, West? You're no drifting gunhand. You've got intelligence."

"Anybody who wishes to do so can read, Marshal. And most of us can think and reason. That's who I am. Good night, Marshal."

Buck picked up his hat from the bar and walked out into the night.

"More to him than meets the eyes, Marshal," the deputy observed.

"Yeah," said the marshal. "But it's that unknown about him that I'm afraid of."

Buck spent the next three days loafing and listening around Challis. He read a dozen six-month-old newspapers, bought a well-worn book of verse by Shelley and began reading that. He played a little poker, winning some, losing some, and ending up breaking about even. Twice he saw a couple of the most disreputable-looking men he'd seen in years. He knew they were mountain men, and he knew they were checking on him. The men had to be close to seventy years old, but they still looked like they could wrestle a grizzly bear. And probably win.

Some of the so-called "good people" of the community sniffed disdainfully at the sight of the buckskin-clad old men, snubbing them, having highly uncomplimentary things to say about them. Buck wanted to say, "But these men opened the way west. These men faced the dangers, most of the time alone. And many of their compadres were killed opening the way west. Had it not been for them, you folks would still be waiting to make the trek westward. These men are some of the true heroes of our time; living legends. You should welcome them, praise them, not snub and insult them."

But Buck kept his mouth shut, knowing he would be wasting his words. He recalled the words of that fellow called Thoreau: If a man does not keep pace with his companions, perhaps it is because he hears a different drummer. Let him step to the music which he hears, however measured or far away.

But Buck knew there was more to it than that. And he silently cursed his lack of education, vowing to read and retain more wisdom of words. He had left his books, his precious books, back at the cabin in that lovely lonely meadow, where he had buried his wife and son. Nicole and Arthur. He knew someday he'd return to that valley. If he lived through his mission.

He leaned back in his chair on the boardwalk, his back to a storefront, and pondered away a few moments, wondering why so many people built false and unworthy idols. These old mountain men were, in some cases, like military men. Looked down on and cursed until the need for them arises, then, as that moment passes, they are once more shunted aside. Like those signs Buck had been seeing on sóme stores: No Irish wanted here.

Buck's philosophical meanderings were shoved aside as his eyes found the two men walking slowly down the center of the dirt main street.

Phillips and Carson. Both of them wearing two pistols. Their hands were near the pistols, ready to draw. With a sigh, Buck stood up and looked around him. Then he remembered: Marshal Dooley and his deputy had left that morning to ride out to a ranch; something about rustling.

"Get out in the street, West!" pig-face Phillips yelled.

Buck stepped off the boardwalk, slipping the leather thongs from the hammers of his .44s as he walked.

Front doors and windows facing the street banged shut as the residents headed for cover. Gunfights were nothing new to these people. They just wanted to view it from a safe place.

"It doesn't have to be this way, boys!" Buck called. But he knew it did. With people like Carson and Phillips, winning was the only way. So-called "loss of face" was totally unacceptable. Reasoning was beyond their comprehension.

Something is wrong with this method of settling disputes, Buck thought. And something is very wrong with my own personal vendetta. But the young man, self-educated as far as his education went, knew that, at this point in the advancement of civilization, a dusty street and the smell of gunsmoke was judge and jury.

But he also knew that lawyers weren't the final answer,

either. They mucked matters up too much, twisting and reshaping the truth.

There had to be a better middle ground. But damned if he knew what it was.

"You ready to die, boy?" Carson yelled.

Buck cut his eyes for just an instant. Standing in front of a saloon was one of the men from back at the trading post. What was his name? Jerry. Yeah. Big Jack's buddy. And standing a few yards from him, an old buckskin-dressed mountain man. The mountain man, old and big and still solid, cradled a Henry repeating rifle in the crook of one massive arm.

"We all have to see the elephant sometime," Buck said. He could tell the men facing him were nervous. Since he had whipped them that night, Buck had heard stories about Carson and Phillips. They were thugs and ne-er-do-wells. Shiftless troublemakers. Buck had heard that the pair had used guns before, but were not gunhands, per se. They were back-shooters, cowards. But of course, as Buck knew well, most bullies were cowards.

Buck stood in the center of the street, standing tall and straight, his big hands, rough and work-hardened, close to his guns.

There was fifty feet between the men when Carson and pig-face Phillips stopped. Buck could see the sweat on the men's faces. Buck knew he could not afford to draw first. Even though the men were trash, this was their town; Buck was a stranger. They had to draw first in order for it to be called self-defense. Even if it was two on one.

Buck stood quietly, waiting.

"You had no call to scar us up like you did," Carson yelled. "You don't fight fair."

Buck waited.

Then Buck knew what had been wrong with his philosophical thinking of a few moments ago. These men were mentally ill-equipped to face the day-to-day struggles of living peacefully. But was that Buck's fault? Was he, and others like him, responsible for Carson and Phillips and others like them? What would happen if he presented them with an armload of books, saying to them, "Here, gentlemen, within these pages lie the answers. Here is a thousand years of wisdom. Understand this and you'll learn how to cope; how to live decently . . ." Buck shook those thoughts away.

We are all put here on this earth with the capability to learn to reason. These men, and others like them, don't want to learn. Therefore, it lies on their head, not mine. We come into this world naked and helpless and squalling. Yes. But we are equal to the task of learning.

Buck mentally settled it.

To hell with them!

"Ain't you got no tongue?" Phillips hollered. "Cain't you talk?"

"What do you want me to say?" Buck asked.

"Beg and we'll let you turn tail and run on out of here!" Carson yelled.

"I beg to no man," Buck's words were softly offered.

"Then die!" Phillips screamed. He reached for his gun.

Buck let him clear leather before he drew his right-hand .44. He fired twice, one slug taking Phillips in the belly, the second slug hitting the man in the center of his chest. Phillips fell backward, mortally wounded.

Carson had not drawn. The man's face was chalky white. He watched as Buck holstered his .44. Buck waited patiently.

The street was silent as a hundred pairs of eyes watched in awe and disbelief, the incredible speed of the tall young man an astonishing thing to witness. His hand had been like a blur as he drew, cocked, and fired.

"Back off, Carson," Buck said. "Just turn around and walk away and it's over. How about it?"

A hundred pairs of ears heard him offer the man his life.

A hundred pairs of ears heard Carson refuse the offer.

"Hell with you!" Carson snarled, and went for his gun.

Born with the gift of ambidextrousness, Buck was as fast with his left hand as with his right. In a heartbeat, Carson lay dead on the dusty street. The man's bootheels and spurs beat a death march on the dirt as his spirit joined that of Phillips, winging their way to their just rewards.

Buck reloaded his .44s and holstered them. He walked across the street to his chair and sat down.

People began streaming out of offices and stores and saloons. They gathered around the fallen pair of would-be gunhands. They looked at Buck, sitting calmly on the boardwalk.

"Mind if we get the man to take your picture?" some called.

Buck didn't mind at all. He wanted Stratton and Potter and Richards to hear of this.

The town's only photographer gathered up his bulky equipment and came on a run.

Buck sat calmly, waiting for the marshal.

5

"When you gonna tell the boy you still alive and kickin'?" Beartooth asked the mountain man who had been following Buck.

He was called Beartooth because he didn't have a tooth in his mouth. And hadn't had in forty years. No one knew what his Christian name was, and it wasn't a polite question to ask.

"I might not never," the mountain man said. "He thinks I'm dead. Might be best to keep it thataway. I'm only goin' in if and when he needs help."

"He'll need help," Dupre said. "Plenty guns up at Bury. And they all going to be aimed at your friend."

Dupre had drifted up from New Orleans in the late '20s. His accent was still as thick as sorghum.

"You ain't seen Smoke—'scuse me, *Buck*, git into action," the mountain man said. "He's hell on wheels, boys. Best I ever seen. And I seen 'em all."

"Don't start lyin', Preacher," Greybull said.

Greybull was a mountain of a man. It took a mule to pack him around.

"What do you think about it, Nighthawk?" Preacher asked.

"Ummm," the old Crow grunted.

"Whutever the hell that means," Tenneysee said. "Damned Injun ain't said fifteen words in the fifty year I been knowin' him."

"Ummm," Nighthawk said.

"Might make the lad feel better if'n he knowed you was still breathin'," Pugh said. Pugh was commonly referred to as "Phew!" He hated water. "Then again," Pugh said. "It might make him irritable. He probably said all sorts of kind words 'bout you. An' thinkin' of enough kind words 'bout you to bury you probably took him the better part of a month."

"Phew," Preacher said. "Would you mind changin' positions just a tad. Right there. Don't move. Now the wind is right. Why don't you take a bath? Damn, you'd make a vulture puke."

"Well, if you ask me—" Audie said.

"Nobody did," Beartooth said. "Hell, nobody can *see* you."

Audie was a midget. About three and a half feet tall. And about three and a half feet wide. He was a large amount of trouble in a very compact package.

"As I was saying," Audie said, "before your rudeness took precedent." Audie had taught school in Pennsylvania before the wanderlust hit him and he had struck out for the west, on a Shetland pony. When the Indians had seen him, they'd laughed so hard they forgot to kill him. "I think it best that Preacher keep his anonymity for the period preceding our arrival in Bury. Should Preacher reveal his living, breathing self to the young man, it might prove so traumatic as to be detrimental to Jensen's well-being."

"Ummm," Nighthawk said, nodding his head in agreement.

"Whut the hale's far you shakin' your head about, you dumb Injun?" Greybull said. "You don't know no more whut he said than us'ins do."

"Ummm," Nighthawk said.

"Whatever Audie said, I agree with him," Matt said. Matt was a Negro. Big and mean and one-eyed.

Matt was probably the youngest man present. And he was at least sixty-five. He had lost his eye during a fight with an angry mountain lion. Matt had finally broken the puma's back.

"Good Gawd, Audie!" Deadlead said. "Cain't you talk American? What the hell did you jist say?"

Deadlead had earned his nickname from being a crack shot with a pistol. Like most of the mountain men, no one knew what his Christian name was.

"Ummm," Nighthawk said.

"I say we break camp and meander on up towards Bury," Powder Pete said. "Old as we is, some of us might not make the trip if we wait much longer."

"I opt fer that myself," Tenneysee said. "What do you say, Nighthawk?"

"Ummm."

"I'll not have this town filled up with would-be gun-hands looking to make themselves a reputation," Marshal Dooley said. "Get your truck together and hit the trail, West."

"Friendly place you have here, Marshal," Buck said with a double-edged smile.

"Yes, it is," Dooley said, ignoring the sarcasm in Buck's tone. "Something about you invites trouble, boy." He waved a hand absently. "I know, I know. You didn't start the fight. And I understand from talking with witnesses you even tried—slightly—to back away from it. That's good. But not good enough. Clear out, West."

"In the morning soon enough?"

Dooley wavered. He nodded his head. "Stay out of the saloons tonight and be gone by dawn."

Buck stepped out of the office onto the boardwalk. He didn't object to being asked to leave town. He didn't

blame the law. It was time to be moving on. And there
was no point in delaying his departure until morning.
Buck was getting that closed-in feeling anyway. And so
was Drifter. Last time he'd looked in on the animal,
Drifter had rolled his eyes and tossed his head. And then
proceeded to kick in the back of his stall.

Buck walked to the hotel, gathered up his gear, and
headed for the stable. He had bought his supplies earlier and was ready to go.

"Ready to go, Drifter?" Buck asked the stallion.

Drifter reared up and smashed the front of his stall.

"Guess so," Buck mumbled.

The band of mountain men met Lobo at the base of
Greyrock Mountain, about halfway between the Sawtooth Wilderness area and Challis. Lobo briefed the
men on what he'd seen in town.

It was rumored that Lobo had once lived with wolves.

"Faster than greased lightnin'," Lobo said. "I never
seen nothin' like it afore in my life. An' the lad didn't
even blink an eye doin' it."

"Tole you!" Preacher said to the men, grinning.

"Don't start braggin'," Powder Pete told Preacher. "It's
bad 'nuff jist havin' to look at you." Powder Pete was so
called because of his expertise with explosives.

"Did the law run him out of town?"

"Don't know. Didn't hang around to see. Law might
ask him to leave. But if that there boy gits his back up,
there ain't nobody gonna *run* him nowheres."

"Wal, les' us just sorta amble on toward the northeast,"
Preacher said. "If I know Smoke—and I do, I raised him—
he'll take his time gettin' to Bury. He'll lay back in the
timber for a day 'er so and look the situation over. We'll cross
the Lost River Range, head acrost the flats, and turn north,
make camp in the narrows south of Bury. I know me some
Flatheads live just west of Bitterroot. Once we set up camp,

I'll take me a ride over to the Divide, palaver some with 'em. They'll be our eyes and ears. That sound all right to you boys?"

"Quite inventive," Audie said.

"Ummm," Nighthawk grunted.

Buck crossed the Salmon to the east bank and began following the river north. He stayed on the fringe of the timber that made up the northern edge of the Lemhi Range. He would follow the river for about thirty-five miles before cutting to the east for about ten miles. That should put him on the outskirts of Bury. Once there, he would make camp south of the town and look it over.

The dozen mountain men, with about six hundred years of survival and fighting experience between them, were riding hard just south of Challis. With their rifles held across the saddlehorns, their fringed buckskins and animal-hide caps and brightly colored shirts and jackets and sashes, the last of the mountain men were returning for one more fight. They were riding hard to help—if he needed it—the youngest mountain man. One of their own. A young man who had chosen the lonely call of the wilderness as home. A young man who preferred the high lonesome over the towns and cities. A young man they had taken under their wing and helped to raise, imparting to him the wisdom of the wilderness, hopefully perpetuating a way of life that so-called civilized people now sneered at and rejected. This gathering, this aging motley crew, knew they were the last—the very last—of a select breed of men. After this ride, never again would so many gather. But hopefully, just maybe, their young protege would live on, known for the rest of his life, as the last mountain man.

6

The town of Bury, with a population of about five hundred, sat on a road first roughed out by Mormon settlers in the mid-1850s. Bury had a bank, probably the best school in that part of the country—a large, two-story building—a large mercantile store, a weekly newspaper, several saloons, several cafes, a large hotel, a sheriff, several deputies, a jail, a leather shop, and several other businesses, including a whorehouse located discreetly outside of town. The town also boasted several churches. A handful of ranches lay around the town, and a lot of producing mines as well.

And nearly all of it was owned by three men: Stratton, Potter, and Richards.

Bury also had a volunteer fire department. They were going to need a fire department before Buck was through.

The business district of Bury was three blocks long, on both sides of the wide street. It was down that street that Buck rode at midmorning. He had camped some miles from the town, watching the one road for two days. A stagecoach rolled in every other day. Wagons bringing supplies rolled by. Peddlers and tinkers and snake-oil salesmen rattled past.

Booming little town, Buck thought. For a while longer, that is.

The first thing Buck noticed in his slow ride up the street was the number of gunhands lounging about on the boardwalk, and not just in front of the saloons. A couple always seemed to be in front of the bank, as well. Buck guessed there had been some attempts to hold up the place. Or perhaps the Big Three were just cautious men.

He located the livery stable and arranged a stall for Drifter, warning the stable boy not to enter Drifter's stall.

"He's got a mean eye for sure," the boy said, eyeballing the stallion.

"He killed one man," Buck said, knowing that tale would soon spread throughout the small town.

The boy solemnly nodded his head. ·

Buck handed the boy a five-dollar gold piece. "Just between you and me, now. Make certain he gets an extra ration of grain."

"Yes, *sir!*"

"Both Drifter and the packhorse, now."

"Yes, *sir!*"

Taking his personal gear and his rifle, Buck stashed the rest of his gear in Drifter's stall. He walked toward the hotel. As he walked, he passed by a very pretty, dark-haired, hazel-eyed young woman. He smiled at her and she blushed. Buck paused and watched her walk on toward the edge of town. Buck crossed the street to better watch her and saw her push open the gate on a small picket fence and walk up onto the porch of a small house. She disappeared from view.

"Nice," he muttered.

"Sure is," a voice came from behind him.

Buck slowly turned around to face the sheriff and one of his deputies. Neither one of them would win any prizes for good looks.

"Sheriff Reese. This is Rogers, one of my deputies. I don't know you."

That's good, Buck thought. But you will, Sheriff. You will. "Buck West."

"Ahh," Reese said. "Now I know you. The gunhand."

"Some say I am."

"Going to be in town long?"

"That depends."

"On what?"

"On how fast I get rested up, resupplied, and find out more about this Smoke Jensen and how I go about collecting the reward money."

Reese smiled. "First you have to catch him, hombre."

"I'll catch him," Buck said, without changing expression.

Reese stared at the young man. Something about this tall young man was just slightly unsettling. Even for a man like Dan Reese, who had worked on both sides of the law nearly all his life. Reese had worked the hoot-owl trails many times, in several states, ducking and dodging the law that sought him.

Beside him, Rogers stood and glared at Buck, forming an instant dislike for the young man. Rogers was big and solid, including that space between his ears. He was not just dumb; he was stupid. And very dangerous. He had killed more times than he could remember—with fists, guns, knife, or club.

"You stay away from Sally Reynolds," Rogers said. "I got my eyes on her. 'Sides, she likes me."

Buck cut his eyes to the deputy. He doubted that even Rogers's own mother liked him very much. Sally Reynolds. He wondered what the pretty lady did in Bury? "Sally Reynolds is one of our schoolteachers," Reese said. "She wouldn't want notin' to do with no damned bounty hunter like you, West."

"Uh-huh," Buck said. "You're probably right, Sheriff. Anything else I need to know about Bury and its citizens?"

Reese got the accurate impression that he had just been dismissed by Buck. The feeling irritated him. "Jist stay out of trouble."

Buck turned his back to the men and walked on up the boardwalk, toward the hotel.

"I don't lak him," Rogers said. "I think I'll kill him."

"I don't like him either. But you don't do nothin' 'til you're told to do it. You understand that, Rogers?"

"Yes, sir."

"Let's find out what Stratton thinks about this West."

"What's your impression of him?" Stratton asked.

Reese hesitated, then leveled with one of his three bosses. He didn't much care for Buck West, but he knew better than to play the game any way other than straight. "I think he's who he says he is. And I think the rumors are right. He's one hell of a gunfighter."

"Keep an eye on him."

"Yes, sir."

Buck checked into the hotel, a very nice one for a town so far away from the beaten path, and stowed his gear. He bathed, took a shave, and dressed in a dark suit, white shirt and black string tie, polished boots. He checked and cleaned his .44s, and belted them around his waist, tying down the low-riding holsters.

He stepped out onto the boardwalk, carefully looked all around him, as was his habit, and then headed for the cafe, preferring that over the hotel dining room. He took a seat one table over from Miss Sally Reynolds. They were the only customers in the cafe, the lunch hour over. He felt eyes on him and looked up into her hazel eyes. He smiled at her.

"Pleasant day," Buck said.

"Very," Sally replied. "Now that school is out for the summer, it's especially so."

"I regret that I don't have more formal education," Buck said. "The War Between the States put a halt to that."

"It's never too late to learn, sir."

"You're a schoolteacher?"

"Yes, I am. And you . . . ?"

"Drifter, ma'am."

"I . . . don't think so," the young woman said, meeting his gaze.

Buck smiled. "Oh? And why do you say that?"

"Just a guess."

"What grades do you teach?"

"Sixth, seventh, and eighth. Why do you wear two guns?"

"Habit."

"Most of the men I've seen out here have difficulty mastering one gun," Sally said. "My first day out here I saw a man shoot his big toe off trying to quick-draw. I tried very hard not to laugh, but he looked so foolish."

Buck again smiled. "I would imagine so. But I should imagine the man minus the toe failed to find the humor in it."

"I'm sure."

Conversation waned as the waitress brought their lunches. Buck just couldn't think of a way to get the talk going again.

Deputy Rogers entered the cafe, sat down at the counter, and ordered coffee.

Rogers glared at Sally as she said to Buck, "Will you be in Bury long?"

"All depends, ma'am."

"Lady of your quality shouldn't oughta be talkin' to no bounty hunter, Miz Reynolds," Rogers said. "Ain't fittin'."

Buck slowly chewed a bite of beef.

"Mr. Rogers," Sally said. "The gentleman and I are merely exchanging pleasantries over lunch. I was addressing the gentleman, not you."

Rogers flushed, placed his coffee mug on the counter, and abruptly left the cafe.

"Deputy Rogers doesn't like me very much," Buck said.

"Why?" Sally asked bluntly.

"Because . . . I probably make him feel somewhat insecure."

"A very interesting statement from a man who professes to have little formal education, Mr. . . . ?"

"West, ma'am. Buck West."

"Sally Reynolds. Western names are very quaint. Is Buck your Christian first name?"

"No, ma'am. But it might as well be. Been called that all my life."

"Are you a bounty hunter, Mr. West?"

"Bounty hunter, cowhand, gunhand, trapper. Whatever I can make a living at. You're from the east of the Mississippi River, ma'am?"

"New Hampshire. I came out here last year after replying to an advertisement in a local paper. The pay is much better out here than back home."

"I . . . sort of know where New Hampshire is. I would imagine living is much more civilized back there."

"To say the least, Mr. West. And also much duller."

Hang around a little longer, Sally, Buck thought. You haven't seen lively yet. "Would you walk with me, Miss Reynolds?" Buck blurted. "And please don't think I'm being too forward."

"I would love to walk with you, Mr. West."

The sun was high in the afternoon sky and Sally opened her parasol.

"Do you ride, Miss Reynolds?" Buck asked.

"Oh, yes. But I have yet to see a sidesaddle in Bury."

"They ain't too common a sight out here."

"*Ain't* is completely unacceptable in formal writing and speech, Mr. West. But I think you know that."

"Yes, ma'am. Sorry."

She tilted her head, smiling, looking at him, a twinkle in her eyes. As they walked, Buck's spurs jingled. "Which line of employment are you currently pursuing, Mr. West?"

"Beg pardon, ma'am?"

"Bounty hunter, cowhand, gunhand, or trapper?"

"I'm lookin' for a killer named Smoke Jensen. Thirty thousand dollar reward for him."

"Quite a sum of money. I've seen the wanted posters around town. What, exactly, did this Jensen do?"

"Killed a lot of people, ma'am. He's a fast gun for hire, so I'm told."

"Faster than you, Mr. West?"

"I hope not."

She laughed at that.

A group of hard-riding cowboys took that time to burst into town, whooping and hollering and kicking up clouds of dust as they spurred their horses, sliding to a stop in front of one of the saloons.

Buck pulled Sally into a doorway and shielded her from the dust and flying clods.

When the dust had settled, Buck stepped aside and Sally stepped once more onto the boardwalk. "Those are men from the PSR Ranch," she said. "Rowdies and ruffians, for the most part."

"PSR?" Buck asked, knowing full well what the letters stood for.

"Potter, Stratton, Richards. It's the biggest ranch in the state, so I'm told."

"How do they get their cattle to market?" Buck asked. "I know they don't drive them over the Divide."

"They haven't made any big drives yet. I understand that so far they've sold them to people in this area. Leesburg, Salmon, Lemhi. Small communities within a fifty- to seventy-mile radius. The big drive is scheduled for late next spring. They'll be using a hundred or more cowboys."

"Quite an undertaking."

"Oh, yes."

A door opened behind them. A very pretty lady emerged from the dress shop. "Sally," she said. She gave Buck a cool glance and walked on down the boardwalk.

"That is, ah, Mr. Richards's mistress, Buck. Her name is Jane."

Buck had just seen his sister for the first time in almost ten years.

7

"You have an odd look in your eyes, Buck," Sally said.

"I never have gotten used to being snubbed, I suppose. But I suppose I should have, by now. But to be snubbed by a common whore irritates me."

"She may be a whore, but she isn't common," Sally corrected that. "I'm told she speaks three languages very fluently; her home is the showcase of the state; and her carriage was built and brought over from France."

"Oh?" Now where in the devil did Janey learn three languages? he thought. She quit school in the eighth grade.

"Here she comes now," Sally said.

It was a grand carriage, all right. The coachman was a black man, all gussied up in a military-looking outfit. Four tough-looking riders accompanied the carriage. Two to the front, two to the back.

As the carriage passed, Buck removed his hat and bowed gallantly.

Even from the boardwalk, Sally could see the woman in the carriage flush with anger and jerk her head to the front. Sally suppressed a giggle.

"Oh, you made her mad, Buck."

"She'll get over it, I reckon." Buck remembered the time, back before the war, when he had rocked the family outhouse—with his sister in it. She'd chased him all over the farm, throwing rocks at him.

"That funny look is back in your eyes, Buck. What are you thinking?"

"My own sister," he said.

"Does Jane remind you of her?"

"Not really. I haven't seen the sister I remember in a long time. I'll probably never see that girl again."

Sally touched his arm. "Oh, Buck. Why do you say that?"

"There is nothing to return to, Sally. Everything and everyone is gone."

He took her elbow and they began to walk toward the edge of town. They had not gone half a block before the sounds of hooves drumming on the hard-packed dirt came to them. Two of the bodyguards that had been with Jane reined up in the street, turning their horses to face Buck and Sally.

Buck gently but firmly pushed Sally to one side. "Stand clear," he said in a low voice. "Trouble ahead."

"What—?" she managed to say before one of Richards's gunhands cut her off.

"You run on home now, schoolmarm. This here might git messy."

Sally stuck her chin out. "I will stand right here on this boardwalk until the soles of my shoes grow roots before I'll take orders from you, you misbegotten cretin!"

Buck grinned at her. Now this lady had some *sand* to her.

"What the hell did she call me?" the cowboy said to his friend.

"Durned if I know."

The cowboy swung his eyes back to Buck. "You insulted Miss Janey, boy. She's madder than a tree full of hornets. You got fifteen minutes to git your gear and git gone."

"I think I'll stay," Buck said. He had thumbed the thongs off his .44s after pushing Sally to one side.

"Boy," the older and uglier of the bodyguards said, "do you know who I am?"

"Can't say I've had the pleasure," Buck replied.

"Name's Dickerson, from over Colorado way. That ring a bell in your head?"

It did, but Buck didn't let it show. Dickerson was a top gun. No doubt about that. Not only was he mean, he was cat quick with a pistol. "Nope. Sorry."

"And this here," Dickerson jerked a thumb, "is Russell."

Buck hadn't heard of Russell, but he figured if the guy rode with Dickerson, he'd be good. "Pleased to meet you," Buck said politely.

Dickerson gave Buck an exasperated look. "Boy, are you stupid or tryin' to be smart-mouthed?"

"Neither one. Now if you gentlemen will excuse me, I'd like to continue my stroll with Miss Reynolds."

Both Dickerson and Russell dismounted, ground-reining their ponies. "Only place you goin' is carried to Boot Hill, boy."

Several citizens had gathered around to watch the fun, including one young cowhand with a weather-beaten face and a twinkle in his eyes.

"Stand clear," Buck told the crowd.

The gathering crowd backed up and out of the line of impending fire. They hoped.

"I've bothered no one," Buck said to the crowd, without taking his eyes from the two gunhands facing him. "And I'm not looking for a fight. But if I'm pushed, I'll fight. I just wanted that made public."

"Git on your hoss and ride, boy!" Russell said. "And do it right now."

"I'm staying."

"You a damn fool, boy!" Dickerson said. "But if you want a lead supper, that's up to you."

"Lead might fly in both directions," Buck said calmly. "Were I you, I'd think about that."

Some odd light flickered quickly through Dickerson's eyes. He wasn't used to being sassed or disobeyed. But damn this boy's eyes, he didn't seem to be worried at all.

Who in the devil was they up against?

"That's Buck West, Dickerson," the young cowboy with the beat-up face said.

"That don't spell road apples to me," Russell said. He glared at Buck. "Move, tinhorn, or the undertaker's gonna be divvyin' up your pocket money."

"I like it here," Buck said.

"Then draw, damn you!" Dickerson shouted. He went for his gun. Out of the corner of his eye, he saw Russell grab for his .45.

Buck's hands swept down and up with the speed of an angry striking snake. His matched .44s roared and belched smoke and flame. The ground-reined horses snorted and reared at the noise. Dickerson and Russell lay on the dusty street. Both were badly wounded. The guns of the PSR men lay beside them in the dirt. Neither had had time to cock and fire.

"Jumpin' jackrabbits!" the young cowboy said. "I never seen nothin' like that in my life."

Buck calmly punched out the spent brass and dropped the empties to the dirt. He reloaded and holstered his .44s, leaving the hammer thongs off.

Sheriff Dan Reese and Deputy Rogers came at a run up the wide street. Many townspeople had gathered on the boardwalks to crane their necks.

"Drop those damn guns, West!" Reese yelled before arriving at the scene. "You're under arrest."

"I'd like to know why." Sally said, stepping up to stand beside Buck. Her face was very pale. She pointed to Dickerson and Russell. "Those hooligans started it. They ordered Mr. West to leave town. When he refused, they threatened to kill him. They drew first. And I'll swear to that in a court of law."

"She's right, Sheriff," the young cowhand said.

Reese gave the cowboy an ugly look. "Which side are you on, Sam?"

"The side of right, Sheriff."

Dickerson cried out in pain. The front of his shirt was covered with blood. The .44 slug had hit him squarely in the chest, ricocheted off the breast bone, and exited out the top of his shoulder, tearing a great jagged hole as it spun away.

Russell was hardest hit. Buck's .44 had struck him in the stomach and torn out his lower back. The gunhand was not long for this world and everybody looking at him knew it.

"Any charges, Sheriff?" Buck asked, his voice steady and low.

There was open dislike in Reese's eyes as he glared at Buck. He stepped closer. "You're trouble, West. And you and me both know it. I hope you crowd me, gunfighter. 'Cause when you do, I'll kill you!"

"You'll try," Buck replied in the same low tone.

Reese flushed. He stepped back. "No charges, West. It was a fair fight."

Russell groaned, blood leaking from his mouth. He jerked once on the dirt and died.

"Have his full name recorded," Buck said, playing the part of the hard hunter. "There might be a reward on him."

"You're a sorry son of a you-know-what," Reese said. "Ain't you got no feelin's at all?"

"Only for those who deserve it," Buck said. He turned and took Sally's elbow. "Shall we continue?"

As the tall young gunfighter and the pretty lady strolled off, the young cowpuncher named Sam looked at them. He thought he knew who the gunfighter was, and his name wasn't Buck West. But Sam thought he'd keep that information to himself for a time. Might come in handy.

"Your first gunfight?" Buck asked as they walked.

"Yes. And I hope my last."

"It won't be. Not if you continue living out here. It's a big, wild, raw country still. The laws are simple and straight to the point. Justice comes down hard. Out here, a man's word is his bond. That's the way it should be everywhere. Tinhorns and shysters and crooks don't last long in the west."

"And you, Buck?"

"What do you mean?"

"Will you last long out here?"

"No way I can answer that. I hung up my guns once. Thought I would never put them on again. It didn't work out. Maybe I can walk away from it one more time. I don't know. Worth a try, I guess."

They paused at Sally's front gate. "Would you like to have supper with me this evening?" Buck asked. "At the hotel dining room?"

"You're awfully young to have already retired once from gunfighting."

"Some of us had to start young, Sally."

"Yes, I suppose. It's an interesting land, your wild west. I'll be ready at six. Good afternoon, Mr. Buck West." She smiled. "Or whatever your name is."

Jane looked out the window of her bedroom. Ever since she had seen the arrogant young man she had struggled to recall where she'd seen him before. She knew she had. But where? She just could not remember. And now the startling news that the young man had bested Russell and Dickerson in a stand-up gunfight.

Incredible.

She sighed and turned away from the window that overlooked the northern vastness of the PSR ranchlands. She had time for a bath before Stratton and Richards and wives came out for their monthly business and dinner meeting.

The face of the tall gunslick remained in her mind. His name would come to her in time.

* * *

Sheriff Dan Reese had gone through all his dodgers twice, looking for anyone who resembled Buck West. Nothing. But anybody that fast and sure had to have a backtrail. Trick was in finding it. Russell and Dickerson were both hard men. Or had been. And they both had been almighty quick. Yet this Buck West had handled them as easily as children. Just blew in out of nowhere. Probably came from Texas, way down on the border.

Sheriff Reese stood up and stretched. One thing for certain, he thought: Buck West was trouble. Best way to handle him was to get him on the PSR payroll. He'd talk to Richards about it. First thing this evening.

He glanced up at the clock. Had to shave and bath now, though. Get out to PSR headquarters.

The dozen old mountain men made their camp about ten miles south of the town of Bury, in the timber of the Lemhi Range. As soon as they were set up, Preacher changed ponies and headed east, toward the Continental Divide and the Bitterroot Range. At first light, Dupre was to head into Bury for a look-see. Pick up some bacon and beans and coffee and salt and keep his ear open.

"Better wash them jug-handle things first," Beartooth told him. "Probably git five pounds of dirt out of 'um."

"I'd talk," Dupre retorted. "Last time you took a bath it killed the fish for five miles downstream."

"Ummm," Nighthawk said.

8

Buck had ordered his one suit pressed, had bought a new set of longhandles and a new pearl-gray shirt, and was ready to knock on Miss Sally Reynolds's door promptly at six.

As he walked the short blocks from the hotel to Sally's house, Buck had been conscious of eyes on him. Not unfriendly eyes, but curious ones. He had passed several ladies during his walk. They had batted their eyes and swished their bustles at him. Buck had smiled at the ladies and continued walking, his spurs jingling.

He had spoken to the crowd of little boys that had followed him—at a safe distance. He had noticed that several of them were wearing two wooden guns in makeshift holsters, the leather tied down low.

Buck didn't know whether he liked that or not. He didn't want any young people aping his lifestyle. But he didn't know what he could do about it.

Miss Sally Reynolds was dressed in gingham; a bright summer color with matching parasol. The light, bright color setting off her dark hair. She wore just a touch of rouge on her cheeks.

Dusk when they closed the gate to her picket fence and began their stroll to the hotel dining room. The crowd of boys had been called in to supper by their mothers, so Buck and Sally could walk in peace.

They had just left Sally's house when two carriages, accompanied by half a dozen outriders, rolled stately past them.

"Wiley and Linda Potter in the first carriage," Sally said. "Keith and Lucille Stratton in the second carriage. They're going out to Josh Richards's. He lives on the PSR Ranch. They have a monthly dinner and business meeting. The sheriff will be there too, I should imagine."

"Same time, every month?" Buck asked.

"Oh, yes. Very punctual and predictable."

Buck smiled at that. But his smile was only to hide his true inner feelings. And those thoughts were dark and dangerous.

For one hot, flashing instant, Buck's thoughts were flung back in time.

La Plaza de los Leones—Square of the Lions, later to be renamed Walsenburg—was a major farming and ranching community in 1869, when Smoke and Preacher rode in from the west.

They were met by the town marshal and told to keep on riding.

They planned to do just that. But first they wanted to know about the Casey ranch.

"Southeast of here. On the flats. Casey's got eight hands. They all look like gunnies."

"You got an undertaker in this town?" Smoke asked.

"Sure. Why?"

"Tell him to dust off his boxes—he's about to get some business."

Ten miles out of town, they met two hands riding easy, heading into town.

"You boys is on the TC range," one of the riders warned. "Get the hell off. The boss don't like strangers and neither do I."

Smoke smiled. "You boys been ridin' for the brand long?"

"You deef?" the second hand asked. "You been told to git—now git!"

"You answer my question and then maybe we'll leave."

"Since '66. That's when we pushed them longhorns up here from Texas. If that's any of your damned business. Now git!"

"Who owns TC?"

"Ted Casey. Boy, are you plumb crazy or jist stupid?"

"My Pa knew a Ted Casey. Fought in the war with him— for the Gray."

"Oh? What be your name?"

"Some people call me Smoke." He grinned. "Jensen."

Recognition flared in the eyes of the TC riders. They grabbed for their guns. They were far too slow. Smoke's left-hand .36 belched flame and smoke as Preacher fired his Henry one-handed. Horses reared and snorted and bucked at the noise. The TC gunnies dropped from their saddles, dead and dying.

The one TC gunhand alive pulled himself up on one elbow. Blood poured from two chest wounds, the blood pink and frothy, one .36 ball having passed through both lungs, taking the rider as he turned in the saddle.

"Heard you was comin'," he gasped. "You quick, no doubt 'bout that. Your brother was easy." He smiled a bloody smile. "Potter shot him low in the back; took him a long time to die. Died hard. Hollered a lot." The TC rider closed his eyes and died.

Smoke and Preacher burned the house down, driving the men from it after a prolonged gunfight. They took only Casey alive.

"What are you figurin' on doin' with him?" Preacher asked.

"I figure on going back to town and hanging him."

"I don't know how you got that mean streak, boy. Seein' as how you was raised—partly—by a gentle old man like me."

Despite the death he had brought and the destruction wrought, Smoke had to laugh at that. Preacher was known throughout the West as one of the most dangerous men ever to roam the high country and vast Plains. The old mountain man had once gone on the prowl, spending two years of his life tracking down and killing—one by one—a group of men who ambushed and killed a friend of his, stealing the man's furs.

Smoke tied the unconscious Casey across a saddle. "'Course you never went on the hunt for anyone, right?"

"Well . . . mayhaps once or twice. But that was years back. I've mellowed a mite since then."

"Sure." Smoke grinned. Preacher was still as mean as a cornered puma.

By the banks of a creek outside of town, a crowd had gathered for the hanging. Marshal Crowell was furious as he watched Smoke build a noose.

"This man has not been tried!" the marshal protested.

"Yeah, he has," Smoke said. "He admitted to me what he done."

The marshal looked at the smoke to the southeast.

"House fire," Preacher said. "Poor feller lost everything."

Casey spat in the direction of the crowd. He cursed them.

"This is murder!" the marshal said. "I intend to file charges against you both."

"Halp!" Casey hollered.

A local minister began praying for Casey's poor wretched soul.

Casey soiled himself as the noose was slipped around his neck.

The minister prayed harder.

"That ain't much of a prayer," Preacher opined sourly. "I had you beat hands down when them Injuns was fixin' to skin me alive on the Platte. Put some feelin' in it, man!"

The local minister began to shout and sweat. The crowd swelled; some had brought their supper with them. A hanging was always an interesting sight. There just wasn't that much to do in small western towns. Some men were betting how long it would take for Casey to die—providing his neck didn't snap when his butt left the saddle.

A small choir had assembled. The ladies lifted their voices to the sky.

Shall We Gather At The River, they intoned.

"I personally think Swing Low would be more like it," Preacher opined.

A local merchant looked at Casey. "You owe me sixty-five dollars."

"Hell with you!" Casey tried to kick the man.

"I want my money!" the merchant shouted.

"You got anything to say before you go to Hell?" Smoke asked Casey.

"You won't get away with this!" Casey screamed. "If Potter or Stratton don't git you, Richards will."

"What's he talkin' about?" the marshal asked.

"Casey was with the Gray—same as my Pa and brother," Smoke explained. "Casey and some others waylaid a patrol bringing a load of gold into Georgia. They shot my brother in the back and left him to die. Hard."

"That was war," the marshal said.

"It was murder."

"Hurry up," a citizen shouted. "My supper's gettin' cold."

"I'll see you hang for this," the marshal told Smoke.

"You go to hell!" Smoke told him.

Casey swung in the cool, late afternoon air.

"I'm notifying the territorial governor of this," the marshal said.

Casey's bootheels drummed the air.

"Shout, man!" Preacher told the minister. "Sing, sisters, sing!" he urged the choir.

"What about my sixty-five dollars?" The merchant shouted.

All the memories had flashed through Buck's mind in the space of two heartbeats.

"You've gone away again," Sally said.

Buck looked at her. She was smiling up at him. "Yes, I guess I was, Sally. I apologize for that."

They continued walking toward the hotel. Sally said, "Buck, are you here to slay dragons or to tilt at windmills?"

"Beg pardon?"

"Are you familiar with Cervantes?"

"Is he a gunhand?"

She looked at him to see if he was serious. He was. "No, Buck. A writer."

"No, I guess I missed that one. I know what slaying dragons means. But what's that about tilting windmills?"

"Oh, I suppose you're not. I didn't notice Sancho riding in with you."

Now Buck was thoroughly confused. "I never had a Mex sidekick, Sally."

"I have a copy of Don Quixote—somewhere. I'll find it and loan it to you. I think you'll enjoy it."

"All right." Buck was well-read, considering his lack of formal education and allowing for the locale and his lifestyle. But he sure as hell had never heard of any Don Quixote.

Heads turned as they entered the dining room. Some dining there gave the young couple disapproving looks. A few smiled. They took a table next to the wall, affording them maximum privacy, and ordered supper. PSR beef, naturally, with boiled potatoes and beans, and apple pie for dessert.

Neither admitted it, for separate reasons, but both wondered what might be taking place at the grand house of the PSR ranch.

"And it was a fair fight?" Josh Richards asked Sheriff Reese.

"Stand up and square," Reese said. "I didn't see it, but Sam did. He said he ain't never seen nothin' like that Buck West's draw. Lightin' fast. Neither Dickerson nor Russell got a shot off. And they drew first."

"And he's a bounty hunter?" Stratton asked. He was a big man gone to fat. Diamond rings glittered on his soft fat fingers.

"That's what Jerry told me."

"Jerry saw him fight back at the trading post, that right?" Potter asked.

"Yes, sir."

Wiley Potter, like his two partners, had pushed his past from him. He almost never thought of his outlaw and traitor days. He was a successful man, a man under consideration to be territorial governor. And he played his political power to the hilt. He was always well dressed, well groomed.

Josh Richards listened, but had little to say on the subject of the bounty hunter, Buck West. If this West was as good as described, Richards wanted him on the payroll. Of the three men, Richards had changed the least. Physically. He was still a powerful man. Something he had always been proud of. That and his reputation with the ladies. But he knew it was time for him to be thinking of settling down. And while Janey's reputation was a bit scarlet, she was, nevertheless, the woman he planned to marry. She was just as ruthless and cunning as Richards. Would do anything for money. They made a good team.

"I'll see him in the morning," Richards said. "Let's eat. I'm hungry."

Potter was big politically—the front man, all smiles and congeniality, territory-wide. Stratton was the local big shot—the president of the bank and so forth. But Richards ran the show, always staying quietly in the background. That's the way he wanted it.

The men trouped out of the study into the dining

room. Richards looked at Jane. "Something the matter?" he asked in a whisper.

"That Buck West. I've seen him before. Somewhere."

"Can you remember where?"

She shook her head. "Not yet. But I will." She looked him directly in the eyes. "He's trouble, Josh."

"Your imagination, my dear. He'd be a good man to have on our side."

"Watch him," she cautioned. "I don't trust him."

"You don't even *know* him, Jane!"

"Yeah, I do. I just can't remember where I met him, that's all."

"It'll come to you."

"Bet on it."

9

Buck knew he wasn't going to tolerate much living in the hotel. He didn't like the closed-in feeling. The sheets were clean, and that was nice, but the bed was soft and made his back hurt. Buck was not accustomed to the finer things in life. So-called finer things. To Buck, the finer things were the clean smell of deep timber; the high thinness of clean air in the mountains; the rush of a surging stream, wild white water whipping and singing; the cough of a puma and the calling of a bird. Now *that* was fine living!

He walked down to the cafe in the coolness of the early morning. The eastern sky was just beginning to streak with silver, but the cafe was busy, the smell of bacon and eggs and frying potatoes filling the air.

Conversation stopped when Buck walked in and took a seat at a far table, his back to the wall. When the waitress came to take his order, Buck said, "If the food's as good as it smells, I'll take one of everything on the menu."

The waitress smiled at him. Buck ordered breakfast and said, "The owner must make a fortune in this place, the food's so good."

"The owner?" the waitress asked, a curious look in her eyes.

"Yes. Are you the owner?"

She laughed. "Not hardly, sir. Mr. Stratton is the owner. Mr. Stratton owns everything in Bury. Every building and every business."

"Interesting," Buck said. "*Everything?*"

"Everything, sir."

Buck mulled that over in his mind while he ate. The buzz of conversation had returned to normal and the townspeople were ignoring Buck, concentrating on eating. Eating was serious business in the west. Not to be taken lightly. Not at all. Buck thought, the waitress might think Stratton owns everything in sight, but Potter and Richards are right in there as well.

So no one owns their own business. Good. That will make it easier when I burn the damn place to the ground.

Buck was halfway through his breakfast when Deputy Rogers blundered in, closing the door just a bit too hard. Obviously, he wanted everyone to know he had arrived.

Rogers plopped down in a chair facing Buck and said, "Mr. Richards wants to see you."

"When I finish eating. Now go away."

Rogers could not believe his ears. "Hey, gunslick! I said—"

"I heard what you said. So did the entire crowd. I'll see Mr. Richards when I'm finished. Now go away."

Rogers wanted to start something. He wanted it so badly he could taste his personal rage. But he had orders to leave Buck alone. Uttering an oath, he stumbled from the table and slammed the door behind him.

The cafe was totally silent. Even the cook had stepped out and was staring in disbelief at Buck. The one collective thought among them all was, *No one, absolutely* no one *keeps Mr. Richards waiting.*

The front door opened. Josh Richards stepped in. He nodded politely to the crowd and walked to Buck's table, pulling out a chair and calling to the waitress to bring him coffee.

"Ham and eggs are real fine," Buck said. "I recommend them."

Richards smiled. "All right. Ham and eggs, Ruby!"

"Yes, sir."

Buck held out his right hand. "Buck West."

Richards took the offered hand. "Josh Richards. You don't much care for Deputy Rogers, do you Mr. West?"

"I don't think he's got both hands in the stirrups, that's for sure."

"Quaint way of putting it. I'll have to remember that. Oh, you're right, Mr. West. Rogers is a bit weak between the ears. But he does what he is told to do."

"That's important to you, Mr. Richards?"

"Very."

"Money's right, I can be as loyal as any man. More than most, I reckon."

"I imagine you can. Are you looking for a job, Mr. West?"

"I'm lookin' for Smoke Jensen, sir. But that gunhand's backtrail is some cold."

"Yes. I've had a lot of men looking for Jensen. So far, to no avail. Tell you what I'll do, Mr. West. I can put you on the payroll today. Right now. Fighting wages. That's good money. Five or six times what the average puncher makes. You hang around town, the ranch. Just let your presence be known. Every now and then, I'll have a job for you. Sometimes, Mr. Stratton, Mr. Potter, or myself have to transfer large sums of money from place to place. Highwaymen have taken several of those pouches. I need a good man to see that it doesn't happen again. How about it?"

"All right," Buck said with a smile. "Oh, one more thing?"

"Certainly."

Buck pointed with his fork. "Eat your breakfast. It's getting cold."

* * *

Buck met Stratton and Potter. It was all he could do to conceal his raw hatred from the men. He shook hands with them and smiled, nodding in all the right places.

When the meeting was over, he returned to his hotel room and washed his hands with lye soap. They still felt dirty to him.

He saw to his horses and found the livery boy true to his word. Both Drifter and the pack animal were getting extra rations of grain.

He walked the town, getting to know the layout of Bury. As he walked, he noticed a buckskin-clad old mountain man leaning against the wall of the not-yet-opened general store. The mountain man appeared not to be watching Buck, but Buck knew he was watching him. His name came to Buck. Dupre. The Louisiana Frenchman. He remembered him from the rendezvous at the ruins of Bent's Ford, back in . . . was it '66? Buck thought it had been.

Dupre looked as old as time itself, and as solid as a granite mountain. Buck had been raised among mountain men, and he knew these old boys were still dangerous as grizzly bears. Not a one of the mountain men still left alive could tell you how many men they'd killed. White men. Indians didn't count.

When Buck again caught his eyes, Dupre was talking to the store owner. Not owner, Buck corrected himself—manager. The two men went inside. Buck continued walking. Unlike most men who spent their lives on the hurricane deck of a horse, Buck enjoyed a good stroll.

It was a pretty little town, Buck thought. And not just thrown haphazardly together, like so many frontier towns. He took his time, speaking to the men and doffing his hat to the ladies he passed. He noticed suspicion in many of the eyes; open hostility in a like amount. He wondered about that.

"You're up early," a voice called from Buck's left.

He stopped and slowly turned. Sally Reynolds sat on her front porch, drinking what Buck guessed was coffee.

"I enjoy the early morning, Sally."

"So do I. Would you care for a cup of tea?"

"Tea?"

"Tea."

"Sure. I guess so. Never acquired much of a taste for it."

"I can make coffee."

"No, no. Tea will be fine." He pushed open the gate and took a chair on the porch.

It wasn't fine. Buck thought he was going to gag on the stuff. It didn't taste like nothing. But he smiled bravely and swallowed. Hard.

Sally laughed at him. "Please let me make you some coffee, Buck. It will only take a few minutes."

"Maybe you'd better. I sure would appreciate it. This stuff and me just don't get along."

Buck sat alone on the small porch and watched as Dupre rode past, riding slowly, his Henry repeating rifle held in one hand, across the saddle. As he rode past, the old mountain man nodded his head to Buck. "Nice mornin', ain't it, son?"

"Yes, it is. Have yourself a good day."

"My good days are twenty year down my backtrail," Dupre said. "But I still manage to git by." He rode on, soon out of sight.

"Who in the *world* was that?" Sally asked. She placed a cup of coffee on the small table between their chairs.

"You probably read about them in school," Buck said. "Mountain men?"

"Oh, yes! But I thought they were all dead."

"Most of them are. The real mountain men, that is. But there's still some salty ol' boys out there, still riding the high lonesome."

"The high lonesome? That's beautiful, Buck. Do I detect a wistful note in your voice?"

"Wistful?"

"Means a longing, or a yearning for something."

Could he trust her? Buck didn't know. She could very well be a spy for Stratton or Potter or Richards. Then he remembered how she had stood up to Sheriff Reese. He made up his mind. All right, he would tell her just enough to bait her.

"I guess so, Sally. I came out here just a boy. Alone," he lied. "I grew up in the mountains. Met a lot of mountain men. They was, were, old men even then. But tough and hard as nails. They knew their way of life was about gone, even then. But it was a fine way of life—for them; not for everybody."

"And for you, Buck?"

"For me? Do you mean did I enjoy it?"

She nodded.

Buck smiled. "Oh, yes. I'll get a burr under my saddle one of these days and you won't see me for several days. I'll have to shake the staleness of town off me; head for the high country. Me and the horses. But I'll be back. If it matters to you, that is."

She was silent for a very long moment. So long that Buck thought he had offended her with the statement.

"Yes, Buck. I think it does matter to me. In . . . a way that I can't explain. Not just yet. Buck, I am a very perceptive person . . ."

"A what kind of person?"

"Perceptive. That means I have a keen insight, or understanding, of things."

"Terrible to be as ignorant as I am," Buck said.

Sally did not pursue that, for she did not believe Buck to be an ignorant person. Just a person who was hiding something. For whatever reason.

"And your insight tells you what about me, Sally?"

"That you don't fully trust me."

"I don't fully trust anybody, Sally. Out here in the west,

trust is something that has to be earned. It has to be that way 'cause your life might depend on it."

"Yes. I've heard that from several people since I've been out here."

"It's very true. You have a lot of outlaws working out here. You have a half-dozen Indian tribes on the warpath. Long as you stay close to Bury, you probably won't have to worry about the Indians attacking. It's too big for them. But get a mile away from town, and your life is in constant danger. You've got to know the man or men you ride with. Will they stand with you or turn tail and run? See what I mean about earning trust?"

"Yes. I suppose so. I won't tell you what else my insight tells me about you, Buck. Not until I've earned your trust. Do you suppose that will happen?"

"I imagine so."

Buck checked in with the Big Three's office manager, the office located in a building in the center of town, and told the dour-faced and sour-dispositioned little man he was riding out; be gone for a day or two. Give his horse some exercise.

MacGregor grunted and told Buck to be back day after tomorrow. He had to ride south to deliver a pouch.

"I'll be back."

He rode north out of Bury, following the Salmon River. He headed for a small town called Salmon. A rough-and-tumble mining camp.

He had no intention of going to Salmon; Buck just wanted to see if he was being followed. He wanted to test how much trust Richards had in him.

"Not much," Buck grunted. He was back in the deep timber, hidden, watching his backtrail. He was watching a half-dozen riders slowly tracking him. Using his spyglass, Buck pulled them into closer view. He knew their faces, having seen them loafing around Bury, but didn't know their names.

Buck rode deeper into the timber, making a slow circle, coming out of the timber behind the riders. Now he was tracking them. He wore an amused look on his face as he watched the gunhands slowly circling, having lost Buck's trail, trying to once more find it. Buck rode up to within five hundred or so yards of the men and sat his horse, watching the men.

One rider finally lifted his head, feeling, sensing eyes on him. "Crap!" the man's voice drifted faintly to Buck. "He's watchin' *us*, boys."

The PSR riders bunched and rode slowly toward Buck, reining up a respectable distance from him. One said, "This ain't nothin' personal, partner. We ride for the brand, just like you."

"No offense taken, boys. Town was closing in on me. I wanted some space. You know what I mean?"

"Know exactly what you mean," a scar-faced rider said. "We got biscuits and coffee and it's 'bout noon. Let's build a fire and jaw some."

Cinches loosened, bits out, the horses ground-reined, they grazed. The riders sat on the ground, munching biscuits and drinking cups of strong black coffee. The scar-faced rider was Joiner. The oldest of the men, a hard-eyed puncher, was Wilson. Buck took an immediate dislike for Wilson and he sensed the feeling was mutual. McNeil had practically nothing to say. But he kept eyeballing Buck. The man's head was totally bald. Long was short and stocky. He wore one gun tied down low and his second gun in a shoulder-holster rig. Davis was a long lean drink of water; looked like a strong wind would blow him slap out of the saddle. Simpson was big and mean-looking.

"You familiar with Brown's Hole?" Joiner asked Buck.

"Been there. Went there lookin' for Jensen. Grave

close to the base of Zenobia Peak. Looks like that's where Jensen planted his pa."

"You dig the grave up?" Wilson asked.

"*Hell*, no!"

Davis said, "That'd be a sin. Sorry no good would do that. Let a man rest in peace."

Wilson looked pained. "Mayhaps that'd be where the gold is buried."

"How would a dead man do that?" Simpson asked.

Wilson nodded his head. "Ain't thought about that. You right."

Then another piece plopped into place in Buck's mind.

10

1867. Emmett Jensen's horses had been picketed close to the base of Zenobia Peak. His gear was by his grave, covered with a ground sheet and secured with rocks. The letter from his pa, given him by the old mountain man, Grizzly, was in Smoke's pocket.

"You read them words on that paper your pa left you?" Preacher asked.

"Not yet."

"I'll go set up camp at the Hole. I reckon you'll be along directly."

"Tomorrow. 'Bout noon."

"See you then." Preacher headed north. He would cross Vermillion Creek, then cut west into the Hole. Smoke would find him when he felt ready for human company. But for now, the young man needed to be alone with his pa.

Smoke unsaddled his horse, Seven, and allowed him to roll. He stripped the gear from the pack animals, setting them grazing. Taking a small hammer and a miner's spike from his gear, Smoke began the job of chiseling his father's name into a large, flat rock. He could not remember exactly when his pa was born, but he thought it about 1815.

Headstone in place, secured by rocks, Smoke built a small fire, put coffee on to boil in the blackened pot, then sat down to read the letter from his pa.

Son,

I found some of the men who killed your brother Luke and stolt the gold that belonged to the Gray. Theys more of them than I first thought. I killed two of the men work for them, but they got led in me and I had to hitail it out. Came here. Not goin to make it. Son, you dont owe nuttin to the Cause of the Gray. So dont get it in your mind you do. Make yoursalf a good life and look to my final restin place if you need help.

Preacher kin tell you some of what happen, but not all. Remember—look to my grave if you need help.

I allso got word that your sis Janey leff that gambler and has took up with an outlaw down in Airyzona. Place called Tooson. I woodn fret much about her. She is mine, but I think she is trash. Dont know where she got that streek from.

I am gettin tared and seein is hard. Lite fadin. I love you Kirby-Smoke.

Pa

Smoke reread the letter. Look to my grave. He could not understand that part. He pulled up his knees and put his head on them, feeling he ought to cry, or something. But no tears came.

Now he was alone. He had no other kin, and he did not count his sister as kin. He had his guns, his horses, a bit of gold, and his friend, Preacher.

He was eighteen years old.

* * *

Now, five years later, it all came back to him. Sure, he thought. His pa had dug his own grave, put the gold in the bottom, and then crawled in on top of it to die. The old mountain man, Grizzly, had buried him.

Well, the gold could just stay there. Damned if he'd dig up his pa's grave for it.

"Where else you been lookin' for this Smoke?" McNeil asked.

"Name someplace. I thought I had him cornered over near Pagosa Springs, but he gave me the slip. I drifted down into New Mexico Territory after him. But he was always one jump ahead of me. He's slick."

"He'll screw up," Long said.

"When he does I'm gonna be there," Buck said. And he noticed out of the corner of his eyes that the men seemed to relax. He had passed their test.

Buck prowled the area about Bury for two days, planting a permanent map in his brain. He would remember the trails and roads and landmarks. They would come in handy when Buck made his move and sought his escape.

And he learned from the PSR gunhands about the townspeople of Bury. They were a pretty scummy lot, according to the riders. There were men who had skipped out on partners back east: men who were wanted for everything from petty crimes to murder. In exchange for loyalty, the Big Three had offered them sanctuary and a chance to bury their past. After twenty years, the businesses they ran for the Big Three would revert to the shopkeepers. Free and clear.

So Buck could expect no help from them.

In a way, that knowledge made it easier.

The saddlebags handed to Buck by MacGregor were heavy. The canvas and leather saddlebags were flap-secured by padlocks. Buck did not ask what was in the bags; the sour little Scotsman did not volunteer that information.

"It's about a sixty-five-mile ride," Buck was told. "Head out east to the Lemhi River and follow it down. Little mining operation down in the Lemhi Valley. Town ain't got no name. So it's called No Name. Be a man there waitin' for you. Name is Rex. Give the saddlebags to him, wait 'til he checks them out, and he'll give you a receipt. Come back here."

The Scotsman turned away and stumped back to his rolltop desk, leaving Buck with the heavy bags. Buck smiled. "Gimme some expense money, friend."

The Scotsman sighed and reached into a tin box, pulling out a thin sheaf of bills. He made Buck sign for them. "Bring back anything that's left. Not that I think there will be anything left, that is."

Buck rode out at nine that morning. He stopped by Sally's place and found her sitting on the front porch. Drinking that damnable tea. "Be back in about three days." He smiled. "I'll bring you back a couple of pounds of coffee." He wheeled Drifter and was gone.

Staying close to the timber, with the flats to his left, Buck let Drifter pick his own pace. About ten miles out of town he reined up and sat his horse. He rubbed his eyes in disbelief. Was that an elf up ahead, sitting on a spotted pony? Buck walked Drifter slowly toward the sight. Sure looked like an elf.

"Since I care nothing for life in caves or other subterranean dwellings, I can assure you that I am not a troll," the little man said, when Buck was within earshot.

"A what?"

"Never mind, young man. My name is Audie. I, along with others of our vanishing breed, have made our meager camp just to the west of where we are now engaged in this somewhat less than loquacious confabulation."

Buck blinked. "Huh?"

Audie sighed. "Very well." He took a deep breath. "Me

and them there other ol' boys who was pards with Preacher is a-camped over yonder." He jerked his thumb.

"Oh. All right. For a little fellow you got a smart mouth, you know that?"

Audie jerked out a .44 with the barrel sawed off short. "But I carry a very large friend, do I not?"

"I'd say so. An' quick with it, too."

"Did you think I might be an elf?" Audie smiled after the question.

"Well, sir. Ah . . . yeah!"

"How quaint," the remark was very drily given. "But . . . given the fact that elves are rumored to engage in somewhat capricious interference in human affairs, and are usually represented in diminutive human form, I suppose your first impression might be forgiven. But I cannot, for the life of me, envision Greybull as an elf."

"Mister Audie, I don't *even* know what it is you just said."

"We're watching you," Audie plunged onward, undaunted. "We'll be there when you need us." He wheeled his pony around and trotted off.

Buck watched him disappear from view. Buck removed his hat and scratched his head. "I've seen the seasons change, the birthing of human life, and been in love. But I ain't *never* seen nothin' like that!"

At No Name, Buck tied up in front of a building with the name PSR on the false front. *Rex Augsman* was painted on the door. Buck pushed open the door and stepped inside, pausing for a moment to allow his eyes to adjust to the dimmer light.

"You Rex Augsman?" Buck asked the man who was rising from behind his desk.

"That's me."

"You got some proof of that?"

He pointed to a diploma hanging on the wall. Mining engineer. Rex M. Augsman.

"I'm from PSR headquarters up in Bury." He held out the saddlebags. "I'm supposed to give this to you."

"You look like you might just have some sense," Rex said. "A definite improvement over the others." He opened the padlocks and looked inside. He smiled and said, "Welcome to the team. You passed the final test."

"What do you mean?" Buck asked.

The engineer dumped the contents of the heavy saddlebags onto the counter. The bags had been filled with cut-up pieces of newspaper and lots of rocks.

"The young man is not exactly a paragon of intelligence," Audie said. "But there is something about him that suggests there might be a glimmer of hope."

"Smart as a whip, you dwarf!" Preacher fired at the former schoolteacher. Halfway to the Divide, Preacher had run into a band of friendly Flatheads. Yes, they had been into Bury many times to trade. Yes, they would keep their eyes and ears open and report back to Preacher. Preacher had returned to the base camp.

"No doubt you speak nonprejudicially," Audie said.

"Don't you cuss me!" Preacher warned. "I'll rap you up-side the head."

Audie reached for the sawed-off .44. Preacher reached for his Colt.

Lobo suddenly growled like a wolf and the two old friends settled down, dropping their hands from the butts of pistols.

"Sorry 'bout that, little friend," Preacher said.

"I, too, offer my sincere apologies, Preacher," Audie said. "It's the tension of waiting for the unknown."

Dupre grinned and walked to his bedroll. He pulled two clay jugs out of the blankets. "I tink perhaps we have a drink or three," he said.

"Right good idee," Greybull said.

"I could stand a taste myself," Matt said. "How 'bout you, Nighthawk?"

"Ummm."

* * *

Buck had asked for a receipt for the newspapers and rocks. Back in Bury, he solemnly presented it to MacGregor. The Scotsman looked at Buck, then the receipt, and a sour smile slowly formed on his lips.

"You're a damn fool for staying, boy," MacGregor said. "I told Richards you were an honest man. That impressed him. But honest men won't last long in a town filled with scalawags and hooligans. Tell him I said it, if you wish—but you won't. You've stepped into a snake pit, young man. There isn't a handful of people—men *and* women—in this town and surrounding area that is worth spit. Oh, I know why you're here, Mr. Kirby Jensen, aka Smoke, aka Buck West. You're here to avenge your wife, your son, your father, your friend Preacher. You're so full of hate it's consuming you, eating you alive. If you let it, boy, it will destroy you."

"How many others know who I am?" Buck asked, keeping his voice calm.

"I think the red-haired gunman, Sam, probably knows. Sam is quite like you. An honest man. The schoolteacher you've been sparking about, Sally. She probably suspects. Don't worry about me, Buck. I am a federal marshal."

11

Buck had asked the Scotsman how he had known about him. MacGregor had shown him a wanted dodger on Smoke. He had cut off the hair and added a beard. It was eerie; almost like looking into a mirror.

"Your skill and speed with your guns gave you away, Buck," MacGregor said. Then he smiled. "What are you planning to do here?"

"I'm going to kill Potter and Richards and Stratton and then burn this damn town to the ground."

"Warn me before you start putting your suicidal plan into action. I need to gather up my evidence and get out of here."

Buck had looked at the smaller man, not knowing how to take the man. "But you're a federal marshal, Mac-Gregor. Aren't you going to arrest me?"

"On what charges, Buck? I'm not aware of any federal charges against you. You haven't committed any acts of treason against the government of the United States. You haven't robbed any federal mints. You haven't assaulted any federal agents or destroyed any federal property. Hell, I personally hope you are successful in destroying this cesspool. Good day, Mr. West."

Buck stabled Drifter and went back to the hotel for a

bath and shave. MacGregor hadn't told him very much as to the why of a federal marshal being in Bury; just that if he, MacGregor, was successful, another chapter in that regrettable bloody insurrection referred to as the Civil War would be closed. And perhaps a young man would finally be at peace with himself.

MacGregor had left it at that.

After cleaning up, Buck walked to Sally's house carrying a small package wrapped in brown paper. He found her working in the yard, planting flowers. She turned at the sounds of his bootheels and the jingle of his spurs and smiled at him.

Brushing off her hands, Sally asked, "Did you have a good trip?"

"Oh, yes." Buck held out the package. "Brought you something."

She waved him onto the porch and they both took chairs. She opened the package and laughed out loud. Two pounds of coffee.

"I'll grind these beans and make some coffee right now," she said. "While it's perking I'll clean up. It won't take me five minutes."

They chatted away the remainder of the morning. Sally fixed sandwiches for lunch, then the two went for a stroll around town. While resting on the cool banks of a creek, Buck said, "Sally, I want to tell you something."

She glanced at him. "Sounds serious."

"Might be. Sally, if I ever come to you and tell you to pack up and get out of town, don't question it. Just do as I say. If I ever tell you that, it's because a lot of trouble is about to pop wide open."

"If there is an Indian attack, wouldn't it be safer in town rather than outside of town?"

"It won't be Indians, Sally."

"There are children in this town, Buck," she reminded him.

"I'm aware of that."

"Are you saying the sins of the father are also on the head of the son?"

"No," Buck's reply was given slowly, after much thought. "Why would I think that?"

She touched his face with her small hand. "Who are you, Buck?"

And just before his lips touched hers, Buck said, "Smoke Jensen."

"Well, this cinches it," Richards told MacGregor. "I've got a man I can trust. You agree?"

"Oh, most assuredly," the Scotsman said. "I like the young man."

Richards gave his bookkeeper a sharp glance. Damned little sour man had never seemed to like anybody. But if MacGregor gave his OK to Buck West, then Buck was all right.

"Boss," Jerry stuck his head into the office. "Some range-rider just reported a group of old mountain men's gatherin' south and west of here."

"Mountain men?" Richards said. "That's impossible. All those people are dead."

"No, sir," Jerry respectfully disagreed with his boss. "There's still a handful of 'um around. They old, but they mean and crotchety and not to be fooled with. Dangerous old men. I've run up on 'um time to time. And Benson over to the general store reports that one was in his place 'bout three days back. Bought supplies and sich."

"Mountain men," Richards vocally mused. "Now why would those old characters be hanging around here?"

Neither Richards nor Jerry noticed the faint smile on MacGregor's face. The Scotsman now knew what Buck/Smoke was up to. And it amused him. But, he cautioned himself silently, you damn sure don't want to be around when Buck and his friends lift the lid on Pandora's Box. Best start making arrangements to pull out. It isn't going to be long.

"Don't know, boss," Jerry said. "Just thought you'd want to know about it."

"Yeah, right, Jerry. Thanks."

MacGregor watched the men leave the office. The undercover federal marshal sat down at his desk and took up his pen, dipping the point into the inkwell. He returned to his company ledger book. But he had a difficult time entering the small, precise figures. His shoulders kept shaking from suppressed laughter.

"I must keep reminding myself that I'm a lady," Sally told Buck. But the twinkle in her eyes told Buck that while a lady she might be, there were a lot of hot coals banked within.

"Aren't you going to run away, screaming in fear?" Buck asked her. "After all, I'm the murderer, Smoke Jensen."

"You took an awful chance, telling me that."

"Maybe I have some insight, too."

"Yes, I suppose you do. Now tell me about Smoke."

She listened attentively for a full ten minutes, not interrupting, letting him tell his painful story, his way. Several times during the telling he lapsed into silence, then with a sigh, he would continue.

When he had finished, she sat on the cool creek bank, her long skirt a fan of gingham around her, and mentally digested all she had heard.

Finally she said, "And to think I work for those creatures." She hurled a small stone into the water. "Well, I shall tender my resignation immediately, of course."

Buck's smile was hard. "Stick around, Sally. The show's just about to begin."

"What would you do if I told you . . . well, I am quite fond of you, Buck?"

"What would you want me to do?"

"Well," she smiled, "you might kiss me."

Just as their lips touched, a voice came from behind them. "Plumb sickenin'. Great big growed-up man a-moonin' and a-sparkin' lak some fiddle-footed kid. Disgustin'."

Buck spun around, on his feet in a crouch, his hands over the butt of his guns. His mouth dropped open.

"Shut your mouth, boy," Preacher said. "Flies is bad this time of year."

"*Preacher!*" Buck croaked, his voice breaking.

"It damned shore ain't Jedediah Smith," the old man said drily. "We lost him back in '35, I think it was. Either that or he got married. One and the same if'n you's to ask me."

Buck ran toward Preacher and grabbed him in a bear hug, spinning around and around with the old mountain man.

"Great Gawd Amighty!" Preacher hollered. "Put me down, you ox!"

Buck dropped the old man to the ground. His big hands on Preacher's shoulders, Buck said, "I can't believe it. I thought you were dead!"

"I damn near was, boy! Took this old body a long time to recover. Now if'n you're all done a-slobberin' all over me, we got to make some plans."

"How'd you find me, Preacher?"

"Hell's fire, boy! I just followed the bodies! Cain't you keep them guns of yourn in leather?"

"Come on, Preacher! Tell the truth. I know you'd rather lie, but try real hard."

"You see how unrespectful he is, Missy?" Preacher looked at Sally. "Cain't a purty thang lak you do no better than the laks of this gunslick?"

"I'm going to change him," Sally said primly. She was not certain just how to take this disreputable-looking old man, all dressed in buckskins and looking like death warmed over.

"Uh-huh," Preacher said. "That's whut that white wife of mine said, too."

"White wife!" Buck looked at him. "You never had no wife except squaws!"

"That's all you know, you pup. I married up with me a white woman that was purtier than Simone Jules Dumont's mustache."

"Heavens!" Sally muttered.

Simone Jules Dumont, also known as Madame Mustache, was either from France or a Creole from the Mississippi Delta region—it had never been proven one way or the other. She'd showed up in California during the 1849 gold rush and had soon been named head roulette croupier at the Bella Union in San Francisco. Eventually, Simone had moved on to a livelier occupation: running a gambling saloon/whorehouse at Bannack, Montana. It was there she is rumored to have taught the finer points of card dealing to Calamity Jane. And her mustache continued to grow, as did her reputation. She killed what is thought to be her first husband—a man named Carruthers—after he conned her out of a sizable amount of money. She moved on to Bodie, California, mustache in full bloom, and killed another man there when he and another footpadder tried to rob her one night. She lost most of her money in a card game on the night of September 6, 1879, and passed on through the Pearlies that same night after drinking hydrocyanic acid.

"Did you have any children from that union, Mister Preacher?" Sally asked.

"Durned if'n I know, Missy. I lit a shuck out of there one night. Walls was a-closin' in on me. I heard she took up with a minister and went back east. I teamed up with John Liver-Eatin' Johnston for a time. He lost his old woman back in '47 and went plumb crazy for a time. Called him Crow Killer. He kilt about three hundred Crows and et the livers out of 'em."

Sally turned a little green around the mouth. Buck had heard the story; he yawned.

"I didn't think crows were good to eat, Mister Preacher," Sally said.

"Not the bird, Missy," Preacher corrected. "The Indian tribe. You see, it was a bunch of Crows on the warpath that kilt Johnston's old woman. John never did lak Crows after that. Et a bunch of 'em."

"You mean he was a ... *cannibal?*"

"Only as fer as the liver went," Preacher said blandly. "He got to lookin' at me one night while we's a-camped in the Bitterroot. Right hongry look in his eyes. I took off. Ain't seen him since. Last I heard, old Crow Killer was a scout for the U.S. Army, over on the North Plains."

Sally sat back on the bank, averting her eyes, mumbling to herself.

"I wish you had gotten word to me that you were still alive, you old coot," Buck said.

"Couldn't. I were plumb out of it for a couple of months. By the time I could ride out of that Injun camp, Nicole and the baby was dead and buried and you was gone. I'm right sorry about Nicole and the boy, Smoke."

Buck nodded. "Better get use to calling me Buck, Preacher. You might slip up in town and that would be the end of it."

"I ain't goin' into town. Not until you git ready to make your move, that is. You wanna git a message to me, Smoke, they'll be a miserable-looking old Injun in town named Hunts-Long. Flathead. Wears a derby hat. He'll git word to me. Me and the boys was spotted last yesterday, so we'll be changin' locations." He told Buck where. "T's tole you met up with Audie." That was said with a grin.

"I thought I was seeing things. I thought he was an elf."

"He's the furrtherest thang from an elf. That little man will kill you faster than you can spit. Yessir, Smoke, you got some backup that'll be wrote up strong when they writes about the buryin' of Bury. Got Tenneysee,

Audie, Phew, Nighthawk, Dupre, Deadlead, Powder Pete, Greybull, Beartooth, and Lobo. And me. 'Course I'm a better man than all them combined," Preacher said, in his usual modest manner. "And Matt."

"Phew?" Sally said. "Why in Heaven's name would you call a man that?"

"'Cause he stinks, Missy."

"I know Matt. The negro."

"That's him. Ol' one-eye." Preacher stuck out his hand. "Be lookin' at you, Smoke. You take care, now." He whistled for his pony and the spotted horse trotted over. Preacher jumped onto the mustang's back and was gone.

Sally looked at Buck. A load seemed to have been removed from his shoulders. His eyes were shining with love as he watched the old man ride out. He seemed to stand a little taller.

He met her eyes. "It's sad. When those men are gone, a . . . time will have passed. And it will never be again."

"That is not entirely true, Smoke Jensen," Sally said.

"Oh? What do you mean?"

"You'll be here to carry on."

12

The day after seeing Preacher, Buck was witness to a scene that lent credence to what MacGregor had said about the men and women who made up the population of Bury. Buck was sitting on the boardwalk in front of one of Bury's hurdy-gurdy houses, leaned back in his chair, when a man and woman and three children walked up the main street. The man and woman wore rags and the kids looked as though they had not eaten in days. The ragged little band of walkers stopped in front of the large general store. Buck drifted over that way just as the red-headed cowboy, Sam, walked over from another direction. Buck and Sam looked at each other and nodded greetings.

"Watch this," Sam said out of the corner of his mouth. "This might change your mind about the men you're working for. And the sorry people in this town."

"You get your money out of the same hand that pays me," Buck reminded him.

"But I don't have to like it . . . Smoke."

"Do I know you from somewheres else?" Buck asked.

"I was in Canon City when you and that old mountain man drew down on Ackerman and his boys. Took me awhile to put it all together. But I knowed I'd seen you before."*

*The Last Mountain Man.

"Why haven't you tried to collect the bounty on my head, then?"

Sam hesitated. "I don't know," he finally admitted. "Mayhaps I'm havin' some second thoughts 'bout the way my life's been goin' up to date. And then mayhaps I just want to hang around and see the show. 'Cause I know when the time gets right, you're goin' to put on one hell of a show."

"You gonna watch my back?"

"I don't know. Talk to you later. Listen to this."

The ragged emaciated-looking man was talking to the store manager. "I'm begging you, mister. Please. My kids are starving and my wife is worn out. I ain't asking nothing for myself. Just a bite of food for my wife and kids. I'll work it out for you."

The storekeeper waved his broom at the ragged man. "Get on with you. Get out of here. Go beg somewhere else."

"I'll get down on my knees and beg you, mister," the man said. He was so tired, so worn out, he was trembling.

The man who ran the leather shop next to the general store stepped out onto the boardwalk to watch the show. "What happened to you, skinny?" he called to the ragged man.

"Indians. They ambushed the wagon train we was on. We didn't have time to circle. They split us up. Most of the others died. We lost everything and have been walking for days. Brother, can you find it in your heart to give my kids and woman something to eat?"

"Only if you got the money to pay for it. If you don't, then haul your ashes on, beggar."

The man's shoulders sagged and tears began rolling down his dusty face.

Buck could not believe what he was hearing and seeing. But he knew he could not afford to step out of character—not yet. He watched and waited.

Other shopkeepers had gathered on the boardwalk. The man who ran the apothecary shop laughed and said, "There's a joyhouse down the end of this street. Why don't you put your woman in there? Clean 'er up some and she'll make enough to get you goin' again." The gathering crowd roared with laughter.

Sam explained. "Man poisoned his partner back in Illinoise," he said. "Then stole his woman and come out here. Real nice feller. Name's Burton."

"Yeah," Buck returned the low tone.

The hotel manager stepped out. He waved his arms at the ragged little band. "You ne'er-do-wells get out of here. That little girl looks like she's got galloping consumption. No one here wants to catch that. Stir up the dust and get gone from here."

"Morgan," Sam said. "Ran a hotel in Ohio until he burned it down. Killed several sleepers. Another nice feller."

"I just don't believe the heartlessness of these people," Buck said.

"You ain't seen nothin' yet, partner," Sam said. "Stick around."

"The Lord helps those who help themselves," Reverend Necker said, appearing on the scene. "But He frowns on shirkers. Now be gone with you."

"A minister?" Buck whispered.

"About as holy as you and me," Sam said. "Come from Iowa, so he says. He's a drunk and a skirt-chaser."

The woman had gathered her children close to her and was fighting back tears. The man's shoulders were slumped in defeat.

Sheriff Reese and Deputy Rogers walked up. "You vagabonds keep on moving," the sheriff ordered. "Get on with you now before I put a loop on you all and drag you out of town."

"I don't believe I'm seeing this!" Sally shouted from the fringe of the crowd. Her hot eyes found Buck and bored invisible holes into his heart. She swung her eyes back to the merchants gathered on the boardwalk.

"What is the matter with you people?"

"Warn her off," Sam whispered. "You and me will get some grub and clothes for them people; give it to them on the outskirts of town. But warn her off, Buck. She's treadin' on dangerous ground."

"How?" Buck whispered.

Sam grunted. "Good question, I reckon. That lady would stand up to an Injun attack armed with a broom, I'm thinkin'."

"You people should be ashamed of yourselves!" Sally shouted. "Look at those children. *Look at them!* They're starving."

"This ain't none of your business, Miz Sally," Sheriff Reese said. "You just go on back home and tend to your knittin'."

"Well, I'll make it my business!" Sally flared, sticking her chin out and standing her ground. She looked at the ragged, starving family. "You people come with me. To my house. I'll give you all a hot meal."

"No, you won't, Miss Reynolds," the voice came from the edge of the crowd.

All heads turned to stare at Keith Stratton, mounted on a showy white horse.

"What do you mean, Mr. Stratton?" Sally asked.

"Those people are losers, Miss Reynolds," Stratton said. "No matter what or how much one does for them, they will be begging again tomorrow. Trash. That's all they are. All they ever will be. And you don't own that house you're living in. I do. You are staying there rent-free. And you are paid to teach school, not meddle in town affairs. Now please leave."

"And if I choose to stay?" Sally asked.

"You will neither have a job, nor a place to stay," Stratton warned.

"Stratton just stepped into a pit full of rattlers," Sam projected accurately. "All dressed up in gingham."

"Yep," Buck said.

"I see," Sally said. "Will you allow me the time to gather up my personal belongings, or do you intend to seize those along with the house?"

"You're about to make a very bad mistake, Sally," Stratton informed her.

"There is quite a popular phrase out here, Mr. Stratton," Sally said. "It is said that out in the west, a person saddles their own horses and kills their own snakes."

"I'm familiar with the saying," Stratton said, his triple chins quavering as he spoke. The sunlight glinted off his diamond rings.

"Then I stand by that maxim, sir."

"A what?" Sam whispered.

"Don't ask me," Buck said.

"You're a very foolish and headstrong young woman, Miss Reynolds. But if that is your decision, then you have one hour to gather up your possessions and vacate that house."

Sally nodded and looked at the ragged family. "You people come with me."

Buck started toward Sally. She waved him back. "You have made your choice, Buck. So long as you work for the other side, I do not wish to see you."

She winked at him.

Buck hid his smile, knowing then what Sally was doing. She was jeopardizing her own position in order to strengthen his own. *Gal had guts,* Buck thought. *But where in the hell was she going to stay the night?* he wondered.

"She's going to stay *where?*" Buck shouted at Sam.

Sam backed up. "Easy now, partner." He kept his hands away from his guns. "She's gonna stay down at Miss Flora's place."

"A whorehouse!"

"It wasn't my idea, Buck. It was Miss Flora's. She likes Sally 'cause Sally was always nice and polite to them, ah, ladies that work the Pink House."

"Sally Reynolds in a whorehouse!"

The red-headed cowpuncher-turned-gunslick took another step backward. The last thing in this world he wanted was for Buck to reach for those guns. Sam was fast, but Lord knows not nearabouts that fast. "Miss Flora done closed the doors to the Pink House, Buck. Shut 'er down tight. She's been wanting to pull up stakes for a year. Take her girls and head out. Stratton and them blocked that move. Made her mad. Now she's locked the doors to the Pink House. This is liable to bring things to a head 'round here, Buck."

Buck began to relax as the humor of the situation struck him. He had been told that the Big Three built the joyhouse to keep their randy gunhands happy. If Miss Flora had indeed shut the Pink House down, a lot of gunhands were going to be walking around with a short fuse.

Leave it to Sally to light the fuse.

Buck asked, "What happened to that poor family?"

"Sally give 'um a big poke of food and money enough to buy clothes and a wagon and horses. You knew she was rich, didn't you?"

"Sally? Rich?"

"Folks is. Her daddy owns a lot of factories and such back east. Her momma has money too. Stratton and Potter and Richards just might have grabbed ahold of a puma's tail this time. I hear Wiley Potter was all upset about what Stratton done today. He sent word to Sally to go on back to her little house and forget what happened. Sally told him, through Miss Flora, that she would forget only when pigs fly."

Deputy Rogers walked up, a grim look on his face. "Buck West! You go see Mr. Richards over to the office. And you, Sam, is fired. Them words come from Mr. Stratton. He's done found out about you helpin' them dirt farmers over in the flats. Git your gear and be out of town by sundown." He looked at Buck. "Move, West!"

Buck silently stared the big deputy down. With a curse, Rogers wheeled around and stalked away.

"What dirt farmers, Sam?"

"It's a big country, Buck. They's room for lots of folks. The Big Three don't object to farmers comin' in, but only if they agree to the terms set up by Potter and Stratton and Richards. If they don't, they git burnt out and run off the land. I don't hold none with the likes of that. A young couple with two little kids moved in last year. Just after I joined up. Started homesteadin'. Richards sent some of his hardcases in. When the man got his back up, Long shot him dead. Becky—that's the widder woman's name—stayed on the place, workin' it herself. I kinda helped along from time to time. I was raised on a farm in Minnesota. Guess they heard about my helpin' out."

Buck looked hard at the man. Could he trust him, or was this a set-up? He decided to play along, test Sam. "You stick around. I'm going to see Richards. When I'm through, we'll take a ride out to the Widow Becky's place. OK?"

"All right, Buck. I'll be at the livery."

Buck walked to the PSR offices. Richards was waiting for him. He pointed to saddlebags on the counter. "No test this time, Buck. The corporation is buying more land. Those bags contain gold dust and the contracts. Man named Gilmore is waiting for you in Challis. Get the papers signed, give him the dust, and get back here."

"Yes, sir."

Buck picked up the saddlebags and walked to the stable. Sam was waiting for him, talking with the little boy Buck had given the gold piece to. Sam grinned at Buck.

"This here is Ben. This stable is his home. His pa was kilt in a cave-in a couple of years ago. He ain't got no ma. He's a good boy. Keeps his mouth shut. And he don't like none of the Big Three. Stratton took a whip to him last year. Marked him up pretty good. Richards kicked him off the boardwalk later on. Bust a rib. He's all right, Buck."

"You go to school, Ben? Buck asked.

"No, sir. Mister Rosten won't let me. Says I gotta work here all the time."

Ben looked to be about nine years old.

Buck nodded. He mentally added Rosten's name to his list of sorry people. "You seen an old Indian around? Wears a derby hat?"

"Hunts-Long. Yes, sir. When he's in town he camps down by the creek yonder." Ben pointed.

"You go tell Hunts-Long I said it's time. Get the word out. He'll know what you mean." Buck gave the boy some coins. Ben took off.

"We can't be seen leaving town together, Sam. Where do you want to meet?"

"Crick just south of town, 'bout four mile. I'll meet you there in a couple of hours."

Buck nodded. "If you playin' a game, Sam, workin' for the other side, you'll never live to see the game finished."

"I believe you, Buck. Or Smoke. No games. I'm done with that. See you at the crick."

Buck watched the cowboy ride out. He wondered if he was going to have to kill him.

13

Buck took his time saddling Drifter. He watched the old Flathead, Hunts-Long, ride out. He was conscious of Little Ben looking at him.

"You know Miss Flora, boy?"

"Yes, sir. Down to the Pink House."

"After I'm gone, you walk down there and tell Miss Sally Reynolds I said to keep her head down. She'll know what I mean. You got that?"

"Yes, sir. Mister Buck? Sam's a nice feller. He ain't no real gunhand. He got backed into it."

"How's that, Ben?"

"Story is—I heard some men talkin'—a deputy over in Montana Territory pushed Sam hard one day. Sam tried to get out of it, but the deputy drew on him. Sam was faster. Kilt the man and had to take the hoot-owl trail." The boy grinned. "Sam's sweet on Miz Becky."

"Sam told me he was from Minnesota."

"Yes, sir. That's what I heard, too. Sam wants to go back to farmin', way I heared it."

"A lot of us would like to be doin' something other than what we're doin', Ben. But a man gets his trail stretched out in front of him, sometimes you just got to ride it to trail's end, whether you like it or not."

"You be careful, Mister Buck."

"See you, boy."

Buck rode out easy. He could feel ... *something* in the air. A feeling of tension, he thought. And he wondered about it. The pot was about to boil over in Bury, and Buck didn't know what had caused the fire to get too hot. But he knew that sometimes just the slightest little push could turn over a cart—if the contents weren't stacked right.

A mile out of town, Buck cut off the road and reined up, hidden in the timber. He waited for half an hour. No riders passed him. He rode out of the timber, heading for the creek.

"Buck, this here is Becky," Sam said. He was trying very hard not to grin, and not being very successful.

Becky's hair was as red as Sam's, her tanned face pretty and freckled across the nose. She was a slender lady, but Buck could sense a solid, no-nonsense quiet sort of strength about her. Two red-headed kids stood close by her. A boy and a girl. About four and six, Buck guessed. They grinned shyly up at Buck. He winked at them and they both giggled.

Buck took the lady's hand and was not surprised to find it hard and callused from years of hard work.

After talking with Becky and the kids for a few moments, Buck took Sam aside. "You stay here with her, Sam. Until I get back from Challis. Don't be surprised if you spot some old mountain men while I'm gone. I'm going to swing by their camp and tell them I'm just about ready to strike. I'll tell them about your lady friend here, too. They'll probably ride by to see if they can get her anything. And they'll be by. They don't hold with men who hurt womenfolks."

"Who are your friends, Buck? These mountain men, I mean?"

Sam stood open-mouthed as Buck reeled off the

names of some of the most famous mountain men of all time. Sam finally blinked and said, "Those are some of the meanest old codgers that ever forked a bronc."

"Yeah," Buck said with a grin as he swung into the saddle. "Ain't they?"

He waved good-bye to Becky and the kids and pointed Drifter's nose south. A mile from Becky's cabin, Buck turned straight east, toward the new camp of Preacher and his friends. Even Buck, knowing what to expect, drew up short at the sight that soon confronted him.

Greybull and Beartooth were wrestling. Dupre was fiddling a French song while Nighthawk and Tenneysee were dancing. Together. Audie was standing on a stump, reciting pretty poetry to the others.

"I hate to break this up," Buck said.

"Then don't!" Preacher said. "Jist sit your cayuse and listen and learn. Go ahead, Audie. Tell us some more about that there Newton."

"*Isaac* Newton, you ignorant reprobate! I was merely stating Sir Newton's theory that to every action there is always opposed an equal reaction: or, the mutual actions of two bodies upon each other are always equal, and directed to contrary parts."

"Then direct it to him," Buck said, pointing at Preacher. "'Cause he sure is contrary."

Audie looked pained while the others laughed. He glowered at Buck. "If I had you in a classroom I'd take a hickory stick to the seat of your pants, young man."

"I don't know nothing about Newton," Buck said, still sitting on Drifter. "But I did like that poetry. Can you say some more of that?"

"But of course, young outlaw called Smoke," Audie said with a wave of his hand. "Dismount and gather around."

Dupre had stopped his fiddling, Nighthawk and Tenneysee their dancing, Greybull and Beartooth their wrestling.

"'I came to the place of my youth'", Audie said, "'and

cried, The friends of my youth, where are they? And echo answered, Where are they?'"

"That don't make no damn sense," Phew said.

"And it don't even rhyme," Deadlead growled.

"It doesn't have to rhyme to be poetry!" Audie said. "I have told you heathens that time and again."

"Say something that's purty," Preacher said.

"Yeah, that fits us'ns," Powder Pete said.

"What a monumental task you have verbally laid before me," Audie said. "Very well. Let me think for a moment."

"And I don't reckon it has to rhyme," Matt said.

Audie smiled. He said, "'And in that town a dog was found. As many dogs there be, both mongrel, puppy, whelp, and hound, And curs of low degree. The dog, to gain some private ends, Went mad, and bit the man. The man recovered of the bite, The dog it was that died.'"

Still smiling, Audie stepped off the stump and walked off, leaving the old mountain men to scratch their heads and ponder what he'd just said.

"Is he callin' us a bunch of *dogs?*" Lobo asked.

"I don't think so," Preacher said.

Deadlead looked at Nighthawk. "What do you think about it, Nighthawk?"

"Ummm."

Buck's ride to Challis was uneventful. He found the man named Gilmore, completed his business, and headed back. When he rode into Bury, past Miss Flora's Pink House, he noticed the front door was closed, a hand-lettered sign hanging from a string. *Closed,* the sign read. Smiling, Buck rode to the PSR office and handed the receipt to MacGregor. The Scotsman had a worried look on his now-more-than-ever dour face.

"What's wrong?" Buck asked.

"New territorial governor was just named. It wasn't Potter. He's fit to be tied."

"You knew it wouldn't be all along, didn't you?"

"I had a rather strong suspicion."

"Now what?"

"I don't know. I haven't got enough evidence to bring any of the Big Three to court and make it stick. The Big Three violate a number of *moral* laws. But they run their own businesses on the up and up—so far as I've been able to find out. They have committed murder—either themselves or by hiring it out—but since this town, and all the people in it, belong to the Big Three, no one will talk. But there is a sour, rancid feeling hanging in the air, Buck, Smoke—what *is* your real name?"

"Kirby."

MacGregor nodded absently. "I gather those mountain men in the timber are friends of yours?"

"Preacher helped raise me. I know most of the others." He named them.

MacGregor chuckled. "Old bastards!" he said, with no malice in the profanity. "Did you know Audie is the holder of several degrees?"

"Yes. How did you know about that?"

"Oh, ever since I came out here, fifteen years ago, I have maintained a journal of sorts. I should like to take all those pages and turn them into a book someday. A book about mountain men. I've talked with many of them. But my God, they *lie* so much. I can't tell what is truth and what is fiction."

"I've discovered that most of what they say is true."

"Really now, Smoke! A human being cannot successfully fight a grizzly bear and win!"

"Negro Matt fought a mountain lion with his bare hands and killed it. Preacher fought a bear up on the North Milk in Canada and killed it. Jedediah Smith fought a grizzly and killed it—by himself. Bear chewed off one of his ears, though. Shoo Fly Miller had a grizzly bear for a pet. Those old boys are still about half hoss, half alligator."

"My word!" MacGregor said.

"Stick around, Mac," Buck said cheerfully. "If you live through what's coming up shortly, you can write the final chapter to the lives of the mountain men."

It was going sour, Buck thought, walking from the PSR offices back to his hotel. He could sense it; an almost tangible sensation. The gunhands that were constantly in view were behaving in a surly manner. Cursing more and drinking more openly. Buck noticed a distinct lack of kids playing on the boardwalks and streets. He noticed a couple of loaded-down wagons parked in front of the general store.

Buck stopped in front of a saloon and asked the scar-faced Joiner, "What's going on?"

"Two schoolteachers and their families pullin' out. Didn't like the way Miz Sally was treated. The boss is some sore, let me tell you."

Buck smiled.

Joiner looked sourly at him. "You find something funny about that, West?"

"Just that a man can't push some women, is all."

Joiner grunted. It was obvious to Buck that he was looking for a fight. And Buck wasn't.

When Joiner saw that Buck wasn't going to fight, he said, "There can't be much sand to your bottom, boy."

Buck met him eye to eye. "If you want to get a shovel and start digging for that sand, Joiner, feel free to do so. But I'd suggest you make one stopover first for a little digging."

"Oh? And where's that?"

"Boot Hill." Buck turned and walked on up the street. As he turned, his right side blocked to Joiner's view, Buck slipped the hammer thong off his .44.

He could feel Joiner's eyes boring into his back as he walked.

"Buck West!" Joiner shouted. "Turn and fight, you tin-horn!"

Buck heard Joiner's hand as his palm struck the wooden grips of his pistol.

Turning, Buck drew, cocked, and fired, all in one fluid motion. Joiner's pistol clattered to the wooden boardwalk as the .44 slug from Buck's gun hit him squarely in the center of the chest. Joiner staggered backward, grabbed at a wooden chair for support, missed the arm of the chair, and sat down heavily on the boardwalk, one hand supporting himself, holding himself up, the other hand covering the hole in his chest.

"You bassard!" Joiner hissed at Buck.

"You pushed me, Joiner," Buck reminded the man.

Joiner groaned and let himself slump to the boards.

Burton ran out of the apothecary shop, crossed the street, and knelt by the dying Joiner. When he looked up at Buck, his face was flushed with hate. "If you're so damned good with a gun, why didn't you just shoot the gun out of his hand? You didn't have to kill him."

"I ain't dead!" Joiner protested weakly.

"You ain't far from it," Burton told him.

"Get me a preacher!" Joiner said.

"He'd probably do you more good than a doctor," Burton agreed.

Buck punched out the spent brass and slid a live round into the chamber. He dropped the empty brass to the dirt of the street just as the sounds of a carriage approaching rattled through the air. The carriage *whoaed* up beside the blood-slicked boardwalk and the tall gunhand standing impassively over the dying Joiner.

"Oh, my word!" the woman seated in the carriage said.

"Help me, Miz Janey!" Joiner cried.

A group of Cornish miners, in town from their work at a nearby silver mine, gathered around, beer mugs in callused hands.

"The bloke's nearly done," one immigrant from Cornwall observed. "Shall we sing him a fare-thee-well, mates?"

"Aye. Let's."

A half-dozen voices were raised in song, drunkenly offering up a hymn.

A jig dancer from the hurly-gurly in front of which Joiner lay dying stepped out. "Can I have your pockets, love?" she asked Joiner.

"Get away with you!" Reverend Necker said, running up. "You filthy whore!"

"Careful, Bible-thumper," the jig dancer said. "Or I'll tell everybody where you was the other evenin'."

Necker flushed and bent down over the dying Joiner.

"He kilt me!" Joiner said, pointing a trembling finger at Buck.

"Damn sure did," Necker said.

Buck raised his eyes to look squarely at the woman seated in the fancy carriage.

Janey met the tall young man's direct stare.

The elegantly dressed woman flushed as Buck's eyes stared directly at her.

"Save me, Preacher!" Joiner groaned. "I don't wanna go to Hell. I got a family to take care of."

"Where are they, son?" Necker asked. He looked at the blood on his hands. Joiner's blood. "Yukk!" Necker said.

"Damned if I know," Joiner said. Then he closed his eyes and did the world the greatest favor men of his ilk could do. He died.

Janey stared at Buck. Her eyes widened as Buck smiled. She watched as Buck turned and walked away.

It couldn't be! she thought. That was impossible. Kirby was back in Missouri, probably working that damned hardscrabble farm.

But she knew the man who had killed Joiner. She knew him. It was her brother.

14

Janey stood in her bedroom, absently gazing out the window. So Buck West was really Kirby Jensen, aka Smoke. She laughed, but the laugh was totally void of mirth. She suddenly remembered all the good times they'd shared as children, back in Missouri. It had been a hard life, but despite that, there had been plenty of love to go around. Never enough money for nice things, but none of them had gone hungry.

"Crap!" Janey said, turning away from the window. She didn't know what to do. The gunfighter was blood kin, but Janey felt no warmth toward him. She looked around her. Damned if she was going to give all this up for a man she hadn't seen since he was a snot-nosed kid tryin' to farm forty rocky acres with a damned ol' mule.

She walked downstairs, searching for Josh.

"Gone, ma'am," the Negro houseman informed her.

"Gone, where?"

"Up to the north range to inspect the herds, ma'am. Won't be back for several days."

"Bull-droppings!" Janey blurted.

The houseman's eyes widened.

"Thank you, Thomas," Janey said. "That will be all."

Now she sure didn't know what to do.

* * *

MacGregor ceased his pacing, his mind made up. He would not leave Bury, as had been his original plan. He would stick it out here. If Buck West, aka Smoke Jensen, was successful in his plan, what a book that would make! And, the Scotsman smiled grimly, he could close the federal pages on Potter, Stratton, and Richards.

"He's really the outlaw Smoke?" Flora asked Sally.

"He's Smoke Jensen, but he's no outlaw," Sally told the gathering of joy-girls.

"We can't get out of town, Miss Sally," Rosa said. "The little boy, Ben, says Potter and Stratton gave orders to that nasty Rosten not to rent us wagons or horses. We're stuck."

Sally nodded. As Josh Richards had once explained to her, the Pink House was one of the best constructed buildings in town. The two-story structure was built of logs, with excellent craftsmanship in the construction, with carefully fitted corners. Instead of a mixture of clay and moss filling the chinks, solid mortar had been used. With a little rearranging of furniture, the house could easily withstand any stray bullets.

"All right, ladies," Sally said. "Here's what we'll do . . ."

"What's happening!" Deputy Rogers said. "I don't understand none of it. It's like . . . it's like ever'thang was just fine one day, and the next day it's all haywire!"

Sheriff Dan Reese knew what was happening, but he didn't feel like explaining it to this big dummy standing before him. He'd seen boom towns go sour before. And he knew that sometimes a feller could skin the clabber off the top and salvage the milk. Not often, but sometimes.

But he had a sinking feeling it was too damn late for Bury.

"Shut up, Rogers," he said. He looked at his other

deputies, Weathers and Payton. "You men check them
shotguns and rifles. Git over to the store and stock up on
shells. I don't know why, but something tells me everything that's happenin' is the fault of that Buck West.
Damn his eyes!"

"So we is gonna do what?" Payton asked. Like Rogers,
Payton was no mental giant.

"I think the bosses is gonna tell us to kill him."

Potter turned from the second-floor window of the
PSR offices to look at Stratton. "You feel it?" he asked.

"Yes," Stratton said with a sigh. "Whatever *it* is."

"I had the territorial governorship in the palm of my
hand," Potter said. "And suddenly, for no reason, I lose it.
Why? A seemingly intelligent, reasonable young woman, a
very capable school teacher, suddenly falls for a gunslick.
Why? And now I discover that Buck West—or whatever his
name is—is buddy-buddy with Sam, and Sam is sharing the
blankets with a squatter. What's happening around here?"

"Don't forget the mountain men gathering up in the
deep timber."

"That's right."

The two men looked at each other and suddenly their
brains began to click and hum in unison.

"Mountain men helped raise Kirby Jensen," Stratton
said.

"We've all heard the rumors that Preacher wasn't killed,"
Potter said.

"All our troubles started when Buck West arrived in
town."

The men sent a flunky for Sheriff Dan Reese.

"Anybody have any idea whatever happened to old
Maurice Leduc?" Deadlead asked.

The mountain men were camped openly and brazenly
about two miles outside of Bury. They knew their reputation had preceded them, and they likewise knew that none

of the Big Three's gunhands were about to attack the camp. For one thing, they held the vantage point—the crest of a low hill. For another, no twenty-five cowboys-turned-gunhands were about to attack a dozen old hardbitten mountain men; especially not the most notorious bunch of mountain men to ever prowl the high lonesome. No matter that none of the mountain men would ever see seventy years of age again. That had nothing to do with it. Even at seventy, most of them could still outshoot and outfight men half their age.

Lobo said, "Last I heard, ol' Leduc come back up to near Bent's fort and built hisself a cabin; him and a teenage Mex gal. Took up gardenin'." That was said very contemptuously.

"Hale's far!" Powder Pete said. "That was back in '58."

"Wal, what year is this here we're in?" Dupre asked.

"Oh . . . about '75, I reckon," Tenneysee said.

"You don't say," Greybull said. "My, time does git away from a man, don't it?"

"If that is the case," Audie said. "And I will admit that I don't even know what year it is, not really, I was born seventy-one years ago."

"And got uglier every year," Preacher said.

"You should talk. You're so ugly you could pose for totem poles."

"I 'member the furst time I seen one of the things," Phew said. "Up in Washington Territory. Like to have plumb scared me out of my 'skins."

"That'd probably been a good thing for all concerned," Matt said. "Least you'd a took a bath then. You ain't been out of them skins in fifty year."

"I wish Smoke would git things a-smokin' down yonder," Beartooth said. "I'm a-cravin' a mite of action."

"He'll start stirrin' it up in a day or three," Preacher opined. "And then we'll all have all the action we can handle. Bet on it."

"Reckon whut he's a-doin' down there?" Lobo asked.

"Probably tryin' to spark that schoolmarm," Preacher said. "He's shore stuck on her."

"What do you mean, I can't come in?" Buck said, standing on the front porch of the Pink House.

"Buck," Sally's voice came through the closed door. "You'd better get out of town. Little Ben just slipped up to the back door and told us Sheriff Reese and his deputies are looking for you. Word just drifted into town that you're Smoke Jensen."

So the cat was out of the bag. Fine. He was getting tired of being Buck West. "You . . . ladies have plenty of food and water?"

"Enough for a month-long siege. Go on, Buck."

"Call me Smoke."

15

Smoke slipped around the side of the Pink House and into the weed-grown alley in the rear. He carefully picked his way toward the rear of the stable. He felt sure the front of the stable would be watched.

For the first time since he had arrived in Bury, the town was silent. No wagons rattled up and down the streets. No riders moving in and out of town. No foot traffic to be seen in Bury. A tiny dust devil spun madly up the main street, picking up bits of paper as it whirled away.

Smoke slipped from outhouse to outhouse, both hammer thongs off his .44s.

Reese and his deputies apparently believed Smoke would not take to the alleys, but instead stroll right down the center of the main street, spurs jingling, like some tinhorn kid who fancied himself a gunhand. But Smoke had been properly schooled by Preacher, whose philosophy was thus: if you're outnumbered, circle around 'hind 'em and ambush the hell out of 'em. Ain't no such thang as a fair fight, boy. Just a winner and a loser.

Smoke didn't want to open the dance just yet. He was in a very bad position, being on foot and armed with only his short guns.

And he was still about a block and a half from the

stable. His eyes picked up the shape of a small boy, frantically and silently waving his arms. Little Ben. Smoke returned the wave. Ben disappeared into the stable and returned seconds later, leading a saddled and ride-ready Drifter. Smoke grinned. Drifter must have taken a liking to Little Ben, for had he not, the stallion would have stomped the boy to death.

"Jensen!" The harshly spoken word came from his right, from the shadows of an alley.

Out of the corner of his eye, Smoke could see the young man had not drawn his pistol. The cowboy was a PSR rider, but Smoke did not know his name.

Smoke slowly turned, facing the young rider. "Back away, cowboy," Smoke stated softly. "Just walk back up the alley and no one will ever have to know. If you draw on me, I'll kill you. Turn around and you'll live. How about it?"

"That thirty thousand dollars looks almighty good to me, Jensen," the puncher replied, his hands hovering over his low-tied guns. "Start me up a spread with that."

"You'll never live to work it," Smoke warned him.

Ben was slowly leading Drifter up the alley.

"Says you!" the cowboy sneered.

"What's your name, puncher?"

"Jeff Siddons. Why?"

"So I'll know what to put on your grave marker."

Jeff flushed. "You gonna draw or talk?"

"I'd rather not draw at all," Smoke again tried to ease out of the fight.

"You yellow scum!" Jeff said. "Draw!" His hands dipped downward.

Jeff's hands had just touched the wooden handles of his guns when he felt a terrible crushing double blow to his chest. The young cowboy staggered backward, falling heavily against the side of the building. Smoke was already turning away from the dying cowboy as light faded in Jeff's eyes. "Ain't no human man that fast!" Jeff spoke his last words, sitting in his own dusty blood.

Smoke looked back at the dying cowboy. "Just remember to tell Saint Peter this wasn't my idea."

But he was talking to a dead man.

He heard the drum of bootheels on the boardwalk, all running in his direction. He turned just as a voice called out, "Hold it, Jensen!"

Smoke ducked in back of the building just as a shot rang out, the bullet knocking a fist-sized chunk of wood out of the building. Smoke dropped to one knee and fired two fast shots around the side of the building, then he was up and running toward Ben and Drifter, ignoring the howl of pain behind him and in the alley. At least one of his snap shots had struck home.

"That damned little stable boy's helpin' Jensen!" a man's voice yelled. "I'll take a horsewhip to that little son of a bitch!"

Smoke reached Ben and Drifter. "Run to Miss Flora's Ben. Them women won't let anything happen to you. Run, boy, run!"

Ben took off as if pursued by the devil. Smoke mounted up. His saddlebags were bulging, so Ben must have transferred a lot of his gear from the packs normally borne by the pack animal. He looked back over his shoulder. Sheriff Reese was leading a running gang of men. And they weren't far behind Smoke.

"Hold up there, Jensen!" Reese yelled, just as Smoke urged Drifter forward and cut into the alley where the dead cowboy lay. Reese lifted a double-barreled coach gun and pulled the trigger. The buckshot tore a huge hole in the corner of the building.

Drifter leaped ahead and charged through the alley, coming out on the main street. Smoke turned his nose north for a block and then whipped into another alley, coming out behind Reese and his men. Smoke had reloaded his Colts and now, with the reins in his teeth, a Colt in each hand, he charged the knot of gunslicks headed by Sheriff Reese.

"I want that thirty thousand!" a man yelled. Smoke recognized the man as Jerry, from back at the trading post.

"Hell with you!" Reese said. "I want that—" He turned at the sound of drumming hooves. "Jesus Christ!" he hollered, looking at the mean-eyed stallion bearing down on him.

The charging stallion struck one gunhand, knocking the man down, the man falling under Drifter's steel-shod hooves. The gunnie screamed, the cry cut off as Drifter's hooves pounded the man's face into pulp.

Reese had jumped out of the way of the huge midnight black horse with the killer-cold yellowish eyes, losing his shotgun as he leaped. One of Drifter's hooves struck the sheriff's thigh, bringing a howl of pain and a hat-sized bruise on the man's leg. Reese rolled on the ground, yelling in pain.

"You squatter-lovin'son!" Jerry screamed at Smoke, bringing up a .45.

Smoke leveled his left-hand .44 and shot the man between the eyes.

As blood splattered, the foot-posse broke up, fear taking over. Men ran in all directions.

Smoke urged Drifter on, galloping up the alley and once more entering the main street. He looped the reins loosely around the saddlehorn and screamed like an angry cougar, the throaty scream, almost identical to a real cougar's warcry, chilling the shopowners who were huddling behind closed doors. Stratton, Potter, and Richards had promised them a safe town and lots of easy money; they hadn't said anything about a wild man riding a horse that looked like it came straight out of the pits of Hell.

Preacher sat straight up on his blankets. He slapped one knee and cackled as the gunshots drifted out of Bury. The shots were followed by the very faint sounds of a big mountain lion screaming.

"Hot damn, boys!" Preacher hollered. "Somebody

finally grabbed holt of Smoke's tail and gave 'er a jerk. Bet by Gawd they'll wish they hadn't a done it."

"He a-havin' all the fun!" Beartooth gummed the words.

"They's plenty to go around," Lobo growled. "When he needs us, he'll holler."

"Ummm," said Nighthawk.

"How eloquently informative," said Audie.

Leaning close to Drifter's neck, presenting a low profile, Smoke charged up the main street. He was not going to shoot up the town, for he did not want to harm any woman or child. He had made up his mind that he was going to give the shopkeepers and the storeowners and their families a chance to pull out. But he was doing that for the sake of the kids only. To hell with the adults; man or woman, they knew who they worked for. One was as bad as the other.

Ten minutes later, Smoke had reined up and dismounted in the camp of the mountain men.

"Howdy, son!" Preacher said. "You been havin' yourself a high old time down there, huh?"

"That's one way of putting it," Smoke said, putting one heavily muscled arm around the old man's wang-leather-tough shoulders.

"You grinnin' like a chicken-eatin' dog, boy," Preacher said. "What you got a-rattlin' 'round in 'at head of yourn?"

Smoke looked at Powder Pete. "You got any dynamite with you?"

"Only time I been without any was when them durned Lakotas caught me up near the Canadian border and wanted to skin me. Since I was somewhat fond of my hide, I were naturally disinclined to part with it."

Smoke laughed aloud, and the laughter felt good. He felt as though he was back home, which, in a sense, he was. "What happened?"

"The chief had a daughter nobody wanted to bed down

with," Powder Pete said, disgust in his voice. "Homeliest woman I ever seen. 'At squaw could cause a whirlwind to change directions. The chief agreed to let me live if'n I'd share Coyote Run's blankets. How come she got that name was when she was born the chief had a pet coyote. Coyote took one look at her and run off. Never did come back. 'At's homely, boy. I spent one winter with Coyote Run, up in the MacDonald Range, on the Flathead. Come spring, I told 'at chief he might as well git his skinnin' knife out, 'cause I couldn't stand no more of Coyote Run. Chief said he didn't know how I'd stood it this long. Told me to take off. I been carryin' dynamite ever since. Promised myself if'n I ever got in another bind lak 'at 'air, I'd blow myself up. Whut you got in mind, Smoke?"

"One road leading into and out of Bury."

Powder Pete and the other mountain men grinned. They knew then what was rattlin' around in Smoke's head.

"If you men will, find the best spots to block the road to coach and carriage travel. Set your charges. I'm going to give those who want to leave twenty-four hours to do so. I want the kids out of that town. I'd prefer the women to leave as well, but from what I've been able to see and hear, most of the women are just as low-down as their men."

"Simmons's old woman is," Dupre said. "I knowed her afore. Plumb trash."

"I still want to give them a chance to leave," Smoke said. "And I especially want Sally and the women in the Pink House out, along with MacGregor and Little Ben. The rest of the townspeople can go to hell."

Deadlead and Greybull picked up their rifles. Deadlead said, "Us'n and Matt and Tenneysee will block the horse trails out of town. Rest of ya'll git busy."

"Preacher," Powder Pete said, "you take the fur end of town. I'll scout this end. I'll hook up with you in a couple hours and plant the charges."

"Done." Preacher moved out.

"I shall make the announcement to the good citizens

of Bury," Audie said. "My articulation is superb and my voice carries quite well."

"Yeah," Phew said. "Like a damned ol' puma with his tail hung up in a b'ar trap. Grates on my nerves when you git to hollerin'."

Audie ignored him. "Considering the mentality of those who inhabit that miserable village, I must keep this as simple as possible. Therefore, the Socratean maieutic method of close and logical reasoning must be immediately discarded."

"Umm," Nighthawk said.

"Whut the hell did you say?" Lobo growled. "Sounded like a drunk Pawnee. Gawdamnit, you dwarf, cain't you speak plain jist once in a while?"

"Rest your gray cells, you hulking oaf," Audie responded. "I'm thinking."

"Wal, thank to yoursalf, you magpie!"

"Silence, you cretin!"

Smoke let them hurl taunts and insults back and forth; they had been doing it for fifty-odd years and were not about to quit at this stage of the game. He turned to face the direction of Bury.

He would give them more of a chance than they had given his brother or father. Ever so much more of a chance than they had given his baby son and his wife, Nicole. Ever so much more.

He let hate consume him as he recalled that awful day. . . .

He had made a wide circle of the cabin, staying in the timber back of the creek, and slipped up to the cabin. Inside the cabin, although Smoke did not as yet know it, the outlaw Canning had taken a blanket and smothered Baby Arthur to death. Nicole had been brutally raped, and then her throat had been crushed. Canning scalped the woman, tying her bloody hair to his belt. He then skinned a breast, thinking he would tan the hide and make himself a nice tobacco pouch.

Kid Austin had gotten sick watching Canning's callousness. He walked outside to vomit.

Another outlaw, Grissom, walked out the front of the cabin. Grissom felt something was wrong. He sensed movement behind him and reached for his gun. Smoke shot him dead.

"Behind the house!" Felter yelled.

Another of the PSR riders had been dumping his bowels in the outhouse. He struggled to pull up his pants and push open the door at the same time. Smoke shot him twice in the belly and left him to die on the craphouse floor.

Kid Austin, caught in the open, ran for the banks of the creek. Just as he jumped, Smoke fired, the lead taking the Kid in the buttocks, entering the right cheek and tearing out the left.

Smoke waited behind a woodpile, the big Sharps buffalo rifle Preacher had given him in his hands. He watched as something came sailing out the open back door. His dead baby son bounced on the earth.

The outlaws inside the cabin taunted Smoke, telling in great detail of raping Nicole. Smoke lined up the Sharps and pulled the trigger. A PSR rider began screaming in pain.

Canning and Felter ran out of the front of the cabin, hightailing it for the safety of the timber. In the creek, Kid Austin crawled upstream, crying in pain and humiliation.

Another of the PSR riders exited the cabin, leaving one inside. He got careless and Smoke took him alive.

When he came to his senses, Smoke had stripped him, staked him out over an anthill, and poured honey all over him.

It took him a long time to die.

Smoke buried his wife and son amid a colorful profusion of wild flowers, stopping often to wipe away the tears.

16

"What are you thinking, young man?" Audie asked.

"About what Potter and Stratton and Richards ordered done to my wife and son."

"Preacher told us. That was a terrible, terrible thing. But don't allow revenge to destroy you."

"When this is over, Audie, it's over. Not until."

"I understand. I have been where you are. I lost my wife, a Bannock woman, and two children to white trappers. Many many years ago."

"Did you find the men who did it?"

"Oh, yes," Audie smiled grimly. "I found them."

Smoke did not have to ask the outcome.

"There will always be men who rise to power on the blood and pain of others, Smoke," the former-school-teacher-turned-mountain-man said. "Unfortunate, certainly, but a fact, perhaps a way, of life."

"The people who run the shops in that town can leave," Smoke said. "Even though I know they are, in their own way, as bad as Potter, Stratton, and Richards. I'll let them go, if they'll just go."

"They won't," Audie prophesied. "For most of them, this is the end of the trail. Behind them lies their past, filled with crime and pettiness. For most of them, all that waits behind them is prison—or a rope. Theirs is a mean, miserable existence." He waved his hand at the mountain men. "We, all us, remember when that town was built. We sat back and watched those dreary dregs of society arrive. We have all watched good people travel through, look around them, and continue on their journey. I, for one, will be glad to see that village razed and returned to the earth."

Audie walked away. About three and a half feet tall physically, about six and a half feet of man and mind and courage.

Smoke sat back on his bootheels and wondered what razed meant.

He'd have to remember to ask Sally. She'd know. And with that thought, another problem presented itself to Smoke's mind. Sally. He knew he cared a lot for the woman—more than he was willing to admit—but what did he have to offer someone like her? When news of what he planned to do to Bury reached the outside, Smoke Jensen would be the most wanted man in the west. Not necessarily in terms of reward money, for if he had his way, Potter, Stratton, and Richards would be dead and in the ground, but more in terms of reputation. A hundred, five hundred, a thousand gunhawks would be looking for him to make a reputation.

Back to the valley where Nicole and Baby Arthur were buried?

No. No, for even if Sally was willing to come with him, he couldn't go back there. Too many old memories would be in the way. He would return to the valley for his mares; he wanted to do that. Then push on and get the Appaloosa, Seven.

Then . . . ?

He didn't know. He would like to ranch and raise horses. And farm. Farming was in his blood and he had always loved the land. A combination horse and cattle ranch and farm? Why not? That was very rare in the west—almost unheard of—but why not?

Would Sally be content with that? A woman of class and education and independence and wealth? Well, he'd never know until he asked her. But that would have to wait. He'd ask her later. If he lived, that is.

Deputy Rogers was the first to report back to Potter and Stratton and Sheriff Reese. Josh Richards was still out in the field; he knew nothing of the true identity of Buck West. Not yet.

"North road's blocked 'bout three miles out of town," Rogers reported. "An' I mean blown all to hell. Brought a landslide down four-five hundred feet long."

Deputy Payton galloped up and dismounted. "South road's blocked by a landslide. A bad one. Ain't nothing gonna get through there for a long time. They's riflemen stuck up all around the town, watchin' the trails. Old mountain men, looks like."

"I should have put it all together," Stratton said with a sigh. "I should have known when that damn Jensen came ridin' in, bold as brass. Should have known that's who it was."

"What are we going to do, Keith?" Wiley Potter asked.

"Wait and find out what Jensen wants. Hell, what else can we do?"

Audie had made himself a megaphone out of carefully peeled bark. He had stationed himself on a ridge overlooking the town of Bury.

"Attention below!" Audie called. "Residents of Bury, Idaho Territory, gather in the street and curb your tongues."

"Do what with a tongue?" Deputy Rogers asked.

"Don't talk," Stratton said.

"Oh."

"Armageddon is nigh," Audie called. "Your penurious and evil practices must cease. *Will* cease—immediately. The women and the children will be allowed to leave.

You have twenty-four hours to vacate and walk out with what meager possessions you can carry on your backs. Follow the flats south to Blue Meadows. Where you go from there is your own concern. Twenty-four hours. After that, the town of Bury will be destroyed."

"What's that about arms?" Dan Reese asked.

"Armageddon," Reverend Necker said. "Where the final battle will be fought between good and evil." He looked around him. "Has anybody got a jug? I need a drink."

"I ain't gonna hoof my tootsies nowhere," Louise Rosten said. "They's wild savages out there."

"Just head straight across the flats toward the east," her husband told her. "They's a settlement 'bout thirty miles over yonder. Pack up the kids and git gone. Hell, you can outshoot me."

"Hunts-Long and his Flatheads will escort the women and children to safety," Audie's voice once more rang out over the town. "They'll be waiting on the east side of the creek. You have twenty-four hours. This will be my last warning to you."

"I ain't travelin' with no damned greasy Injuns!" Veronica Morgan said. "I ain't leavin' the hotel."

Her husband looked at her. "Get those snot-nosed brats of yours and get out. I'm tired of looking at your ugly face and listening to those brats squall."

Veronica spat in her husband's face and wheeled about, stalking back to the hotel.

"Potter! Stratton! Richards!" Smoke's voice boomed through the bark-made megaphone. "This is Smoke Jensen. I'm giving you a better chance than you gave my pa, my brother, and my wife and son."

None of the town's residents had to ask what Smoke was talking about. They all, to a person, knew. They knew the town was built on stolen gold and Jensen blood. They all knew the whole bloody, tragic story. And they had consented to live with that knowledge.

Stratton's heavy jowls quivered with rage and fear. He

turned his little piggy eyes to Potter. "Now what?" he demanded.

"Just stay calm and keep your senses about you, man," Potter said. "Look at facts. We've a hundred and fifty men in this town. Thirty of them are hardcases drawing fighting pay. Josh is out there," he waved his hand, "with fifteen or twenty other gunhands. We're up against a handful of old men and one smart-aleck gunhawk who is too sure of himself. We've both known Hunts-Long for years. He's a peaceful, trusting Indian and so is his tribe. Send the women and kids out and we'll make ready for a siege. The stage is due in three days. We'll have someone there to meet it, turn it around, and get the Army in here from the fort. Then we'll hang Smoke Jensen and his damned old mountain men and be done with it once and for all."

Stratton and the others visibly relaxed. Sure, they thought. That was a damn good plan. Some of them began to laugh at how easy it would be. Soon all those gathered in the street were laughing and slapping one another on the back. The women were cackling and the men hoo-hawing.

"Sounds lak they havin' a celebration down thar," Lobo said. "Wush they'd let us in on it."

"They're thinking about the stage," Smoke said. "If they could turn it around with a message, they could get the Army in here and chase us all the way to Canada."

"Les' we had someone down thar to meet it with a story," Phew said.

Smoke smiled at that. "That's what we'll do, then."

"Now what?" Dupre said.

"We give them twenty-four hours, just like I promised."

"I can't help but feel sorry for the kids," Smoke said.

"There isn't a child down there under ten or eleven years of age," Audie observed, watching through binoculars.

"They are past their formative years; or very close to it. They are just smaller versions of their parents."

The sun had been up for an hour and the women and children of Bury were moving out. On foot. Had Smoke and the mountain men been able to hear the comments of the men, it would have left no doubt in any of their minds.

"I shore am glad to see that bitchin' woman clear out," Hallen said. "Hope I never see her again."

Morgan watched his wife—common law, since each of them was still married, to someone else—and her brats walk out of town. "I hope they're attacked by Indians," was his comment.

Simmons watched his wife trudge up the road. "Old lard-butted thing," he said, under his breath. "God, I hope I never see her again."

Like comments were being shared by all the men as they watched the women and kids move out.

Linda Potter and Lucille Stratton had elected to remain with their men. True to the end. Or 'til the money ran out—whichever came first.

Hunts-Long and his Flatheads were waiting by the creek. They had orders from Preacher to escort the women to the flats and keep them there until the matter was settled in Bury—one way or the other.

"You can't know that for certain," Smoke said, looking at Audie, who had lowered his binoculars from the stream of humanity.

"With very little exception, my young friend. It doesn't hold true always, but water will seek its own level."

"We're gonna have to keep a sharp lookout for Richards's men, boy," Preacher said. "Them fifteen-eighteen riders he's got is all gunhands. Now you listen to me, boy," Preacher spun Smoke around to face him. "Them gold and silver mines that belong to them Big Three assayed out high. One mine, they got the gold assayed out at more than one hundred thousand dollars a ton. You know anything about gold, boy?"

Smoke shook his head.

"Two hundred dollars a ton is a workable mine, Smoke. So them boys ain't gonna just sit back and let you and us'ns destroy a fortune for 'em. We gonna have to be ready for nearabouts anything."

"I done warned them far'ners at the mines to stand clear of Bury," Matt said. "They took it to heart."

"How about the other miners?"

"Some of the miners here now was at the mining camp on the Uncompahgre," Preacher said. "The bettin' is high and fast."

"Who is the favorite?"

"Hell, boy," Preacher grinned. "Us'ns!"

17

According to the calendar, it was still the middle of spring in the mining country of East–Central Idaho. Someone should have told Mr. Summer that. By noon of the day of the pull-out, the temperature had soared and the sun was blisteringly hot. Bury, located in a valley, lay sullen and breezeless, the pocket in which it lay blocking the winds.

And the tempers of those trapped in the town were beginning to rival the thermometer.

One of Richards's men had discovered the blocked road and had hightailed back to the PSR ranch, informing Josh. Janey had just informed him as to Buck's real name. Josh Richards stood in the lushly appointed drawing room of the mansion and stared out at all the PSR holdings. Slowly, very slowly, a smile began playing at the corners of his mouth.

"What do you find so amusing, Josh?" Janey asked, watching the man.

"I will soon be the richest man in all of Idaho Territory," Josh replied. He carefully lit a cigar and inhaled slowly.

"I don't follow you."

"Think about it, Janey. We—you and I—are in the best

possible position. Your brother is going to take some losses at Bury. He might even get himself killed. We can hope for that, at least." She shrugged. Whatever happened to Kirby didn't concern her at all. "All we have to do is pull the PSR men off the range, leaving only a skeleton crew with the herds, and station them around the house in armed circles. Let Smoke and his mountain men kill off as many as they can in Bury. For sure, Smoke will kill Stratton and Potter—that's what he came here to do. By the time the siege is over at Bury, Smoke's little army will be shot up and weakened; no way they could successfully attack this place. When they start to pull out, that's when I take my men and wipe them out." He grinned hugely. "Simple."

"So you're tossing Wiley and Keith to the wolves," she said matter-of-factly.

"Sure," he replied cheerfully. "Do you care?"

"Hell, no!" the woman said. "And there's something else, too."

"Oh?"

"You know the Army and the marshals will be in here investigating after it's over."

"Yeah. Sure. What about it?"

"Well, you just tell them some crap about Potter and Stratton. Tell them you found out about some illegal dealings they were involved in; you broke away from them. Tell the investigators you didn't want any part of anything illegal. You can even tell them you and your men joined up with Smoke and the mountain men in the assault on Bury. But," she said, holding up a warning finger, "that means that *everybody* has to die."

"You're a cold-blooded wench, Janey," he said with a great deal of pride and admiration.

"Just like you, love."

"Oh, I like it. I *like* it!" Josh began to pace the floor. He began to think aloud, talking as he paced. "I've got the best of the gunhands out here. Most of these men have been with me for years. They're loyal to me, and to me alone.

They'll stand firm. I'll put all the newer men out on the range, looking after the cattle. Put the range-cook out there with them with ten days-two weeks of supplies and tell the boys to stay put." He grinned again, looking at Janey Jensen. "Love, we are going to *rule* Idaho Territory."

"I always wanted to be a queen," Janey said.

Josh and Janey began laughing.

To put a lid on the growing tempers in Bury, Stratton and Potter ordered free drinks at the town's many saloons and hurdy-gurdy houses. Then one drunk cowboy suggested they kick in the doors to the Pink House and have their way with the women barricaded inside.

About fifty men, in various stages of inebriation, marched up the main street and gathered in front of the Pink House. They began hooting and hollering and making all sorts of demands to the ladies. The hooting abruptly dipped into silence when the ladies inside shoved shotguns out through the barricaded windows. The sounds of hammers being jacked back was loud in the hot, still air.

The men took one look at a dozen double-barreled express guns pointing at them and calmed down.

"We are *closed*!" Miss Flora's voice came to the crowd. "You gentlemen have ten seconds to haul your ashes out of here. Aim at their privates, girls!"

A dozen shotguns were lowered, the muzzles aimed crotch-high.

The suddenly-sobered crowd hauled their ashes. Promptly.

Preacher watched it all through field glasses. He chuckled. He could not, of course, hear what was going on, but he could guess. "Them gals done read the scriptures to them ol' boys," he said. "I don't think the ladies is gonna be bothered no more after this."

One trapped PSR so-called gunhand emptied his pistol

at the ridge overlooking the town. He stood in the center of the street and hurled curses at Smoke and the mountain men. Preacher reached for his Spencer and sighted the gunslick in. He emptied the tube, plowing up the ground around the man's boots. The cowboy shrieked in terror and dropped his pistol, running and falling and crawling for cover. He took refuge in the nearest saloon.

"We havin' fun now, Smoke," Preacher said, reloading. "But it's gonna turn ugly right soon."

"I know."

"You havin' second thoughts 'bout this, boy?"

"Not really. But if those men down there, with the exception of Potter and Stratton, wanted to leave, I wouldn't try to stop them."

"I's a-hopin' you'd say that. Audie! Bring Smoke that there funny-lookin' thang you built."

Smoke took the megaphone and moved down the ridge, being careful not to expose himself. He lifted the megaphone to his lips.

"You men of Bury!" Smoke called. "Listen to me. It's Potter and Stratton and Richards I'm after. Not you. You don't owe them any loyalty. Any of you who wants to toss down his weapons and walk out can do so."

There was no reply of any kind from the town.

Smoke called, "I'm giving you people a chance to save your lives. The men you work for murdered my brother. They shot him in the back and left him to die."

"Rebel scum!" a voice called from the town.

Smoke shook his head. "The men you work for killed my pa."

"Big deal!" another voice shouted.

"Real nice folks down there," Audie muttered.

"The men you work for ordered out the men who raped and tortured and killed my wife, and killed my baby son," Smoke spoke through the megaphone.

Laughter from the town drifted up to Smoke and the mountain men. The laughter was ugly and taunting.

"She probably wasn't nothin' but a whore anyways!" a voice shouted.

"I can't believe it," Smoke said, looking at Preacher. "I can't understand those types of people."

"I can," Audie said. "If you were my size, you would know just how cruel many people can be."

"Rider comin'," Tenneysee said.

Sam rode up and dismounted, walking to the edge of the ridge. He waited until Smoke and his friends climbed back up. "Givin' them folks a way out, Smoke?" he asked.

"I tried," Smoke replied.

"They ain't worth no pity," Sam said. "Lord knows I ought to know. I worked for them long enough. I seen them people do things that would chill you to the bone. I ain't never seen a bunch so hard-hearted as them people down there. Lie, steal, cheat, kill—them words don't mean nothing to them people. Simmons at the general store worked his momma to death. And I mean that. Then buried her in an unmarked grave. Cannon at the newspaper is so bad he's barred from the Pink House. Likes to beat women, if you know what I mean. And them ranchers out from town"—he spat on the ground—"hell, they just as bad. They run down and hanged a twelve-year-old boy when they found him leadin' off unbranded stock. He was just tryin' to feed his sick ma. It was pitiful. I seen some sights, but that one made me puke. Don't feel no sorrow for them folks down there, boys. They ain't worth spit."

"Come and get us, gunhawk!" a voice yelled from the town. "We'll give you the same treatment the rest of your family got."

Smoke tossed the homemade megaphone to one side. "I tried," he said. "I tried."

The owners of the three other ranches located near Bury gathered at the home of Josh Richards. The owners had brought their so-called cowboys, many of whom were outlaws and gunfighters. Richards explained the situation at Bury—tactfully and pointedly leaving out that when his partners were dead, he would own it all.

"Well," Marshall of the Crooked Snake spread said, "I can see why we can't rush the town. Them mountain men would pick us off afore we got close enough to do any real damage."

The other two owners, Lansing of the Triangle and Brown of the Double Bar B, nodded their agreement. Lansing looked at Richards and asked, "You got a plan?"

"Not much of one. And my plan is rather self-serving, I'm afraid."

"Self what?" Marshall asked.

"It helps us but doesn't do much for those trapped in Bury," Richards explained.

"Hell with them!" Brown said. "We can always get more shopkeepers to come in."

No one mentioned Stratton or Potter. The men just looked at each other and smiled. Honor among thieves, and all that.

"Let's hear it," Lansing said.

"I don't understand it," Sam said. "Richards has about twenty gunhands out there at the ranch. And by now he's called in Marshall and Lansing and Brown. Together, the four of them could put together forty-fifty men. That many men could put us in a box. I wonder what they're waiting for?"

Audie was thoughtful for a moment. "Perhaps this Richards person is hoping to gain from all this."

Smoke looked at him. "Sure. If Stratton and Potter get dead, Richards has it all."

"The loyalty of those men is overwhelming," Audie said drily.

"I wanted to burn down the town," Smoke admitted.

"And I wanted revenge against those who killed my brother and pa, and who sent those men after me and my family. But as sorry as those people are down there in Bury, I don't want their blood on my hands."

Preacher seemed to breathe a sigh of relief. He knew the young man well, and knew Smoke did not want needless killing on his mind.

"Mayhaps you won't have to kill none of them down there," Preacher said.

"You chewin' 'round on something, Preacher," Beartooth said. "Spit 'er out."

"Well, lets us'ns slip word to Potter and Stratton that Richards is gonna lay out of this here fight. Kinda see what happens after that."

"An' juice it up a mite, too," Tenneysee said with a grin.

"Why, shore!" Preacher returned the grin. "Ain't nothing no better than a good joke." He thought about that for a moment. "At our age, that is."

18

Audie wrote out the first message to be delivered to the citizens of Bury. But it was so filled with big words nobody on the ridge knew what it said.

YOUR SO-CALLED CONFIDANTS HAVE ELECTED NOT TO CROSS THE RUBICON. THEY HAVE NOW SHOWN THEIR TRUE COLORS. THE MOMENT OF TRUTH IS NIGH. TO FIGHT US WOULD BE FOLLY. YOUR TRUE ADVERSARIES ARE YOUR ONE-TIME INTIMATES.

Tenneysee looked at the note and said, "I et Injun corn and sweet corn and flint corn, but I ain't never et no rubycorn. Whut the hell does food have to do with this here matter?"

"Imbecile!" Audie snapped at him. He opened his mouth to explain then closed it, knowing that if he tried to explain about the river it would only confuse matters further.

Audie stood and watched as Smoke laboriously printed another message, pausing often to lick the tip of the pencil stub.

Smoke tied the note to a stick, slipped down the ridge to within throwing distance, and tossed the message onto the main street.

Then Smoke, Sam, and the mountain men sat back and waited for the fun to begin.

* * *

Deputy Rogers had retrieved the stick. Since he couldn't read, he had no idea what was going on. He took the stick to Sheriff Reese. Reese read the message and took off at a run for Stratton and Potter.

"It's a trick!" Stratton said, his fat jowls quivering.

"I don't think so," Potter said. "You know perfectly well that by now all the ranchers know the road is blocked. There isn't a day goes by a dozen or more cowboys don't come into town to raise hell. Janey makes her grand appearance in town every day, weather permitting. No, I think we've been tossed to the lions. God*damn* Richards!"

"What are we gonna do?" Reese asked.

"I don't know. Give me time to think."

"If they try to send someone out of town, let them," Smoke said. Turning to Sam, he said, "And the one person they're going to meet will be you."

"I don't follow you," the puncher said.

"Your being fired was just a sham. A trick to get you on my side and see who I really was. You make them believe you're still working for Richards. Tell whoever they send out that Richards isn't going to interfere with me—he wants me to destroy the town, and everybody in it. Think you can pull that off?"

Sam grinned in the twilight. "You just watch me."

Sam rode out toward the north, reining up several miles from town. The mountain men built campfires to the south, the west, and the east of Bury. They deliberately left the north dark.

"That damned Jensen is so sure of himself he's not even guarding the north road," Reese said. He cursed under his breath.

"We got to be sure," Potter said. "Reese, send one of your men out to the ranch. Or as close to it as he can get. I've been thinking about something else, too." He looked at Reese. "Who gave the orders to fire Sam?"

"Richards said Mr. Stratton did."

"I never gave any such orders! You're sure Richards said it was my idea?" Stratton demanded.

"Well, yes, sir. But maybe he just used your name and forgot to tell you about it?"

"Why would he do that?"

"Because Sam worked for you, kinda."

But the seeds of suspicion had already been planted and were taking root. "Bull!" Stratton said.

"Looks bad, Keith," Potter said. "I'm beginning to think that just maybe Richards may have sent for Smoke."

"Yeah," his partner replied. "That would fit. That no good—" He bit back the profanity.

"Reese, you go snoop around town while your man is riding out. Go."

"Hold up!" Sam called from the darkness.

Deputy Rogers reined up and tried to peer through the gloom. "Sam? That you, Sam?"

"Yeah. Don't let none of them other riders catch you out here. They'll shoot you on sight."

"What other riders?" Rogers pulled in close to Sam.

"Crooked Snake, Triangle, Double Bar B—and any of Mr. Richards's gunhawks."

Rogers sighed. "Then it's true, Sam?"

"It's true." An idea began to form in Sam's head. He thought Smoke would like it. "I'm ridin' between town and the ranch, carryin' messages back and forth."

"Well, heck!" Rogers took off his hat and scratched his head. "I ain't got no messages to give you. Sorry."

"That's all right." You big dummy! Sam thought. "I got one for you to carry to Potter and Richards."

"They figured it out, Sam."

"Figured what out?"

"That you was all the time not fired and really workin' for Richards."

Sam breathed a bit easier. "I figured they would."

"And Mr. Richards sent for that there Smoke Jensen, didn't he?"

"I think so." This was gettin' better and better, Sam thought. But, he reminded himself, don't drop your guard. Rogers was big and stupid, but still a cold-blooded killer and cat quick.

"What's your message for them in town?"

Sam thought hard. "They're comin' in at noon, tomorrow."

"Well, then, I got a message for you. You tell 'em we'll be a-waitin'."

"No, we won't be waiting!" Stratton said.

"Huh?" Rogers was getting confused.

"Damn right!" Potter said.

"How we gonna get past Smoke and them mountain men?" Reese asked.

"Go holler up the hill," Stratton said. "Tell Smoke I wanna talk to him."

"What do you want?" Smoke called out of the high darkness.

"It was Richards that ordered your brother killed!" Potter yelled. "Me and Stratton didn't have nothing to do with it."

Smoke knew the man was lying. Knew it because of the dying confession of a TC hand a few years back. Smoke knew Potter had shot his brother. But since Sam had hightailed it back and told them all what he'd done, Smoke had agreed it was a fine idea. He'd play along.

"All right. I never knew who it was. But you was part of it," Smoke returned the darkness-shrouded shout.

"I won't deny that." Stratton's voice. "Neither of us. But what's done is done. I still have nightmares about it, though. If that makes any difference to you."

"That lyin' poke of buffalo chips!" Preacher said. "Only nightmares he ever has is someone stealin' his money."

"Yeah, I know," Smoke told his mentor. Raising his voice, he called, "What'd you want to talk to me about?"

"Ain't no call for us to be fightin' each other, Jensen. We know that Josh sent for you, probably payin' you good money, but whatever he's payin' you, we'll triple it. How about it? You're a hired gun. What difference does it make who pays you?"

"He's payin' me what's on that dodger. All in gold. You want to triple that, I'll take it in greenbacks or double eagles. Send MacGregor up here with the money. Let all the women leave the Pink House. Send them up here with Mac."

"And you'll do what?"

"I'll stand aside and let you three fight it out among you. Deal?"

"Who is Sam working for?" Potter called.

"Richards. But I know where he is, so I can get word to him."

"All right. It'll take us about an hour to get that much money together. We'll have to open the bank."

"I'll be here. In the meantime, you let those women go free. Deal?"

"It's a deal, Jensen."

"Sally?" Smoke called. "You hearin' all this?"

"Yes!" Sally's voice rose faintly from the edge of town.

"Then get some clothes and blankets together and come up here. You won't be harmed."

"We're on our way. And Mister Potter and Mister Stratton?" she yelled.

"We're right here, Miss Sally."

"We'll all be armed!"

No one could hear Stratton or Potter's muttered response. Probably just as well.

19

"Thank Sam for this," Smoke told Sally, as the women scampered up the hill and over the crest of the ridge. "He come up with this idea."

"Came up with," Sally corrected.

"Yes, ma'am," Smoke said.

"Lord have mercy!" Preacher muttered. "Rest of you boys look out now, 'cause them two gonna git to sparkin' and a-moonin' and a-carryin' on like who'd-a-thunk-it."

"Shut up, Preacher," Smoke told him.

"Most unrespectful young'un I ever hepped raise," Preacher said.

"*Dis*respectful," Sally corrected automatically.

"Lord, give this old man strength," Preacher mumbled, walking away.

About forty minutes after the women arrived, MacGregor called up the hill. "Do you actually expect one aging bookkeeper to behave as a pack animal and carry all this money up this mountain?"

"Comin' down," Smoke called.

"Any trouble?" Smoke asked, facing Mac on the hillside.

"Not a bit. Come on, let's walk." He tossed his suitcase to Sam and split the sacks of money between Smoke and himself. When they were out of normal earshot, Mac said,

"I told Stratton and Potter I was no gunhand. I wanted out. They dismissed me without a second thought. Tell you the truth, I was relieved to get out. What in the world is going on, Mr. Jensen?"

"Let them destroy each other," Smoke said. "I'll clean up what's left."

"Very good thinking, young man. But what if one side or the other discovers your ruse?"

"My what?"

"Your trickery?"

"I'll worry about that if and when it happens."

"I think I would not like you for an enemy, young man," Mac said.

"When this is over, Mac, you'll probably never see me again. I intend to drop out of sight, change my name, hopefully get married, and settle down."

"I wish you luck, Kirby Jensen."

"Thank you, Mr. MacGregor."

With much good-natured grumbling among the mountain men, the ladies were settled in for the night. Guards were posted on the ridges, although none believed they were really necessary. The lights in the town of Bury blazed long into the night as the men prepared for war. Around midnight, very late for a western town, the lanterns and candles began to go out and the town was a dark shape in a velvet pocket.

The town was stirring before the first silver fingers of dawn began creeping over the mountains, touching the valleys and lighting the new day.

On the ridges, the men and women watched the citizens of Bury saddle horses and check out equipment.

"Mines is shut down tight," Dupre told Smoke. The Frenchman had just completed a night-long tour of the country.

"The miners?"

"They around, but they keepin' their heads down and their butts outta sight. They know all hell's about to break loose around here."

"You see any PSR riders?"

"Several. They watchin' the town. Been there all night. I allow as to how they know 'bout the deal you made with Potter and Stratton. Seen one haul his ashes back towards the spread, hell bent for leather.

Smoke's grin was visible on the rim of the tin cup full of scalding black coffee. "Going to be a very interesting day," he said.

"So Wiley and Keith sold out to Smoke Jensen," Josh mused aloud. "Interesting. Thank you for that news." He waved the cowhand away and concentrated on his breakfast, conscious of the eyes on him as he ate.

Marshall and Lansing and Brown sat at the long table in the dining room. Marshall finally said, "They got us outnumbered just a tad."

"Not enough to cause us any concern," Josh replied. "As soon as they start pulling out, my riders will come fogging with the news and we'll have time to get ready. Besides, they're shopkeepers and store owners, not gunfighters."

Brown dashed cold water on that remark. "Josh, there ain't a man among them ain't a veteran of either the Civil War or a dozen Injun fights. They may be scoundrels and the like, but they ain't pilgrims."

Josh laid his knife and fork aside. He patted his mouth with a napkin. "Yes, you're right. They aren't going to just roll over and give up." He was thoughtful for a moment. He picked up a tiny silver bell and rattled it, bringing the houseman to the dining room. The other ranchers hid their amusement at that. "Thomas," Josh said to the black houseman, "tell Wilson and McNeil I wish to see them. Now!"

* * *

"Boss," Wilson said, uncomfortable in the lushly appointed dining room with carpet and heavy drapes and expensive chandelier. McNeil stood by his partner's side. The men held their hats in their hands.

"Pick a half-dozen boys from each ranch and take a dozen of our men. Ambush the men from town. To get to here, they've got to come through Levi Pass. Hit them there. Draw enough ammo and food for several days in the field. And, Wilson . . ." He met the man's eyes. "If you fail, don't bother coming back."

"Yes, sir."

Smoke stood on the ridge overlooking the now-deserted town of Bury. His eyes were bleak. Savage-looking. Sally stood by his side, gazing up at him.

"What are you thinking, Smoke?" she asked.

"Take a good look at Bury, Sally."

"I see it. What about it?"

"'Cause this is the last time you'll be able to see it."

"Are we pulling out?"

"No. Not yet."

"Then . . . ?"

"I'm going to burn it to the ground." He checked both his Colts and picked up his Henry repeating rifle. He slowly walked down the hill, Matt, Preacher, Tennessee, and Greybull following him.

Sally stood on the crest of the ridge, Audie by her side—standing on a large rock. Little Ben joined them, rubbing sleep from his eyes.

"What are your feelings toward and for that young man?" Audie asked.

"I love him," Sally said quietly.

"It bloomed very quickly between you two. Are you certain of your feelings?"

"Yes."

"When this is over," Audie said, "I believe the burning hate within him will vanish. It's been an all-consuming thing with him for a long time. But hear me out, young woman. No matter where you two go . . ."

"Three," Sally said, putting her arm around Ben's shoulders.

Audie smiled. "No matter where the *three* of you go, Smoke's reputation will follow. No matter how hard he tries, he will never be able to completely shake it. This is wild and savage country, and it will be so for many years to come. If you settle somewhere to ranch, there will be outlaws who will try to take what is yours, and Smoke will stand up to them. Word will get around, and tinhorns and would-be gunhands will follow, the only thing in their minds being the desire to be the man who killed the fastest gun in the west. Then you will have to leave and settle elsewhere, for Smoke is not the type of man to back down. He desperately wants to settle down, live a so-called normal life, but it is going to be extremely difficult. You're going to have to be very strong."

"Yes," Sally said, not taking her eyes from her young man. And she knew he was hers. "I am aware of that. Mr. Audie . . ."

"Just Audie. My last name is no longer important."

"Audie. I am a woman of some means. I recently came into quite a large sum of money. Perhaps Smoke will consent to go back east and live."

Audie smiled. "What would he do, Sally? Can you imagine him in some office, with a tie and starched collar?"

She laughed softly. She could not imagine that.

"He is a man of the west, of the frontier. This is his land. He would not be happy anywhere else."

And I would not be happy anywhere without him, she thought. Odd that I have known him for so brief a time and yet am so certain of my feelings. But I am certain.

* * *

Only a few people remained in town, and those looked very suspiciously at Smoke and the mountain men. Their suspicion soon turned to hard reality.

"Pack up and clear out," Smoke informed them. "Get your gear together, and move out!"

"You can't just come in here and force us out!" a man protested.

Smoke looked at the man, open contempt in his eyes. "You did what before you came here?"

The man shuffled his feet and refused to reply. He dropped his eyes.

Smoke looked at the small group left behind in the town. "You all knew you were working for crud and crap. And you didn't care. All you cared about was money. And it didn't make a damn to any of you where that money came from, or how you earned it. I have no sympathy for any of you. Get your gear together and get out of here."

They got.

"Round up all the pack animals you can find," Smoke asked the mountain men. He waved all but four of the men down from the ridge, leaving those as guards. "We're gonna give some of these homesteaders in this area a second chance. Food, clothes, boots, guns, equipment. We'll pass it out later. Let's get to work."

What couldn't be packed out on horses and mules was passed up the hill like a bucket brigade. Soon the stores were emptied. The town was strangely silent and ghostlike. Audie summed it up.

"This town had no heart," the little man said. "One cannot feel sorry for destroying something that never lived."

Smoke tossed the first torch into a building. The dry wood was soon blazing, spreading to the adjoining building. Black greasy smoke began pouring into the sky in spiraling waves. The dry pine began popping like six-guns. Soon the heat was so intense it forced the men back to the coolness of the ridge.

"Soon as them people see this smoke, they'll get the message," Preacher said.

"Those that are left alive," Smoke said softly.

20

Levi Pass lay sullen under the heat of the sun. Bodies littered the pass; men and animals sprawled in soon-to-be bloated death. The first contingent of men, led by Deputy Payton, had been knocked from their saddles in a hard burst of rifle fire from the rocks above the pass. Among the first to die were Rosten, the stable manager; Simmons, who ran the general store; and Deputy Payton. A sheriff back in Iowa would never learn that he could destroy the murder warrant he held for Payton.

Among the gunhands in the rocks, McNeil and a rider from the Crooked Snake and Triangle lay dead. The moaning of the wounded, on both sides, softly drifted out of and above the dust and gunsmoke of the pass.

Then the men saw the smoke belching into the skies.

"What the hell?" Wilson muttered from behind his shoulder on the ridge.

"That bastard Jensen has torched the town!" Potter said.

"Oh, my God!" Stratton said, his face dusty and his elegant clothing torn and dirty. "All our records."

Wilson laughed. "Looks like your boy done turned on you!" he called down into the pass.

"Our boy!" Potter yelled. "He started out workin' for you."

"You lie!" Wilson yelled. "You brung him in!"

"What the hell are you talking about?" Stratton screamed.

Wilson's long-unused gray cells began working. "Now wait just a minute," he called. "You tryin' to claim you didn't hire Jensen?"

"Sure we did," Potter yelled. "But we hired him away from Richards. Last night. Richards brought him in to kill us."

"You're crazy!" Wilson yelled. "Just hold on a second. Everybody stop shootin'. We got to talk about this."

"I don't trust you!" Potter screamed. "You're up to something."

"I ain't up to nothin', you fat hog!" Wilson yelled. "You and Stratton was the ones who wanted it all. Ya'll caused all this trouble."

Wilson stood up from behind the boulder.

Sheriff Reese lifted his rifle and shot the man in the stomach. The .44 round knocked the gunhand backward. He died with a scream on his bloody tongue.

A Crooked Snake rider shot Cannon, the newspaper editor, in the center of his forehead. Cannon was dead before he hit the rocky ground of the pass road.

Levi Pass erupted and rocked with pistol and rifle fire. Britt, a rider for the Crooked Snake, crouched behind his cover and mulled matters over in his mind. He was getting the feeling that that damned Smoke Jensen had set them all up; made fools out of everybody; sitting back and laughing while they were shooting at each other.

He slipped from his cover and inched his way toward the timber, where the horses were tied. He spurred his mount, heading for the PSR spread. He wanted to tell his boss what he'd just heard.

Behind him, the savage gunfight continued, the air filled with shouts and curses and the screaming of the wounded and the silence of the dead.

* * *

"Now wait a minute!" Josh said. "Tell me again what you heard back at the pass."

Britt repeated what he'd heard between Wilson, Stratton, and Potter.

Lansing went to a window of the mansion and looked toward the town. Though miles away, he could clearly see the black smoke pouring into the sky. "Shore nuff on fire," he said.

"He played us against each other," Richards said. "And I played right into his hands. He set me up like a kid with a string toy. That damn gunhawk *knew* what I'd do." He sat down heavily. "I don't like being made a fool of. I don't like it worth a damn!"

"He shore done 'er though," Marshall rubbed it in a bit. Marshall and the other ranchers were every bit as tough as Richards, with no back-up in them. They were all thieves and murderers, their pasts as black as midnight.

Richards's gaze was bleak. "Gather up the men. We're ridin'."

"Richards is anything but a fool, Smoke," Sally told him. Standing beside her, Sam solemnly nodded his head. "If he puts all this together, then you've lost your element of surprise."

"I don't think either side wiped the other out in that pass," Preacher opined. "And we ain't heared no gunfire in more'un an hour. I think they got to talkin' and figured things out."

Smoke looked at Tenneysee. "The supplies hidden?"

"B'ar couldn't find 'em."

"We'll get the women over to Becky's place and leave them there. We'll head for the timber and make them come after us."

"The ranches lay in a half circle around Bury," Sam said. "Marshall, Lansing, and Brown will have most of their men out looking for you; only a handful will be at the ranches. The real cowhands and punchers will be with the herds. They're cowboys, not gunslicks."

"Then we'll leave them be," Smoke said. "When we get ready to scatter the herds, we'll tell the punchers to take off for new ground."

"They'll go," Sam said.

"Let's ride."

Leaving what was once the Idaho Territory town of Bury still smoking and burning behind them, the outnumbered band of ancient mountain men, gunhands, and ladies saddled up and drifted into the deep timber, with Sam leading the way. At Becky's small farm, Sam explained the situation to Becky and she agreed to help any way she could. Little Ben introduced the kids to the mountain men. Becky's kids had seen a lot during their time in the west, but absolutely nothing compared with the sight of the old mountain men, all dressed in buckskins and colorful sashes and armed to the teeth. And they certainly had never seen anything to match Audie. No taller than the children, the tiny mountain man captivated the kids. When he jumped up on a stump and began telling fairy tales, the kids sat around him listening, spellbound.

Sally and Smoke walked a short distance from the cabin. "Do we talk now, Smoke?" she asked.

"I reckon so." He waited for her to correct his grammar. She did not.

"Very well. I want to see the west, Smoke. And I want you to show it to me."

"Dangerous, Sally. And not very ladylike. You'd have to ride astride."

She hid her smile. Her father had paddled her behind several times as a child for doing just that. "I'm sure I could cope."

Buck let that alone. "What is it you want to see?"

"The high lonesome," she said without hesitation.

"It's all around you here."

"You know what I mean, Smoke. The real high lonesome.

The one you and the other mountain men talk about. When you speak of that, your voice becomes soft and your eyes hold a certain light. That's the high lonesome I would like to see."

"You'll have to learn to shoot," Smoke said dubiously.

"Then I shall."

"Camp and live out in the wilderness."

"All right."

"It won't be easy. Your skin will be tanned and your hands will become hard with calluses."

"I expect that."

Smoke kept his face noncommittal. He had hoped Sally would want to see his world; the world that he knew was slowly vanishing. There would be time.

He hoped.

"All right," he said.

She rose up on her tiptoes and kissed him on the cheek. "You come back to me," she said.

He did not reply. That was something he could not guarantee.

"Nothing left, Boss," Long reported back to Josh Richards. "Jensen burned the whole place to the ground."

Potter and Stratton were now once more joined with Richards. The opposing sides had ceased fighting in Levi Pass and begun talking. The men were chatting amicably when Richards, Marshall, Lansing, and Brown rode up with their men.

"Nothing?" Burton asked. "My apothecary shop is gone?"

"There ain't nothing left," Long said. "And Jensen and them old bastards is gone. Took the women and left. I cut their sign but lost it in the rocks."

"Sam?" Richards asked.

"No sign of him."

"That was a nice hotel," Morgan said wistfully.

326 *William W. Johnstone*

"Beautiful church," Necker said. "Takes a heathen to destroy a house of God."

Simpson spat on the ground. "You damned fake!" he told Necker. "You ain't no more no preacher than I is. I knowed all along I'd seen you 'fore. Now I remember. I knowed you up in Montana Territory. Elkhorn. You was dealing stud and pimpin'. You kilt Jack Harris when he caught you cold-deckin' him."

"You must be mistaken, my good man," Necker said. But his face was flushed. "I came from—"

"Shut up, Necker. Or whatever your name is," Lansing said. "Now I'm gonna tell you all something. Or remind you of it. Remind you all of a lot of things. They ain't none of us clean. We all—*all of us*—got dodgers out on us. Now we can't none of us afford to lose this fight. 'Cause you all know damn well when that stage reports the town is burnt, the Army's gonna come in here and start askin' a bucket full of questions. That means all them pig farmers and nesters in this area's gotta go in the ground. Cain't none of 'em be allowed to live and flap their gums." He glared at Richards. "I tole you time after time that I didn't trust that there Scotsman. He ain't what he appears to be. Bet on it. When the trouble started, he shore wanted to leave in a hurry, didn't he?"

"Yes, he did," Stratton said. "And it appeared that he and Smoke Jensen were friends."

"They got to die," Marshall said. "All of them."

"What about them farmers' kids?" a gunhand asked.

"Them, too," Brown said. "Cain't nobody be left alive to point no finger at us."

"I want Smoke Jensen!" Dickerson gasped from his blankets on the ground. Still gravely wounded, the outlaw had insisted upon coming to the pass rather than leaving with the men Smoke had ordered out before burning the town.

The men ignored him. Dickerson's wounds had reopened, and all those present knew the outlaw and murderer was not long for this world.

"Ya'll hear me?" Dickerson said.

"Aw, shut up and die!" Necker told him. "We're busy."

Dickerson fell back on his dirty blankets and died.

Smoke, Sam, and the mountain men rode west, toward Marshall's Crooked Snake spread. The Frenchman, Dupre, was ranging ahead of the main body of men. About two miles from the ranch, Smoke pulled up, waiting for Dupre to return with a scouting report.

During this quiet, which, all knew, would soon become very rare, Preacher talked with Smoke. "You beginnin' to feel all the hate leave your craw, boy?"

"Yes," Smoke admitted.

"That's good. That's a mighty fine little gal back yonder at that nester place."

"She wants to see the high lonesome."

"Be tough on a woman. You gonna show her?"

Smoke hesitated. "Yes."

Preacher spat a stream of brown tobacco juice on the ground, drowning a bug. "Soon as this here affair is done, you two best git goin'. High lonesome will soon be gone. Civil-lie-say-shon done be takin' over, pilgrims ruinin' everything. Be a fine thing to show that woman, though. She's tough, got lots of spunk. She'll stand by you, I's thinkin'."

"Us, you mean, don't you?"

"You mean the boy?"

Smoke shook his head. "I mean Sally, Little Ben, me, and you."

"No, Smoke," Preacher said. "I'll be leavin' with my pards. They's still some corners of this land that's high and lonesome. No nesters with their gawddamned barbed wire and pigs and plows. Me and Tenneysee and Audie and Nighthawk and all the rest—wal, our time's done past us, boy. Mayhaps you'll see me agin—mayhaps not. But when my time is nigh, I'll be headin' back to that little valley where you hammered my name in that stone. There, I'll jist lay me down and look at the elephant. I'll warn you now, son. This will be the last ride for Deadlead and Matt. They done tole me that. They real sick. Got that disease that eats from the inside out."

"Cancer?"

"That'd be it, I reckon. They gonna go out with the reins in they teeth and they fists full of smokin' iron. They'll know when it's time. You a gunhand, boy; you understand why they want it thataway, don't you?"

"Yes."

"All right. It's all said then. When it's time for me and the boys to leave, I don't want no blubberin', you understand?"

"Have you ever seen me blubber?"

"Damn close to it."

"You tell lies, old man."

Preacher's eyes twinkled. "Mayhaps one or two, from time to time."

"Here comes Dupre."

"We gonna be runnin' and ridin' hard for the next two-three days, son. We'll speak no more of this. When this is over, me and boys will just fade out. 'Member all I taught you, and you treat that there woman right. You hear?"

"I hear."

"Let's go bring this to an end, boy."

21

"If you're cowboys, turn those ponies' noses west and ride out. If you're gunhands, make your play," Smoke said.

The three riders on the Crooked Snake range slowly turned their horses, being very careful to keep their hands away from sixguns. They sat and stared at the mountain men and at Smoke.

"We're drawin' thirty a month and found," one said. "That ain't exactly fightin' pay."

"You got anything back at the bunkhouse worth dyin' over?"

"Not a thing."

"You boys ride out. If you've a mind to, come back in three-four days. They'll be a lot of cattle wandering around with no owners. You might want to start up some small spreads in this area."

"You be the outlaw, Smoke Jensen?" a cowboy asked.

"I'm Jensen. But I'm no outlaw."

"Mister, if you say you're an African go-riller, you ain't gonna git no argument from me," another cowboy said.

"Fine. You boys head on toward the Salmon. Drift back in three-four days. We'll be gone, and so will the ranches. The homesteaders will still be here, though. Unless you want to see me again, leave them be. Understand?"

"Mr. Jensen, I'll even help 'em *plow!*"

Smoke smiled. "Take off."

The punchers took off.

"Five, maybe six gunnies at the ranch," Beartooth said, riding up.

Smoke looked at Powder Pete. "Got some dynamite with you?"

"You don't have to say no more." Powder Pete wheeled his mustang and took off for the ranch, Smoke and Sam and the mountain men hard after him.

"How do you boys want it?" Smoke called to the deserted-appearing ranch.

A rifle shot was the only reply.

"Hold your fire," Smoke told his people. Raising his voice, he shouted, "Your boss payin' you so much money you'd die for him?"

"Hell with you, Jensen!" the shout drifted to Smoke. "Come git us if you got the sand to do it."

Smoke looked at Powder Pete. "Blow 'em out!"

The old mountain man grinned and slipped silently away. About five minutes later, the bunkhouse exploded, the roof blowing off. A dynamite charge blew the porch off the main house, collapsing one side of the house. Smoke and the mountain men poured a full minute of lead into the house.

"I'm done with it!" a man shouted from the dynamite-ruined and bullet-pocked house. "Lemme ride out and I'm gone."

"Take what's on your back and clear out!" Smoke yelled. "How 'bout you other men?"

"There ain't no other men," the man shouted, a bitter edge to his voice. "Two was in the bunkhouse. Rafter got another in here. Lead took the others. I'm it!"

"Clear out and don't come back."

"You just watch my dust, Jensen."

They watched it fade out, the gunhand riding toward the west. He did not look back.

"Check the house for wounded, then burn it all," Smoke said.

"You got a mean streak in you," Preacher said. "Shore didn't git it from me."

Smoke grinned at the man who had helped raise him. Preacher was as mean and vindictive as a wounded grizzly.

"I allow as to how we ain't gonna bury them gunhawks in the house," Preacher said, not putting it in question form.

"Somewhere, sometime, they had a ma," Smoke said. "She'd wanna know her boy was buried proper."

"I'd afraid you say that," Preacher bitched. "I ain't never found no shovel to fit my hand."

"There goes my ranch," Marshall said, looking west into the sky. There was no bitterness in his voice, only a grudging admiration.

The hundred-odd men sat their saddles and stared at the black smoke pluming into the sky.

"We can still save the cattle," one of his men said.

"You want them, you save them," Marshall replied. "I'm headin' out."

"Where the hell you think you goin'?" Lansing asked.

"I'm pullin' out. You boys got any smarts, you'll do the same. I just realized that we ain't gonna stop this Jensen. If'n a man's right, and he jist keeps on comin', ain't nothing or nobody gonna stop him. And you know what, boys? Jensen's right."

"*Right*?" Potter squalled. "He comes in here and ruins everything we worked to build and you sit there and say the man's right?"

Marshall chuckled grimly. "That's it, boys. Everything we got we built on stole money and the blood of others. Hell with it. I'm pullin' out." He wheeled his horse and turned his back to the others.

Josh Richards jerked up his rifle and shot the man in

the back. Marshall fell from the saddle, his spine severed. He lay on the ground, looking at the men through pain-filled eyes. "Should have known one of you would do that," he gasped.

Stratton shot the man between the eyes.

Potter looked at what remained of Marshall's men. "Stay with us. All his cattle, his mine holdings—everything is yours if we win this fight."

"We'll stay," one hard-faced Crooked Snake gunnie said. "I never liked Marshall no how."

"Let's ride."

"What do we do with the cattle?" Audie asked.

"Leave them for those cowboys," Smoke said. "They seemed like pretty decent boys to me."

"The cattle on Richards's place?" Tenneysee asked.

"That's another story. We'll give them to the nesters and the miners."

"Seems fair enough," Lobo said. "I damned shore don't want 'um."

"Someone has to meet the stage and turn it around," Smoke said. "Any volunteers?"

"McGregor said he'd do it," Sam spoke. "But I don't like the idee of one man waitin' out there all alone with a hundred or so gunhands on the prowl."

"You go back and meet the stage with him," Audie suggested. "I should imagine you and your ladyfriend will be settling in this area. So the less you have to do with this matter, the better. Agreed, Smoke?"

"Good idea. Take off, Sam. I'll see you when this is over."

Reluctantly, Sam agreed and rode out, back to Becky's cabin.

"Lansing's Triangle is almost due north from here," Matt said. "We hit there next?"

"That's what they would expect us to do, isn't it?" Smoke asked, a hard grin on his lips.

"Oh, you sneaky, boy!" Preacher said. "You as sneaky as a rattler."

"Whut you two jawin' about?" Phew asked.

"We head straight east," Smoke explained. "For Brown's Double Bar B. I'm betting Richards and all the rest are hightailing right now to set up an ambush around Lansing's spread."

"At's rat good thankin', boy," Beartooth said. "I can tell Preacher hepped raise you."

Preacher stuck out his skinny chest. "Done a damn good job of 'er, too."

"Don't start braggin'," Greybull said. "I been listenin' to you bump them gums of yourn for fifty years. Sickenin'."

"Hush up, you mule-ridin' giant!" Preacher told him.

The other mountain men joined in.

They were still grousing and bitching and hurling insults at one another as they rode off.

"We're spread thin," Brown said to Richards. "Real thin."

"But when they come," Stratton said, "we'll have them in a circle. All we have to do is close up the bottom of the pinchers and trap them."

"If they come," Lansing said. "I don't trust that damned Jensen. He's a devil."

"He's just a man," Sheriff Reese said sourly.

"A hell of a man," Richards said. "Janey's brother."

"What!" Potter shouted.

"Janey told me before I left the ranch. She knew all along that she'd seen him somewhere, but she didn't put it together until a few days ago."

"What'd she say do with him?" Stratton asked.

Richards shrugged. "Kill him."

Dawn broke hot and red over the valley that Brown called his Double Bar B spread. During the night, Dupre and Deadlead had slipped into the ranch area and found it deserted except for the cook. They had put him on the road after he told them that all the men drawing fighting pay were out with the boss. Just punchers riding herd on the cattle. Give them a chance, and they'd haul their ashes quick.

That was what Smoke was now doing. Alone.

The punchers looked up as the midnight-black stallion with the tall rider approached their meager camp. They all knew, without being told, who they were facing.

"We're cowboys, not gunhawks," one puncher said. "We ain't lookin' for no trouble."

"Then you won't have any," Smoke told him. "Get your gear, pack it up, and ride out." He made them the same offer he had made the Crooked Snake cowboys.

"Sounds good to me," a puncher said. "We gone, Mister Jensen."

Smoke watched them ride out, leaving the herd without a backward glance.

He waved the mountain men in. Lobo inspected the main house.

"Place is a damned pigsty," he reported back.

"Well, let's roast some pigs," Smoke said.

"That son of a bitch!" Brown shouted, jumping up, his eyes to the east. "He's fired my ranch."

Richards looked at the smoke pouring into the sky. There was a look of grudging admiration on the man's cruel face.

"I've had it!" Morgan said. "Me and Burton and Hallen and some of the others been talkin'. We're pullin' out, headin' west."

The others looked at the rifles in the men's hands. Potter stepped in before gunfire could start.

"All right!" he shouted. "How many of you are leaving?"

Nearly all the men from town were leaving, with the exception of Sheriff Reese and his so-called deputies.

"I gather you're going to join your families?" Richards said with a smile on his face.

"That's crap!" Reverend Necker said. "I don't care if I ever see that old bat again."

"Don't any of you ever set a boot in this part of the country again," Stratton warned.

"Don't you worry," Burton said.

The townspeople rode out without looking back.

Looking around them, the ranchers and gunhands could see where others had deserted them during the night. Quietly slipped away into the darkness. What remained were the hardcases.

"They wasn't much help anyways," a gunnie from the Crooked Snake said. "I never did trust none of them."

"Rider comin' hard," another gunslick said, looking toward the southeast.

Simpson reined up, his horse blowing hard. "Miners quit!" he said. "All of 'em. Said they ain't workin' for none of you no more."

Stratton started cursing. Potter and Richards let him curse until he ran down.

"Where's all them townies goin'?" Simpson asked.

"Turned yeller and run," Long told him.

"Let 'em go. They's only in the way." He looked at Richards. "That smoke back yonderways—that the Double Bar B?"

"Yeah." He twisted in the saddle, the leather creaking. He looked at the men gathered around him. "Any the rest of you boys want to turn tail and run?"

That question was met by silence and hard eyes.

"We gonna make them mountain men and Mister Jensen come to us," Richards declared. "Where's the nearest nester spread from here?" He tossed the question to anyone.

"'Bout ten miles," a gunslick said. "Next one is about four miles from that one."

"Dent," Richards looked at a mean-eyed rider. "Take a couple of boys and go burn them out. Black, you take a couple men and burn out the next pig farmer's family. That ought to bring Mister High-And-Mighty Jensen on the run." Richards started laughing. "And while you're doing that, the rest of us will be setting up an ambush."

"What about the wimmin and kids?" a gunhawk named Cross asked.

"What about them?" Potter asked.

"I thought we agree on that?" Stratton said.

"They have to die," Richards said. "All of them."

22

The homesteader's cabin appeared deserted when Dent and the others galloped into the front yard, the horses' hooves trampling over a flower bed and a newly planted garden. Normally, that action alone would bring the wife on a run, squalling and flapping her apron. It was a game the punchers liked to play with nesters, for few cowboys liked nesters, with their gardens and fences.

This time their destructive actions were met with silence.

Inside the cabin, the man lifted a finger to his lips, telling his wife and kids to be still. The wife nodded and moved to a gun slit in the logs, a .30-30 in her hands. Her husband held a double-barreled shotgun, the express gun loaded with buckshot. That painted lady from town had ridden by the day before, warning them to be on guard. All them ladies from the Pink House was riding around, warning the other homesteaders what was happening. First time he'd ever met a . . . a . . . one of them ladies. Nice looking woman.

He eased the hammers back on the shotgun.

"Set the damned place on fire!" Dent yelled. "Burn 'em out."

Those were the last words Dent would speak in his life. The homesteader's shotgun roared, the buckshot from both barrels catching Dent in the chest and face. The charge lifted the gunhand from the saddle, tearing off most of his face and flinging him several yards away from his horse.

The homesteader's wife shot the second rider in the chest with her .30-30 just as the oldest boy fired from the hog pen. Three riderless horses stood in the front yard.

The homesteader and his family moved cautiously out of hiding. "Take their guns and stable their horses," the man said. "Mother, you get the Bible. Son, you get a couple shovels. We'll give them a Christian burial."

Black lifted himself up to one elbow. The pain in his chest was fierce. He coughed up blood, pink and frothy. Lung-shot, he thought.

Black looked around him. Douglas and Cross were lying in the front yard of the pig farmer's cabin. They looked dead. *Hell*, they were dead!

Who'd have thought it of a damned nester?

Black looked up at the damned homesteader in those stupid-looking overalls. Man had a Colt in each hand. Damn sure knew how to use them, too.

"Never thought a stinkin' pig farmer would be the one to do me in," Black gasped the words.

"I was a captain in the War Between the States," the man spoke calmly. "First Alabama Cavalry."

"Well, I'll just be damned!" Black said.

"Yes," the farmer agreed. "You probably will."

Black closed his eyes and died.

"No smoke," Lansing observed.

"Thought I heard gunfire, though," Potter said.

"Yeah," Stratton said. "But who is shootin' who?"

Richards's stomach felt sour, like he'd drank a glass of clabbered milk. Sour. Yeah, that was the word for it. Sour. Whole damned business was going sour. And all because of one man. He looked around him. Something was out of whack. Then it came to him. About ten or so men were gone, had slipped quietly away. Hell with them. They still had fifty-sixty hardcases. More than enough to do the job.

Or was it?

He shook that thought away. Can't even think about that. He wondered what that damned Smoke was doing right now.

Janey had never seen a more disreputable-looking bunch of men in all her life. *God!* They looked older than death.

Except for her brother.

Janey looked at the dead gunhands lying in the front yard. The gunhands Josh had left behind to protect her. That was a joke. But there wasn't anything funny about it.

"Hello, brother," she said.

"Sis," Smoke returned the greeting.

"Well, now what?" Her voice was sharp.

"How much money you have in the house, sis?"

"You going to rob me?"

"No."

She shrugged. "Quite a bit, I guess, brother. Yeah. Lots of money in the house."

"Can you ride astride?"

"Kid," she laughed, "I've ridden more things astride than I care to think about."

Smoke knew what his sister meant. He ignored it. "Change your clothes, get what money you can carry, and clear out. I don't care where you go, just go. I don't ever want to see you again."

Her laugh was bitter. "You always could screw up every plan I ever made."

"Don't you care what Richards did to your pa and brother?" he asked.

"Hell, no!"

He remembered his pa's letter. "I guess Pa was right, Janey. He said you were trash."

"Rich trash, baby brother. Doesn't that bother you?"

"Money rich, sis. That's all."

"And you don't think that's sufficient?"

"If you do, I feel sorry for you."

"Then that makes you a fool, Kirby!"

He shrugged. "One hour, Janey. That's all the time I'm giving you. Pack up and clear out."

She nodded and turned her back to him. She stopped and turned around. She gave him an obscene gesture, spat on the porch, and walked into the house.

"You rat sure there wasn't some mixup in babies when she were birthed?" Preacher asked. "You sure she's your sis?"

"I'm sure."

Janey left riding like a man and holding the rope of the pack animal.

"Aren't you the least bit worried about your man?" Smoke had asked her.

"Shoot the son of a bitch as far as I'm concerned," had been her reply. She had spurred her horse and ridden off without looking back.

"What a delightful young woman," Audie said, the crust about an inch thick in his voice.

Smoke watched his only living relative—that he knew of—ride away. He knew he should feel something—but he didn't.

Yes, he did, he corrected.

Relief in the fact that he had found her alive and had offered her a chance to live and she had taken it.

He shook his head.

So he still felt something for her.

But damn little.

"Burn the house to the ground," he said. He looked around him. Deadlead and Matt were gone. His eyes met Preacher's gaze.

"They gone to buy us some time," the mountain man said. "They won't be back."

Smoke nodded his head.

"I tole 'em not to kill Stratton, Potter, or Richards," Preacher said. "You wanted them yourself."

"I do. Thanks."

"Think nuttin' of it. I give 'em to you fer your birthday. Rest of us be takin' off shortly. You know what I mean."

Smoke knew.

Two riders left their saddles before the sounds of the rifle fire reached the column of outlaws. The two men were dead before they hit the ground.

"What the hell?" Reese yelled.

"Ambush!" Stratton screamed.

Two more men were flung backward and to the ground, dead and dying.

"There they are!" Rogers hollered, pointing to a ridge. "Come on, let's get 'em!"

A dozen riders looked at each other, nodded minutely, and slowly wheeled their horses, riding in the opposite direction.

"Come back here, you cowards!" Potter screamed.

"Let them go," Richards said calmly. "Nobody fire at them."

His partners looked at him strangely.

"It's over," Richards said. "We're walking-around dead men and don't even know it."

"What do you mean?" Stratton's scream was tinted with hysteria.

"Look," Richards said, pointing toward his ranch house.

A huge cloud of black smoke was filling the air.

"The PSR house!" Reese yelled.

"Yeah," Richards said. He smiled. "And you can bet my darling Janey has taken all the cash in the house—which was considerable; she'd need a pack animal to carry it off—and is gone. Her brother wouldn't kill her."

"Well, you're taking it damned calm," Potter said.

"No reason to get upset. What is done is done."

One of the dying gunhawks on the ground moaned.

"Hosses comin' at us," a gunnie said. "Holy crap!" he yelled. "We're being charged!"

Deadlead and Matt were in the middle of the riders before the gunhands could really believe it was all taking place. With the reins in their teeth and their fists wrapped about the butts of .44s and .45s, the old mountain men emptied their pistols and had shucked their rifles before any-one else could fire a shot. Richards had trotted his horse off a few hundred yards and was sitting quietly, watching it all, Potter and Stratton with him. Stratton's face was ashen, his hands trembled, his once fine clothes were torn and dirty.

Eight more riders had joined the four on the ground before the mountain men were blasted from their saddles. Matt rose to his boots, roaring as his blood poured from his wounds.

"Somebody kill that damned nigger!" a gunslick yelled.

Matt shot the man between the eyes with a pistol he'd grabbed from off the ground.

Deadlead jerked a gunhawk off his horse and snapped his neck as easily as wringing the neck of a chicken.

Twenty guns roared. The riddled bodies of the mountain men fell to the already-blood-soaked dust.

Deadlead lifted his bloody head and looked at Sheriff Dan Reese. "Thank you, boys." He fell to the ground, dead, beside his lifelong friend.

"He *thanked* me!" Reese said, horror in his voice. "Thanked me? For *what*?" he screamed.

"If you don't understand," Richards said, "there is no point in my trying to explain it to you." He looked around him. "Long! Take a couple of boys. Get over to that woman's cabin Sam is sweet on. Kill her and them snot-nosed brats."

"With pleasure," the short, stocky gunhand said with a grin. "I just might get me a taste of that gal 'fore I do."

"Your option," Richards said.

Long took Deputy Weathers and rode toward the nester cabin. The were, despite all that had happened, in high spirits. Becky was a one fine-lookin' piece of woman. They rode arrogantly into the front yard, scattering chickens and trampling the flower garden.

"You in the house!" Long called. "Get your tail out here, woman."

The door opened and Nighthawk stepped out, his big hands wrapped around .44s. He blew Long and Weathers clean out of their saddles. He tied the dead men to the saddles and slapped the horses on the rump, sending them home.

"Those two won't bother me again," Becky said.

"Ummm," Nighthawk replied.

23

The ever-shrinking band of outlaws and gunhands looked toward the west. Another cloud of black smoke filled the air.

Lansing began cursing. "How in the hell are them old men doin' it?" he yelled. "We're fightin' a damned bunch of ghosts."

"Are you stayin' or leavin'?" Stratton asked.

"Might as well see it through," the man said bitterly. Those were the last words he would speak on this earth. A Sharps barked, the big slug taking the rancher in the center of his chest, knocking him spinning from his saddle.

"I've had it!" a gunhand said. He spun his horse and rode away. A dozen followed him. No one tried to stop them.

"Look all around us," Brown said.

The men looked. A mile away, in a semicircle, ten mountain men sat their ponies. As if on signal, the old mountain men lifted their rifles high above their heads.

Turkel, one of the most feared gunhawks in the territory, looked the situation over through field glasses. "That there's Preacher," he said, pointing. "That'un over yonder is the Frenchman, Dupre. That one ridin' a mule is Greybull. That little bitty shithead is the midget, Audie. Boys, I don't want no truck with them old men. I'm tellin' you all flat-out."

The old men began waving with their rifles.

"What are they tryin' to tell us?" Reese asked.

"That Smoke is waiting in the direction they're pointing," Richards said. "They're telling us to tangle with him—if we've got the sand in us to do so."

Potter did some fast counting. Out of what was once a hundred and fifty men, only nineteen remained, including himself. "Hell, boys! He's only one man. There's nineteen of us!"

"There was about this many over at that minin' camp, too," Britt said. "They couldn't stop him."

"Well," Kelly said. "Way I see it is this: we either fight ten of them ringtailed-tooters, or we fight Smoke."

"I'll take Smoke," Howard said. But he wasn't all that thrilled with the choices offered him.

The mountain men began moving, closing the circle. The gunhands turned their horses and moved out, allowing themselves to be pushed toward the west.

"They're pushing us toward Slate," Williams said. "The ghost town."

Richards smiled at Smoke's choice of a showdown spot.

As the old ghost town appeared on the horizon, located on the flats between the Lemhi River and the Beaverhead Range, Turkel's buddy, Harris, reined up and pointed. "Goddamn place is full of people!"

"Miners," Brown said. "They come to see the show. Drinking and betting. Them old mountain men spread the word."

"Just like it was at the camp on the Uncompahgre," Richards said with a grunt.* "Check your weapons. Stuff your pockets full of extra shells. I'm going back to talk with Preacher. I want to see how this deal is going down."

Richards rode back to the mountain men, riding with one hand in the air.

*The Last Mountain Man.

"That there's far enuff," Lobo said. "Speak your piece."

"We win this fight, do we have to fight you men too?"

"No," Preacher said quickly. "My boy Smoke done laid down the rules."

His *boy*! Richards thought. Jesus God. "We win, do we get to stay in this part of the country?"

"If'n you win," Preacher said, "you leave with what you got on your backs. If'n you win, we pass the word, and here 'tis: if'n you or any of your people ever come west of Kansas, you dead meat. That clear?"

"You're a hard old man, Preacher."

"You wanna see jist how hard?" Preacher challenged.

"No," Richards said, shaking his head. "We'll take our chances with Smoke."

"You would be better off taking your chances with us," Audie suggested.

Richards looked at Nighthawk. "What do you have to say about it?"

"Ummm."

Richards looked pained.

"That means haul your ass back to your friends," Phew said.

Richards trotted his horse back to what was left of his band. He told them the rules.

Britt looked up the hill toward an old falling-down store. "There he is."

Smoke stood alone on the old curled-up and rotted boardwalk. The men could see his twin .44s belted around his waist. He held a Henry repeating rifle in his right hand, a double-barreled express gun in his left hand. Smoke ducked into the building, leaving only a slight bit of dust to signal where he once stood.

"Two groups of six," Richards said, "one group of three, one group of four. Britt, take your group in from the rear. Turkel, take your boys in from the east. Reese, take your people in from the west. I'll take my people in from this direction. Move out."

Smoke had removed his spurs, hanging them on the saddlehorn of Drifter. As soon as he ducked out of sight, he had run from the store down the hill, staying in the alley. He stashed the express gun on one side of the street in an old store, his rifle across the street. He met Skinny Davis first, in the gloom of what had once been a saloon.

"Draw!" Davis hissed.

Smoke put two holes in his chest before Davis could cock his .44s.

"In Pat's Saloon!" someone shouted.

Williams jumped through an open glassless window of the saloon. Just as his boots hit the old warped floor, Smoke shot him, the .44 slug knocking the gunslick back out the window to the boardwalk. Williams was hurt, but not out of it yet. He crawled along the side of the building, one arm broken and dangling, useless.

"Smoke Jensen!" Cross called. "You ain't got the sand to face me!"

"That's one way of putting it," Smoke muttered, taking careful aim and shooting the outlaw. The lead struck him in the stomach, doubling him over and dropping him to the weed-grown and dusty street.

The miners had hightailed it to the ridges surrounding the town. There they sat, drinking and betting and cheering. The mountain men stood and squatted and sat on the opposite ridge, watching.

A bullet dug a trench along the wood, sending splinters flying, a few of them striking Smoke's face, stinging and bringing a few drops of blood.

He ran out the back of the saloon and came face to face with Simpson, the gunhawk having both hands filled with .44.

Smoke pulled the trigger on his own .44s, the double hammer-blows of lead taking Simpson in the lower chest, slamming him to the ground, dying.

Quickly reloading, Smoke grabbed up Simpson's guns

and tucked them behind his gunbelt. He ran down the alley. The last of Richards's gunslicks stepped out of a gaping doorway just as Smoke cut to his right, jumping through an open window. A bullet burned Smoke's shoulder. Spinning, he fired both Colts, one bullet striking Martin in the throat, the second taking the gunnie just above the nose, almost tearing off the upper part of the man's face.

Smoke caught a glimpse of someone running. He dropped to one knee and fired. His slug shattered the hip of Rogers, sending the big man sprawling in the dirt, howling and cursing. Reese spurred his horse and charged the building where Smoke was crouched. He smashed his horse's shoulder against the old door and thundered in. The horse, wild-eyed and scared witless, lost its footing and fell, pinning Reese to the floor, crushing the man's stomach and chest. Reese howled in agony as blood filled his mouth and darkness clouded his eyes.

Smoke left the dying man and ran out the side door.

"Get him, Turkel!" Brown screamed.

Smoke glanced up. Turkel was on the roof of an old building, a rifle in his hand. Smoke flattened against a building as Turkel pulled the trigger, the slug plowing up dirt at Smoke's feet. Smoke snapped off a shot, getting lucky as the bullet hit the gunhand in the chest. Turkel dropped the rifle and fell to the street, crashing through an awning. He did not move.

A bullet removed a small part of Smoke's right upper ear; blood poured down the side of his face. He ran to where he had hid the shotgun, grabbing it up and cocking it, leveling it just as the doorway filled with men.

Firing both barrels, Smoke cleared the doorway of all living things, including Britt, Harris, and Smith, the buckshot knocking the men clear off the rotting boardwalk, dead and dying in the street.

"Goddamn you, Jensen!" Brown screamed in rage, stepping out into the street.

Smoke dropped the shotgun and picked up a bloody rifle from the doorway. He shot Brown in the stomach. Brown howled and dropped to the street, both hands holding his stomach.

Rogers leveled a pistol and fired, the bullet ricocheting off a support post, part of the lead striking Smoke's left leg, dropping him to the boardwalk. Smoke ended Rogers's career with a single shot to the head.

White-hot pain lanced through Smoke's side as Williams shot him from behind. Smoke fell off the boardwalk, turning as he fell. He fired twice, the lead taking Williams in the neck, almost tearing the man's head off.

Ducking back inside, grabbing up a fallen shotgun with blood on the barrel, Smoke checked the shotgun, then checked his wounds. Bleeding, but not serious. Williams's slug had gone through the fleshy part of the side. Using the point of his knife, Smoke picked out the tiny piece of lead from Rogers's gun and tied a bandana around the slight wound. He slipped further into the darkness of the building as spurs jingled in the alley to the rear of the old store. Smoke jacked back both hammers on the coach gun. He waited.

The spurs jingled once more. Smoke followed the sound with the twin barrels of the express gun. Carefully, silently, he slipped across the rat-droppings-littered floor to the wall that fronted the alley. He could hear breathing directly in front of him.

He pulled both triggers, the charge blowing a bucket-sized hole in the old pine wall.

The gunslick was blown clear across the alley, hurled against an outhouse. The outhouse collapsed, the gun-hand falling into the shit-pit.

Silently, Smoke reloaded the shotgun, then reloaded his own .44s and the ones taken from the dead gunnie. He listened as Fenerty called for his buddies.

There was no reply.

Fenerty was the last gunhawk left.

Smoke located the voice. Just across the street in a falling-down old building. Laying aside the shotgun, he picked up a rifle and emptied the magazine into the storefront. Fenerty came staggering out, shot in the chest and belly. He died face down in the littered street.

"All right, you bastards!" Smoke yelled to Richards, Potter, and Stratton. "Holster your guns and step out into the street. Face me, if you've got the nerve."

The sharp odor of sweat mingled with blood and gunsmoke filled the still summer air as four men stepped out into the bloody, dusty street.

Richards, Potter, and Stratton stood at one end of the block. A tall, bloody figure stood at the other. All their guns were in leather.

"You son of a bitch!" Stratton screamed, his voice as high-pitched as a woman. "You ruined it all." He clawed at his .44.

Smoke drew and fired before Stratton's pistol could clear leather. Potter grabbed for his pistol. Smoke shot him dead, then holstered his gun, waiting.

Richards had not moved. He stood with a faint smile on his lips, staring at Smoke.

"You ready to die?" Smoke asked the man.

"As ready as I'll ever be, I suppose," Richards replied. There was no fear in his voice. His hands appeared steady. "Janey gone?"

"Took your money and pulled out."

"Been a long run, hasn't it, Jensen?"

"It's just about over."

"What happens to all our holdings?"

"I don't care what happens to the mines. The miners can have them. I'm giving all your stock to decent, honest punchers and homesteaders."

A puzzled look spread over Richards' face. "I don't understand. You did . . . all *this*!" he waved his hand—"for nothing?"

Someone moaned, the sound painfully inching up the street.

"I did it for my pa, my brother, my wife, and my baby son."

"But it won't bring them back!"

"I know."

"I wish I had never heard the name Jensen."

"You'll never hear it again after this day, Richards."

"One way to find out," Richards said with a smile. He drew his Colt and fired. He was snake-quick, but hurried his shot, the lead digging up dirt at Smoke's feet.

Smoke shot him in the right shoulder, spinning the man around. Richards grabbed for his left-hand gun and Smoke fired again, the slug striking the man in the left side of his chest. He struggled to bring up his Colt. He managed to cock it before Smoke's third shot struck him in the belly. Richards sat down hard in the bloody, dusty street.

He opened his mouth to speak. He tasted blood on his tongue. The light began to fade around him. "You'll . . . meet . . ."

Smoke never found out who he was supposed to meet. Richards toppled over on his side and died.

Smoke looked up at the ridge where the mountain men had gathered.

They were gone, leaving as silently as the wind.

24

After MacGregor filed his report with the commanding officer at the fort, the Army made only a cursory inspection of what was left of Bury, Idaho Territory, and the burned ranches around it.

Wanted posters were put out for the outlaw and murderer Buck West. MacGregor wrote the description of the man, thus insuring he would never be found.

A lot of small ranches sprang up around the area. Very prosperous little farms and ranchers. The ladies from the Pink House stayed. They all got married.

Sam married Becky.

The last anyone ever saw of Smoke Jensen and Sally Reynolds, the two of them were riding toward the mountains, toward the High Lonesome, leading two packhorses.

"You think we'll ever see them again?" Becky asked Sam.

Sam did not reply.

But as Nighthawk might have said, "Ummm."